CW01640623

The Tea Planter's [illegible]e

A Story of Intrigue and Passion:
(The India Tea Series: Book 2)

Janet MacLeod Trotter

This is a work of fiction. Names, characters, organizations, places, events, and incidents are either products of the author's imagination or are used fictitiously. Any resemblance to actual persons, living or dead, or actual events is purely coincidental.

Text copyright © 2014, 2021 by Janet MacLeod Trotter
All rights reserved.

No part of this book may be reproduced, or stored in a retrieval system, or transmitted in any form or by any means, electronic, mechanical, photocopying, recording, or otherwise, without express written permission of the publisher.

Published by MacLeod Trotter Books Ltd

www.janetmacleodtrotter.com

Cover design by Michael Star

ISBN-978-1-908359-69-8

The India Tea Series

In the fertile valleys of India, the passionate and resourceful women of the Belhaven and Robson tea planter families have always dreamt big, even in the momentous early years of the twentieth century. From the majestic mountains of Assam to the industrial streets of northern Britain, they must learn to cope with hidden secrets, forbidden love, betrayal and adversity as they strive to make life better for themselves and their loved ones. But as they embark on epic adventures across a fast-changing world, will the upheavals of war and the dying days of the British Raj stop their dreams from becoming a reality?

Praise for The India Tea Series

'Irresistible'
Sunderland Echo

'A wonderfully moving, deeply emotional tale'
Daily Record

'Trotter uses her experiences and imagination to bring strength and depth to her novels. Another thought-provoking book'
Lancashire Evening Post

'Another action-packed, emotionally charged page-turner'
Newcastle Journal

'A moving saga set against the backdrop of the thriving tea trade in turn-of-the-century Tyneside'
Peterborough Evening Telegraph

'A gripping and heartrending novel... An unforgettable novel of courage, suffering and enduring love'
Bolton Evening News

Titles by Janet MacLeod Trotter:

The Raj Hotel Series
The Emerald Affair – Book 1
The Sapphire Child – Book 2
The Diamond Daughter – Book 3

The India Tea Series
The Tea Planter's Daughter – Book 1
The Tea Planter's Bride – Book 2
The Girl from the Tea Garden – Book 3
The Secrets of the Tea Garden – Book 4

HISTORICAL
In the Far Pashmina Mountains

The Jarrow Trilogy
The Jarrow Lass
Child of Jarrow
Return to Jarrow

The Durham Trilogy
The Hungry Hills
The Darkening Skies
Never Stand Alone

The Tyneside Sagas
A Handful of Stars
Chasing the Dream
For Love & Glory

The Rebellious Woman Sagas

The Suffragette
A Crimson Dawn

Scottish Historical Romance

The Flower of Scotland (formerly The Jacobite Lass)
The Beltane Fires
Highlander in Muscovy

MYSTERY/CRIME

The Vanishing of Ruth
The Haunting of Kulah

TEENAGE

Love Games

NON-FICTION

Beatles & Chiefs

Dedication

This novel is dedicated to the fond memory of my grandparents, Bob Gorrie (known as jungli Gorrie) and Sydney Easterbrook, who went to live and work in India in the 1920s – and to my beloved mother, Sheila, who lived there until she was eight years old.

PROLOGUE

India, 1907

Sophie stood on tiptoes, peering through the tangle of creepers that blocked her view from the veranda to the path below. She was impatient for her birthday party to begin; for friends from the neighbouring tea gardens to come and share the cake and apple pie that cook had made; to play blind man's buff, and hide-and-seek. This strange, creaky house with its shaded veranda and overgrown garden was perfect for hiding. They were playing drums for her down in the village; they had started before dawn and had been playing for hours. She pestered her mother.

'When will they come, Mama? When will they *come*!'

'Wheesht, lassie,' her mother sighed. 'It's too far for children to come just for tea.'

'No it's not!' Sophie shook her head of honey-coloured curls. 'We go for hours and hours to see people.'

'This year is different. How many times do I have to tell you?'

Sophie looked at her mother in disappointment; she hadn't even made the effort to change into an afternoon dress, as if she knew no one was coming. Sophie had put on her best blue dress the moment she had woken, without any help from her nanny, Ayah Mimi, though she had allowed Ayah to brush out her hair and button her shoes with the special metal hook.

Sophie brightened. 'We can ask some village children then.'.

She had seen them splashing in the river pool when Papa had given her a riding lesson down the drive and along the track that led deep into the forest. Some of them had laughed and waved to see her perched high in the saddle, her legs straddled like a boy's with her father leading the reins.

Her mother ignored this. 'Ayah will set out your toy tea set and you can have a party with your dolls.'

'No!' Sophie stamped her foot in frustration. Today, she was six years old and wanted a proper tea party at the grown-ups' table. She didn't like the wax-faced dolls her parents had given her two years running, ignoring her pleas for a toy train. The only doll she had ever loved was a soft one in a velvet jacket with a long dark plait like Ayah Mimi's, but it had gone mouldy and disintegrated in last summer's rains. 'I want a proper party!'

'Don't shout,' her mother snapped, 'you'll disturb Papa.' She gave an anxious glance into the dark interior of the house. All was quiet but for the new kitten mewling.

'Will Papa get up today?' Sophie asked. 'If I can't have a party, will he take me fishing?'

'Not today. No one's going anywhere today.'

'Why not?'

Her mother twisted and twisted a ring around her finger.

'Next year, God willing, I promise you will have a party.'

'I don't like it here – I want to go home.' Sophie ran to the veranda steps and plonked herself down to wait; she refused to believe that no one would come.

'Keep out of the sun,' her mother fretted, 'and don't go further than the bottom of the steps.'

'Why?'

'Cause I say so.'

Ayah Mimi's soft tread came out of the shadows. The slim woman with a mole on her chin popped Sophie's *topee* on her head and coaxed her out of the fierce light.

'Lime juice and story time,' said Ayah with a smile, 'then lots of cake.'

When Sophie looked round, her mother had already gone.

***

They were arguing – men's voices. Her father's was hoarse and querulous, the other man's deep and booming. The wide veranda was in darkness. Someone had covered her with a cotton sheet – it smelled of cloves like Ayah Mimi – as she had lain napping in the low hammock.

The sky was red and angry; the drumming from the village louder, sending birds screaming into the trees. Sophie sat up in alarm. Her mother was screaming too.

'Just go! You're making things worse!'

And why was that kitten wailing? The dusk made everything sound bigger than it was.

Sophie scrambled out of the hammock, stumbling into heavy furniture and knocking over a pot plant. She peered down the steps; a large black horse was tethered to a post. She could just make out its tail flicking in the dying light, but no one was tending it. No cooking fires burned in the compound beyond the jungle of garden.

Was it still her birthday? She looked down at the limp dress stuck to her prickly skin. It must be.

'Ayah?' Sophie called out. 'Ayah Mimi!'

She wanted her nanny to come and be with her while the grown-ups shouted and the fireworks went off in the village and the drumming went on pounding like it was inside her head.

Suddenly the shouting was spilling through the door. Sophie pressed back into the shadows.

'Jessie, you're not safe here. There have been threats. You must come—'

'I'm going nowhere. Stop interfering! You being here is what makes it not safe.'

The man with the booming voice strode from the house and down the steps. Sophie heard the big horse snort as he mounted and kicked it forward with a final shout, 'On your own heads be it!'

Her father's ranting continued after the rider had gone – his 'fever shouting' as her mother called it – and it rang around the old house.

As she crouched in the dark, too anxious to move, Sophie heard hushed women's voices – urgent, tearful – and hurried footsteps making the uneven floorboards squeak.

A flash of pink sari dashed down the steps. Sophie jumped up.

'Ayah Mimi! Wait!'

The woman turned, startled. She was clasping something; the kitten's basket.

The next moment her mother was grasping her arm. 'Quiet, let her go.'

'Where's she going?'

Her mother's face looked pained, like she had toothache.

'On an errand.'

Sophie was frightened. Ayah Mimi shouldn't be going anywhere without her. And who was the shouty man who had upset Papa? And why did her mother look like she was crying? It was the worst birthday ever and she hated the noise and the bangs coming from the village that seemed to be getting closer, and the flaming torches licking the night sky. All this she wanted to say to her mother. Instead she burst into tears and wailed, 'And I never got to play hide-and-seek!'

'Hush, lassie,' her mother said, briefly putting an arm about her. She pulled a cotton handkerchief from her sleeve. 'Blow your nose.'

All at once, there was an explosion of noise at the compound gate. Sophie's father started bellowing again. Her mother gasped. She turned and pushed Sophie across the veranda.

'Go and hide now.'

'Are we playing hide-and-seek?' Sophie felt fear and excitement.

'Yes, now quickly. Be still as a mouse and don't make a sound.'

Immediately, Sophie felt better. 'Don't look.' She grinned and scampered off.

She hid in the linen chest, burrowing deep into the spicy-smelling sheets. Listening out for her mother's footsteps, all she heard was the muffled drumming and the crackle of fireworks. Her mother didn't come; Ayah didn't come. Only the rain came. Sophie heard it battering off the roof, louder than any village drum. The air cooled. Then she slept.

***

Finally, they found the child curled up in the laundry chest, squinting at the sudden light. She was shocked and mute as they lifted her out, hair damp and matted against her flushed cheeks. But it was the eyes – dark pools full of terror – that shook them the most. It was a look that haunted, and left them worrying just how much the girl had seen.

Chapter 1

Edinburgh, June 1922

Sophie Logan leapt up the spiral steps two at a time, the clatter of her shoes on the worn stone echoing up the gloomy tenement stairwell. She burst through the door of the second-floor flat, unpinning her hat, kicking off her shoes and calling, 'Auntie Amy! I'm back.'

The sound of hammering stopped. 'In here, dearie.'

Sophie peered into the chaotic room her aunt used as a workshop for furniture making, breathing in the smell of newly cut wood and varnish. Amy Anderson looked up, grinning under a mop of fading, frizzy fair hair, her trim body enveloped in dusty overalls. The walnut bookcase was nearly finished.

'Good day, dearie?'

'Bedlam, Auntie. I had to run the office while Miss Gorrie went over to Duddingston to interview a new cook for the home. The telephone didn't stop ringing. What did people do before they were invented?'

'Wrote letters and had a bit of patience.' Amy snorted.

Sophie laughed. Stepping over planks, she ran her hand over the hand-carved decoration of flowers and leaves.

'It's beautiful – so lifelike.' She put her nose to the wood and breathed in the nutty, spicy smell. Her insides fluttered at the spark of memory; the smell of trees, of India.

'Don't eat it,' her aunt teased, 'or you'll spoil your supper.'

The memory evaporated. 'Shall I put the kettle on, Auntie?'

'A pot of tea would be grand. Oh, and talking of letters; there's one come for you from Newcastle.'

'Tilly?' Sophie gasped in excitement. Her aunt nodded. 'It's about time. What are the arrangements for her twenty-first birthday?'

'Believe it or not,' said Amy, 'I haven't steamed it open.'

'We'll read it over a cup of tea.' Sophie smiled. 'The suspense must have been killing you.'

‘Cheeky wee madam,’ her aunt said with a mock wagging finger.

While the kettle boiled on the gas range in the tiny kitchen, Sophie dashed into the sitting room, slit open her cousin Tilly’s letter with an ivory-handled letter opener and stood in the light of the window to read it. There were reams of pale blue notepaper covered in Tilly’s neat slanting writing, telling her in great detail of the goings-on in the Watson household and life in the bustling industrial city a hundred miles south of Edinburgh.

The cheery Watsons had been a lifeline for her when she’d been shipped back from India, orphaned and dislocated, and given into the care of her mother’s older sister Amy. Sophie remembered so little of her first six years: snapshots of colour – white light filtering through lime green leaves, the salmon pink of her Ayah’s sari – and a birthday without a party. She had long forgotten the faces of early childhood.

Her spinster aunt had tried her best to provide a home and soon involved her clinging niece in her every activity – suffrage meetings, Kirk on Sundays, trips to the timber yards – but it was the holiday visits to her aunt’s cousins in Newcastle that had brought the laughter and words back to Sophie’s plump lips.

‘Cousin Johnny’s been posted to somewhere called Pindi,’ Sophie called out to her aunt. ‘Have you heard of it?’

‘Rawalpindi,’ Amy answered, appearing in the doorway. ‘It’s an army station in the north Punjab. Your parents married and honeymooned near there in a hill station called Murree.’

‘Did they?’ Sophie glanced at the silver-framed photograph on the mantelpiece of a handsome couple in elaborate wedding clothes. It always struck her how sombre they looked but Amy had assured her that her parents were merely keeping still for the camera.

‘Jessie loved it there.’ Amy smiled. ‘Didn’t mind that it was winter and snowing; it had a healthy Scottish bluster.’

‘Wasn’t that a long way from Assam?’

Amy shrugged. ‘Aye, but we had a church connection there – a mission with a boarding house – I suppose they got a good rate at that time of year. And your mother always loved the hills.’

Sophie waited for more; her aunt rarely talked about her mother in case it upset her but Sophie craved these nuggets of information. Amy nodded towards the kitchen.

'Don't boil that kettle dry.'

Later, with cups of tea poured and shortbread eaten, Sophie read out the long letter. There was talk of Tilly's mother going to stay with her eldest married daughter in Dunbar for the summer where the sea air would do her chest good.

'*I'll probably have to go with her,*' Sophie read aloud, '*unless you can think up an excuse for me. What are the chances of Auntie Amy taking us to Switzerland on the train again? It was the best holiday I've ever had in my life. Beg her for me, will you?*'

Amy Anderson laughed. 'Tilly spent the whole time complaining about walking up mountains. But it was a grand trip, wasn't it? It was thanks to the bequest from the Oxford Tea Company that we could afford to go.'

'Yes, the company have been good to me, haven't they?'

'Well, your father was a respected employee – the company was only doing what was right by putting a bit in trust for you – seeing you through your education. And, from what I hear, they made huge profits during the War.'

'Still, it was kind of them,' said Sophie, returning to the letter.

'*Johnny's dear friend Clarrie Robson is back on leave from Assam with her small daughter Adela. She's just as much fun as ever and the girl is a pretty dark-eyed thing, already talking ten to the dozen. Clarrie's handsome husband isn't with her (more's the pity!) but Wesley will be here in the autumn to take them back, when things aren't so hectic in the tea gardens—*'

'Is that the woman who ran the tea room in West Newcastle?' Amy interrupted. 'What was it called?'

'Herbert's.' Sophie nodded. 'Named after her first husband. Her stepson Will was a good friend of Johnny's, remember? Me and Tilly had such a massive crush on Will. I think it was the floppy hair – and he was always teasing us younger girls but in a nice way.'

'Oh aye, the poor laddie who died after the war ended.'

'Yes,' Sophie sighed. 'Tilly said Clarrie was heartbroken – and Johnny too.'

'Well, it's grand that she found happiness again with one of the Robsons,' said Amy.

'Listen to this.' Sophie read on, '*Wesley's cousin, James Robson, is also on leave in Newcastle, though he and Clarrie don't really get on. It's the first time he's been back to England since before the Kaiser's War.*'

'James Robson?' Amy gasped.

Sophie looked up quickly. 'Is he the Robson who worked with my father in Assam?'

'Aye he is.' Her aunt was giving her an odd look.

'And?'

Amy hesitated. 'He was the man who brought you back after your parents . . .' Her voice softened. 'Don't you remember him?'

Sophie shrugged. 'No, not really. I remember the big ship and feeling seasick, but that's all. Tell me about him.'

But Amy said, 'Read on, dearie, and see what Tilly has to say.'

Sophie went back to the letter.

'*He called on Mama last week with letters from Johnny and photos of the wedding in Calcutta. My new sister-in-law Helena looks ever so pretty. Apparently the wedding dress was sent for from Paris. Mama put on a brave face but she's still upset that they chose to rush into marriage instead of waiting till next year when she could come out. But Helena's family are mostly in Calcutta and Delhi so it suited them – and, between you, me and the gatepost, Mama would never survive a trip to India with her bad chest. So I can't blame Johnny for wanting to get on with it.*

'*Mr Robson isn't a bit like his cousin Wesley. Isn't it funny how different members of the same family can be? He's not as tall – more square like a prize-fighter – and he's older – his hair has already gone grey, though his thick moustache is still brown. He's what you would call weather-beaten and he couldn't sit still for two minutes.*

'*I don't think he's used to female company as he really didn't have much to say for himself, except when Mama got him on to talking about dogs and horses. He's missing his animals on the tea estate, especially his favourite – a retriever called Rowan. He made a real fuss over our fat Flossy and she seemed to take to him too. Mama said it was a bit of a relief when he went, but, out of politeness, she insisted on him coming to my twenty-first birthday party next Saturday.*

'*Come a day early if you can, so you can stop Mama and Mona fussing too much. You are so lucky not to have a bossy older sister – but Mona will be so much nicer to me if you are there! Auntie Amy is to come too of course. It won't be grand, just a nice tea and a bit of dancing to keep you happy. I can't wait to see you. Let us know on which train you plan to arrive.*

'*Your loving cousin and best friend, Silly Tilly.*'

Sophie looked up, her brown eyes shining with excitement. 'Let's go on the motorcycle – give The Memsahib a run out.'

Amy rolled her eyes. 'Lassie, I'm not sitting on that flapper seat for all the tea in India.'

'I'll get the garage to fix the sidecar back on again.'

'You've never driven it that far before.'

'Almost as far. We could stop off in the Borders for a night on the way. Miss Gorrie said I could take a few days off.'

Sophie was eager for the trip away; she had done little for her own twenty-first birthday a month ago, just helped out at a fundraising hop for Miss Gorrie and had a cake baked by her aunt.

Amy saw the determination in her niece's face; it was useless to argue with her when she got an idea into her wilful pretty head.

'So,' said Sophie, pacing to the window, 'we'll get to meet this James Robson again.' She was intrigued by the thought of meeting someone who had known her parents in India.

'Aye, and you can thank him in person for his kindness to you,' her aunt pointed out. 'Even if you don't remember it.'

Sophie gazed down the street opposite, to the yellow gorse and green slopes of Salisbury Crags. She never tired of the incongruous sight of the rocky outcrop so close to the heart of the soot-blackened city. She was seized with renewed impatience to be out in the countryside again. She would never really be a city girl, however long she lived here; not like Tilly who loved libraries, theatre trips, shopping or just sitting in a fuggy parlour endlessly reading. Dear Tilly.

As Sophie folded the letter, she noticed a post scriptum scrawled on the back.

'Johnny and Helena have invited me out to India. Mama thinks I should go. I think they are plotting to get me married off to someone suitable. What do you think I should do? You always come up with the right answer. We shall discuss it next week.'

Sophie felt a pang of anxiety.

'What's wrong, lassie?' Amy asked. She passed her aunt the final page.

'Oh, I see,' Amy said, understanding at once. 'You're worried Tilly will stay and not come back.'

Sophie nodded, gulping down the panic inside. She relied so completely on Tilly's friendship that she couldn't imagine her not being close enough for them to meet up every few months as they had done since childhood. India was so very far away.

'Don't go worrying about something that might never happen,' Amy advised. She knew that underneath the smiles and chatter, her niece still had a fear of losing people close to her. She had learnt when young that bad things did happen.

'You're right, Auntie,' Sophie said, putting on a brave face and dismissing the thought.

Chapter 2

Sophie rode out of Edinburgh on a blustery June day with a roar of engine and a belch of blue exhaust smoke, her Auntie Amy snug under a rug and tarpaulin in the open sidecar and their luggage secured in its trunk. Sophie, in jodhpurs, cast-off army jacket and goggles, and her fair ponytail lifting in the wind, gripped the juddering handlebars as The Memsahib rose and dipped along the route to Dalkeith and the south.

She had learnt to drive at seventeen in the last year of the war when she had worked at the Red Cross depot. Soon tiring of counting supplies, she had volunteered to deliver clothes and linen to the various hospitals and convalescent homes, always finding time to chat to the invalids. One amputee, a major with the Scottish Horse, had been so grateful for her cheerful banter and broad smile that he had given her his old Enfield motorcycle. Sophie, who loved things mechanical, had learnt to grapple with its eccentricities, change a tyre (punctures were frequent), thin the oil and clean the plugs. Sophie Logan and her noisy motorcycle were a common sight in south Edinburgh and on the steep winding roads of the nearby Pentland Hills. Her aunt loved to be taken on picnics into the countryside or down the coast, usually returning with the sidecar crammed with driftwood or fallen branches for her to fashion into cigarette boxes or spurtles for stirring porridge.

They stopped in Lauder for lunch and Jedburgh for afternoon tea.

'Let's press on, Auntie Amy,' urged Sophie, the cramp in her arms from holding the heavy bike on the twisting roads having eased. 'The rain's holding off and it's still hours till nightfall.'

Soon they were out of the town and heading through dense woods. An open lorry full of men overtook them with a boisterous hooting. Some of the men waved and whistled through their fingers but Sophie could only imagine the ribald comments they would be making at a woman driver. She glanced sideways to see her aunt returning a regal wave, which caused much amusement among the grinning workmen as the lorry sped away in a cloud of acrid smoke that set the women coughing.

Shortly afterwards, they were leaving the lush farmland and grinding upwards into bleak moorland whose monotony was broken only by swaying plantations of young conifers. The higher they climbed, the more the wind strengthened until it was hard to keep the bike steady. At the steepest incline, the sky abruptly darkened and rain came on, sudden and heavy.

Sophie stopped to struggle into waterproofs.

'Shall we go back to Jedburgh?' Amy shouted from under a black sou'wester.

'No, it's too far,' Sophie called through the rain, 'and we're nearly at Carter Bar. We'll get over the top and stop at Otterburn if we have to.' Silently, she was still determined to get to Newcastle that day and surprise Tilly, who wasn't expecting them until tomorrow.

The Memsahib wouldn't start. The engine coughed and died. Sophie tried again, and a third time. From the smell of oil she knew she'd flooded it. Why had she stopped? She had already been soaked before putting on waterproofs, and the delay had only given further discomfort to her aunt.

'I need to change the oil,' she explained. Amy, stoic but grim-faced, began to climb from the sidecar. 'No, please, Auntie, don't get out.'

Pushing her goggles on to her head, Sophie peered through the horizontal rain; the road ahead disappeared into mist. It was miles back downhill since they had passed the last isolated farm but she could smell wood smoke on the wind, so there must be some habitation close by. If she couldn't get it started, they would have to beg for shelter.

With numb fingers she began to fumble with the tool box where a can of spare oil was kept. Her oilskin cape billowed up and flew in her face, the wind blowing her sideways.

Amy watched with concern, and lost patience. 'This is ridiculous – you'll catch your death. We need to find a bothy. There'll be one in the woods for the shepherds.'

'Just give me a minute,' Sophie protested.

'Come on, lassie,' Amy said, just as stubborn, 'leave the wretched beast – at least till the rain eases off.'

On the point of giving up, there was a sudden rumbling noise and a truck rattled out of the mist. It trundled past the waving women, slowed, stopped and reversed towards them. A lean young man jumped down from the cabin.

'Hello, ladies, can we help? Me and Boz wondered where you'd got to,' he grinned, pushing a slick of wet hair out of his eyes. 'Run out of petrol, have you? We've got spare.'

'No.' Sophie felt foolish. 'I just need to change the oil.'

'Looks like you need a change of clothes too.'

She blushed at his assessing look. He was scruffily dressed but his Scots accent was educated. 'It's nothing I can't manage.'

'Let us help,' he insisted. 'Your poor mother is getting drenched.' 'Thank you, young man,' Amy called, already out of the sidecar and accepting his offer with alacrity.

He went straight across to help her, taking her by the elbow and steering her towards the truck. 'Jump aboard and we'll take you back to the camp to dry off.'

A tall, red-headed man with large ears loped around the back of the vehicle.

'Boz, get their luggage,' the driver ordered as he lifted a dripping Amy to safety. He turned back to Sophie. 'In you get, quick as you can.'

Soon, both women were perched up high, squeezed in between the two men.

'I'm Tam Telfer,' the driver introduced himself as he turned the lorry around, 'and this is William Boswell, but everyone calls him Boz.'

The red-haired friend smiled bashfully and nodded in agreement.

Amy introduced them in return. 'How fortunate that you came along when you did; an answer to our prayers.'

'That's not how we're usually described,' Tam laughed. 'But to tell you the truth, we've been keeping an eye out for you coming over the top. When the rain came on hard, Boz and I thought we should go looking for the damsels in distress.'

Amy glanced at Sophie and raised an eyebrow. 'How very observant.'

'How did you know we were heading for Carter Bar?' Sophie was curious.

Tam turned and winked. 'You were packed for a journey and this road only goes to England.'

Boz spoke up, his accent thicker. 'We've been watching the bike frae the plantation. Tam was takin' bets as to whether you'd make it up the brae.'

'Was he now?' Sophie felt annoyance.

But Amy laughed. 'You're foresters then?'

'Student foresters,' Tam said, 'at Edinburgh University. The reason we're so long in the tooth is we had an extended holiday in Flanders, courtesy of the Kaiser, before starting our degree.'

'Good for you, laddies.' Amy nodded with approval.

'Was it you who overtook us south of Jedburgh?' Sophie asked, remembering the lorry of laughing men.

'Yes,' Tam admitted, his look amused as he steered the truck between a break in the trees and pulled up outside a long, low hut.

'So how much did you win in your bet that I wouldn't make it to the top?' Sophie challenged.

Tam pulled on the brake and cut the engine. He looked at her with bright blue eyes full of merriment. 'I lost two bob,' he replied. 'I was the only man bet you would get to the top before it rained.'

A huge beam spread across Sophie's bedraggled yet still pretty face.

***

The men gave up one of their bunkrooms for the women, brought in hot water in a zinc tub and left them to change.

'Sorry, Auntie,' Sophie apologised, brushing out her wet hair and pulling on a Fair Isle jumper. 'I shouldn't have insisted on leaving Jedburgh. Looks like we're here for the night.'

'This is no hardship,' Amy said brightly, 'and maybe they can be a new source of cheap timber.' She winked.

In the spartan communal mess room they sat around a scrubbed table with a dozen students and ate ham and egg pie, peas, kale and steamed potatoes.

'The lecturers don't stay here,' Tam explained. 'They prefer a comfy billet in Jedburgh or to drive out from Edinburgh for the day – make sure we haven't thinned the wrong trees or raided over the border.'

He was delighted to find Amy's interest in trees and they talked animatedly about different types of wood, their grains and suitability for furniture. Sophie observed him. There was an energy about him and a sense of fun that immediately appealed. Despite a beaky nose, he was handsome with a strong jaw, sharp blue eyes and a lean athletic build. She noticed a scar on the back of his head where the hair had not grown back and wondered how he had got it.

'And do you share your aunt's passion for wood, Miss Logan?' he was quick to include her.

'I'm in awe at what she does with it' – Sophie smiled – 'but I prefer my trees alive. I love nothing better than to walk through wild forests.'

Tam's look was quizzical. 'You can't get much opportunity to do that around Edinburgh?'

'No, but The Memsahib allows me to reach the Border forests or get up to Perthshire.'

For a moment Tam was lost for words.

'She means her motorcycle.' Amy chuckled.

'Ah! Why *memsahib*?'

'I grew up in India till I was six,' Sophie explained. 'It's a bit tongue in cheek I suppose – my motorcycle is the boss, not me, I'm afraid.'

Tam laughed. 'How interesting. Some of us boys are training for the Indian Forest Service – me and Boz – and Rafi over there.' He thumbed down the table at a dark-haired Indian who nodded and gave an attractive smile. Sophie noticed how at ease he seemed among them, yet there was something unsettling about him. Maybe it was just the mention of India again so soon after Tilly's letter.

'You're going to work in India?' Sophie's interest quickened.

Tam nodded. 'Just another month of practical, then exams in early September and we're off.'

Boz interjected. 'Not forgetting a month in France and Switzerland in August learning from their foresters.'

'Switzerland?' Sophie cried. 'Lucky you!'

'You know it?' Tam asked.

'Auntie Amy took me and a cousin there before the war. I fell in love with it.'

'They say the foothills of the Himalayas look like Switzerland.' Tam called down the table to the Indian. 'Isn't that right, Rafi?'

Rafi shrugged and laughed. 'I wouldn't know, Telfer – you can't see them from downtown Lahore.' His voice betrayed little of an Indian accent.

'You're such a city boy,' Tam teased. 'Don't know how you're going to cope in the jungle.'

'Just like you Telfer – by getting the natives to do all the hard work.'

Tam barked with laughter. 'Don't be fooled by Rafi's *sahib* act.' He winked at Sophie. 'Five years in the army and three as a student have turned him into a terrible radical. Surname should be Lenin, not Khan.'

They took mugs of tea and sat around a fire that filled the room with aromatic wood smoke. Tam brought out cards and the women joined in a game of rummy. Boz struck up on a guitar and they joined in popular war songs and Scottish ballads.

'Sophie can play,' Amy told them.

'I haven't for ages, Auntie.'

'Go on,' Tam encouraged. 'We've had Boz singing out of tune all week – please take it off him.'

Sophie strummed and sang 'The Skye Boat Song'. Then Amy requested some North Country songs that her Watson cousins had taught her. The students clapped and sang along; Tam told her she had a voice as sweet as honey. She knew he was the type who flirted with women but she was enjoying the attention. What harm would it do for one evening? She would probably never see him again.

They retired to bed with the rain still drumming on the corrugated iron roof, Tam and Boz promising to rescue her bike in the morning.

Sometime in the early hours the rain stopped and the silence woke Sophie. She lay and dozed, but Amy's snores prevented her from falling back asleep. After pulling on clothes, she padded barefoot into the mess. Her boots were still damp but she put them on and went outside.

The sun was watery and yellow, rising over the treetops, the air fresh and smelling of pine and damp earth. Sophie closed her eyes and breathed it in.

'Best part of the day, isn't it?'

Startled, she spun round. Tam was standing in shirt and khaki trousers, hair still ruffled from sleep, smiling at her. Her stomach lurched.

'Yes,' she agreed, pushing loose, unbrushed hair behind her ears, self-conscious at her dishevelled state. 'I didn't think anyone would be up. I thought I'd walk – couldn't sleep.'

'Can I come with you?' he asked. 'Or do we need a chaperone?'

'My chaperone is sound asleep.'

'Shall we risk it?'

Sophie nodded. 'I'll behave myself if you will.'

Tam grinned in delight at her teasing.

For a while they walked in silence, Tam leading her along a track through the woods, then he stopped to point out trees they had marked and fence posts they had cut and hammered into the ground.

'Tough work,' he said, 'but none of us are shy of getting our hands dirty. It's what the army taught us – don't ask a man to do a job you're not prepared to do yourself.'

She asked him about the war. He'd started as a private in the Scottish Horse then transferred to Artillery; finished up as a captain in the mortar division.

'Boz and I were 'mortar-mongers' – went through the whole thing together.'

'Did you know Major Bruce MacGregor in the Scottish Horse?' Sophie asked.

'Knew a captain of that name – must be the same man. Tall with a bushy moustache.'

'Walks on crutches now; lost a leg,' Sophie said. 'The Memsahib belonged to him. He wouldn't let me pay for it. Said my befriending him was worth ten motorcycles.'

Tam gave her a sidelong look. 'I think I'm jealous of the major.'

She laughed and blushed. 'Tell me more about France.'

But Tam seemed reluctant to talk of the war.

'You tell me about India first. I need to know all there is before I go.'

Sophie sighed. 'I'm afraid I'm the wrong person to ask; I remember so little. You see, my parents both died of fever when I was six; it was all terribly sudden. I know my father was a tea planter in Assam and my mother came out from Edinburgh to marry him, but I wouldn't even know what they looked like if Auntie Amy hadn't kept their photo on the mantelpiece. Isn't that sad?'

Tam stopped and put a hand on her shoulder. 'You poor girl. No brothers or sisters?'

'No, just Auntie and my second cousins in Newcastle.'

Tam squeezed her shoulder. 'Well, from what I can see, Auntie Amy's been as good as any mother could be – worth at least ten motorcycles.'

Sophie's eyes pricked with tears as she smiled back. 'Yes, she is. And Cousin Tilly's worth another half a dozen.'

'There you are then – rich in relations,' Tam declared.

They walked on, comfortable in each other's company, swapping stories about life in Edinburgh. Tam lived to the west of the city in Roseburn and talked with affection about his formidable mother and older sister Flora who had been suffragists before the war and now were passionate about Christian Science.

'What's that exactly?' Sophie asked.

'I suppose it's about the power of prayer – and the mind – to overcome weakness in the body; to heal.' He gave her a wary look as if she might find such talk embarrassing.

'Go on,' she encouraged.

'Rather than just sit and listen to a sermon and be told what to think,' he went on, 'we Christian Scientists read to each other and concentrate the mind on making each other better – doesn't matter where you are in the world.'

'Like positive thinking?'

'More than that,' Tam said, enthusing. 'It's tapping into the creative force – mother, father, God – whatever you want to call it.' He looked at Sophie with eyes that shone. 'Sometimes, in the trenches, I'd get so exhausted that I could hardly drag myself out of my billet – completely physically and mentally done in. Then this friend I met – an American – encouraged me to do some Science. I thought it sounded a madcap idea but did it just to please. Suddenly I had all this energy again – the lads thought it was the toffees Mother sent me,' Tam smiled, 'but I knew it was more than that. Christian Science gave me the strength to carry on and now my mother and sister practise it regularly too. They like the idea that the philosophy was started by a woman.' There was a note of defiance in his voice. 'I can see from your look that now you think I'm quite mad.'

Sophie shook her head and smiled. 'I think you look extremely fit, so there must be something in it.'

Tam laughed. 'I like you, Sophie Logan.'

They walked on and suddenly were through the woods; the view opened up, taking Sophie's breath away. The hills rolled into the misty shimmer of dawn, a skylark trilling high above.

While she gazed into the distance, Tam studied her, entranced by her fresh pink-cheeked looks, huge brown eyes and full lips parted in wonder. Her blonde hair fell in untidy waves about her shoulders, and he imagined her soft tresses spread across his pillow on the bunk bed he had vacated for her. Dangerous thoughts, he warned himself.

‘Can I see you again, Sophie?’ he asked, though he hadn’t meant to.

She turned and smiled in surprise, her face suffused in the morning light. He took her hand and held it in his for a moment, warming it in his rough, dry palm. Sophie’s insides fluttered with desire.

She swallowed hard and replied, ‘Yes, Tam, I’d like that very much.’

Chapter 3

Newcastle

Tilly was watching at the bay window of the terraced house in Gosforth and flew outside at the noisy arrival of the motorcycle. Flossy the West Highland terrier waddled at her heels, barking. Small children stopped play to gape at the women on the bike; the pony of a tea delivery van whinnied and stamped in alarm in the normally quiet street.

Tilly flung plump arms about the dismounting Sophie. 'You must have driven like the wind to get here so quickly.'

'We came from Carter Bar this morning.' Sophie grinned and hugged her cousin.

'Carter Bar?' Tilly exclaimed.

'Aye, we were kidnapped by wild forest men,' Amy said, clambering stiffly out of the sidecar.

'How exciting!' said Tilly, nearly tripping over fat Flossy as she went to help. 'But with you two, nothing surprises me. Welcome, Auntie Amy.' She kissed her on the cheek and chattered non-stop as she helped her up the steps, while Sophie carried in their bags.

When Tilly's father had been alive, the Watsons had employed a butler-cum-footman to fetch and carry, but since his death after the war, the family had lived more modestly. The paintwork of the once grand frontage was peeling and Tilly had confided recently that the house was becoming too much for her mother to manage.

Tilly's oldest sister, Mona, appeared and greeted them. 'Let Tilly carry one of those cases,' she fussed. 'How was your journey? I can't imagine why you didn't come by train.' Useless for Sophie to explain that the motorcycle was her one bit of adventure, for Mona continued without pause. 'We'll have tea in the drawing-room just as soon as you're settled. I'll tell Cook you're here. Mother's resting. She's having a bad day with her chest – probably the pollen.'

'I'm sorry to hear that,' said Amy.

'You can go in and see her later. Oh, Tilly!' Mona called after her sister while holding on to Flossy. 'Do be careful with that case; you're bashing it off the banister.'

'Oh, silly me,' Tilly said, flustered.

'It doesn't matter,' Sophie reassured, 'the case is ancient.'

'But the banister isn't,' Mona replied. 'Lift the case higher; that's it.'

Pausing for breath on the landing, Tilly rolled her eyes. 'I'll still be five years old in Mona's eyes when they're wheeling me about in a bath chair.'

'Us both.' Sophie grinned.

'No.' Tilly shook her head. 'She may pretend to disapprove but she secretly admires your independent spirit. All we Watsons do.'

Over tea and sponge cake, they caught up on news. Tilly's other sister Jacobina was doing well as a governess near Inverness but was too far away to attend the birthday party. Mona dominated the conversation. When she'd exhausted the topic of her married life in Dunbar and how well her husband's grain business was going, she turned her critical eye on her youngest sister who was feeding titbits to their old dog.

'You shouldn't feed her cake, you know, she's fat enough as it is. Would you like more tea, Aunt Amy? Of course Walter's been very good about me coming down here to help with Tilly's birthday celebrations. She has an admirer, has she told you?'

'Hardly that,' Tilly said, her round face going crimson under her mop of red curls. She began a vigorous patting of Flossy.

'Called twice this week and sent a huge bouquet of flowers, and it's not even her birthday yet.'

'They were for Mother too.'

Sophie noticed how Tilly's hazel eyes shone and her cheeks dimpled at the teasing. 'Tell me more at once. You said nothing in your last letter about bunches of flowers.'

'There's nothing to tell.'

'James Robson,' Mona said on her sister's behalf, 'the tea planter. I'm surprised Tilly hasn't mentioned him – especially with your father's connection to the Oxford Tea Company. They were managers together, weren't they? Mr Robson said he knew you as a child before your parents' sudden passing away.'

'Mona, I don't think Sophie wants reminding . . .'

'I don't mind, really,' Sophie said at once. No one had ever understood that it was the not speaking about her parents that she found the hardest to bear. She gave Tilly a quizzical smile. 'Mr Robson, eh? The one who got on so well with Flossy?'

'He – he's quite sweet really,' Tilly stammered and fiddled with a strand of wavy red hair.

'A bit on the old side,' said Mona, 'and you've got to wonder why he's got to the age of forty-five and never married.'

'How on earth do you know his age?' Tilly exclaimed.

'I asked Clarrie Robson of course; she knows everything about the Robsons with her being married to James's cousin. Was a bit guarded when I asked her opinion, but admitted he was shrewd in business.'

'Mona! You had no right to go asking about Mr Robson – not on my behalf. I hardly know him.'

'Precisely,' said Mona. 'That's why I needed to make enquiries. Didn't want our little Tilly making a fool of herself over him. More tea, Aunt Amy?'

'Thank you.' Amy held out her cup. 'I'm sure Tilly is quite able to assess Mr Robson for herself, Mona dearie.'

'And Cousin Johnny knows him, doesn't he?' Sophie said. 'Trusted him to bring back his wedding photos.'

Mona pursed her lips. 'Met him over a few whiskies in some club in Shillong, which is hardly a recommendation.'

Tilly protested at this. 'It wasn't like that. Clarrie and Wesley introduced them when Johnny was posted to Shillong as doctor to the Ghurkha regiment there. James Robson was suffering terribly with a bad tooth and, as there wasn't a dentist for hundreds of miles, Johnny extracted the tooth. Mr Robson was so grateful, he gave our brother a couple of days shooting in return.'

'So your Mr Robson is toothless as well as old?' Sophie grinned.

‘Oh be quiet, he’s not my Mr Robson.’ Tilly giggled and slapped Sophie’s hand, making her spill tea down her skirt.

‘Tilly, look what you’ve done,’ Mona scolded. ‘You are the clumsiest girl!’

‘Sorry, Sophie.’ Tilly thrust her linen napkin at her friend.

Sophie dabbed. ‘It’s fine – and I deserved that.’

‘Tell me about your wild foresters, Auntie Amy,’ Tilly said, steering the conversation away from the Robsons.

‘Wild foresters?’ Mona repeated, alert to fresh gossip.

Amy briefly described their rescue in the rain.

‘And you stayed with them overnight in their camp?’ Mona gasped in shock.

‘And lived to tell the tale,’ Sophie said dryly. ‘Some of them are training for India.’

‘I wonder if any of them will go to Assam?’ Tilly asked. ‘Clarrie will be interested. She and Wesley helped fund a young Indian friend through forestry training at Dehra Dun.’

‘Indian?’ Mona frowned. ‘Whatever for?’

‘He’s the great nephew of her old head servant or some such. Fought in Flanders.’

‘There was an Indian among the Edinburgh students,’ Amy said. ‘Rafi Khan they called him. That’s a Mohammedan name.’

Tilly shook her head. ‘No, that wasn’t it but we’ll ask Clarrie at the party.’

‘Goodness me!’ Mona cried. ‘Let’s change the conversation from forestry men and Indians before Mother comes in.’ She rang the bell for Cook to remove the tea tray. ‘And, Tilly, you had better help Sophie change out of her wet skirt and give it a sponge down before it stains.’

The friends jumped up at the opportunity to escape upstairs.

***

Tilly’s messy bedroom was crammed with books and postage stamp albums; an old nursery table was covered with envelopes and piles of stamps still to be sorted, mounted and labelled.

'Johnny's sent me some Indian ones – and he's friendly with an Australian padre who's going to collect for me too. I do miss Johnny, though.' Tilly sighed and plonked down on the bed. 'No one to stick up for me when Mother and Mona are nagging.'

Sophie changed out of her skirt. 'I'll have to put my jodhpurs back on – I only brought one skirt and a dress for the party.' She dabbed at the stain with cold water from the washstand. 'So you think you'll go out and visit Johnny then?'

'I may have to.' Tilly shrugged, sounding suddenly dejected.

'What do you mean?'

Tilly twirled hair around her finger; a sign of nervousness that Sophie knew well.

'Tell me.' Sophie abandoned the skirt and sat down beside her cousin.

'I'm not supposed to say until after the party.'

'You can tell me anything,' Sophie encouraged, 'you know I'll keep it secret.'

Tilly's shoulders sagged. 'Mother is going to live with Mona.'

'Yes, you said in your letter. But just for the summer?'

'No' – Tilly sighed– 'for good. Mother is selling the house. I offered to be housekeeper here, do the cooking, if it meant Mother could stay on, but Mona and Walter said it's out of the question and that I couldn't possibly cope.'

'Yes you could!'

'No, it's worse than I realised.' Tilly said. 'There are debts to pay. Johnny's medical training took all my parents' savings. Walter says the sale of the house will pay them off and leave a bit over for them to keep Mother in comfort.'

'But what about you and Jacobina?' Sophie cried. 'This is your home too.'

'Not for much longer. And Jacobina doesn't mind like I do; she loves the Highlands and won't ever return to a life in the city.'

Sophie saw the tears welling in Tilly's eyes. She put arms about her friend's plump shoulders.

'Don't worry, it won't be that bad. Dunbar is a pleasant town and it'll be nearer for us to visit each other.'

Tilly shook her head. 'Mona has convinced Mother that it would be better for me to go to India and stay with Johnny and Helena – my best chance of finding a husband. Mona doesn't want me in Dunbar being a drain on their household.'

Sophie snorted. 'She was boasting about how well Walter's business is doing.'

Tilly gave an unhappy look. 'That's just Mona putting on a brave face. Things are tough for farmers since the war ended.'

Sophie asked. 'What do you want to do?'

Tilly was torn. 'I want to see Johnny again of course . . . But I don't know what's more terrifying; being married off to someone I hardly know or not finding anyone who wants to marry me and being sent back to Mother and Mona as a failure.'

'Oh, Tilly!' Sophie exclaimed. 'I bet the young officers in Pindi will be queuing up to marry you. You're the prettiest, kindest girl I've ever known.'

Tilly blushed and suppressed a smile. 'Nonsense.'

'Not nonsense,' Sophie declared. 'And if you don't find anyone worthy of you, then you can come back to Edinburgh and live with me and Auntie.'

'Can I?' Tilly brightened.

'Of course.'

A tear spilled from Tilly's eye and her chin wobbled. 'You are the best friend anyone could ask for,' Tilly gasped, and they hugged each other tight.

Chapter 4

Stepping from the dusty drab street of Newcastle's West End into Herbert's Tea Rooms, Sophie was assaulted by colour. It was decorated with party streamers and Chinese lanterns, the tables laid with starched white cloths, vases of multi-coloured flowers and tiers of dainty sandwiches, fruit scones and slices of chocolate cake – Tilly's favourite.

Sophie gazed at the Egyptian-style decor of golden sphinx, bejewelled pharaohs and black hieroglyphics painted on to bright yellow walls, with palm fronds standing in brass holders on the black and white tiled floor. Incongruous, she thought, to pass from the gritty working-class quarter and the clank of industry into this dazzling oasis of gaudy glamour and the strains of a string quartet.

Tilly gripped Sophie's arm in alarm. 'Why is it set out for so many? I only wanted something small.'

A handsome dark-haired woman in an old-fashioned tea dress rushed to greet them.

'Happy birthday, Tilly!' she planted a kiss on her flushed cheek. 'How bonny you look in blue.'

'Clarrie, this looks wonderful,' Tilly gasped at her hostess. 'You've gone to so much trouble. I don't deserve it.'

'Of course you do, and it's no trouble at all.' Clarrie smiled. 'Lexy and the girls have done all the hard work.' She turned to Sophie, her eyes widening at the sight of the shapely young woman in a short cream crêpe de chine frock, jaunty green hat and kid gloves. 'Can this beautiful young lady be little Sophie Logan? Do you still like custard tarts?'

Sophie laughed and shook hands. 'Yes I do! Are you still making the best ones in the land?'

Clarrie put a hand on her arm. 'Still a little charmer, I see. And yes, they are just as good. You'll please Lexy no end if you eat as many as you can.'

'It's such a beautiful cafe,' Sophie enthused. 'Better than anything I've seen in Edinburgh – and we do cafes very well.'

'Again I can't take the credit – my sister Olive redesigned it all to suit modern tastes,' Clarrie said. 'Since I went back to live in India, she helps Lexy run this place. My husband and I really only help with the finances now.'

'Where's Adela?' Tilly asked. 'I hoped she'd be here.'

'Olive is looking after my wild lass this afternoon – she's being spoilt rotten by her big cousins.'

'I know the feeling.' Sophie grinned and slipped her arm through Tilly's.

Clarrie welcomed in Tilly's mother and sister, finding Mrs Watson a chair at once, noticing her laboured breathing and pasty look. Mona stood guard at the door, pulling Tilly firmly by the hand so she wouldn't escape greeting friends and acquaintances as they arrived. Sophie caught Tilly's pleading look and hovered close by, amazed at the number of guests trooping in, while Tilly stuttered a bashful welcome. When the tea room had filled up, Sophie steered Tilly away from Mona and introduced Clarrie to Auntie Amy.

'A suffrage friend of mine spoke highly of you, Mrs Robson,' Amy said, 'for allowing your cafe to be used for the census protest before the war.'

'Oh, what a night that was, partying till dawn!' Clarrie clapped her hands. 'Who was your friend?'

'Florence Beal. She thought you very brave as you hadn't been open long and no doubt there were plenty who disapproved.'

'Dear Florence! Yes, plenty disapproved,' Clarrie admitted, 'including my eldest stepson. But I used to find that if something incensed Bertie then it was usually a cause worth fighting for.' She gave a wry smile. 'Now,' she turned to Tilly, 'you lasses must find friends your own age. Why don't you join the group over there? Church friends, are they?'

'Tennis club mainly,' Tilly said, glancing anxiously across.

'Tennis?' Sophie said in surprise.

'I play more bridge there than tennis admittedly.' Tilly giggled. 'Mona must have invited them.'

Sophie saw Tilly's reluctance and slipped an arm through hers. 'Come on, introduce me to your sporty friends, then we'll stuff ourselves with cake.'

With her cousin at her side, Tilly found the party less of an ordeal. She was happiest in a small group of people she knew well, but Sophie could speak to anyone and soon had the tennis crowd laughing at stories about their childhood holidays together; camping in the Pentland Hills and visiting Great Uncle Daniel, a retired weaver, in Perth.

'He taught us to fish,' Sophie said. 'It was the only thing he knew how to cook so we had fish nearly every day. When it came to gutting them, Tilly would announce she was feeling suddenly vegetarian and disappear with a book.'

'Oh, I couldn't bear all those slippery innards.' Tilly pulled a face. Sophie nudged her.

'But you converted back quickly to fish eating by the time they were cooked.'

'And he took us to the music hall,' Tilly reminisced, 'but told us never to repeat any of the jokes or Mother and Auntie Amy would never let us stay again.'

There was general agreement that Great Uncle Daniel sounded just the sort of special uncle that everyone should have. The young men began to request dances and fill up the girls' dance cards. Sophie noticed how Tilly kept glancing at the entrance and suspected she was watching out for James Robson and wanting to keep some dances free for him. She too was intrigued to meet the tea planter, and thought it rude he was so late.

Then Mona beckoned Tilly to join her in the middle of the room while waitresses went around with tray-loads of small glasses of punch for toasting. Mona, on behalf of her mother, made a short speech of welcome to their family and friends.

'I'm very fond of my youngest sister,' said Mona, 'even if she has driven us all mad over the years with her head in the clouds and her clumsiness. But you couldn't ask for a kinder heart and a sweeter nature. I'm sad that neither our sister Jacobina nor our dear brother Johnny can be here today – and of course we all miss dearest Father – but they are here in thought and spirit. So let us raise our glasses to Tilly!'

'To Tilly!' they chorused and drank. People looked at the birthday girl expectantly.

'Th-thank you.' Tilly blushed. She could think of nothing else to say, quite overawed to be the centre of attention.

'Well,' Mona said, 'what Tilly wants to say is, please enjoy the tea and the dancing and thank you for coming.'

Tilly nodded and smiled and wished the floor would swallow her up.

Sophie slipped to her friend's side, took her elbow and murmured, 'Cake now,' then steered her back to the table.

Two of the men from the tennis club claimed the cousins in the first dance; a sedate two-step. Tilly then managed a waltz without treading too much on her partner's feet, followed by a Gay Gordons with the son of their family doctor, which left her dizzy and declining the next few. She watched Sophie doing a sprightly polka and wished she had half her grace and nimbleness. The young men queued up to dance with her pretty cousin, and somehow Sophie seemed to know all the latest dances, including the racy foxtrot, which brought a disapproving look from Mona.

The dance was nearly over, and Tilly had given up hope that James Robson would come when she noticed his stocky figure standing near the door, dressed in a crumpled linen suit and smoking hard. His weathered face looked ruggedly handsome above the stiff white collar. He was staring in her direction so she half rose with a tentative wave, then realised he was looking beyond her. She turned to see that it was Sophie who had caught his attention, twirling around the dance floor in a Scottish reel. Glancing back at James's mesmerised look, she felt a wave of disappointment and sat back down.

Mona pounced on James and pulled him over to greet the family. Tilly's mother gave a distracted hello; she was feeling the strain of too many people and the heat as much as Tilly. Auntie Amy, though, was all smiles as she shook hands.

'So glad to meet you again, Mr Robson.' She beamed. 'Sophie is looking forward to seeing you too. She's dancing over there.'

'I thought that must be her – the likeness to her mother is striking.'

'Yes it is,' Amy agreed. 'She wants to thank you in person for helping her through school.'

James grunted. 'No need.'

He turned to Tilly and held out a present. 'Happy birthday, Matilda.' His expression was almost a scowl. For a second Tilly wondered who Matilda was; no one had called her that since she had left school at fifteen.

'Thank you.' She took it, not wanting to open it in front of curious eyes. 'May I open it later?'

'Whatever you wish,' James said, aware of her discomfort. Perhaps he had been wrong to come, he thought. The attentions of an older man were obviously embarrassing. 'It's only a papier mâché trinket box bought in the bazaar.'

Tilly went even redder and couldn't think of a polite reply.

'How very useful,' Mona came to the rescue. 'Please sit down with us, Mr Robson, and we'll order a fresh pot of tea. We did think you'd be here earlier. The dancing is nearly over. The band has another engagement at five o'clock.'

James's colour deepened. 'I'm not one for dancing, I'm afraid.'

'Well, that's something you and my sister have in common,' Mona said bluntly.

James sat down gingerly on a dainty chair, his legs anchored firmly either side as if he feared his bulk would break it. Ever watchful, Clarrie appeared with a waitress carrying a fresh pot of tea and replenished the sandwiches. They greeted each other warily, then Clarrie bustled away again.

Amy attempted to engage him in conversation. 'How was the voyage?'

'Fine, thank you.'

'How long are you in England?'

'Six weeks.'

'Not long then. So you return . . .?'

'In four weeks.'

'Perhaps you'll have time to pay us a visit in Edinburgh?'

'Perhaps,' James said, glancing again at the dancing Sophie and stirring sugar vigorously into his tea, causing it to spill over the cup on to the saucer. He was aware of the women exchanging glances and wished they would talk among themselves. He was so out of practice in polite conversation, largely content with his own company and that of his dogs in his remote home. He spent his days talking business with his undermanagers and workers, and after a day in the saddle was too tired to go socialising. Besides, the nearest neighbours were miles away and just as busy as he.

Amy tried again. 'The tea gardens are doing well, I hope?'

'We do our best.' He took a slurp of tea. Herbert's Tea Rooms served a quality blend, he thought with grudging admiration. Now tea he could talk about. 'Things have been harder since the war. There was a great deal of stockpiling at the docks that flooded the market once shipping could sail safely again. And the growers had been encouraged to produce as much as possible during the war, so there was massive overproduction.'

'Good for us tea drinkers, surely?' Amy asked. 'The price of tea has come down.'

'Yes,' Mona joined in. 'As someone who has to keep a rein on the household purse, a drop in tea prices is to be welcomed.'

'A slump in the price is not good in the long run,' James curbed his impatience. 'If we don't get a good price, we can't invest in new machinery and then we become inefficient or go out of business – then a couple of years down the line you'll see the price of tea rising sharply.

'We've had to cut back on production – and our labour force was hit hard by Spanish flu so we've had extra recruitment costs to bear.'

'Oh yes, there was quite a storm in the papers recently over tea workers,' Amy remembered. 'Lots of them leaving because of sickness and bad conditions.'

'Stirred up by outside agitators,' James snapped. 'That troublemaker Gandhi sent in his followers to try to start a revolt among the coolies. But it's all died down now. We don't have any trouble at the Oxford, though some gardens have gone to the wall.'

There was an awkward pause. Tilly looked anxiously at the faces around the table. Her mother looked ill; Mona was raising eyebrows at an amused Amy, while James looked annoyed. She wanted to make him feel at ease as well as demonstrate that she knew something about the tea trade. It was obviously the way to his heart.

'Clarrie says that your cousin Wesley is doing very well at Belgooree,' she piped up. 'She says that specialist small growers are becoming popular again, after all the inferior tea people had to drink through the war. Is that what you're doing at the Oxford gardens, Mr Robson?'

To her dismay, he looked incensed.

'Certainly not! Wesley has allowed his heart to rule his head. He's only done it to please Clarrie because she grew up there. It's never made a profit even in old Jock Belhaven's day. Belgooree will never be as prosperous as the Oxford; it's only because Wesley's ploughed so much money into it – I don't know how he hoodwinked the shareholders into the foolhardy venture. He's quite misguided.'

The dancing finished and, as the band packed up, Sophie came over breathless to the family table. She noticed at once Tilly's burning cheeks and eyes brimming with tears. Whatever had upset her?

Amy broke the strained atmosphere, introducing a bulldog of a man with a thick red neck and piercing blue eyes. 'Sophie, this is Mr James Robson.' He stood, nodded and, after a moment's hesitation, took her hand in a crushing handshake.

'So pleased to meet you, Mr Robson.' Sophie smiled, pulling her hand free and trying not to wince. Something about his square shoulders and jutting chin gave her a frisson of remembrance.

He gave a half-smile. 'You look like your mother.'

'Do I?' Sophie was suddenly overcome with the thought that this man had known her parents; had been the one to rescue her from India and bring her to Scotland. Her eyes smarted. 'I'm very grateful for what you did for me – and helping me and Auntie financially.'

He cleared his throat, embarrassed by such talk. 'Nothing really. Was pleased to do it. Friend of your parents. Such a tragedy.'

Sophie was bursting with a hundred questions. 'There's so much I want to ask you about India – about my parents. I remember so little.'

'Perhaps now is not the time or place,' Amy said gently. 'I hope that Mr Robson might visit us properly before his leave is over, so we can repay him for some of his kindness.'

'Oh yes,' Sophie enthused, 'please come.'

James smiled, flattered by the pretty young woman's eagerness. A thought half formed in his mind. He began to ask her questions about her life in Edinburgh. She told him about her work for the Scottish Servants' Charity, her driving in the war for the Red Cross and her passion for motorcycling. James was entranced, though a little shocked at her modern ways. Her upbringing with spinster Amy Anderson appeared somewhat lax. Sophie's father, Bill Logan, would not have approved at all. But, as the other guests said their thanks and left, James felt energised by Sophie's chatter and was reluctant to leave.

Abruptly, Tilly stood up.

'Mother, you don't look at all well; would you like to go home now?'

Mrs Watson nodded with relief and reached for her stick.

'Oh, Mother, I'll take you home,' Mona took command. 'Tilly, you stay and say goodbye to your guests.'

'Most people have gone and I'd rather come too.' Tilly gave a pleading look. 'I don't feel well either.'

'Too much cake?' Sophie teased. Tilly's expression was so tearful that Sophie jumped up too. 'Sorry, Tilly, I didn't mean—'

Tilly shook her off. 'Don't fuss.'

'Yes,' Mona sniffed, 'I think it's time we all went home.'

Sophie stood back, baffled. Mona turned to James. 'This has all been a bit much for Mother. I hope you enjoy the rest of your visit in Newcastle, Mr Robson. Goodbye.'

'Perhaps I could call round this coming week?'

'We shan't be there,' Mona said rudely. 'Mother and Tilly are returning with me to Dunbar on Monday.'

Sophie gave Tilly a look of surprise but her cousin did not deny it.

Mona signalled to Clarrie, who sent a waitress into the street to hail a cab. James, feeling suddenly snubbed by the Watsons, gave a curt goodbye and left. As the family thanked the staff at Herbert's, Clarrie took Tilly's hands in hers.

'I hope you've had a grand time?'

Tilly nodded and gulped back tears.

'James Robson hasn't been upsetting you, has he?'

'Why should I care about Mr Robson?' Tilly tried to laugh.

Clarrie lowered her voice. 'He's a man's man – not very comfortable around lasses – but he'd be mad not to see such a bonny one right under his nose,' Clarrie said kindly.

Tilly smiled, trying to smother her jealousy that James appeared too captivated by her cousin to notice her.

Back at the Gosforth house, Mrs Watson retired to bed and Amy offered to sit with her and read, leaving the cousins alone.

Mona was quick in her condemnation. 'What a rude man, turning up when the party was almost over and then lecturing us all on the economics of tea, as if we had the slightest interest.'

'I don't want to talk about it,' Tilly said, collapsing into a chair with a book.

'And the way he criticised dear Clarrie in front of us all and ticking you off as if you were a child. The man has no manners.'

'What did he say?' Sophie asked. 'I knew something had upset you.'

'You're one to talk,' Mona rounded on her young cousin. 'Monopolising him you were. It was *Tilly's* birthday, not yours. I do think you could have been a bit more considerate.'

'I'm sorry.' Sophie was contrite. 'I was just trying to keep the conversation going – nobody seemed to be saying anything.'

'Sometimes it's more ladylike to talk less and listen more,' Mona scolded.

'Tilly, forgive me.' Sophie sat down beside her friend. But Tilly would not look up from her book.

'Well,' Mona huffed, 'it's as well to find out now what a bore he is. Drank his tea like a navvy as well. No, I don't think he's husband material at all. You can do a lot better than James Robson.'

Sophie said, 'That's not very kind. I think he was just a bit overwhelmed in female company. Probably doesn't see much of it in Assam.'

'Another reason for Tilly not to encourage him,' Mona said. 'She doesn't want to live in the back of beyond with no polite society for a hundred miles.'

'Tilly could live anywhere as long as there's a supply of books.' Sophie nudged her friend.

Tilly threw down her book and sprang up. 'You don't know what I want – either of you! But I'm not encouraging him because it's obvious he cares nothing for me and I don't care for him. So you're welcome to him, Sophie.'

Tilly rushed from the sitting room and stamped upstairs, leaving the other women open-mouthed.

Mona stopped Sophie going after her. 'She'll see that it's all for the best when she goes out to join Johnny and Helena in Rawalpindi. My new sister-in-law is very well connected in India – army family – been there for three generations. She'll find a suitable young officer for my sister – and maybe instil more household skills into her than I've been able to.' Mona warmed to her theme. 'Robson's only in trade – they come pretty far down the pecking order in India, so I'm told.'

'But you can tell Tilly's fond of him,' Sophie pointed out, 'or she wouldn't be making such a song and dance of pretending she isn't.'

'Fondness is for dogs,' Mona was sharp. 'Marriage is more important than that. What matters is financial security and being of the same class. If you rub along together like I do with Walter, then that's an added bonus.'

Ignoring Mona's advice to leave Tilly alone, Sophie knocked on her door and tried to enter. The door was locked and her cousin would not answer her calls.

'I'm sorry, Tilly,' she said through the keyhole. 'Don't let this come between us. I only wanted to speak to Robson about my parents, that's all. He's about the closest link I've got to them. Don't be mad with me.'

But Tilly remained silent and Sophie gave up with an exasperated, 'Oh, silly Tilly!'

***

Tilly lay on her bed wrapped in a soft woollen shawl that Johnny had sent to her from India, feeling wretched. She wanted to rush to the door and let Sophie in, so why didn't she? Why was she punishing her best friend? She understood that Sophie didn't care for James Robson and saw him merely as a friend of her dead parents; she knew her well enough to know that, even if Sophie felt even a flicker of interest in the tea planter, she would do nothing to encourage him, out of loyalty to her. That was not the problem.

What hurt was the look of admiration and desire on James's face the moment he had set eyes on Sophie; his handsome blue eyes had never lit in such a way for her, and she knew they never would. She would be for ever in the shadow of her much prettier, more vivacious cousin. Sophie didn't even realise the power she had to attract men. At that moment, Tilly made up her mind that she would go and live with Johnny and Helena as the family wished, so that she would forge a new life thousands of miles away and out of Sophie Logan's shadow. She would marry whomever would have her, and then she could hold her head up high among her relations who thought her so unremarkable and believed that she would never amount to anything.

Chapter 5

Plunging into an ice-filled bath, James submerged his head and came up roaring with the cold. It was the best way to dampen down his troublesome sex drive on this trip to England. He did not know where to go in Newcastle to relieve his ardour and would not risk bumping into anyone he knew. At home – strange how Assam felt like that now even though the British there constantly harked on about England being home – he found that riding hard was just the antidote to a sex problem. Or, when things got really bad, he would take himself down to Tezpur and spend a night with one of the girls at The Orchid on the edge of the bazaar.

As he washed himself vigorously with hard carbolic soap, James wondered again if the whole trip had been a mistake. Ever since he had arrived in the country he had felt like a fish out of water, bewildered at the changes in post-war England: the fashions, the music, the traffic, the pace of life and lack of deference, the new dances he would never be able to master. He found it hard not to stare at all the flesh on show, with skirts so much shorter and bare arms flaunted in summer and in evening frocks. He was pretty sure that the wives and daughters of his tea planter friends were still wearing the high-necked, full-skirted dresses that their mothers had worn when he'd first gone out to Assam in Queen Victoria's day. But then he so seldom socialised at the club or accepted invitations to dinner that perhaps he just hadn't noticed.

Why had he not spent his leave travelling in the colonies? There was good sport to be had in Australia and South Africa, so he was told. He ducked his soapy head underwater one more time. No, he had come back to Newcastle for one specific reason; to find a wife. It was time he looked to the future and the next generation of Robsons who would take on the mantle of running the Oxford Tea Company, its plantations and exports. They had expanded into tea rooms before the war but sold those at a handsome profit to invest in land in East Africa; his cousin

Wesley was supposed to have gone out to supervise their new tea gardens there.

Wesley, he thought with irritation, had turned out such a disappointment. The brightest and most able businessman in the family, Wesley had lost his head over the strong-willed Clarrie Belhaven, married her and returned to her childhood home at Belgooree in the Khasi hills. So far they had produced only their dark-eyed daughter Adela, so there was no heir to the family firm. And with Clarrie's dubious heritage – her mother had been half Assamese, which didn't bother him unduly but made her socially outcast in India – Wesley had sacrificed any chance of taking on leadership of the family firm when he, James, decided to retire.

So he needed a wife young and robust enough to survive the tropical heat of Assam and bear him sons. Besides, a woman on the domestic front to provide a few comforts and make his house, Cheviot Cottage, more homely wouldn't be a bad thing, and it would please his neighbours, the Percy-Barratts, who for years had been badgering him to marry. Muriel Percy-Barratt had taken it upon herself to oversee his servants and order his household, but James knew that the long-suffering Reggie Percy-Barratt thought his wife spent too much time over at Cheviot Cottage.

James leapt out of his cold bath and towelled himself down. Muriel would approve of Tilly; the youngest Watson daughter looked robust and seemed eager to please. She would be the sensible choice. Then Sophie Logan's athletic figure and pretty face pushed their way into his thoughts again. How alike she was to her bonny mother Jessie. With a pang of longing that he had not felt in years, he allowed himself to think of Jessie Logan. All the young tea planters had been in love with Logan's wife. Perhaps that had been the real tragedy.

As he dressed, James decided on action. The waspish Mona Watson had said that her family were leaving for Dunbar tomorrow, so that meant Sophie and her aunt would be too. Even though it was Sunday and he suspected the Presbyterian Watsons would not welcome social calls on a day of rest, this might be his last chance. If his proposal came to nothing, then he would leave Newcastle immediately and head to France for some boar hunting. James struggled once more into a tight starched collar and flattened down his thick, wiry hair with brilliantine, wondering why he should feel more nervous now than he had done when coming face to face with a bear on a hunting trip in Upper Assam.

***

'Oh, Mr Robson?' Mona's mouth turned down in disapproval. 'I am surprised to see you here again.' She guarded the door and did not invite him in. James curbed his impatience.

'I'm sorry to call unannounced, but you did say you were leaving for Dunbar this week and I thought this might be my only opportunity—'

'I'm afraid we aren't receiving visitors,' Mona interrupted. 'Mother is resting and my sister is too busy packing.'

'It's Miss Logan that I wish to speak to,' James said, standing his ground.

Mona gave a little gasp and her mouth tightened. 'Well, I'm sorry to disappoint you, but Sophie and her aunt are out taking the air with Clarrie Robson. They met at the kirk this morning and Clarrie suggested a picnic. I don't really approve of such things on Sunday, but Aunt Amy allows Sophie whatever she wants, as far as I can see.'

'Mona, who's at the door?' Tilly called down the stairs, Flossy panting at her heels.

'Mr Robson,' Mona said, 'but I'm just explaining—'

'Well, let him in,' Tilly cried, hurrying down. 'He'll think we Watsons have no manners.'

Tilly flushed pink at the bow James Robson gave her and couldn't believe her luck that he had decided to call on her again. She had long grown tired of packing and regretted not going on the picnic with Sophie. But then she would have missed James's visit; he had obviously called to make amends for arriving late and being offhand at her party.

'Please come in,' she smiled. 'Would you like tea? The maid's off duty but I can boil up a kettle.'

Flossy went straight to James, licking his large hands when he bent to fondle her.

'Hello, old girl.'

'Tilly, he hasn't come to see you,' Mona said, as James fussed over the dog.

'Oh?' Tilly's face fell. How stupid she was to think that he had. Of course, it was Sophie that he wanted to visit.

James stepped forward, annoyed by Mona's thoughtlessness. 'I'd be pleased to take tea with you, Matilda. May I call you Matilda?'

'Of course.' Tilly brightened. 'Though I'd rather you called me Tilly. Matilda reminds me of being told off for spilling ink at school.'

James raised an eyebrow. 'Tilly it is then.'

'Well, I haven't time to sit around chaperoning you.' Mona was dismissive. 'I have all Mother's things to pack.'

'You have nothing to fear' – James gave an amused grunt – 'and I won't be staying long.'

Tilly felt her insides plunge at his words; he was here under sufferance. Mona left them standing awkwardly in the drawing room.

'Please sit down, Mr Robson.' Tilly pointed at a sturdy wing-backed chair by the empty grate. 'My father liked to sit there.'

James gave it a wary glance.

'Sorry, I don't know why I said that.' Tilly flushed. 'I just meant that it's a good chair for a large man like you. Not that you're large – just manly – it's all the outdoor pursuits you mentioned – that make you . . . Oh dear' – Tilly's hands flew to her hot cheeks – 'I really don't know how to speak to you, Mr Robson. I'm so used to Mother or my sisters doing the talking for me. You must think me very stupid and dull.'

James hesitated, then took her by the elbow and steered her on to a faded brocade sofa and sat beside her. Flossy flopped down at his feet.

'Not dull or stupid. Your open manner is refreshing, Tilly. I usually find the gossiping of women quite tedious.'

Tilly eyed him and then let out a throaty laugh. 'Well, that's very candid of you too. Tell me about the women in India, Mr Robson. Are they very different from us?'

'The British or the natives?' James asked.

'Both.'

'Well, the native women are very hard working; they are nimble with their fingers and make good tea pickers.'

'Do you speak to them in their language?'

James was surprised by the question. 'I don't really get to speak to them; my subordinates deal with them directly.' Her gaze made him uncomfortable. 'But I do speak a few words of Bengali – most of the house staff come from Bengal – and I can make a stab at Hindustani.'

'So these women are workers, not friends?'

James felt uneasy as he thought of the women at The Orchid he occasionally paid for sex; they would hardly think of him as a friend. He nodded. 'That's just the way it is in India.'

Tilly looked pensive for a moment, and he wondered if she thought less of him for having no native friends. But she let it pass.

'And the British in India?' Tilly asked.

James felt on firmer ground. 'The British women in Assam are full of pluck, on the whole. There are fewer these days who can't endure the heat or who succumb to sickness.'

'Like Sophie's mother?' Tilly asked.

James nodded briefly, not wanting to be reminded of the Logans and his reason for calling. 'But most of them make the most of it and thrive on the life.'

'That's what I imagine my new sister-in-law Helena is like,' Tilly enthused. 'Johnny's letters are full of their social life – gymkhanas and dances and dinners and picnics – it must be so much fun. Do you like Helena?'

James was taken aback by the blunt question. His impression of Johnny's new wife was of a social climber who hadn't wanted a mere *boxwallah* – a man in trade – like him at her wedding. But perhaps he was being unfair.

'She was jolly enough,' James said.

'Oh dear,' said Tilly, 'you don't like her, do you?'

James laughed with embarrassment. 'Your brother adores her and that's what matters.'

'Yes it is.' Tilly smiled wistfully. 'He used to think the world of me too.'

'He still does,' James said gallantly.

'Really?'

'Yes.'

'What did he tell you about me?' Tilly grinned expectantly.

James recalled vividly. Johnny was just as open and friendly as his youngest sister, with the same refreshing candour that might not go down well with some of his superiors and probably wouldn't with Tilly.

'You don't have to make up something nice to say that wouldn't be true,' Tilly pressed him. 'So what did my brother say?'

'That you're good with dogs and never ill.'

To his surprise, Tilly roared with laughter. 'Well, that's the truth!'

Flossy raised her head and gave a small bark at her mistress's mirth. They both reached for the dog at the same time and their hands knocked against each other's. Tilly pulled back first. James thought how pretty she looked when she blushed.

'Would you like that cup of tea now?'

James glanced around the room hoping there might be something stronger. He craved a large whisky and soda but he suspected the Watson women were teetotal as he had never been offered more than tea here.

'Tea would be grand.' He forced a smile.

'Good,' said Tilly. 'You might as well come with me or you'll only be sitting here on your own twiddling your thumbs.'

Meekly, he followed her out of the drawing room and through the green baize door that separated the front of the house from the servants' domain. Yet it was all strangely quiet, unlike the chatter and singing that rang around his kitchen compound at home. James paced around the gloomy kitchen with its smoky range while Tilly coaxed a blackened kettle to boil enough water for a pot of tea and talked to Flossy about sharing biscuits. The shelves were almost empty of supplies and the coal scuttle was largely filled with dross. Perhaps the Watsons' circumstances were more straitened than Johnny had led him to believe; or was he unaware of the family situation?

Tilly reached for a canister of tea and spooned three heaps into the warmed teapot. 'You'll drink the cold dregs, won't you, Flossy? None of our tea gets wasted.'

James could tell by smelling it that the tea was inferior Dust tea, but he said nothing. He was enjoying Tilly's animated conversation and felt suddenly protective towards her; she deserved better than this dispiriting place. Picking up the tray, he insisted on carrying the tea things, barging at the baize door with a broad shoulder and sweeping back into the drawing room with Tilly chattering behind him about Flossy's love of Assam tea. As he put down the tray, he glanced out of the bay window and saw Sophie and her aunt turning into the street. The moment he had waited for was almost here. His heart missed a beat at the sight of her fair face laughing as she held on to her hat in the breeze, blonde hair escaping its pins.

Tilly followed his look and caught sight of her cousin too. She felt suddenly deflated; she had been enjoying having this energetic man's company all to herself. Alone, he was much more relaxed and appeared to have a sense of humour too. She struggled to hide her disappointment. 'Oh, there they are. I'd better fetch two more cups.'

James turned. Her hazel eyes held his gaze for an instant; kind beseeching eyes like those of a faithful hound. It struck him in that moment that Tilly really did care for him. On his earlier visits that month he had hoped to cultivate a mutual regard between them, even friendship. James had immediately liked her brother Johnny but had found Tilly overshadowed by her bossy sister Mona; until now. He couldn't remember the last time he'd felt so at ease in a woman's company. He had a sudden gut instinct what to do.

'Tilly, I've come here today—' he began to explain.

'I know why you've come, Mr Robson,' she said with a sad smile. 'It's Sophie you want, isn't it?'

For a long moment James said nothing. Tilly held her breath though she already knew his answer. It had been exciting pretending for a while that this man might be interested in her. She bent down to hug Flossy; at least the dog's love was wholehearted and constant.

'Tilly, you're wrong,' James said in a stern voice. 'Will you marry me?'

Startled, she looked up. 'Did you say *marry*?'

James reached down and pulled her to her feet. His grip dug into her fleshy arms. 'Yes I did. So will you?'

'Mr Robson, I thought—'

'Don't think,' James was impatient. He wanted her answer before Sophie walked in and he changed his mind or lost his nerve. 'Please, Tilly; say you'll be my wife.'

'Wife?' Tilly echoed, then let out a gurgle of delight. 'Yes, Mr Robson, I will!'

James let go his iron hold and, clamping his hands either side of her head, planted a robust kiss on her plump mouth.

'Thank you.' He grinned in relief. Tilly liked him and wanted him; and she'd saved him from making a fool of himself over the Logan girl, who probably would have turned him down flat. 'We'll get wed before I return to India. You can follow on later – it'll take a while to sort out a passage and I'll need time to fix up the house – but there's nothing to stop us marrying straight away, is there?'

'I suppose not,' Tilly gasped, her head reeling from her sudden change in fortune.

They heard the front door open; the chatter between Sophie and Amy grew closer.

'Pinch me.' Tilly snorted with mirth.

'Pinch you?' James frowned.

'So I know I'm not dreaming this.'

Instead, he seized her hand and crushed it in his, as much to give himself courage as to reassure Tilly.

Chapter 6

Sophie had hoped to return to Edinburgh by the same route they had come south on, but Mona insisted that they call in at Dunbar for a night, so they motored up the coastal road.

James Robson's hasty proposal to Tilly had taken everyone by surprise. Mrs Watson was tearful but relieved; Mona was not so accepting.

'Engaged?' Mona had cried, once James had left. 'You hardly know the man!'

'You've been nagging me to find a husband for the past two years,' Tilly protested.

'You can do better than a tea planter,' her sister blustered. 'Johnny will find you a young officer with good prospects.'

'He won't need to now.' Tilly was triumphant. 'Mr Robson runs a very good business – he's a wealthy man – and I won't need to be beholden to anyone. Assam sounds amazing – full of exotic animals and polo matches and tea.'

'You're frightened of wild animals and you hate sport,' Mona said.

'Well, I love tea,' Tilly replied.

'I think Tilly will make a wonderful planter's wife,' Sophie defended her friend. 'Her house will be open to everyone. James Robson is a lucky man.'

'Well that's true,' Mona conceded. 'We Watsons are known for our hospitality.' This prompted her to insist on Sophie and Amy staying at Dunbar on their way home. 'Can't have you breaking down in the middle of nowhere and being at the mercy of wild foresters again.'

Sophie kept to herself that that was exactly what she had hoped might happen, for she had thought a lot of the dashing, smiling Tam Telfer over the past couple of days. She was pleased for Tilly, who seemed so happy at her sudden engagement, but it stirred up mixed feelings in Sophie. Tilly would be leaving England for good and the Watsons' home in Newcastle would be sold. After the wedding, she would never be able to visit them again; it would be a painful tearing up of roots.

And Tilly would be going to live in India, the place of Sophie's birth and first six years of life, the place where her parents had lived, died and were buried. She felt a strange envy that it was to Assam that her cousin was going, and yet also relief that it wasn't her. Deep down, Sophie still feared the place – feared India and Indians – though she knew it was irrational. But India had taken her parents away – a quick, cruel overnight fever – and her beloved Ayah Mimi had vanished too.

What had happened to her nurse? Perhaps she had merely gone off to another job. Sophie had never asked and no one had thought to tell her. But she had been left with a huge pain inside and a feeling of being deserted.

Leaving Dunbar a couple of days later and promising Tilly to return for the early July wedding in Newcastle, Sophie relished the ride up the Berwickshire coast, buffeted by a salty wind and clearing her head of troublesome thoughts. She sang songs at the flapping seagulls and her aunt shouted out the choruses above the noise of the engine.

Sophie went straight back to work the following day and Miss Gorrie kept her busy with paperwork and answering the telephone. Sophie decided that they needed extra storage and spent a happy day sawing planks, hammering nails and erecting shelves in the office. More than anything, she relished doing practical, physical jobs, and Amy had taught her to be a competent joiner.

Each evening on returning home, she would call to her aunt, 'Any post for me?'

'No, dearie,' Amy would say. 'But you can't expect Tilly to be writing long letters when she has a wedding to arrange.'

But it wasn't from Tilly that Sophie wanted to hear; she still hoped that the handsome, friendly forestry student, Tam, might get in touch. He had asked for her address and she had encouraged him, but he had neither written nor called. Perhaps they were still away at camp, or maybe he had already left for his month of forestry practice on the Continent? She tried to recall when that was to be.

After three weeks of hearing nothing, she decided that Tam had forgotten about her or had lost her address. Either way, she hadn't caught his interest in the way he had caught hers. Better to forget about him. She booked train tickets for Amy and herself to attend Tilly's wedding, travelling down and returning the same day. By all accounts, the Watsons' house was half packed up and Sophie could not bear the thought of staying there with Tilly gone.

Walking home across the Meadows to Clerk Street the evening before the wedding, Sophie saw a group of young men playing cricket, probably students enjoying post-exam freedom. She lingered in the pleasant sunshine, in no hurry to go back to the flat.

She became aware of one of the men staring at her as he fielded close by. He looked foreign; handsome in a swarthy way with thick black hair. He smiled and gave a half wave but she had no idea who he was so didn't wave back. He must have mistaken her for someone else. Uncertainty crossed his face and he turned away. A moment later, the ball came hurtling in his direction, speeding along the ground. He dived to stop it, picked it up and threw it back with powerful shoulders, preventing the batsmen from taking a second run.

The over finished and the fielders changed positions. Sophie was about to move on when a tall, red-haired man sauntering towards her called out, 'Hello there! Miss Logan, isn't it?'

She recognised his sticky-out ears at once. William Boswell, Tam's friend.

'Boz!' She grinned. 'How are you?'

'Very well. And you?'

'Fine thanks. I'm just on my way home from the office.'

Boz gave an appreciative glance at her smart skirt and blouse. 'Not on The Memsahib today?'

'No, she's just for days off. In fact she's in the garage having her starter pedal soldered back on.' Sophie smiled and rolled her eyes. 'Probably won't be able to afford her for much longer.'

'Well, I'm glad to see you got safely back from Newcastle.'

'Thanks.' Sophie hesitated then asked, 'Is Tam playing too?'

'No, Tam's a rower and tennis player.'

'Oh, I love tennis.'

'Come on, Boz!' his bowler called over. 'This isn't a tea dance.'

Boz went scarlet. 'Got to go, sorry.'

'No, I'm sorry for getting you into trouble,' Sophie said, aware of being stared at by the athletic fielder. She remembered him now; the Indian from the forestry camp. Somebody Khan.

'It's nice to see you again.' Boz gave a bashful smile. He turned away, then called over his shoulder. 'Would you like a game of tennis sometime?'

'Yes, of course.' Sophie smiled.

'Tomorrow?' he asked eagerly.

'Not tomorrow, but I'm free on Saturday. Auntie Amy would love to play too. Can we make up a foursome?'

He hesitated for a fraction. 'Of course, that would be grand! I'll call and collect you. Clerk Street, isn't it?'

'Yes, number seventy-one. How did you . . .?'

'Tam mentioned it.' Boz grinned. 'I'll book a court for two o'clock.'

They waved goodbye and Sophie carried on, feeling ridiculously light-headed that she had stumbled upon Tam's good friend so unexpectedly. She felt sure it would be Tam who would make up the foursome.

It was only as she arrived home and raced up the stone stairs to give Amy the news that she wondered why Tam had never called. He had remembered where she lived and talked about her to his close friend. But then he had obviously forgotten the number; Boz had only known the name of her street. Saturday couldn't come soon enough.

***

The day of Tilly's wedding broke grey and drizzly, but the gloomy weather couldn't dampen her excitement. Jacobina had arrived the night before from Inverness, filling the house with good-humoured chatter, and a telegram from Johnny expressing his pleasure and good wishes had been better than any present.

Sophie and Amy came on an early train, in time for a late breakfast and to help her dress and make ready.

'Mona allowed me to have her wedding gown altered,' Tilly explained. 'Wasn't that kind of her?'

Sophie eyed the elaborate long dress with its flouncy lace collar and full skirts. It was a style that had been popular before the war and its gathered-in waist and puffed sleeves showed off Tilly's curvy figure far better than the modern straight dresses.

'Very kind of Mona,' Sophie approved, 'and it suits you perfectly.'

Sophie as bridesmaid was dressed modestly in a plain blue dress of crêpe de chine, long cream gloves that had belonged to her mother and a new straw cloche hat anchored on to her flyaway fair hair with a large steel hatpin. She was in charge of Tilly's long lace train.

'Mona is convinced I'm going to trip over it and break my ankle,' grimaced Tilly, 'or, worse still, tear the blessed thing.'

'You won't,' Sophie assured. 'But if you do, you have that *manly* James Robson to catch you!'

Tilly snorted with laughter. She had recounted her awkward conversation with James several times to her cousin, and now Sophie delighted in teasing her about having called the tea planter large and manly.

At the moment of leaving the house for the Presbyterian kirk in Newcastle's West End, Sophie felt a lump form in her throat.

'Tilly, you look beautiful.' Tears brimmed in her eyes. 'I'm so happy for you.'

Tilly smiled back, radiant. 'Thank you. I can't tell you how much it means to have you with me.'

'This is going to be a great day, Tilly Watson – soon to be Robson.' Sophie grinned and kissed her on the cheek.

Tilly's insides curdled with nervousness at the thought. She had very little idea what to expect beyond the ceremony and tea party, which Clarrie had insisted on having at Herbert's Tea Rooms as a gift from her. This time, Tilly had declared it would be a very small affair with just close family, and this appeared to suit James too.

'I don't like fuss,' he had agreed, 'and most of the Robsons are in their graves or scattered abroad.'

He had invited only an elderly aunt and some distant cousins called Landsdowne. The Landsdownes had declined and the elderly aunt had said she would come to the service but that the tea party would be too much for her liverish constitution. For best man, James had rustled up a retired planter called Fairfax living in Tynemouth who had befriended him when he'd first gone out to India in the 1890s and had taught him how to play polo and track tigers.

James had booked them into a hotel somewhere on the coast for two days, and then he would have to leave for Liverpool and his passage back to India. Tilly didn't know if she was more frightened at the thought of being alone with the formidable tea planter for two whole days or of being separated from her new husband for several months until she joined him in December. He had organised for her to be chaperoned on the voyage out by another tea planter's wife, Muriel Percy-Barratt, who would be on leave in Yorkshire till the autumn, settling her youngest boy into boarding school.

'Tilly, are you ready?' Walter, her portly brother-in-law asked, offering her his arm. In the absence of any Watson men, Walter had agreed to give her away in marriage. He was a genial, quiet man and Tilly thought him a saint for enduring Mona's bossiness. But she missed her dear father and brother Johnny, and she was suddenly overcome by their absence.

'Here, take this,' Sophie murmured and thrust a handkerchief into her hand. From the look of compassion on her cousin's face, Tilly knew she understood. She blew her nose into the scented handkerchief, dabbed her eyes and handed it back.

Sophie winked and pulled Tilly's veil into place. 'Anchors away,' she whispered.

Clutching on to Walter's arm and heading down the aisle of the plain, lofty church, Tilly was astonished to see James standing smartly in morning coat and striped trousers. It was the first time she had seen him wearing clothes that weren't crumpled or a little stained. His ruddy neck still strained against his collar but his dimpled chin was well-shaved, his moustache trimmed and hair cropped short, making him look younger.

He gave her an anxious smile as if he had doubted she would turn up, and she knew in that moment that they were both equally nervous and keen to make a go of it.

She trembled as they made their vows and her hand shook as James thrust the gleaming wedding band on to her finger, so that he had to clutch at her fingers to keep them still. Tilly tried not to wince at his strong grip. Then organ music erupted around them and the small group of wedding guests began a lusty hymn singing. When the moment came to head off down the aisle on the arm of her new husband, Tilly caught sight of her mother's grey face beaming and tearful, and a sob caught in her own throat. Even Mona was sniffing and smiling encouragement. Glancing behind, Tilly saw that Sophie was arranging the long trail of lace, her face pink with emotion. They exchanged loving smiles. Tilly felt suddenly blessed to be surrounded by people who loved her just the way she was.

'Come on, my dear,' James's voice boomed over the music. He jammed her arm possessively in his and marched her out of the church.

Clarrie laid on a delicious tea at Herbert's, screening off an area of the tea room to give them privacy and laying on a fiddle player to entertain.

'We can push back the tables if you'd like a dance or two?' Clarrie offered.

'I'm no dancer,' James said stiffly, his neck turning red. Tilly already knew this was a sign of his embarrassment.

'Me neither,' she said hastily, 'but thank you, Clarrie – we're just enjoying hearing the music.'

Although the tea plates groaned with sweet fancies that Tilly would normally have wolfed down, her stomach was so knotted she could hardly eat. Sitting in her finery, she drank two cups of tea, terrified of spilling a drop on Mona's precious gown, and forced down a finger of wedding cake, which only made the aching worse.

Her sisters were talking loudly and laughing at things Amy and Sophie were saying; even her mother had colour in her cheeks and was in deep conversation with the elderly tea planter, Fairfax. Clarrie was trying to make small talk with James, who wouldn't sit down, but he seemed ill at ease and lost for words. He kept taking out his pocket watch and checking the time, frowning and throwing her glowering looks. It made Tilly all the more nervous; was he bored or already regretting their momentous step?

Clarrie gave up on talking to James and came to her side, James following.

'I've been telling your husband that he must bring you across to visit us at Belgooree, once you are settled at Cheviot Cottage.'

'Thank you, I'd love that.' Tilly gave a grateful smile. 'Isn't that kind?' She looked at James but couldn't yet bring herself to use his first name.

'It's a long way between the Oxford gardens and the Khasi hills – two days' travel,' James muttered.

'A day and a half,' Clarrie countered. 'So when you come you must stay. Adela would be so pleased to see you too. But we can talk about that more before you leave for India.'

'Well, Mrs Robson,' James growled, 'it's time we left.'

Tilly looked at Clarrie in confusion. Clarrie glanced between them and laughed.

'I think he's talking to you, Tilly, not me!'

Tilly went crimson. 'Of course, silly me. I'm not used to the name yet.'

'You will be soon.' Clarrie smiled. 'And Wesley and I are so happy to have you in the family.'

James ignored this remark and pulled Tilly to her feet. 'I've ordered a cab to take us and Fairfax to Tynemouth.'

Tilly thought him rude for their hasty goodbyes and abrupt departure, but she knew he was awkward at social gatherings and had hardly had time to get to know her family well. She kissed and hugged them all.

'You'll be seeing them again in a couple of days,' James said, not hiding his impatience.

Sophie helped keep her flounces of lace out of the puddles as she stepped into the waiting taxi, while Walter held an umbrella against the worsening rain.

'Come to Edinburgh as soon as you can,' Sophie insisted. 'I want to see as much of you as possible before you go abroad.'

'I will,' Tilly promised and waved through the rain-spattered window at her loved ones huddled in the tea room entrance.

All the way to the coast, James chattered to Fairfax about the tea trade and Assam. The old man pulled on his bushy tobacco-stained moustache and chortled as they reminisced. It was the happiest Tilly had seen James all day and, when they got to their hotel, he invited his old colleague in for a *chota peg*.

'Three large whiskies with soda,' he ordered, before their bags had even been taken to their room. He sank into a comfortable chintz armchair. 'God, I'm in need of a drink.'

'Me too, old boy,' Fairfax agreed. He looked at Tilly warily.

She stood in her wedding dress feeling foolish. 'I've never drunk whisky before.'

'Would you like us to order you tea instead?' asked Fairfax.

'No,' James said, 'Mrs Robson looks more in need of a *chota peg* than we do. Come on, Mrs R, sit down and put your feet up. A whisky is just the thing to steady a bride's nerves.'

Tilly gave a nervous laugh and sat down. When the drink came, she took a sip and grimaced at the sour taste. Her father had taken a 'wee dram' as he had called it, only on special occasions like seeing in the New Year. She couldn't imagine how anyone found the taste enjoyable, yet James and his bachelor friend had nearly finished theirs and were ordering another. She persevered and found she quite liked the way the bubbles from the soda tingled around her tongue before she swallowed, and the warmth that spread inside. She relaxed and became giggly at their reminiscences about tiger hunts and elephants running amok in the gardens. After an hour of drinking *chota pegs*, Tilly realised her stomach pains had disappeared.

They ordered a supper of smoked fish and poached eggs with a bottle of red wine; Fairfax needed no persuasion to join them. By the time they had finished, Tilly had developed hiccups and she found it hard to walk without tripping over her dress. She giggled to think how disapproving her mother and sister would be.

'You go upstairs, Mrs R,' James ordered, 'and settle yourself in while I escort my friend home.'

With difficulty Tilly climbed the stairs and only found their room with the help of a chambermaid.

'W-ill you h-help me out of my dress?' she hiccuped.

The girl laughed and stayed to help.

The next thing Tilly knew, she was lying on the double bed in her underclothes, head spinning round like a carousel. The girl had gone, the room was half dark and she knew she was about to be sick. She had no idea where the bathroom was and anyway there wasn't time. She tumbled off the bed and scrambled underneath for a chamber pot, pulling it out just in time. Tilly heaved and spewed into the pot, splashing her face and hair in sick.

She had never felt so ill. When the last retching was over, she sat back in relief. Her stomach felt sore and hollow at the same time. Her hair stank. She felt disgusted with herself. What would James think of her? Where *was* James? By the fading light it must be late evening; she had lost all sense of time.

Too embarrassed to creep along the corridor in search of a water closet in which to flush away the potful of vomit, Tilly carried it to the far corner and covered it with a towel. Perhaps James might not notice. She felt too ill to care. Using water from the china jug on the washstand, Tilly tried her best to wash her face and hair. Then she sprayed on scent from a little bottle given to her by Sophie, hoping it would mask the smell. The flowery scent reminded her of her cousin, and Tilly was suddenly tearful.

James came crashing in at the door half an hour later, to find his new bride shivering in a chair, half undressed, reeking of perfume and crying her eyes out.

'Whatever's wrong?' he slurred, lurching towards her and getting tangled in wedding lace that trailed on the floor. He pitched towards her and grabbed her shoulders to steady himself. She flinched at his touch.

'Ow, that hurts!'

'Your hair's wet.'

'I've been sick.'

'Tilly, y' all right? Not ill?' Clumsily, he stroked her hair.

'I think it was those *chota* things,' she mumbled.

James dropped to his knees and fumbled for her hands. 'Sorry. Thought would help – y' know – first night.'

Tilly felt ill again at the thought that they now had to consummate their marriage. She wasn't sure she wouldn't throw up all over her new husband, who appeared to be quite drunk himself.

'Is Fairfax home safely? You've been a long time.'

'Yes, invited me in for a nightcap. Sorry again.'

'I don't mind.' Right at that moment, all Tilly wanted was to sleep and not wake up until she felt human. She swore she would never touch whisky again.

'Let's getta bed,' James said, pulling himself unsteadily to his feet.

Tilly watched him anxiously as he stumbled around trying to get out of his clothes. Stripped to his drawers and vest, with one shoe and sock still on, James lay back in exhaustion.

'Just give me a minute,' he said.

Silence followed. Tilly climbed out of the chair and went to peer. The next moment, he began a soft snoring. He was half on, half off the bed, but she didn't want to touch him in case he awoke. Snoring next to her was a complete stranger.

She lay down on the pillows wondering how on earth she was going to get through the next two days, and whether, if they didn't consummate the marriage, they could call it all off and she wouldn't have to go and live with this man in India.

***

James woke up with the feel of a bass drum thumping at his temples. His eyes felt small and gritty as he winced in the morning light streaming in at the open window. The curtains billowed and flapped like sails. A strange sour smell mixed with the salty air.

'Good morning, Mr R.'

He turned his head a fraction to see a young woman with red hair scraped back behind her ears, perched on a chair beside the bed eyeing him. She was pale as a sheet, except for her long nose, which was strangely pink. Tilly. His bride. His wife. She looked more like a condemned prisoner. James searched his foggy brain in a panic but could remember nothing of the previous night. Surely he had not mistreated her?

'Good morning,' he mumbled. He tried to sit up, but it made the drumming in his head worse.

Tilly handed him a glass of water. 'I needed one of these too.'

'You did?' James took it gratefully and drained it in one.

'I've ordered tea and toast – couldn't face the thought of a cooked breakfast. The girl is bringing it to the room – don't think I can face sitting in the dining room either – not with the smell of bacon. Have I done the right thing?'

James nodded and groaned. 'Quite the right thing.'

She was wearing a summer dress with a geometric pattern that was making his vision blur. He closed his eyes. When he opened them again, she was standing looking out of the window at the blue-grey North Sea.

'Shall we walk along the beach today?' Tilly asked. 'I'm not sure what else you're supposed to do on honeymoon.'

James snorted. 'I can think of one thing, Mrs R.'

She flung him a look, her pale face abruptly tinged with pink. James felt a jolt of alarm again. He wished he could remember more of last night – he recalled leaving Fairfax's house – but after that his memory failed him. What had he been doing at the old boy's on his wedding night anyway? What a coward he was. He had chosen this young woman on a whim – because she wasn't beautiful or independent-minded like Sophie – but kind and robust and biddable. But now the thought of sharing his life with a girl half his age terrified him; he had no idea how to treat her.

'Tilly.' He swallowed, his throat still parched. 'Did we – last night – you know . . .?'

Her cheeks grew more crimson. 'No, we didn't.'

James swung himself up into a sitting position, noticing how he still had one shoe on. He rubbed his hands over his face and sighed.

'Sorry, I drank too much. It won't happen again.'

Tilly looked him over. His wiry hair stuck out at angles and the skin around his blue eyes seemed more creased than ever. Dark hair sprouted from his broad chest above his crumpled vest, his thick shoulders strangely pale compared to his weather-beaten lower arms. His legs were covered in hair too. It was fascinating and alarming.

'Is something wrong?' He frowned.

She blurted out, 'I had no idea men could be so hairy.'

He gaped at her and then barked with laughter. He clutched his forehead. 'Don't make me laugh, Tilly, my head's too sore.'

There was a knock at the door and the maid came in with a breakfast tray. Tilly motioned to the table in the window and slipped her a shilling. The girl had helped dispose of the chamber pot earlier that morning and deserved every penny.

'The bathroom is two doors up, right-hand side,' Tilly told James. 'Plumbing's noisy but it all works. Why don't you have a wash while the tea brews, Mr R?'

To her surprise, James did as he was told, pulling on a faded paisley-pattern dressing gown, and left with his shaving equipment. He returned shaved and shiny-faced and smelling pleasantly of sandalwood, got dressed behind a screen and joined her for breakfast, polishing off six pieces of toast and most of the tea.

After ordering a picnic lunch, they went out and walked north along the promenade, stopping at Cullercoats to watch the fisherfolk mending their nets in the blustery sunshine, then eating their lunch on the sand at Whitley Bay. Out in the fresh air, they found conversation easy, and Tilly showered him with questions about Assam and what she should expect.

'Muriel Percy-Barratt will keep you right,' he told her. 'She's the *burra memsahib* around the tea gardens – senior lady. Anything you need to know about domestic stuff, Muriel's your woman. She's very pleased to be asked to look after you on the boat back; you'll be able to have all that household chat that I'm no good at.'

Tilly was encouraged to think she already had a ready-made friend.

'And it'll be good having Clarrie Robson not too far away.'

'Belgooree is a great distance from my house,' James was dismissive. 'We hardly ever meet.'

'Clarrie said we could meet in Shillong if I'm there on a shopping trip,' Tilly persisted.

'Shopping?' James queried. 'If there's anything you need, it's far better to order it from Calcutta or have it sent out from home. But Muriel can keep you right about all that.'

Tilly let the matter drop. She didn't want to antagonise him over talk of Clarrie; she was aware that there was a business disagreement with Clarrie's husband Wesley. But it wouldn't stop her being friends with Clarrie, who had been dear to her family for years.

They talked happily about James's pets; his gun dogs, ponies and a talking bird called Sinbad. The fears and doubts of last night seemed ridiculous now, banished by the cheery sunshine and fresh sea air. James's drunkenness had been the result of wedding night jitters, just as hers had been. It made her feel tender towards him that such a mature man should have felt boyish nerves.

That evening, they ate ravenously in the dining room and retired upstairs early. James drew the curtains and they undressed to the sound of seagulls squawking on the window ledge. She kept on her underclothes and climbed under the covers, but James stripped off completely and burrowed in beside her. His skin smelt of sand and sun and her own pale skin glowed from the heat of the day. She held her breath and waited.

‘Can I let down your hair, Tilly?’ he asked.

‘Oh yes, of course.’ She reached behind to loosen it, but he stopped her.

‘Let me do it.’

‘If you’re sure.’

Slowly he unpinned her wavy tresses and pulled them around her shoulders, his fingers brushing her face and neck, sending small shocks down her body.

‘There are so many pins, aren’t there? Mother always complains how many I need and how often I seem to lose them.’

Gently he kissed the wispy tendrils around her forehead and then moved his lips across her lashes and cheeks and chin. His tongue licked at her neck and down her chest as he eased the front of her chemise open, his large fingers clumsy with the dainty ribbon.

‘You taste of the sea,’ he murmured, his voice suddenly soft and deep.

‘Do I? That can’t be very nice.’ Tilly felt her heart begin to thump erratically, a strange warmth creeping down her stomach. ‘I should have thought to have a bath before dinner.’ She tried not to sound breathless, though that was how she felt. ‘But I was so hungry after our day out.’

James pulled away her chemise, releasing her breasts. He gazed down at her and gasped.

‘You’re beautiful, Tilly, like ripe fruit.’

Tilly snorted with sudden laughter. He frowned.

‘What’s funny?’

‘The things you say,’ Tilly spluttered.

He pulled back. ‘I don’t like being laughed at, especially by my new wife.’

Tilly came up on her elbows. ‘I’m not laughing *at* you, I promise.’

‘That’s what it sounds like.’ He sat up and reached for his cigarette case.

Tilly had a sudden panic that they would never consummate this marriage, and if they didn’t do it now, James would sail off to India and change his mind about her and cancel her voyage, and she'd end up a sad old maid living on her sister's generosity in windswept Dunbar. And she knew more than ever that she wanted to make a go of this marriage to James Robson; she had an inkling that the sex side of things could be a whole lot more fun than Mona had indicated during their one brief conversation about preparing for marriage.

She reached out and took the cigarette case and lighter from his beefy hands.

'I'm sorry, I know I sometimes talk and giggle too much, but it's only nervousness. It drives my family mad. Come back and taste the fruit.' She grinned, blushing at her own forwardness. 'I was enjoying it too.'

'Really?' James sounded doubtful.

She guided his hand on to her left breast. 'Here, feel my heart banging like the clappers. It doesn't even race that much in tennis.'

James let out a laugh and plunged his face between her breasts.

'What a feast I'm going to have, Mrs R,' he cried.

Tilly gurgled with laughter as he fondled and kissed her, straddling her with all the keenness of a champion jockey. She thrilled at the exquisite things he did to her fleshy belly and thighs, crying out with joy, revelling in the chaos of discarded clothing and bedding, the heat and sweat of their vigorous lovemaking, not caring how dishevelled she became. She felt like a goddess with her cornucopia of fruit; she may even have said so at the height of their passion.

'Oh goodness, James,' she sighed, as they sank back on the rumpled bed, 'exercise has never been so much fun.'

James chuckled beside her. 'Or with so much commentary.'

'Oh dear,' Tilly said, 'did I talk too much? I'll try not to next time.'

He flung an arm over her soft belly. 'Don't change a thing, Mrs R. You're just right as you are.'

Chapter 7

Edinburgh

William Boswell rang the bell for flat four, seventy-one Clerk Street at a quarter to two. Sophie and Amy were ready in tennis skirts and plimsolls.

Sophie pulled the lever to open the downstairs door but as Boz stepped inside the building she called over the banisters into the stairwell, 'We'll come down and save you coming up.'

She was down the steps, two at a time, her aunt following. In the doorway, she and Boz grinned at each other and shook hands, then Sophie said, 'You remember Auntie Amy from the sidecar?'

'Aye, of course, pleased tae meet you again, Miss Anderson.'

Sophie could see someone standing beyond the half-open outer door; a leg in white flannels and a billow of smoke from a cigarette.

'Tam?' She smiled and stepped outside.

Her face fell as she saw it wasn't Tam Telfer. The Indian from the Meadows cricket match dropped his cigarette, ground it beneath his shoe and held out a hand.

'Hello, Miss Logan; Rafi Khan. We met at the camp – Carter Bar.'

Sophie hesitated. 'Yes, of course.' She took his hand in a brief shake, swallowing down her disappointment.

Amy greeted him more readily. 'From Lahore, wasn't it? Your family's in construction.'

'Well remembered, Miss Anderson.' Rafi smiled.

'And you joined the Lahore Horse because you liked riding more than organising bricks – annoyed your father. I like an independent-minded spirit.'

Rafi gave a delighted laugh. 'And I salute a woman who shook her umbrella at that wily politician Churchill who didn't want you to have the vote and doesn't trust us Indians to run our own country. At least you have won your fight.'

'Rafi, nae politics this afternoon please,' cried Boz, 'the ladies were promised tennis.'

'The one topic shouldn't be at the exclusion of the other,' Amy said, and fell into step with Rafi. 'I passed through Lahore over twenty years ago on the way to my sister's wedding in Murree – wonderful Moghul buildings – and I've never seen such a grand railway station; it was like a palace itself.'

'My grandfather was one of the builders.' Rafi smiled. 'His fledgling company thrived after that – paid for my schooling at Bishop Cotton's in Simla.'

'Simla? Now there's a place I wish I'd visited.'

'Not much different from your Scottish Highlands – or your Scottish weather,' Rafi joked. 'I was well prepared for mist and rain by Simla summers, and for cold winds and snow by Simla winters.'

'So why leave the warmth of Lahore for Scotland, Mr Khan?'

'I like Scottish weather.'

Amy peered at him and realised from his sardonic look that he was teasing her.

'And at Simla I developed a passion for trees. Edinburgh has one of the best forestry trainings in the Empire . . .'

Sophie stepped ahead with Boz, feeling hot with embarrassment that she should have assumed Tam would be making up their tennis four. The sophisticated Khan made her feel quite tongue-tied. Boz seemed to understand.

'Tam is abroad at the moment. He went tae France as soon as term finished.'

'Oh, I see. It's the final forestry camp, is it?'

'No, that's not until August.' Boz glanced at her. 'He's in Paris with his ma and sister. The first holiday they've had together since the end of the war. It was Tam's idea.'

'How kind of him.' Sophie smiled, relieved that Tam's absence had nothing to do with not wanting to play tennis with her. 'He spoke very fondly of them – quite admiring of his older sister.'

'Aye,' Boz agreed. 'Flora's been like a second mother to him – ten years older – so he's always after her approval.'

'Well, taking her to Paris must score a lot of points,' Sophie said dryly.

'Aye, he's out to impress' – Boz nodded – 'show off his bad French and convince her that after surviving a war and a university degree, he's finally a grown man capable of making his own decisions.'

'She sounds formidable.'

'She is.' Boz grunted. 'Any friend of Tam's has to be approved by his sister Flora first.'

'I'll bear that in mind,' Sophie said.

He gave her an odd look. Perhaps he was disappointed that she was taking such an interest in his friend, but surely it must have been obvious at the camp that that was where her feelings lay?

They talked no more of Tam and enjoyed a lively game of doubles; Amy pairing with Rafi, and Sophie with Boz. Her aunt was slower around the court than Sophie, yet her swing was strong, her arms well-muscled from her joinery work. Rafi was also a strong, confident player and had Sophie running all over the court, but Boz, with his lanky height and reach, managed to win many of the shots that Sophie couldn't.

Each pair won a set and then Sophie's pair narrowly won the third. Amy tired and lost the fourth set easily.

'That's enough,' her aunt panted. 'I'm sorry, Rafi, I'm done in.'

'So am I,' Rafi agreed. Though Sophie thought he didn't look tired at all. His handsome face hardly glistened whereas Boz was puce and dripping with sweat. Rafi flicked Sophie a look. 'Well played.' He shook Boz's hand in congratulations but didn't attempt to take hers. 'You make a winning pair.'

Sophie was rankled by his comment; the Indian was mocking her so she ignored him.

'Thanks, Rafi, well played too,' Boz said, wiping his face with a large handkerchief.

'Let me walk you home, Miss Anderson.' Rafi turned away. 'Boz and Miss Logan can have a singles game without us. Your niece still looks full of energy.'

Amy accepted readily and Boz seemed keen to carry on.

'Yes let's,' Sophie agreed, trying not to show her annoyance at Rafi's remark. It was less the words than his teasing manner. 'I don't often get to play and the weather's too nice to be indoors.'

She felt a strange relief when the urbane young Indian walked away with her aunt. He was handsome and humorous, she had to admit, but she didn't feel comfortable in his presence. It was nothing she could readily explain. And the way he looked at her with a coolness that verged on disdain made her suspect that he didn't much like her.

Sophie and Boz played for another half an hour. To her delight, her game improved while he tired, and they drew at five games all.

'Next time I'll beat you,' Sophie said.

'I accept the challenge, Miss Logan.' Boz grinned.

They arranged to play the following Wednesday evening and walked back to the Clerk Street flat together, Sophie inviting him up for some of Amy's home-made lemonade to quench his thirst. She felt a flutter of nerves as she entered the flat; the Lahori would be lounging in a comfortable seat smoking and spouting politics with her aunt.

'Your friend Mr Khan wouldn't stay to tea, Mr Boswell,' Amy explained. 'Said he had some studying to do.'

'That's Rafi.' Boz grunted. 'Always striving tae be the best.'

'I admire his dedication,' Amy said. 'It must be hard for him so far from home and family.'

She gave Sophie one of her steely looks as if it had somehow been her fault Rafi had not stayed.

'Aye, suppose it must.' Boz shrugged. 'But Rafi's no been back tae India since the war started, so he canna miss them that much. A man content in his ane company, I'd say.'

***

Sophie played tennis with William Boswell twice the following week after she had finished work. After the second time, he asked her bashfully, 'I was wondering if you'd like to gang tae the Forestry Department hop next Tuesday? It'll no be very glamorous – just in the gym – but they usually get some good student musicians and there's always plenty to eat.'

Sophie hesitated. She didn't want to give Boz false hope that their friendship might blossom into romance. She enjoyed his company but felt nothing deeper.

'I'm not sure—'

'We'll be part of a larger group,' Boz assured. 'You'll no have to dance with me all evening.' She studied his open, genial face. 'It just means I'll no have to be a wallflower for the whole night,' he joked. 'There are never enough lassies. Professor Grant might even give me higher marks for bringing you along.'

Sophie gave a wry laugh. 'Well, if it will help your final degree then I can't say no, can I?'

On Tuesday evening, Sophie raced home late from the office, washed herself at the sink, grabbed a clean blouse from the wardrobe and a lighter skirt for dancing in, pulled a brush through her long hair and swept it up on top of her head in a loose bun.

'Can I borrow your light scarf, Auntie Amy? It's still warm out there and I'll sweat in a coat.'

'Ladies don't sweat,' Amy said, 'they merely glow.'

'They sweat when they dance to ragtime.' Sophie grinned.

'Don't be too late,' Amy tried to be firm, 'you have work in the morning.'

'And I'll turn into a rat at midnight, I know.' She leaned out of the sitting room window, spotted Boz ambling down the street and waved. 'Just coming down!' She turned and planted a juicy kiss on her aunt's soft cheek. 'Don't wait up; I have my key.'

'Enjoy it, dearie.'

Amy watched from the window, her heart squeezing to think how her niece had grown from a clinging, unhappy child into such a lively, attractive young woman who appeared to fear nothing. She walked side by side with the tall red-headed farmer's son, glancing up at him and chattering. Perhaps it would not be long before Sophie would be marrying and leaving home like Cousin Tilly. Amy dreaded the day when Sophie would no longer come clattering up the stairwell and burst through the door with a shout of welcome and a tumble of words about the day's happenings.

She couldn't have loved her more had she been her own child. It grieved her that her sister Jessie had not lived to see her daughter grow up and flourish. Thinking of her tragic sister gave her a pang of foreboding; she prayed that Sophie would not make the same mistake and rush into marriage with someone unsuitable. The tea planter Bill Logan had captured Jessie's heart with his good looks and charm but he had been a jealous and over-possessive man. Amy had instinctively mistrusted him on sight. Strangely, she'd felt the same about Tam Telfer, though she had no grounds for her unease.

She watched until the young pair crossed the road and disappeared towards the Pleasance and the university gymnasium. Lanky William was a cheery soul, but Amy doubted that he would be the one to match Sophie's passionate nature or thirst for adventure.

***

It turned out that Sophie knew one of the other students, Ian McGinty – they had been at the kirk Sunday School together – along with his two younger sisters who were also there to make up the numbers. Rafi walked in with a bohemian-looking older woman in gypsy skirts, a cascade of bangles and bright red lipstick. They stood smoking together by the drinks table; Rafi waved across but didn't come over.

'Some artist's wifie,' Boz felt he had to explain, 'one o' those Pointillists or something. Rafi kens the strangest folk.'

Sophie, forcing herself to stop staring at Rafi and the fascinating woman, entered into the dancing with relish. The musicians were a ceilidh band playing Scottish country dances and not jazz as she had hoped, but she knew all the dances from kirk socials and suffragist fundraisers that Amy had taken her to throughout the years. She danced with Boz and Ian and two other students who had asked to mark her dance card.

Just before the break for supper, Sophie had the strongest feeling she was being observed. As the band announced a Dashing White Sergeant and told the dancers to group into threes, she caught sight of a familiar lean figure standing hands in pockets near the entrance talking to Rafi and the artist's wife but looking directly at her.

'Tam's back,' she gasped.

Boz waved to his friend and called, 'Hey, Telfer! We need another man.'

Sophie's insides did somersaults as Tam left the others and strode across the hall to greet them. He slapped Boz on the back and shook Sophie's hand. 'I'd have come sooner if I'd known the bonniest motorcycle rider in all Scotland was at the dance. Normally it's the professor's granny and her cronies, eh, Boz?'

'Aye, pretty much.' Boz snorted. 'How was Paris?'

Tam's expression tightened. 'A disappointment.'

Boz raised his eyebrows. 'Flora didn't approve?'

'I'll tell you later,' Tam said. 'Come on, let's get in line.' He grabbed Sophie firmly by the hand and pulled her on to the dance floor. Boz took her other hand and she stood between them, thrilled at the unexpected turn of events.

They whirled and shrieked in the lively dance, Sophie's heart pounding every time she had to clasp hands with Tam and duck with him under the arching arms of the opposite dancers. He looked just as handsome as she remembered, his body toned from outdoor labour and his lean face tanned, accentuating the blue of his eyes.

The reel finished and the dancers queued up in the adjoining room for the buffet of pies, sandwiches and fruit cake. Tam found them a table and regaled them with humorous stories about his family in Paris.

'Flora insisted on us going to a show – went on about it all week – then had a fit of the vapours at the lack of clothing on the dancers. Mother kept shouting "They'll catch their death!" and Flora made us all walk out in the middle of the cancan.'

'What were you thinking of, taking them to the Folies Bergère, you daft man?' Boz whistled.

'Never again.' Tam grimaced. 'It's back to North Berwick for Ma and Flora.'

'And you?' Boz asked. 'Did you—?'

'Had my fill of Paris too.' Tam cut him off. 'But tell me what I've been missing.'

'Lots of cricket and tennis,' Boz said. 'Rafi beating me at cricket and Sophie beating me at tennis.'

'Really?' Tam exclaimed.

'Don't sound so surprised,' Sophie laughed, 'I was captain of my school tennis team.'

'Then you need a better opponent,' Tam teased. 'I challenge you to racquets at dawn.'

'Done!' Sophie grinned.

For the rest of the evening Sophie took it in turns to dance with Boz and Tam, but when it came to the final waltz Tam was quick to claim her. She felt ridiculously nervous being held close, his hand clasped firmly in the small of her back, his chin brushing her hair as they spun around the floor. She was impressed by how light on his feet he was.

'You're a great dancer.' He smiled down at her. 'Better than any of the lassies in Paris.'

'I'm glad to hear it,' she said, pleased at the compliment, yet with a twinge of jealousy at the French girls who had danced with him. 'I prefer the modern dances best.'

'Have you been to the new Palais de Danse in Fountainbridge?' Tam asked.

'No,' Sophie was wistful, 'though I hear it's wonderful.'

'So Boz hasn't taken you?'

Sophie shook her head. 'He just asked me tonight to help make up the numbers.'

'So there's no understanding between you?' Tam asked in his forthright way.

'Goodness no,' Sophie said quickly.

'Then, Miss Logan,' Tam said, pressing her closer and murmuring in her ear, 'on Saturday night, you are getting on your glad rags and going to the Palais with me.'

Chapter 8

'You're not going on your own with Mr Telfer, are you?' Amy asked in concern, watching Sophie's elaborate preparation for her night out. She had washed her hair and tightly bound the long strands in rags until they dried; the result was a cascade of blonde ringlets. She had shortened the hem on the blue dress she had worn for Tilly's wedding and was now holding up different pieces of jewellery against the plain frontage.

'The ivory beads or the amber brooch, Auntie?'

'The brooch.'

Sophie pulled a face. 'I think mother's beads look more eye-catching – and they'll go with the ivory bracelet.'

'You're going to wear the bracelet too?' Amy asked in dismay. 'What if you lose it? The catch isn't strong.'

'I won't lose it,' Sophie insisted.

She lifted the ivory bracelet from its battered box – her most cherished possession – given by her parents on her christening. She had a memory of her mother fastening it on to her small wrist; some special occasion like a birthday perhaps? It was more the soft touch of warm fingers and a floral scent that she remembered, and her father laughing in the background; a throaty smoker's laugh. She ran her fingers over the tiny delicately carved elephants' heads and snapped shut the metal catch.

A few years ago, some cheap beads had been strung on to the bracelet so that it would fit her woman's wrist, but Sophie still loved it. The bracelet had been like a talisman for her over the years, a link to her parents and her early life before the tragedy, as if their spirits were conjured up to watch over her whenever she touched it. Yet she could never tell such a superstitious belief to her aunt who was a stalwart of the Kirk.

'Who else will be at the dance hall tonight, Sophie?' Amy persisted, eyeing the macabre bracelet with its decapitated elephant heads; she had never liked it or the way her niece treated it like a holy relic.

'Oh, there'll be a crowd of us,' she answered breezily. 'Boz and the McGintys – folk from the university.'

'Well, Mr Telfer can tell me himself when he comes up to collect you.'

Sophie busied herself pulling on her raincoat. 'I said I'd meet him outside; don't want to miss the bus.'

'But, Sophie—'

'I'll invite him for tea another day, promise.' Sophie grabbed her small evening bag, bought that week in a second-hand shop, gave her aunt a swift kiss and clattered out of the door.

'You'll need a brolly!' Amy called.

'Tam is bound to have one,' Sophie said with a wave and banged the door behind her.

She was a bundle of excitement and nerves; the last thing she wanted was her aunt battering Tam with questions about his family and current affairs like she had with Boz and Rafi. Sophie had the feeling Tam would be less patient with an inquisitive Amy, and she wanted to create a good impression before he was subjected to an inquisition. Pausing in the dim light of the stairwell, she slipped off her dowdy mackintosh, pulled out a lipstick and miniature mirror from her bag and applied a light layer of red. She pressed her full lips together until she was happy with the effect.

Tam was waiting outside with an umbrella against the evening drizzle, dressed immaculately in an evening suit, white scarf and highly polished shoes. Her insides fluttered at his well-groomed appearance and the spicy smell of his shaving soap. He gave her an appreciative look and offered his arm.

'How bonny you look, Miss Logan.' He winked. 'I'll be the envy of every man at the Palais. Come on, in you get.' He indicated the waiting motor cab.

'We're going by taxi?' Sophie cried.

'I'm not having you splashing through puddles in your stockinged legs, my girl.' He grinned.

Sophie flushed with pleasure as he leapt in behind her. Tam chatted easily as they made their way across town, wanting to hear all about the rest of her motorcycle trip to Newcastle and her cousin's twenty-first birthday party. He was astonished to hear that it had resulted in a sudden engagement and marriage a month later.

'This is the dress I wore as Tilly's bridesmaid,' Sophie confessed.

'It's delightful,' Tam assured, glancing at her legs. 'I'm honoured you're wearing it for our evening out.'

Sophie was suddenly self-conscious, pulling at the hem to cover her knees. 'I don't have many smart clothes.'

'You're beautiful whatever you wear.' He smiled.

She knew she was being flattered and no doubt such words came easily to the worldly Tam, but Sophie knew before she even reached the dance hall that she was falling hopelessly in love with him.

They dashed from the taxi and out of the rain into the imposing entrance of the Palais de Danse. Sophie could not believe the difference between the soot-blackened tenements of the street outside and the glittering interior of sweeping gilded pillars, tiled floors and electric lights. At home, the flat was still lit by gas lamps; muted pools of light that never completely dispelled the gloom. Here, lights blazed from chandeliers and wall brackets in a range of colours from dazzling white to soft pink.

After checking her coat into the cloakroom, she took Tam's arm and joined the busy throng of party-goers making for the ballroom, Tam greeting people as they jostled in.

'How was Paris?' a man in evening dress asked.

'Good to see you back Tam,' another clapped him on the back.

'This must be . . .?' a third man in a rowing blazer gave Sophie a glazed look.

'Miss Sophie Logan,' Tam introduced her. 'Tennis champion and motorcycle dispatch rider in the war.'

Sophie laughed with embarrassment. 'Neither of those are true.'

'Tam's a terrible story-teller,' the rower said. 'I can see you are far too young to have been in the war.'

'Young yes,' Tam agreed, 'but she beats Boz at tennis and she does ride a motorbike.'

The man whistled in admiration, swaying slightly on his feet. 'Join us, Telfer, you can't keep the remarkable Miss Logan to yourself.' He introduced himself as Jimmy Scott.

They found a table and Tam went off to get drinks.

Sophie gazed around, amazed at the variety of people; the well-heeled of Murrayfield seemed to be rubbing shoulders with students and office girls like her. She observed the fringed dresses, sequined caps and shorter hairstyles of Edinburgh's young flappers with envy. Perhaps if she saved carefully she could afford a fur stole or at least a feathered headdress? Tam returned with fruit juices. He chatted to his friends from the rowing club about some regatta he had missed.

'No wonder you came a poor third without my muscle,' Tam teased.

'Very selfish of you, Telfer, to swan off to Paris just when you were needed most,' said Jimmy. He reeked of whisky. Tam had told her that some of his friends went drinking before the dance because the Palais was teetotal.

'I don't think he was selfish at all,' Sophie chipped in. 'It was a kind gesture to take his mother and sister on holiday. I'd love to go to Paris.'

Looks were exchanged among the men.

'I'll take you to Paris; just say the word,' Jimmy said, leering at her.

'Say no, Sophie.' Tam laughed. 'Jimmy's never been further south than Prestonpans and doesn't speak a word of French.'

'Whereas you war heroes think you know it all, I suppose?' Jimmy complained.

'We know how to parler avec the lassies,' the beefy man in the dinner suit said. 'Don't we, Tam?'

At that moment they were interrupted by squeals of delight as two young women in matching cream dresses and long lacy mittens clattered up to the table.

'Boys!' the taller one with a dark bob of hair cried as she set about kissing them roundly on the cheek and waving a dance card. 'We can probably squeeze you in.'

'Tam, you came back after all.' Her friend waved a cigarette holder at him. 'I told Nell you would.'

'No, I told you, Catherine,' Nell contradicted. 'Tam's an Edinburgh boy. He would miss us far too much.'

Seats were pulled up for the new arrivals and introductions made. Nell knew the men from the student debating society; Catherine was her school friend. They looked at Sophie with curiosity. She felt unusually tongue-tied amid the quick-fire chatter and teasing; they were all so sophisticated and well educated compared to her. What she yearned to do was dance to the wonderful band music pulsating from the dozen musicians on the dais at the end of the ballroom.

Abruptly, Tam stood up and led Sophie on to the dance floor for a foxtrot.

'They're good lads,' he said, 'but it's difficult to get a word in edgeways.'

'The girls too.' Sophie gave a wry smile.

'Debating society.' Tam grinned. 'Thought you would approve of lassies who can speak up for themselves?'

'I do. But I want to dance with you more than I want to listen to your friends.'

Tam's eyes widened, then he laughed and squeezed her tighter.

The evening sped by and Sophie hardly had time to catch her breath, as Tam and his friends claimed her for every dance. Boz arrived. He gave her a wistful look but seemed happy to dance with Catherine and Nell. Late into the evening as the lights were dimmed, she was surprised to see Rafi appear with Ian McGinty, both men dressed in casual flannels.

'Here come the Bolshies; Khan and McGinty,' Jimmy greeted them drunkenly. Sophie had noticed how he had been swigging from a hip flask throughout the evening. 'Come to spoil our fun, eh?'

'Oh shut up, Jimmy,' Nell said.

But Rafi and Ian were unperturbed. 'Enjoy your bourgeois pursuits while you can, Scott,' Rafi said mildly, raising his glass and blowing out cigarette smoke. 'Come the revolution, we'll put in a word for you with the commissariat.'

'Don't make fun o' me,' Jimmy slurred.

'Come and sit next to me, Rafi,' Nell ordered, 'and tell me about the Empire debate I missed. Tam said you had to give the case for colonial rule. What on earth did you say to win it?'

'Just spouted forth about the benefits of benign Mughal emperors,' Rafi said dryly.

'Not quite what they were expecting.' Tam grunted.

'Makes a change from Britishers going on about railways and missionaries,' said Ian McGinty.

This seemed to rile Jimmy, who was swaying possessively over Nell. 'Khan! Saw you drinking liquor earlier. Thought you Mohammedans weren't supposed to touch a drop.'

Rafi raised his glass of juice in a mock toast. 'Benefits of the Empire, Scott.'

'Bloody hypocrite,' Jimmy snarled. 'S'prised they let you in.'

McGinty stepped towards him aggressively. 'And why shouldn't they? He's as much right to come in here as any of us.'

Jimmy lurched forward and spat out the words, 'Cause he's a bloody wog.'

In a flash, Tam was out of his seat, face contorted in fury.

'Bastard!' he thundered, drew back his fist and landed a punch on Jimmy's nose. Jimmy reeled backwards and fell to the floor. Tam went for him again but Boz and Rafi intervened, blocking his way and holding him back. The beefy rower pulled Jimmy up.

'Get him out of here,' Nell ordered, 'before we all get thrown out.'

Jimmy began to protest but Boz was quick to take his other arm. 'You're drunk; hame time.'

Jimmy was swiftly marched from the hall, clutching his face. It was so quickly over that Sophie could hardly believe it had happened. No one beyond their table appeared to have noticed. Tam stood, breathing hard, his fists still bunched.

McGinty said, 'Well done, Telfer – time someone kicked his imperialist backside.'

Rafi's expression was hard to decipher. Sophie thought he looked more concerned about Tam than himself. Without a word, he put a hand on Tam's shoulder and guided him into a chair. Tam sat staring, clutching the chair arms while he calmed down. There was an awkwardness around the table. Nell stood up and said, 'Come on, Rafi, let's dance.'

They moved off and Sophie watched them until they melted into the throng of dancers. She felt funny watching Nell and Rafi dance together; the violence had upset her and her emotions were all at sea. Boz returned.

'Brown's taken him hame tae his digs. He'll no remember much in the morning. You all right, Tam?'

Tam nodded. Boz looked at Sophie. 'And you?'

'Yes, of course.' She reached for her drink, her hand shaking, and took a long gulp. Boz looked about to say something else, but Tam abruptly stood up.

'Ladies,' he addressed Sophie and Catherine, 'I'm sorry for my barrack-room behaviour.' He stared at his knuckles as if they did not belong to him. 'Please forgive me.'

Catherine waved away his apology. 'Jimmy over-stepped the mark.' She held out a hand to Boz. 'Take me for a tango; we're equally bad at it.'

Left alone, Sophie and Tam regarded each other. 'I've spoilt your evening, haven't I?' Tam looked contrite.

'No,' said Sophie, 'Jimmy did that. And it hasn't really been spoilt – I've been having such a grand evening.'

Tam looked drained. 'Do you mind if we go now?'

Sophie hid her reluctance. 'Of course not.'

Outside, the rain had stopped. Tam revived in the cool air, his former good humour returning.

'Let me walk you home.'

'It's out of your way.'

'I enjoy walking and your aunt will expect me to deliver you safely to your door, won't she?'

'Yes,' Sophie agreed.

'Come on, Miss Logan.' He smiled. 'I don't want Miss Anderson to find an excuse not to let me take you out dancing again.'

They walked arm in arm across Bruntsfield Links and on through the Meadows, the malty smell of the breweries strong on the night breeze.

'You were brave standing up for Rafi,' Sophie said.

'Nothing brave about it. Scott was being a boor in front of you ladies. He drinks too much.'

His expression tightened and she wished she hadn't mentioned it.

'Do you drink alcohol at all?'

'Hardly touch the stuff. Liquor's bad for you; my father died of it.'

'I'm sorry.'

'Don't be. It was a long time ago.' Tam brushed aside her sympathy. 'Besides, Rafi's a good friend; he's twice the man Jimmy Scott will ever be. There's a bond between men like me and Rafi and Boz – boys who made it through the Flanders war. I wasn't going to stand by and see him insulted.'

Sophie squeezed his arm. 'And I admire you all the more for it.'

He stopped and pulled her round to face him, tilting her chin. Sophie's heart thumped at his closeness. Was he about to kiss her? He gazed intently into her eyes. Sophie swallowed, willing him to press his firm mouth to hers.

'I'm not worthy of your admiration,' he said, stepping back.

She felt a wave of disappointment. They carried on walking, Tam making light conversation about Boz and his craving for toffee during the war.

'Rafi says Boz will love all the sweetmeats when we get to India – that's if we all pass the exams.'

Sophie didn't want to talk about Rafi and Boz and exams, or think about Tam disappearing off to India. She wanted Tam to kiss her. She was full of frustration and longing. Surely he could tell?

At the door to her tenement, Tam raised her hand to his lips and gave it a light kiss. He was so gentle that it was hard to believe this was the same man who had lost his temper in an instant with his fellow rower.

'I've enjoyed tonight, Miss Logan. You're a natural dancer.'

'I've enjoyed it too,' Sophie said, fearful he would turn and walk off without making any promise to see her again. 'Tam, how about that game of tennis during the week?'

'Tennis?'

'Racquets at dawn, remember?'

He studied her a moment. 'Of course. I'd like that.'

'Monday?' she suggested.

'I study Hindustani with Downs on Mondays – old hand from the Punjab.'

'Oh.' She waited.

'What about Tuesday after your day at the office?'

'Yes,' she said at once.

'Good.' He smiled.

'Thank you for a magical evening,' she said. 'The Palais was even better than I could have imagined.'

'Well, in you go. I want to see you safely inside and duty done.' He gave a self-mocking salute.

Sophie opened the door. 'Thanks again.' She stepped inside but watched him as he walked away, softly whistling a dance tune. The scar on his head caught in the light of the street lamp. It was a sudden reminder that, young though he was, Tam must have seen and done things that no young man should be expected to endure. She wondered how he had got such a wound but suspected he would resent her asking. Every time he brushed his thick hair around the bald patch it must remind him of war.

Later, she lay in bed unable to sleep, the music going round in her head and images of Tam's handsome face smiling down at her. He liked her, of that she was sure. But there was a reticence about him. Perhaps he didn't want to become romantically involved when in a few short weeks he would be sailing for India and a new life? She felt a stab of envy that he would be going to live in the land of her childhood, but it was madness to allow any feelings for Tam; she had managed so well up until now not to allow any man into her heart. Those you loved too deeply you lost.

As she lay tossing about in her narrow bed, Sophie feared her attraction to Tam was too strong to resist.

Chapter 9

Sophie woke with a start in the early light. She had hardly slept. What had woken her? The image in her head on waking had not been Tam, but Nell dancing with Rafi, moving like swaying grass across the ballroom floor.

Keep away from the grass huts where the natives live. Her father had told her that, she was sure of it. She remembered running across an emerald green lawn and down a dusty track with someone chasing her. It was thrilling and she was laughing. Ahead lay jungle and a pool of brown water where children were splashing and playing. *Keep away!* She'd wanted to join in; she could almost recall the hot pungent smell of ox dung and flowers, hear the shrieks and laughter. On the point of reaching them, someone pulled her back and smacked her legs. She was led bawling back up the track.

Keep her away from there! Her father's furious red face. *No daughter of mine plays with wogs.*

Sophie sat up, trying to shake off the dream. Or had it really happened? Deep down, she knew it to be true. The incident at the Palais between Jimmy Scott and Rafi – the derogatory name Jimmy had used to insult Rafi – was the same one she remembered her father using. It was a common enough term, but it made her sad to think of her father shouting it out for all to hear. And she had no memory of ever playing with Indian children, before or after.

Sophie got up, made a pot of tea and sat at the sitting room window watching a watery yellow dawn behind the dark crags in Holyrood Park. She wished it was an office day. Work would shake off her strange, sad mood; keeping busy always did chase the blues away. She would go to the kirk with her aunt and then take her for a spin in The Memsahib if the rain held off.

Washing in cold water, she dressed, brushed out last night's curls and took a cup of tea into Amy's room to wake her.

Later that day, stopping for a picnic tea in the Pentland Hills with a hazy view over all Edinburgh and beyond to the Forth, Sophie regaled her aunt with the details of the dance but made no mention of Jimmy's drunken behaviour or Tam's aggressive response in case Amy stopped her going again.

'You seem very taken with this Tam Telfer,' Amy said.

'He's invited me to play tennis on Tuesday.' Sophie smiled.

'Singles or doubles with the other boys?'

'Singles.'

Amy gave a direct look. 'I wonder why Mr Telfer did not call or write to you after he said he would at Carter Bar? I hope it's not just because Mr Boswell was showing an interest in you that Mr Telfer has too.'

Sophie was hurt at the suggestion. 'Tam's not like that. He was busy with lectures and then took his mother and sister to Paris; there was no opportunity.'

'Is it really wise to let yourself become attached to a man who is soon to leave the country?'

'Auntie!' Sophie was impatient. 'I can't help who I fall in love with, can I?'

Amy patted her hand. 'I just want you to be cautious. I'm prepared to be won over. And judging by the pink colour he brings to your cheeks by just the mention of his name; it's high time you brought him round to tea.'

'Thank you, Auntie.' Sophie grinned.

As they packed up to leave, Sophie said, 'I had a dream about India last night – it might have been a memory.'

'Was it a nice dream?'

'Not very. I was running away and got smacked and there were children playing but I wasn't allowed to join in. But the colours of the grass and the flowers were so bright I wanted the dream to carry on.'

'Was the place familiar?' Amy asked.

'Perhaps.' Sophie shrugged. 'My father was there.' She gave a troubled look. 'What was he like?'

'I didn't meet him for very long,' Amy said.

'You must have had an impression at least?'

'He was quite handsome and very in love with your mother,' Amy admitted. 'Old-fashioned in his ways, though. A woman's place is in the home where her husband is master, sort of attitude. But then I think the British in India lag behind us by a generation in social progress. Bill Logan certainly didn't approve of my suffrage activities' – Amy laughed – 'or my spinsterhood and independence!'

She saw her niece's sad expression and tried to think of something positive to say about her brother-in-law. 'But he was a family man and Jessie wrote after your birth to say how pleased he was to be a father.'

'Really?' Sophie sighed. 'I just wish I could remember him being like that.'

Buttoning up her cycle jacket, a thought struck her.

'Auntie, did you keep any of my mother's letters?'

Amy paused. 'There may be one or two' – she gave a vague shrug – 'but she wasn't a great correspondent, and after you were born she only wrote at Christmas and birthdays.' She kept to herself the suspicion that Logan intercepted his wife's letters and that some never got sent, for Jessie referred to events and people in her Christmas cards that she expected Amy to know about. And there was that last despairing letter from her sister that she shouldn't really have kept. Guilt that she hadn't kept in better touch with Jessie overwhelmed her anew.

'I hadn't heard from your mother in months that year that she died,' Amy confessed. 'But then your father had moved you all to somewhere more remote and I assumed the postal service was non-existent.'

'We moved away from the Oxford estate?' Sophie asked in surprise. 'Where to?'

'I'm not sure.' Amy frowned. 'Somewhere further into the hills. It was your father who wrote and told me – said your mother's health was growing delicate and the cooler air would do her good. That's why it was even more tragic that they both died of enteric fever there.'

Sophie had a sudden vivid picture of peering through a sun-bleached balcony overgrown with flowering creepers with nothing beyond but trees and jungle. Dressed in a party frock, she'd been waiting impatiently for something or someone. There had been a lot of loud drumming and fireworks; she'd thought they were especially for her.

'I think I remember a bungalow in the hills,' Sophie struggled with the fading image. 'Yes, it was my birthday because I wanted a party but Mother told me I couldn't – it was too far for anyone to come. That must have been the place, mustn't it? The place where my parents died?'

'It's possible.'

'Can you remember where my father said it was, Auntie Amy?'

Amy shook her head. 'Not the area – but I remember the name of the house because it was pretty: White Blossom Cottage.'

'White Blossom Cottage,' Sophie murmured. 'Doesn't sound very Indian.'

'Come on,' Amy became brisk, 'it doesn't do to dwell on the past. I wish your mother had never gone to India, but it's no good having regrets for things you can't undo. Scotland is your home, dearie, so be thankful for that.'

***

The Tuesday tennis was rained off but Sophie invited Tam back to tea to meet Auntie Amy anyway. He was charming and talkative and very admiring of her woodwork, promising to source some beech wood for her next commission. They talked about trees and Switzerland while Sophie refilled the teapot and buttered more scones. He didn't seem to mind the barrage of questions from her aunt.

'And why have you chosen India for your forestry career?' Amy asked.

'It's my second choice,' Tam was candid. 'I had hoped to go to America but that didn't come off. But India offers very good prospects; they have the best forestry service in the Empire. I expect to be a full conservator by the time I'm thirty and an expert in silviculture by thirty-five. I'm already writing articles on all aspects of forestry and getting paid for it. I plan to become an authority so that my expertise will be in demand anywhere in the world.'

Sophie was surprised at the passion with which he spoke about his future and she envied him his single-mindedness. Her aunt, though, had that steely look in her eye.

'I must say, I like a man who knows his own mind,' Amy said, 'and there's nothing wrong with a wee bit of ambition . . .'

'But?' Tam cocked his head. 'You think I'm getting ahead of myself?'

'All you young people seem impatient these days.' Amy laughed. 'Just take time to enjoy life too.'

'I intend to.' Tam grinned. 'There's plenty of tennis and dancing in India, from what I hear. Work hard, play harder; that's Telfer's motto.'

Sophie avoided her aunt's enquiring look; she had no idea if she fitted into Tam's grand plans at all. The thought of going back out to India was both frightening and thrilling. She hardly dared hope it might happen.

Yet after that meeting with Auntie Amy, Sophie saw Tam almost every day for the next two weeks. She took time off work so they could play tennis and walk along Salisbury Crags; if it rained they went ice-skating at Murrayfield ice rink. He took her to tea dances at the North British Hotel and she took him to a concert at the Usher Hall.

'Not very keen on this classical stuff,' Tam was frank, so they left at the interval. But when her employer, Miss Gorrie, gave her spare tickets to Gilbert and Sullivan's *Pirates of Penzance*, Tam clapped and whistled with enthusiasm. On the Saturday, they took off on The Memsahib for a trip to the beach at North Berwick, ate fish and chips, and then dashed back in time to change and go dancing at The Palais. For, above all, they loved to dance together. Each was as passionate as the other. With no other partner had Sophie felt as if she was melded together with another being as much as she did gliding and swirling around the dance floor in Tam's arms.

Sometimes they would meet up with Tam's other friends but Sophie was always impatient to have him to herself. It was after their long day out to North Berwick and the dance hall that Tam, walking her home across the Meadows in the summer half-dark, pulled her under a tree and asked, 'Sophie, can I kiss you?'

'Oh, Tam, I've been longing for this!'

'You have?'

'Yes.' She smiled.

He put his arms around her, squeezing her close, and fastened his mouth on to hers. His kiss was firm and energetic and went on for so long that Sophie was light-headed and gasping for breath when he finally broke away.

'You're quite a girl,' he said, his voice husky.

'I didn't know kissing could be like that.' Sophie grinned, feeling unsteady.

'A pretty girl under a beech tree has that effect on me,' he teased.

She hoped there would be more kissing but Tam took her hand and walked her back to Clerk Street.

As the time drew nearer for Tam and the other students to leave for their forestry camp on the Continent, Sophie's heart grew sore. How would she manage without seeing him for so long? She physically ached with the thought of his absence. And then he would only be back a couple of weeks before going to Oxford to sit his final exams, and after that he sailed for India . . .

She gave herself sleepless nights with tortured thoughts of never seeing Tam again, of him disappearing on his adventure to India where he would be surrounded by young women from the 'Fishing Fleet' – those husband-hunters who sailed out east – all eager to marry a handsome and ambitious Scot with a government job. Perhaps she could go out to India and visit Tilly and somehow engineer to see Tam? But then Tilly was going to Assam to join James Robson, whereas Tam was being posted to the Punjab on the other side of India. Her yearning to return to the country of her birth grew with each day and would give her no peace.

One evening, returning home from dancing and stopping to kiss under their special tree, Sophie spoke of her fears.

'What will happen once you go away, Tam?' she asked. 'What will become of us?'

He laughed. 'I'm only going for a month. We won't pine away and die in that time. And I'll write, of course.'

'But after that,' Sophie persisted, 'what will I do when you go to India?'

For a long moment he was silent. She couldn't read the expression on his lean face as he stood in dark shadow but she felt his thoughts were far away.

'We'll write to each other,' he said breezily, 'and see where it leads.' Then he kissed her again and gave her no more chance to talk.

On the day before Tam left for France and Switzerland, Sophie went to watch him in a rowing race. Boz was there with Rafi and McGinty. Boz was friendly but bashful and soon sauntered off, but Rafi was talking enthusiastically of their impending trip.

'We're going to take a look at our old trenches and some of the wartime haunts,' he said. 'Our first camp's a train ride away from the Somme valley.'

'Really?' Sophie asked in amazement.

'Yes, it's Tam's idea. Has he not told you?'

'No.' She felt a moment's pang that he had told her nothing about his plans, but then she had hardly encouraged him to talk of the trip, resenting that it took him away for so long. 'Why on earth would you want to revisit war sites?'

Rafi took a drag on his cigarette and considered. 'It was a time of camaraderie – living for the day,' he admitted. 'Terrifying at times, but also exhilarating.'

'For those who were lucky enough to survive.' McGinty snorted. 'As a stretcher bearer, I saw too many of the unlucky. I'd never want to go back.'

'I think I understand why you might want to,' Sophie said on reflection.

'Really?' Rafi gave her a long, considering look. She could see that she'd surprised him but she held his look.

'Going back is a bit like laying ghosts to rest?'

He nodded, his smile wistful. 'Yes, I suppose that's it.'

Sophie never had time to question Tam about it. There was tea at the rowing club and then he had to go home and finish his packing. His sister was preparing him a special meal. Sophie hoped he might invite her – she had yet to meet his family – but he joked that he wouldn't subject her to Flora's Christian Science friends until he returned.

'I'll come to see you off at the station tomorrow,' Sophie said. 'I could pick you up on The Memsahib with your luggage.'

Tam gave an awkward laugh. 'Can't have you waking up the street with the noisy Memsahib at such an early hour – or expect you to turn out at dawn.'

'I don't mind.'

'No,' Tam was firm, 'let's just say our goodbyes now. No fuss, eh?'

Sophie felt her throat constrict and tears prick her eyes. There were others at the tram stand and it was too public for a proper farewell. He squeezed her hands in his.

'Don't let me see your beautiful brown eyes looking so sad,' he murmured. 'I promise I will write and tell you everything. And you must write too.'

Sophie nodded, not trusting herself to speak.

'I bet you will have a high old time with Tilly coming to visit' – he smiled – 'and Miss Gorrie will be glad to see you back at work after your absconding with me.'

Sophie smiled and blinked away a tear. The tram rattled to a stop in front of them. Tam bent and gave her a swift kiss on the cheek and pushed her forward. She climbed on, her chest constricting with emotion, and tried to keep him in sight for as long as she could. He stood, looking casually handsome in his rowing blazer and flannels, and waved her away. Sophie sat numbly, silent tears trickling down her face. If parting from Tam for a month was so painful, what would it be like when he sailed for India?

Chapter 10

'So what's the dragon of a sister like?' Tilly asked, as they sat munching potato scones by the gas fire.

'I haven't met Flora yet,' Sophie admitted. She didn't like the look that passed between her cousin and aunt. 'But it's only because he thought I might be intimidated by her evangelising – she's more ardent about Christian Science than Tam.'

'You've never been intimidated by anything,' Tilly retorted.

'Anyway, I'm sure he'll introduce me when he gets back next week.'

'Counting the days?' Tilly teased.

Sophie nodded, unabashed.

'I know how that feels.' Tilly sighed. 'I won't be seeing James until December. It seems a lifetime away. I sometimes think getting married last month was all a dream.'

'So you miss him, dearie?' Amy asked.

'More than I thought I would. I mean, I hardly know him, do I? Between you, me and the gatepost, I only said yes so I didn't have to go to Dunbar with Mother or join the 'Fishing Fleet' of husband-seekers in India, being at the beck and call of my sister-in-law Helena. Is that terribly shallow of me?'

'Very.' Sophie laughed.

'But it's all worked out for the best,' Amy said. 'Your mother wrote to tell me how happy she was at your marriage.'

'Relieved more likely.' Tilly giggled. 'Silly Tilly off her hands.'

'Not a bit of it,' said Amy, 'she could see how happy you both were – but going into it with your eyes open and determined to make a success of it; no unrealistic romantic expectations. That's the recipe for a long partnership, as far as I can see.'

Sophie felt annoyance; she knew her aunt was having a dig at her being so lovestruck over Tam. It had been a source of rancour between them these past three weeks. Why could Amy not be as fulsome over her courtship? When no letters had come from Tam in the first two weeks, Amy had clucked, 'It's probably for the best; he's too ambitious for you.'

Sophie was hurt, insisting the letters had probably gone astray or Tam had been too much on the move. Sharp words had been exchanged.

'You're just being selfish, Auntie,' Sophie had accused. 'You don't want me to marry anyone just so I'll stay here forever and look after you!'

'You ungrateful little madam!' Amy had cried. 'I know a social climber when I see one. He's just toying with your affections! That man's got bigger fish to fry – he'll not settle for less than a governor's daughter.'

But a few days ago she had received a long, affectionate letter from Switzerland and waved it in triumph at her tight-lipped aunt. Tam was full of enthusiasm for his work.

'. . . went to see a log-catching scheme near Interlaken. Very clever the way they use the torrents to float timber downstream from the high mountains; much more simple and efficient than putting in miles of roads. Your aunt would like the wood carving here. Tell her I'm taking photographs for her – pears seem to be popular – give her some food for thought!'

He had ended it with words that she had read and re-read countless times.

'Your letters cheer me up no end. They make me miss you all the more, but don't stop writing as it brings Edinburgh and your dear self so vividly to me. I kiss tenderly the words that have been written by your own fair hand, and must be content with that until I can kiss those sweet lips that I long for more and more each day.'

Sophie's heart had soared at his loving words; she had not thought that a man of action like Tam could have created such a tender letter.

Later that night, when the cousins were bedding down in Sophie's room, she showed Tilly the letter.

'What a romantic this forester of yours is,' Tilly gasped. 'All I've had from James is a telegram telling me he's back in Assam. I don't think it occurs to him to write.'

‘Here’s a photograph of Tam.’ Sophie pointed proudly to an athletic figure in shorts and singlet. ‘It’s his rowing team. I cut it out of the newspaper.’

‘Very good looking,’ Tilly approved. ‘I hope I get to meet him.’

‘You will. I’ll bring him down on The Memsahib to Dunbar for a visit when he’s back, shall I?’

‘Oh yes, do!’ cried Tilly. ‘Mona will need smelling salts; I can’t wait.’

‘I wish Auntie was as enthusiastic as you,’ Sophie said. ‘She likes Tam’s friends better than him – she’s said some hurtful things about him – and he’s so charming to her too.’

‘Auntie Amy doesn’t trust charming,’ Tilly teased.

‘Has she said anything about him to you?’ Sophie asked. ‘Please tell me.’

‘She did say she thought he was a bit full of himself – boasting about how quickly he’s going to climb the ladder.’

‘I don’t see that as a fault,’ Sophie defended. ‘I like him for having ambition.’

‘You know how protective your aunt is of you,’ said Tilly. ‘Until he proposes, she’ll worry about you getting hurt.’

Sophie felt a jolt at Tilly’s words; her friend assumed that she and Tam would get engaged. It gave her a thrill of anticipation.

‘She has no need to worry,’ Sophie said, kissing Tam’s letter, ‘this is proof that he loves me.’

‘I hope he does propose, and quickly,’ Tilly said. ‘Then we could go out to India together. The only thing that makes me sad is the thought of leaving you behind here and not seeing you for years.’

‘Me too,’ Sophie agreed. ‘And I’ve been thinking so much about India these past few weeks that I’m beginning to remember things. It makes me long to go back and see where I lived – try to find out more about my parents and the life they had in Assam.’

They settled down under the covers. ‘Tilly,’ Sophie said, glad that the dark hid her blushes.

‘Umm?’

'What's it like being married?'

'Two days hardly makes me an authority.' Tilly chuckled.

'But you must have – you know – the physical side of marriage,' Sophie whispered.

There was silence and Sophie thought Tilly was cross with her for asking. Maybe sex had been an ordeal.

'It's lovely – hot and messy – but fun.' Tilly gave an earthy laugh. 'Even more fun than ice cream and cakes at Herbert's Tea Room.'

'Ice cream *and* cakes?' Sophie exclaimed. 'Lucky you!'

Sophie had almost drifted off to sleep, warmed by thoughts of Tam and his letter, when Tilly's sleepy voice murmured, 'I think it's India that worries her.'

'Worries who?' Sophie yawned.

'Auntie Amy.'

'Why?'

'Worries about you going back to India if you marry Tam.'

'You mean she'd be frightened of me catching a fever like my parents? But there are just as many dangers here at home – accidents and illness.'

Tilly was quiet, then said sleepily, 'No, not disease. Something else.'

'What then?'

'She said something about not wanting you to make the same mistake as your mother.'

Sophie came awake, a knot forming in her stomach. 'What does she mean by that?'

Tilly turned over. 'Dunno. Ask her in the morning.'

In less than a minute, Tilly was breathing evenly, sound asleep. Sophie was left puzzling over what it was that gave her aunt such concern.

Chapter 11

The next day, Sophie dismissed her worries over her aunt's opposition to Tam. When Auntie Amy got to know him as well as she did, she would take him to her heart too. And her concerns over India were fanciful; Auntie Amy had grown too parochial in her ways and didn't see that India was an exciting place full of opportunity for energetic young people, not a place of which to be frightened.

Yet she was still annoyed with her aunt for favouring Tilly's match with James Robson. Tilly had hardly known James before they married – still knew very little about him – yet Amy gave them her approval.

'Seeing as it's Saturday, I'm going to take Tilly up to see Great Uncle Daniel in Perth,' she declared at breakfast. She ignored Tilly's look of surprise.

'Oh, that's a nice idea.' Amy paused over her toast. 'The old boy will be pleased. We could take the train.'

'I thought we'd take The Memsahib for a spin – she needs a run out.'

'Ah well,' Amy said, 'in that case three would be too many.'

Tilly piped up, 'You can go in the sidecar, Auntie, and I'll cling on to the flapper seat.'

'The sidecar's in the garage being fixed,' Sophie said.

'Let's go on the train then,' Tilly suggested.

Amy looked away. 'No, no; you lassies go and enjoy yourselves. It'll be grand to be out in the fresh air on the motorcycle. I should be getting on with the bookcase. It's taking me much longer than I thought and Dr Forsyth is getting impatient – he wants it twice the size originally agreed, to take all his medical books and journals.'

'Well, it's going to be the grandest bookcase in all Edinburgh when you're finished,' Tilly said, 'so he'd jolly well better be grateful.'

They packed a picnic for the journey, both cousins growing excited at the spontaneous trip. They hadn't been to see old Daniel Anderson since the previous summer. At the point of leaving, Sophie had a pang of guilt for excluding her aunt. She had immediately regretted her high-handed decision to go on the motorbike.

'We could still take the train if you wanted to come,' she said, hovering in the doorway of her aunt's workroom.

Amy, in overalls, looked up from her chiselling, brushing away a strand of unruly hair.

'Away you go and enjoy yourselves!' She smiled. 'I'm just as happy here. And if you're having fun, stay the night. Don't think of driving back in the dark. I won't worry about you till tomorrow teatime.'

'Thanks, Auntie.' Sophie smiled and blew her a kiss across the cluttered room. Amy waved and went back to her work.

After the cousins had gone, Amy found she couldn't settle to her task. She had been sleeping badly and kept waking up listless and anxious. She sighed and went to make a pot of tea. It was Sophie's infatuation with Tam that troubled her. Was her fear of her niece disappearing to India just being selfish? Or was it guilt? She had failed to help her sister, trapped in a loveless marriage. If Sophie went so far away, she would be unable to protect her either. But her niece was now of age and she couldn't stop her rushing after Tam if that's what she wanted.

Amy went to her bedroom and pulled out a battered letter hidden deep in the bottom drawer of her wardrobe. For one final time, she re-read Jessie's unhappy words; '*. . . I'm beginning to despair at Bill's rudeness to others – he takes offence at the slightest things. I can't look at another man (let alone have a conversation) without him flying off the handle. It's not how it used to be – he doesn't even find enjoyment in his daughter anymore and yet Sophie is a delight and her sunny nature is what keeps me going. But then poor Bill has had such a bad bout of malaria that he's not himself. I'm trying to implant the idea of us going away to the hills for a while.*

'Dearest sister, when are you coming back out to see us? I know how busy you are with your campaigning and your carpentry but I long for you to visit. You would so enjoy our wee girl. She reminds me of you – sharp as a pin. I can't see Bill

allowing me to bring her back to Edinburgh for a visit, so you must come to us.

'Your loving sister, Jessie.'

Amy crushed the letter to her breast, a sob heaving in her chest. She had planned to visit that summer – had meant to do so sooner – but by then her sister and brother-in-law were dead, and Sophie was in her care.

Amy went into the sitting room, put a match to the letter and threw it into the grate.

'Forgive me, Jessie,' she whispered, watching till the thin paper was nothing but ash, and then returned to her woodwork with a heavy heart.

***

The Memsahib had a puncture just after the crossing at Queensferry and they had to stop a second time when the engine overheated. So it was early afternoon before they got to the old weaver's cottage on the banks of the River Tay. He gave them a cheery welcome, and though his sight and hearing were worse than before, his mind was as quick as ever.

'*Married*, did you say?' he exclaimed. 'Wee Tilly Watson's got herself a husband!'

'Don't sound so surprised, Uncle Daniel.' Tilly laughed. 'I am twenty-one now.'

'So where are you hiding him?'

'He's gone back to Assam.'

'Assynt?'

'No, *Assam* in India,' Tilly shouted. 'He's a tea planter.'

'Well, well.' Daniel sucked through the gaps in his teeth. 'Tea planter, eh? Just like your father was, Sophie.'

'Yes, Uncle,' Sophie said, 'and he works for the same company.'

'Och well, I hope he's a good man to you, Tilly, so I do.' He hobbled off his stool. 'Tea, eh? We'll have a pot o' tea, right enough. Coming up, lassies. And you're in luck; I've been out and caught a fish this morning. Tilly, you come over here and help me gut its innards.' He chuckled.

They stayed the night, happy to keep the old man company, and talked late into the evening, reminiscing about times past. He was a fund of family stories and anecdotes from the last century when the Andersons had been the elite of weavers in the Perth area. The cousins never tired of hearing them.

'You remind me of my nieces,' he said, puffing on an old clay pipe. 'Aye, Jessie was the home-maker like you, Tilly – but not afraid to travel halfway across the world to be wed and have a family. Aye, that's what she always wanted – a family of her own.'

The cousins exchanged glances across the dim room, Sophie's eyes glinting with emotion that her mother should have had her life snatched away so cruelly.

'And you, Sophie,' Daniel continued his musing, 'just like that headstrong Amy. Always in a hurry to change the world and woe betide any slow fool who got in her way! But just as loving in her own way – no patience – but a loyal heart and a strong sense of justice.'

'I've never thought of myself as being like Auntie Amy,' Sophie said, 'or you like my mother, Tilly. But I like the idea – it's comforting to think Mother was kind like you – it somehow brings her closer.'

The next morning they took Daniel to the kirk and cooked a vegetable broth, which they ate together before they left. A wind was getting up and Sophie was keen to be on the road.

'Aye, there's a storm coming from the west,' Daniel predicted, 'I can smell it on the air.'

They hugged him goodbye and ignored the tutting from his neighbour at their travelling on a Sunday and on such an ungodly machine. They were buffeted around on the journey south, Sophie gripping hard to the handlebars, until her aching arms became rigid and numb. But they pressed on, as blackening clouds rolled in from the west. The storm broke over them as they reached the outskirts of Edinburgh, cold horizontal rain and swirling wind nearly throwing them off the motorcycle.

They reached Clerk Street, drenched and chilled to the bone, and climbed off the bike trembling with relief. Sophie fumbled the key into the outside door with numb fingers and they fell into the dark hallway, gasping and laughing and shaking themselves down.

'You can go first in the tin bath, Tilly,' Sophie offered. 'You've gone blue. Hope Auntie Amy's got something good in for tea. I could eat an elephant.'

Sophie climbed to the second floor with legs buckling from fatigue. She fell in the door first. 'We're back! Drowned as rats but we did it.'

The flat was half dark from the storm outside; her aunt had yet to light the gas lamp in the sitting-room.

'Auntie Amy?' The kitchen was in darkness too.

'She's probably taking forty winks,' Tilly panted, flopping into the battered armchair that had been demoted to the kitchen.

Sophie glanced into the workroom on her way to check her aunt's bedroom. Something wasn't right. The bookcase was lying on the floor. She pushed into the room, peering in the gloom. She couldn't make sense of what she was seeing. There were legs sticking out from under the massive bookcase.

'Oh my God!' Sophie gasped. She sprang round to the other side. Amy's face was staring up at her like a death mask.

'Auntie Amy!' Sophie screamed.

Suddenly, her aunt's eyes flickered open. She tried to mouth something.

'I'm here, Auntie,' Sophie cried. 'Don't move.' She shoved at the heavy bookcase but it didn't budge a fraction.

'Tilly! *Tilly!*' Sophie yelled.

Her cousin came rushing to help.

Chapter 12

The cousins managed to heave the heavy bookcase away from Amy; how long she had lain trapped under it they couldn't tell and she couldn't answer. Her eyes had closed again and she did not respond to Sophie's beseeching. Her limbs were cold and her breathing shallow.

'She's still breathing, Tilly! Auntie Amy, I'm here now, can you hear me? Please open your eyes! You're going to be all right; we're going to get help. *Please* be all right!'

Tilly stood watching and feeling helpless. 'What can I do?'

'I'm frightened to move her,' Sophie said. 'Fetch a blanket to keep her warm. I'll go and get help – the neighbour downstairs has a telephone.' Sophie leapt up. 'Hold on, Auntie, I won't be long.'

Dashing from the flat, she clattered downstairs and hammered on the door below.

'Mr Stronach, please help! Mr Stronach!'

It seemed an age before she heard the lock turn and the bank clerk peered out. Sophie gabbled out her story and at once he was galvanised into ringing for an ambulance.

'You're soaked through,' his wife cried. 'Come and sit down a minute by the fire.'

'No, I must go and be with Auntie,' Sophie said, hardly aware of her bedraggled state. 'But thank you.'

'Let us bring up some hot tea at least,' Mrs Stronach insisted. Sophie nodded gratefully and rushed back upstairs.

In the gloom, Tilly was crouched beside the prone figure, stroking her hair in comfort. Sophie nearly broke down at the tender sight.

'Has she spoken?'

'She was trying to say something before,' Tilly whispered. 'She called me Jessie. But I don't think she can hear me.'

Sophie knelt at the other side and searched under the blanket for her aunt's hand.

'I'm so sorry for leaving you, Auntie Amy,' she whispered, squeezing her limp hand. 'It was selfish of me. We missed having you with us – and Great Uncle Daniel was asking for you – and I'm to give you a kiss.' She leant forward and kissed Amy gently on the forehead. 'And this one's from me' – she kissed her cheek. 'I'm never going to leave you again. You're the best aunt a girl could ever have – more like a mother than my own mother.'

Sophie's voice wavered as a huge lump formed in her throat. She thought she felt her aunt's fingers flutter in hers, yet Auntie Amy appeared unconscious.

'Just hang on tight,' Sophie encouraged. 'Tilly and I are here with you, Auntie. Help's on its way.'

The Stronachs appeared with tea, but Sophie could swallow nothing. Tilly put a blanket around her cousin and slurped at the hot sugary drink to stop her teeth chattering.

Then there was a clattering on the stairs and two ambulance men appeared with a stretcher. The Stronachs steered the young women out of the cramped room and minutes later Amy was being carried from the flat.

One of the men murmured something to Mr Stronach, his expression grim.

'What did he say?' Sophie demanded.

'Miss Anderson is not conscious,' he said. 'The hospital will do their best.'

Sophie made to follow. The bank clerk stood in her way. 'You can't go with them, Miss Logan. Let them do their work. I'll ring later and you can visit tomorrow.'

'Tomorrow? But she needs me with her now,' Sophie fretted.

'You've done all you can for her,' Tilly tried to be reassuring. 'It's a doctor she needs now.'

'Your cousin's right,' Mrs Stronach said firmly. 'Now fetch some dry clothes and you'll come downstairs and get warmed by the fire. I'll not have you lassies catching cold up here. What will your aunt say, if she comes home to find you two with pneumonia?'

Sophie allowed the kindly neighbours to take charge and lead them below.

Mr Stronach rang the hospital but could get no information on Amy except that she had been admitted and her condition was poor. They could visit the following afternoon.

'I can't wait that long,' Sophie cried. It seemed an eternity.

'You'll just have to,' Mrs Stronach said, chivvying the cousins to eat some bread and cheese and later bedding them down by their fire.

Sophie woke in the early hours, amazed that she had slept at all. Tilly lay curled like a hibernating animal under a heavy quilt, her red hair spread across the pillow. She felt a huge surge of gratitude that her cousin was with her, and they were facing this nightmare together. If she were to lose Auntie Amy . . . No! Such thoughts were too frightening. Her aunt had broken her leg or had something that could be fixed. When they visited later today, she would be sitting up in bed, smiling and telling them not to fuss.

Mr Stronach came back at half past twelve for his lunch and rang the hospital again. They were told to visit at two o'clock. Mrs Stronach fixed on an old-fashioned bonnet and set out with the cousins to the hospital.

At the entrance to the ward, they were stopped by a young nurse.

'Matron would like a word,' she said with an anxious look and ushered them into a side room. 'Please sit down.' Only Mrs Stronach did so.

The nurse disappeared. Matron came in with a balding doctor.

'This is Dr MacLean,' she announced.

'What's happened?' Sophie gasped, fearful at their sombre expressions. 'Why can't we see Auntie Amy?'

The doctor cleared his throat. 'You are Miss Anderson's next of kin?'

Sophie nodded. 'Her niece; Sophie Logan.'

'I'm very sorry to have to tell you, Miss Logan, that your aunt passed away an hour ago.'

Sophie stood stunned. Tilly went at once to grasp her hand and guide her to a chair. Seeing that Sophie was speechless, Tilly asked, 'Please tell us what happened, Doctor.'

'Heart failure,' he was frank.

'Her heart?' Tilly frowned.

'We think she had an attack yesterday,' he explained, 'and that's why she reached out and grabbed something heavy as she fell. She had another attack this morning – her heart just wasn't strong enough to survive.'

'But she's fit as an ox,' Sophie cried. 'She's never been ill in her life.'

The doctor gave her a look of sympathy. 'Often there are few signs of heart disease. Perhaps she was a little tired lately or breathless?'

Sophie thought of her aunt playing tennis just a month ago with Boz and Rafi; hardly the signs of a weak heart. But then she had stopped the game early. And she hadn't been working with her usual enthusiasm of late; she had kept putting off finishing the bookcase. Sophie realised she had been too wrapped up in her infatuation with Tam to notice signs of her aunt's illness.

'I should never have left her alone over the weekend,' Sophie agonised.

'You weren't to know,' Tilly said. 'She seemed fit as a fiddle.'

'But if we'd got home sooner and she hadn't been lying unable to move all that time—'

'You mustn't upset yourself with such thoughts,' Mrs Stronach said. 'Her time had come and there's nothing you could have done.'

'Of course I could have done something!' Sophie said. 'It's my fault she was left there so long. Could I have saved her, Dr MacLean? Please tell me the truth.'

A tense silence seemed to suck the air out of the room. The doctor paused then shook his head. 'You couldn't have stopped the heart attacks. You mustn't blame yourself, Miss Logan.'

'See, Sophie?' Tilly comforted. 'It's not your fault.'

Sophie felt her guilt ease a fraction. 'But I could have been there to comfort her,' she whispered. 'I should have been there. She would have wanted me.'

'She knew you were there,' Tilly said. 'She was asking for you when you went for help.'

'Was she?' Sophie gasped.

Tilly swallowed and nodded. 'You were the one who meant the most to Auntie Amy.'

'Thank you.' Sophie threw her arms around her friend and sobbed into her shoulder. Tilly gave way to tears too.

The doctor and matron withdrew and left Mrs Stronach patting the distraught young women and telling them to put on a brave face. Tilly helped Sophie to her feet, her heart aching for her dear cousin, even more alone in the world than before. She would never tell her of the panic in Auntie Amy's eyes when, lying semi-conscious on the cold workroom floor, she had mistaken her for Jessie.

She had turned pained eyes on Tilly and whispered, 'Is that you, Jessie? Don't go away again. Your lassie needs you . . .'

Chapter 13

The day before Amy Anderson's funeral, Tam and the other forestry students returned to Edinburgh. Tilly had written to Tam's mother and sister explaining about the death. His sister Flora had written back to Tilly, passing on condolences, but expressing surprise as she was unaware that her brother was so well acquainted with the family. Tilly only conveyed the message of sympathy to Sophie. She was concerned that Sophie was driving herself too hard. After her showing of grief at the hospital, Sophie had buried her emotions and got on with organising the funeral and sorting out her aunt's affairs. Tilly had called on Mona to come from Dunbar and help.

'You must eat and rest,' Mona had fussed, taking charge of the household. 'I'll not let you waste away. All these other matters can wait. Walter can help with the paperwork, all in good time. Mother's terribly upset at the news of course.'

A large bouquet of flowers arrived from Miss Gorrie and the charity where Sophie worked, but it was a knock on the door late that evening that brought a wan smile back to Sophie's drawn face.

'Tam!' she croaked and fell into his arms, succumbing to tears of relief at seeing him. He rubbed her back.

'My poor girl,' he soothed, 'I'm so sorry about your aunt. I came as soon as I heard. The lads send their condolences too.'

'Don't leave the man on the doorstep, Sophie,' Mona chided, bustling forward. 'You must be the Mr Telfer we've heard so much about? Come in! I'm Cousin Mona – and this is Cousin Tilly.'

Tilly rose and greeted the handsome forester who gave her a firm handshake and ready smile; she understood at once how Sophie had fallen for him.

'I shan't stay long,' he insisted, 'but I wanted to assure you that we shall be there tomorrow to show our respects. Flora saw the notice in *The Scotsman*. And, ladies, if there is anything any of us can do, you just have to ask.'

They enquired about his trip but he told them little. 'I'm glad to be home,' he said. 'The forestry was interesting but my thoughts were often elsewhere.' He gave Sophie a meaningful look. After ten minutes he stood to go. Sophie noticed there was a tired, pinched look to his lean face. It would be selfish of her to try to make him stay longer, though that's what she wanted most. She saw him to the door.

'Be full of courage,' he encouraged, 'I'll be there to support you.' He kissed her swiftly on the cheek and went.

Mona was impressed by his concerned manner and that he had come rushing round after a long and tiring rail journey.

'What a kind young man,' she approved. 'It's obvious how much he cares for you, Sophie.'

'Do you think so?' Sophie's unhappiness lifted a fraction.

'Yes I do,' Mona said. 'Don't you agree, Tilly?'

Tilly nodded. 'And he's just as handsome as you said.'

***

The Church of Scotland on Clerk Street was full of mourners: kirk friends, former suffragists, patrons of Amy's bespoke furniture business, shopkeepers and former pupils from her Sunday School classes. Sophie was astonished at how many people of all ages Amy had known and who now filled the pews and raised the roof with their singing.

But the family took up only one bench: Great Uncle Daniel (who had struggled through on the train and was weeping openly), the Watsons and herself. Jacobina had managed to get down for the funeral but would have to travel back to Inverness that evening. Johnny and Helena had sent a telegram from India. It brought home painfully to Sophie how little family she had left in the world, and all of them on her mother's side. Her father had been the only child of his family to survive into adulthood, and if there were more distant Logan relations, contact had been lost long ago.

Sophie clung to the thought that she had a few loyal and trusted friends who had rallied around her – two girls from school, the invalided Major MacGregor, Miss Gorrie, some friends from the tennis club – and, most importantly of all, Tam, who stood across the aisle, tall and strong-shouldered among his student comrades, his voice booming out above the others.

Afterwards, as they served up refreshments in the kirk hall, Tam stood close by and Sophie felt his strong presence giving her courage as she talked to the dozens of her aunt's friends who wished to reminisce.

As they left for home, Tam said, 'I know this is a time of deep mourning for you but may I call on you in a day or two – to see how you are?'

'Please, I'd like that.' Sophie smiled.

Tam was struck by how beautiful and how sad she looked; her large brown eyes like dark pools in her pale face, her pink lips trembling in the attempt to stay cheerful. Her fair hair was pulled back from her broad, expressive face and hidden beneath a close-fitting black hat; her figure was slim and elegant in a plain black dress and stockings. She looked older; gone was the effusive, happy-go-lucky girl that he had left a mere month ago. His heart ached for her and he wanted nothing more than to crush her in his arms and give her comfort.

Boz and Rafi appeared beside them, shaking Sophie's hand in goodbye.

'If there's anything I can do?' Boz offered.

'We liked your aunt very much,' Rafi added.

'Thank you both.' Sophie smiled. 'It's enough that you came today. It means a great deal.'

Tam felt a ridiculous flood of jealousy. 'I'll see Sophie across the road,' he insisted. 'It's been an exhausting day.'

Boz looked about to argue, then stepped back. Tam took Sophie's arm and steered her from the hall, the Watson family following. Back at the flat, Tam lingered long enough to say, 'I know now is not the time to press you to a social engagement, but when you feel ready, I'd like you to come for a meal to Roseburn and meet my mother and sister. Flora is keen to be introduced.'

Sophie squeezed his hand, her eyes filling with gratitude. 'Thanks, Tam, of course I'd love to meet them.'

***

The days that followed were a blur to Sophie. The Watsons stayed to help sort the flat, which was rented and had to be cleared by the end of the month. Sophie, who could no longer afford to stay on in Clerk Street, was to move to two rooms above Miss Gorrie's office, kindly provided rent-free by her employer. Walter removed the wood from her aunt's workshop, while Mona and Tilly packed up Amy's clothes and books to be sold or go to charity. Their mother declared it was too much of a strain to have to dismantle her cousin's household having just done so to her own, and sat by the sitting room window crying into a lace handkerchief and bemoaning their family fate.

'My dear husband gone – and now Cousin Amy,' she sniffled, 'and Johnny so far away. I know I'll not live long enough to see him again!'

'Nonsense, Mother,' Mona scolded, 'you'll outlive the rest of us. You should be thankful for small mercies; you have Walter and I looking after your every need. Sophie's on her own now and look how brave she is being.'

Sophie didn't feel brave; she felt numb and empty like the small girl who had sailed back from India, shocked at how quickly life could change for the worse and anxious at what new terror lay ahead. She had forgotten those deep feelings of fear and loss – she managed to smother them during the daytime and put on a stoical face – but at night they rose up and threatened to overwhelm her once more. When she did fall into exhausted sleep, she would wake feeling suffocated as if she were buried alive in a hot tomb.

Tilly would hush her and calm her with comforting words. 'You've just had a bad dream; you're quite safe. Go back to sleep.'

What she could say to no one was her dread of going to live in two small rooms by herself. The claustrophobia that had plagued her as a child had returned and the thought of living hemmed in by other tall, soot-blackened tenements with no view of the crags in the King's Park filled her with dread. Yet she felt ungrateful for even thinking it.

But it was Tam who saved her sanity. He came often to visit; breaking off from his revision at the library to take her for a walk or a picnic tea. The Sunday after the funeral, Sophie went over to the Telfers' home in Roseburn – a spartan first floor flat – where she was welcomed by two tall, beaky-nosed women with the same startlingly direct blue gaze as Tam's. Sophie was surprised at their dowdy appearance and modest surroundings; Tam was always dressed immaculately in expensive clothes and spending freely. But Mrs Telfer fussed around her while Flora served up a tea of salad and baked potatoes.

'We're vegetarian,' Flora told her, 'and we enjoy very good health. That's also because we practise Christian Science. We'd be happy to work on you in our prayers. You must be feeling very lost and bereft just now.'

Sophie gulped, her eyes filling with tears. She hadn't expected such directness.

'Flora,' Tam warned, 'you promised not to mention C.S. for at least the first half-hour. You're not to frighten Sophie away.'

'I don't mean to be frightening,' Flora said, looking surprised. 'I'm not frightening you, am I, dearie?'

'No,' Sophie said, then a sob heaved inside. It was her use of Amy's endearment that made her crumble.

Flora rushed around the tea table and thrust a white napkin at Sophie. 'Go on, dearie, let it out. It's your inner self telling you to let go of your sorrow. You haven't lost her,' Flora assured, putting an arm about her shoulders, 'her spirit still lingers keeping watch over you.'

Tam looked on anxiously as Sophie cried and the women took command and prayed over her. Within minutes, Sophie felt as if a huge weight had been dislodged from deep inside. She felt light-headed and suddenly hungry for the first time in over a week.

After that she ate everything they put in front of her and talked for an age about her aunt.

'I feel so guilty that I left her,' Sophie confessed. 'We'd had a disagreement and I was cross with her, so left her out of our trip. If only I'd come back sooner or hadn't gone at all . . .'

'You can't be to blame,' said Mrs Telfer, 'it was your aunt's decision too.'

'That's what I've been telling her,' said Tam. 'Sophie's aunt was quite strong-minded enough to have gone if she'd really wanted. She was just giving you and Tilly a trip to yourselves, while you can still see each other.'

'What was the disagreement about?' Flora asked.

Sophie blushed; she could never admit it had been over Tam.

'Nothing important,' she replied. Flora gave her a penetrating look.

'Well, you'll have no peace of mind if you can't forgive yourself. So you must try. And we will keep you in our thoughts when we are doing our Science, and think positively about you so you will be able to bear your loss.' She gave a sudden flash of a smile. 'Now, more stewed rhubarb and shortbread?'

Later, as Tam walked her home, Sophie slipped her arm through his. 'What kind people you Telfers are. Your mother is sweet, and I do like Flora; she's refreshingly different. I must admit I was nervous at meeting her – Boz made it clear your sister's approval is very important to you.'

Tam snorted. 'So you weren't put off by my relations?'

'Not at all,' Sophie said, 'they were delightful.'

'Well, I can tell Flora likes you too.' Tam smiled, kissing her forehead.

The following week, Mona took her mother back to Dunbar, Walter having gone a few days earlier. Tilly agreed to stay on until Sophie moved into her smaller quarters further into town. 'It's too sad without Auntie,' Sophie admitted, 'and I can't bear to go into her workroom – the thought of her lying in that room—'

'I understand,' Tilly said. 'I'll stay as long as you need me.'

With a few days to go before Tam and his fellow forestry students took the train to Oxford to sit their exams, Tam came rushing round at the end of the day.

'It's a perfect evening,' he enthused, 'I've got a flask of coffee and some of Flora's shortbread and we're going to climb the crags and see the sun setting. I've had enough of studying.'

At once, Sophie's spirits lifted and she grabbed her jacket.

'Tilly, do you want to come too?' Tam asked.

Tilly saw the look on Sophie's face and her eagerness to be alone with Tam.

'No thanks, you know I hate walking unless it's into shops or the theatre. I'll be happy here with Auntie Amy's Walter Scott novels.'

Sophie smiled. It had been a source of amusement for her – and of an argument with Mona – that Tilly had unpacked most of Amy's novels and was re-reading them. Sophie had overruled Mona and said Tilly was to keep whichever ones she wanted.

Tam blew Tilly a kiss, took Sophie's hand and pulled her impatiently from the flat.

***

A quarter of an hour later, Tilly was disturbed by a knock at the door. She opened it saying, 'What did you forget then—? Oh—' she stopped in mid-sentence, 'sorry, I thought it was Sophie returning.'

The broad-shouldered good-looking Indian from Tam's course stood on the doorstep.

'I'm Rafi Khan.' He gave a nod that wasn't quite a bow. 'If Miss Logan's out I can return another time.'

'No, please come in. I'm Cousin Tilly Watson – no that's wrong – Tilly Robson now – I'm still not used to my married name.'

'Yes, I thought so.' He hesitated. 'I'm just returning a book.'

'What book?'

He held it up. 'Poetry. A collection of Scottish ballads.'

'Oh, I love ballads. Sophie and I used to act them out when we were children. She always gave herself the hero's part and I'd be the one who got drowned in a bog or fell off a horse.'

Rafi smiled at this. 'Sounds like me and my brothers – we'd act out the battles of Alexander the Great or the Moghul emperors – and I'd always be the messenger or foot soldier who got killed at the start.'

'A fellow peasant like me.' Tilly laughed. 'Please come in. As I'm a happily married woman there's nothing improper in visiting without Sophie here. I have cold tea or home-made lemonade for weary foot soldiers.'

Rafi chose lemonade and Tilly served it at the table in the window. He took a gulp and said, 'Delicious. Miss Anderson gave me this the last time I called – told me her recipe.'

'You've been before?' Tilly asked. 'Sophie never mentioned it.'

Rafi studied his glass. 'No, I came when she was out. It was Miss Anderson who invited me – she was your aunt too?'

'My mother's cousin actually,' Tilly corrected, 'though I always called her Auntie.'

'I played tennis with your Auntie against Boz and Miss Logan a few weeks ago. I walked Miss Anderson home and she invited me in for lemonade. We talked about poetry and music – she was very knowledgeable and good company – and she invited me back on a couple of occasions.'

'So it was Auntie Amy who lent you the book of ballads, not Sophie?'

Rafi nodded. 'I gave her a translation of Persian poems and she gave me the ballads.' He glugged at his drink. 'I thought I should return the ballads – they belong to Miss Logan now.'

'I think you should keep them,' Tilly said. 'After all, Auntie Amy wanted you to have them and Sophie won't have room to store very much in her new lodgings.'

'So she won't be staying here?' asked Rafi; he'd noticed the bare bookshelves when he'd entered the room.

'No, she can't afford it. Her employer is giving her a smaller flat. I wish I could offer her a home' – Tilly sighed – 'but I'm going to be starting a new life in Assam soon. That's where Sophie lived till she was six. You did know her parents died of fever in the tea gardens, didn't you?'

Rafi nodded. 'Yes, I got the impression she'd like to go back there one day. She said something once about laying ghosts to rest.'

'Did she? That's interesting. Poor Sophie.'

'It surprised me, as I thought she disliked all things Indian.' He reached for a squashed packet of cigarettes and offered her one, asking, 'Do you mind if I smoke?'

'I don't smoke, thank you – but please go ahead.' She fetched a small brass ashtray.

'Made in Benares,' Rafi said, taking it from her and tracing a finger across the metalwork. 'I don't think your aunt was keen for her to go. Mind you, Miss Anderson was fascinated by Indian politics and wanted to discuss the Congress Party's new independence campaign and women's emancipation. I'm afraid I was a big disappointment' – Rafi gave a wry smile – 'as I knew more about what was going on in politics here than in India. After that we stuck to poetry.'

Tilly laughed. 'Dear Auntie Amy.' She poured him some more lemonade. 'But what did you mean by saying Sophie dislikes things Indian?'

Rafi blew out smoke and considered his reply. He shrugged. 'Just her manner. She may not have lived in India since she was six but she has imbibed the ethos of the Raj – the way of looking down her nose at us colonial subjects – we're not quite *pukka*.' His tone was self-mocking.

'I'm sure you're wrong about that,' Tilly defended her friend. 'Sophie is the most warm-hearted person I know. Not stuffy at all. You must have got her on a bad day.'

Rafi laughed. 'I'm glad to hear it. And I'm happy to be proved wrong. You know her far better than I.'

'She's out with Tam just now,' Tilly confided, pointing at the crags, 'having a picnic in the gloaming. Isn't that romantic?'

Rafi gazed out at the rocky precipice glowing in the dying September sun. He felt envy twist his guts. 'Very.'

'Do you think Tam might pop the question?' Tilly asked excitedly. 'It would be the answer to my prayers if he did, then Sophie wouldn't have to go and live in that poky flat and she could come out to India and be near me. Wouldn't that be just grand? Perhaps he's told you his plans? Is Tam going to propose to Sophie? Please tell me if you know!'

Rafi's eyes widened in shock. 'I'd be very surprised. I think Tam is—'

He stopped himself.

'Tam is what?' Tilly frowned.

Rafi thought of the argument between Boz and Tam over a woman they both knew in France with whom Tam was in love. Rafi had stayed out of it but he knew it was a source of friction between the two friends. Boz thought Tam was stringing Sophie along and wasn't serious about her.

'Tam is his own man,' Rafi said hastily. 'He wouldn't confide such things in me, I'm sure.'

He stubbed out his cigarette and immediately lit another one, annoyed with himself for minding. It was obvious Sophie Logan hardly noticed his existence, whereas he couldn't get her lively brown eyes and sensual smile out of his mind, try as he might. He was sure that her shrewd aunt had understood.

'Sorry,' Tilly said at once. 'I didn't mean to put you in an awkward position.'

'You haven't. I don't know what Tam's intentions are, though nothing would surprise me – he's a very impulsive man.'

'So is Sophie,' Tilly said. 'Impulsive, not a man obviously.'

Abruptly Rafi laughed. 'It must run in the family – I hear you married very quickly too, Mrs Robson?'

Tilly blushed and giggled. 'Yes, I did. I can't wait to go out to Assam and join my husband. It all sounds so romantic out there – tiger hunts and tea parties and glorious sunsets while sipping *chota pegs* on the veranda. You see, I'm already learning the lingo. And there will be so many exciting new stamps.'

'Stamps?' Rafi asked in bemusement.

'Yes, postage stamps. I collect them, you see.'

'Ah.' Rafi nodded. 'I used to collect them as a boy too.'

'Did you? Perhaps we could swap some?'

'I'm afraid I threw mine away.'

'Threw them away!' Tilly looked scandalised. 'How could you?'

Rafi looked sheepish. 'Well, they lost their gum in the heat and the album went mouldy in the humidity.'

'Oh dear.' Tilly was dismayed.

'But then I discovered poetry.' He smiled. 'At least if you learn it by heart, it doesn't matter if the book rots.'

Tilly laughed and hoped he was joking about books rotting.

'Well, I'm sure that won't happen where I'll be living. Mr Robson says the climate is perfect. Are you looking forward to going home, Mr Khan?'

He studied her. He felt as at home in Edinburgh as anywhere; this was where he had come on leave from the war with his comrade McGinty and been accepted into his family. It's where his social conscience had been pricked and where he had learnt his politics from McGinty's socialist and bohemian friends. It's where he had grown to like jazz and to dance the foxtrot and drink beer and flirt with women (though the first woman he had ever made love to was the daughter of a French farmer in whose half derelict house he had been billeted before Passchendaele). But it was useless to try to explain; people got embarrassed when he declared Scotland was his home.

'I'm looking forward to seeing my family again,' Rafi said, then immediately changed the subject. 'Tell me what you are reading at the moment. I noticed that Walter Scott's *Waverley* was open on the table when we came in.'

'Oh, Walter Scott,' Tilly enthused. 'Isn't he just one of the most romantic writers that ever put pen to paper?'

***

Tam and Sophie sat at the top of Arthur's Seat, the hill that dominated the city's skyline, catching their breath after the steep climb and gazing at the fiery horizon. The houses lay in a smoky haze but beyond was a clear view to the Firth of Forth and the distant hills.

'I've never seen it so beautiful,' Sophie gasped, seating herself on a rock. Tam poured coffee into two beakers and handed her one.

'Nor I.' He smiled. The look he gave her made her heart continue to race.

They shared out Flora's shortbread from a battered tin while Tam talked animatedly about nearing the end of his degree and the job to come.

'I've been reading up as much as I can about India and the forestry service; there is so much that can be done. Do you know there are over a hundred and fifty different types of timber tree growing there? And those are the ones they know about. There are vast untapped areas in the Himalayas and beyond. One of the challenges is how to extract the timber once it's grown, of course; these places are so remote. But I can't wait to travel to the mountains; it'll be like Switzerland but on a much grander scale.'

He blew hard on the hot coffee and slurped. 'Old Downs, my Hindustani teacher, says there'll be ample work for me in the Punjab without having to go trekking into the wilds,' Tam said, 'but I'm not going to make a name for myself by sitting in some dusty office compiling figures, am I? I'm going to get out into the forests and learn as much as I can. And there'll be plenty of opportunity for sport – bird shoots and game hunting – and getting back in the saddle.'

'It all sounds wonderful,' Sophie murmured.

She saw how his face came alive when he talked of his future work and felt a bittersweet longing. She was glad he had found his calling in life, yet was envious that he had such an opportunity. She too felt excitement at his talk of exploring the Himalayas, of riding and sport in the hills. Yet her future would be confined to office work with the occasional spin on her ancient motorcycle at weekends. Suddenly she couldn't bear the thought. The strength of her yearning to go back to India was overwhelming.

‘Oh, Tam – take me with you.’

A breeze was stiffening around them and a crescent moon lifting into the darkening sky behind. The coffee was finished. She felt foolish for asking; it wasn’t how things were supposed to be done. His silence told her he was embarrassed to be put on the spot.

Tam said nothing as he packed away the empty beakers. He had set out this evening to tell Sophie that, although he cared for her, his heart had been lost to another long ago. Better for her to find a kind man like Boz who could give himself wholeheartedly, for that’s what she deserved. But the more he talked about his pending adventure, the more he saw how suitable the Logan girl would be as his wife. She understood India; she was attractive and sociable and appeared to be in love with him. It would bring his sore heart a bit of solace after his rejection in France by the beautiful, unattainable Nancy.

‘I’m sorry’ – Sophie bit her lip – ‘I’m just desolate at the thought of you going and leaving me behind. I hoped you had brought me here for a special purpose. I love you, Tam!’

He looked startled by her declaration. She saw conflicting emotions cross his face. She steeled herself for words of disappointment; that they would write to each other and keep in touch.

‘You’d really do that for me?’ he asked. ‘Risk everything to follow me out to India?’

‘Of course I would.’

He stared at her with vital blue eyes. ‘I can’t pretend it hasn’t crossed my mind,’ he confessed. ‘I’ve grown very fond of you, Sophie, these past weeks.’

Her heart jumped. ‘Tam, what are you saying?’

He stood and pulled her up beside him. ‘Why don’t we?’ He was seized by the idea. ‘There’s nothing for you here now, is there? And together we could be a wonderful partnership. You can help me in my work and be at my side; you’re plucky and fun and full of spirit – just the sort of girl to thrive out there. It’s all a bit sudden, but if not now when—?’

‘Yes, Tam, *yes*!’ she interrupted. ‘Of course I’ll go with you.’

'Oh, lassie, that's grand!' He grabbed her in a hug. How hadn't he seen the happy solution right under his nose? Sophie Logan was perfect for the life he had now chosen. Her lively optimism would banish all past disappointments. He would put the older, worldly-wise Nancy from his thoughts for good.

'We won't have time to marry before I leave,' Tam was gripped with excitement as he made plans, 'but you can follow me out – give me time to find my feet and get us a house. Bachelors live in digs but we'll need a bungalow. We'll be in Lahore to start off.'

'Tam' – Sophie put her hands to his face – 'just kiss me!'

She thrilled to see the excitement in his handsome face as he bent to kiss her roundly on the lips.

They broke away; Sophie was exultant at her sudden change of fortune. 'This makes me so happy. I hated the thought of you leaving me here all alone.'

'Well, that's not going to happen.' Tam smiled.

Shouldering his knapsack, he took her by the hand and led her back down the steep path. They lingered by Dunsapie Loch as it lay glinting in the bowl of the hill and kissed some more under the brightening moon.

It was dark by the time they reached Clerk Street. By then they had discussed the possibility of Sophie sailing on the same ship as Tilly in November.

'A tea planter's wife, Mrs Percy-Barratt, is going to accompany her,' Sophie said, 'so that she isn't travelling alone. And James's cousin Wesley Robson and wife Clarrie are to be on the same boat too.'

'That's perfect then,' Tam declared with a wink. 'I'll have my fiancée properly chaperoned. The journey out is notorious for illicit romance and snap marriages.'

'Well, I hope Boz will be chaperoning you then,' Sophie replied.

Tam felt a moment of disquiet at the mention of his friend; he would be astonished at the hasty proposal. But then Boz had had his chance with Sophie and she had shown no interest in the tall farmer's son.

'I won't look at any lassie under eighty-five,' Tam teased, 'or dance with anyone under ninety.'

'I wish Auntie Amy was the one who would be coming out to see me married,' Sophie grew tearful. 'I miss her so much.'

'I know,' Tam said, kissing her hair. 'Do you think she would have been pleased at our engagement?'

Sophie hesitated only a moment; 'I'm sure she would have been. All she wanted was to see me happy – and I am, Tam, very happy.'

***

Sophie insisted on Tam breaking the news to Tilly there and then. Tilly clapped her hands and threw her arms around Sophie.

'I knew it! I knew something special was happening. I'm so happy for you both. Congratulations.' She shook Tam's hand.

He stood grinning. 'Thank you. It means a lot to Sophie that you give it your blessing.'

'You make me sound like an old maid,' Tilly teased. 'But if it's blessings you want, then you have them by the score.'

Sophie grabbed Tilly's hand. 'Will you be my matron of honour? We plan to marry in Lahore as soon as I arrive in December.'

'I'd be delighted.' Tilly beamed. 'Mr Rob— er, James and I can come for a holiday over Christmas perhaps.'

Tam said eagerly, 'I'm going to see if I can get Sophie on the same passage out as you and the other Robsons. You could come straight to Lahore.'

Tilly felt herself colouring; she wanted most of all to be reunited with James as soon as possible and to get on with married life.

'I'll write to my husband and see what's best.'

'Good,' Tam said. 'I'm sure you girls can organise it between you.'

'You'll stay for a meal?' Sophie urged.

Tam shook his head. 'I must go and break the news to Mother and Flora. They will have supper ready.'

‘A cup of tea at least?’ Tilly offered. ‘I’m afraid we’re out of lemonade.’

‘Oh’ – Sophie smiled – ‘you can’t have drunk the lot already?’

‘We had a visitor,’ Tilly explained, looking at Tam. ‘Your friend Mr Khan.’

‘Really?’ Tam frowned. ‘What did Rafi want?’

‘He was returning a book of Scottish ballads that Auntie Amy had given him. I said to keep it. Is that all right, Sophie?’

Sophie felt herself colouring for no reason. ‘Of course it is. I have no need of it.’

‘That’s what I said,’ Tilly replied. ‘We had a long chat about books. He’s very good looking, isn’t he? Auntie Amy obviously liked him too; she’d had him round to tea on several occasions.’

‘Had she?’ Tam gave Sophie a curious look. ‘You didn’t tell me Rafi was a regular visitor.’

‘I didn’t know. He certainly didn’t come to see me.’

‘I find that hard to believe.’

‘It’s true,’ Tilly said, detecting a sudden coolness, ‘it was always when Sophie was out. He has the impression Sophie doesn’t think much of him.’

Sophie retorted, ‘I don’t have any opinion, one way or the other. I like him as one of your friends, Tam, that’s all.’ She didn’t like his sudden frosty look or the uncomfortable twist in her stomach at talk of Rafi. ‘It was just Auntie Amy being kind to someone far from home.’

Tam seemed mollified. ‘Of course.’ He took her hand and kissed it. ‘I’m a fool to be jealous. Think nothing of it.’

‘I think it’s sweet the way you’re so possessive over Sophie,’ Tilly teased. ‘I hope my husband is half so attentive.’

‘We had better not tell Mr Robson that you’ve been entertaining an Indian with lemonade and poetry then,’ Sophie joked, glad that the tension had gone.

Tam laughed. ‘So Rafi likes Scots ballads? Who would have thought it?’

***

Tam and his fellow students, Boz, Rafi, McGinty and Jimmy Scott, sat their degree exams and all passed; Tam and Rafi were awarded honours while Jimmy scraped through. By the time they returned from Oxford, there was time for only one more night out at the Palais de Danse and an evening at Roseburn for a supper of fish pie and over-cooked cabbage.

'You'll come and see us, dearie,' Flora insisted, 'even with our Tam away. It'll be awfu' quiet without him.'

Sophie promised she would, grateful for their friendship.

This time Sophie insisted on seeing Tam off at the train station, even though there was no opportunity for a tender farewell. The other four graduates were there too and the platform teamed with tearful relations and porters loading the men's luggage aboard. Flora and Mrs Telfer hovered around Tam until the final moment, showering him with advice on his health and spiritual well-being; Sophie thought he would leave without a kiss. But, as the first whistle blew, Tam embraced his family and then turned to Sophie and pulled her into his arms.

'I can only bear this because I know I'll be joining you in three months,' Sophie said, tears spilling down her cheeks.

Tam's smile was tender as he brushed the tears away. 'Don't be sad, lassie. The time will fly and then we never need be parted again.'

Sophie thrilled at his words. 'I can't wait,' she whispered. 'I love you so much.'

He bent and kissed her swiftly on the mouth as the carriage doors were being slammed closed.

'Hey, Telfer!' Boz shouted from the window. 'You'll miss the train.'

'Aye,' Jimmy called, 'you would think you'd had no breakfast. Leave the lassie be.'

Tam laughed and disengaged from Sophie's arms. Flora gently pulled her away as she told her brother to hurry. 'Take care of yourself, Tammy. You'll always be in our prayers.'

Sophie's heart squeezed in pity. How many times had Tam's sister and mother had to wave him away during the recent war, thinking it might be the last? And here they were, losing him again. It might be three or four years before he was given home leave. What did she have to feel sad about, compared to their sense of loss? Yet they were smiling and stoical and she admired them immensely.

They all waved until their arms ached and the southbound train shrieked and squealed with gathering momentum and vanished out of the cavernous station.

As it was still early, Sophie walked away uphill, too restless just to go home. She made her way to the King's Park and climbed halfway up Arthur's Seat, gazing south down the railway line, even though Tam's train had long gone. She would have given anything to have gone with him, but Tam had been sensible by insisting that he must settle into his job first.

'Don't want to cause a scandal with the new bosses by having an unchaperoned fiancée in tow,' he had been firm. 'We'll do this properly. When you come to live with me, it'll be as Mrs Thomas Telfer.'

Sophie blew a kiss in the direction of Tam's train. She had opened her heart to love and it felt thrilling to be loved in return. For, though Tam had never actually said the words 'I love you' – men like him never did – Sophie knew it to be true. He had been just as hasty as she was in wanting them to be husband and wife, hadn't he?

Chapter 14

Since leaving Liverpool, the sea had been rough for days. Sophie found that sitting up on deck wrapped in a coat and fixing her eye on the grey outline of Portugal and then Gibraltar was the only way to quell the seasickness. She regretted having her hair cut so short in anticipation of living in the tropics; cold air blew down her neck. Tilly sat with her, attempting to read, but rounding Cape St Vincent in a headwind, her book was torn from her cold fingers and carried over the rail.

'I give up,' Tilly cried. 'I'm going into hibernation. Tell me when the sun comes out.'

But then Tilly was moody and queasy a lot these days. It had been a surprise to both her and the family when the cause had been diagnosed a month ago; Tilly was expecting her first baby. It had been the subject of much discussion: Mona and Mrs Watson thought Tilly should stay in Scotland to give birth.

'It's not as safe out there with all the disease and lack of doctors,' Mona had argued.

But, fortified by an ecstatic letter from James, Tilly had stood up to them and insisted on sticking to the plan of travelling out to be with her husband and have the baby born in India.

'I know what'll happen,' Tilly had confided tearfully to Sophie. 'They'll fall in love with the baby and not want it out of their sight. Mona will take over. She'll probably send me out to James babyless and insist that she brings it up in Dunbar because it's a healthier place.'

Sophie had tried to reassure her that Mona would never do such a thing, but Tilly showed a new stubbornness and would not be swayed. It had meant that plans to be Sophie's maid of honour were abandoned as the extra travelling to the Punjab would be too exhausting. James wanted her to travel directly to Assam, so Tilly was to stay on the boat all the way to Calcutta. Sophie had tried to hide her disappointment, but whatever she said seemed to upset her friend.

'You can visit once the baby is born,' Sophie had suggested.

'But that's ages away, and anyhow I won't be able to travel with a baby,' Tilly had snapped.

'Then I'll come to you.'

'I bet you won't. It's so very far and Tam won't want you to leave him once you're married.'

'Just for a visit he will.'

But Tilly had burst into tears. 'I so wanted to be your maid of honour. I don't want this baby.'

'Yes you do.' Sophie had hugged her. 'And you'll make a wonderful mother.'

'I'll be hopeless,' Tilly had sobbed. 'Mona is the one who should be a mother. The whole idea terrifies me.'

Sophie wondered if pregnancy turned all women so emotional and contrary, or whether Tilly was secretly frightened of going so far from her family to be with a man she hardly knew. Well, they were on their way, so it was too late for doubts now, and Sophie was philosophical as she huddled inside a thick tweed coat that had belonged to Auntie Amy.

The stormy weather dogged them through the Mediterranean; a dance and a concert organised by some of the passengers had to be cancelled as people became ill. Sophie hardly heard two words from Muriel Percy-Barratt who was sharing a cabin with her and Tilly. The older woman lay sickly and moaning, refusing to eat anything but water-biscuits. Sophie was thankful that the ship, the S.S. *City of Baroda*, was a modern one with spray baths, but, however much they washed themselves, the smell of vomit still permeated their cabin.

Sophie relied on Clarrie Robson's cheerful company and that of her engaging daughter Adela; though she remained a little in awe of the darkly handsome Wesley who smoked pungent cheroots and shaved on deck.

'What a shame for you young girls about the dance,' Clarrie said as she and Sophie clung to the rail with Adela clasped by the hands between them.

'We'd fall around like skittles if we tried to dance on deck in this,' Sophie joked.

‘It’ll improve soon,’ Clarrie said. ‘In a few days we’ll be crying out for cold weather. Just fill your lungs with fresh salty air while you can.’

‘Salty!’ Adela giggled, trying to jump while thrusting her face up to the spray.

‘You’re such a wee sailor.’ Sophie smiled at the girl and squeezed her hand. ‘Never been sick and no whingeing.’

‘’Ophie lift me up!’

‘No pet,’ Clarrie kept a firm hold, ‘or you’ll be swimming to India.’

Wesley came to find them. Sophie saw the tender look pass between him and Clarrie; they were so obviously still in love. It made her impatient to be with Tam. Wesley grabbed Adela and, ignoring Clarrie’s protests, swung his daughter into his arms and twirled around. Adela squealed with delight.

‘Just look at that beautiful sight,’ Wesley said. ‘The coast of Africa.’

The land lay wreathed in a silvery mist.

‘It reminds me of Benderloch on the west coast of Scotland.’ Sophie gulped, feeling a sudden stab of homesickness. ‘Auntie Amy took me and Tilly on holiday there twice.’

Her emotions see-sawed between deep loss for her Edinburgh home and excitement at going to start a new life with Tam. It was the little things that set her off; the taste of shortbread, the whistle of a Scots tune or mist hanging over the shoreline like now.

Clarrie squeezed her arm. ‘It’s natural to feel a little blue. I missed Tyneside when I first came back to India after the war; then I missed India and Wesley as soon as I was in Newcastle again.’ She gave a rueful smile.

Wesley said cheerily, ‘The journey will help you get in the right frame of mind. By the time the three weeks are over, you’ll be chomping at the bit to get on to Indian soil.’

Sophie gave a weak laugh. ‘If the next two weeks are as stormy as the last eight days, I’ll never want to make the voyage home again.’

With relief, they awoke the next day to a glimmer of sunshine as they sailed between the coast of Tunis and Gallina Island. Over the next couple of days, passengers began to emerge to chat, play deck tennis and dance before dinner. The biggest drawback to the improving weather, Sophie soon discovered, was the revival of Muriel Percy-Barratt. She was soon ordering the young women about and ticking them off for talking to men, no matter how old or married.

'If anyone asks you to dance, you must decline,' she commanded. 'I don't want to have to tell tales to James now, do I, Tilly? And, Sophie; it just isn't seemly for a girl newly betrothed to be flirting with other men.'

'If you mean talking to that retired Colonel Hogg from the Rajputs, he must be at least sixty,' Sophie tried not to laugh, 'and he's chaperoned by his frightening wife. I don't think my virtue's in any danger.'

'But his may be,' snorted Tilly, her good humour returning.

'It's no laughing matter,' Muriel scolded. 'I'm here to ensure nothing improper takes place. You especially, Sophie, should be aware that your carelessness could ruin your future husband's career in the service of India before it's even started. Gossip spreads faster than fever over there.'

'I don't doubt it,' Sophie muttered, rolling her eyes at Tilly. She imagined Muriel was the *burra memsahib* of gossips. But later, Tilly asked her cousin not to antagonise their chaperone or to call her Percy-Battleaxe behind her back in case she overheard.

'It's all right for you – you're escaping at Bombay – I've got the Percy-Barratts as my neighbours for ever more.'

So, for the most part, Sophie sat demurely like Tilly and listened to the advice doled out by the older women like Muriel who were returning from settling their children into schools in Britain. Schooling was a constant topic of conversation.

'Educating children is such a problem in India, isn't it?' Muriel sighed.

'It's all very well up to the age of seven or eight,' said Colonel Hogg's wife. 'I gave my children their lessons till that age, and they came to no harm. But I pitied the older children who were stuck here during the war; mine were safely through school age by then.'

'Yes,' said Muriel, 'I'm thankful the war was all over by the time Henry Junior was ready for prep school.'

'Some of the officers' children who were already at boarding school didn't get to see their parents for the whole of the war, poor blighters,' Mrs Hogg admitted.

'That's awful,' Sophie cried. 'They would hardly know their parents when they returned.'

Muriel gave her a frosty look. 'Hard for the mothers, but at least they knew their children were getting the discipline and educational rigour of first class schools.'

'It's not so bad in the larger stations for younger children now,' said an engineer's wife. 'Places where there are plenty of other British kiddies and nursery schools.'

'Impossible in the countryside where we are,' Muriel declared.

'Mmm,' Sophie mused, 'I certainly have no memory of being sent to school.'

'It's awful having to say goodbye to them,' said the wife of a PWD, Public Works Department Officer, her eyes filling with tears, 'just awful. I'm glad I've still got my Hester with me for another four years, else I couldn't bear it.'

'We all have to bear it,' Muriel was brusque. 'It's what we do best, us wives and mothers.'

Tilly couldn't help putting a possessive hand on her stomach where the roundness was already showing under her straight beige dress. Her baby wasn't even born and she could not imagine sending it so far away from her at such a young age.

'Are there no good schools in the whole of India?' she asked.

'Few for the likes of us,' said Mrs Hogg.

'Even if there were,' Muriel said, 'it would be selfish to keep our children in India after seven years old. They react badly to the climate – lose their strength.'

The engineer's wife nodded. 'They can become lazy like the natives.'

'Quite so,' said Muriel. 'You have to put their well-being before your own feelings, my dear.'

'Still,' the wife of the PWD Officer sighed, 'it's very hard and I hate to think that George might be unhappy in his new school and I'm too far away to do anything about it. How do I know if he's happy?'

Clarrie, who had been playing with Adela among the deck quoits, joined in.

'There are some very good mission schools. I went to one run by Catholic nuns in Shillong. I hope Adela might go there too one day.'

The women were shocked into silence. Adela caught sight of Wesley and went hurtling down the deck towards him. Clarrie smiled at Tilly.

'Things are changing slowly in India, but they are changing. Maybe by the time your bonny baby is eight, he or she won't have to be sent thousands of miles away from you. I have no intention of banishing Adela to boarding school five thousand miles away.'

Clarrie walked off to join her family.

'Well, really,' tutted Muriel, 'the cheek of the woman.'

'How embarrassing,' said the engineer's wife. 'We haven't banished our children.'

'Mrs Robson can be quite forthright,' said Mrs Hogg, standing up. 'I don't think she means to offend.'

'I'm afraid I disagree,' Muriel said. 'That woman doesn't care what she says – and she wasn't even in our conversation.'

'As we're all out on deck,' Mrs Hogg remarked, 'it was hardly private. Now, if you'll excuse me, I'm going for a rest.' She nodded to them and left. Once she was out of earshot, Muriel fuelled her indignation.

'Well, you can guess why Clarrie Robson went to the nuns in Shillong, of course,' she said.

'Is she *Eurasian*?' the PWD Officer's wife whispered the name.

'Exactly. And you just have to look at the child to see the Indian blood coming out in the next generation.'

'Adela is only one-eighth Indian,' Tilly spoke up, 'as if that matters.'

'Oh, I assure you that it does matter,' said Muriel. 'I don't know why they aren't in tourist class.'

'The husband seems nice, though,' said the PWD Officer's wife.

'They're all delightful.' Sophie stood up, tired of their gossiping. 'And they're Tilly's family now, so you shouldn't be rude about them.'

Muriel looked offended. 'Well, from what my husband tells me, your father never gave that woman's family the time of day,' she snapped at Sophie. 'Bill Logan thought Jock Belhaven was letting the side down marrying a half-caste and producing daughters like her – and he wasn't shy in telling Belhaven to his face. It was your father made sure the Belhavens weren't welcome at the club in Tezpur, that's what my Henry said. Your father knew how awkward it was for the other planters and their families. Course that was all before I came to Assam, but I think your father had the right idea.'

Sophie felt winded at this sudden mention of her father and she was shocked to hear he had ostracised Clarrie's family. She swapped looks with Tilly. Was there more to James's disagreement with Wesley than a difference of opinion over methods of producing tea? Perhaps Clarrie was still a social outcast in India and James wanted nothing to do with her?

Tilly gave an embarrassed shrug but said nothing.

'I'm going to change for the tea dance,' Sophie announced, with a defiant look at Muriel. 'I'm glad I don't have children to worry over. I'm going to enjoy a bit of life before getting tied down with all that.'

As she walked off, she heard the tea planter's wife venting her disapproval.

'That cousin of yours thinks she knows it all, Tilly, but the last thing India needs is modern women with their bobbed hair stirring things up. I hope she's not going to give that forester of hers the runaround. He'll need to keep a tight rein or, mark my words, she'll land in trouble.'

***

Sophie soon tired of trying to placate the censorious Muriel and ignored her waspish remarks about Sophie's enthusiasm for the dancing and deck entertainment. She found kindred spirits in young Ella Holland, wife of a surveyor, and a Captain Cecil Roberts, an army engineer who organised impromptu concerts. Sophie sang Scottish songs while the captain badly banged out tunes on a piano. There was a group of Americans going to work for an oil company in the Punjab who were keen on outdoor sports. They helped Cecil, Sophie, Clarrie and Wesley run a sports day for the children, with wheelbarrow races and an obstacle course of quoits and rope netting. It ended in a mass tug of war and buckets of water being hurled at the winners.

'I've heard that Ella Holland and her husband changed their name so that he could progress in the Surveying Department,' Muriel gossiped. 'Used to be called Abrams – obviously Jewish. You just have to look at her.'

'Yes, isn't she pretty?' Sophie said and hurried from the cabin. She didn't know how Tilly could stand the woman's sniping, but her cousin didn't seem to notice. Tilly was constantly tired and showed no interest in joining in the fun.

After nearly two weeks of sailing, the ship docked at Port Said, dropping anchor at midnight. The next morning Sophie badgered a listless Tilly to go ashore to explore. Muriel marched them to the emporium run by Simon Arzt to buy solar *topees*, the ubiquitous sun hats of the British in the tropics.

'Otherwise your brains will fry in the heat,' she warned. 'You can fancify them with a bit of ribbon but you mustn't go anywhere without one.'

'Makes you wonder how anyone survived before they were invented,' Sophie smirked.

'They didn't,' Muriel snapped. 'Ordinary hats don't give British heads enough protection.'

While Muriel was haggling keenly over a blue and yellow vase for her bungalow in Assam, Sophie and Tilly managed to give her the slip. They wandered among the gaudy stalls, admiring the striped shawls and pretty linens and gawping at tea sellers holding high their brass trays loaded with glasses of tea as they wove among the crowds and donkeys.

'Clarrie should employ these boys at Herbert's,' Tilly said. 'How do they not spill a drop?'

'Let's have one,' Sophie said, glad that her friend was showing an interest in something at last, and paid for two glasses of the sweet black tea.

'I can't drink it without milk,' Tilly complained.

'Try it; it's very refreshing. I remember having tea like this as a child. I'd forgotten till now.'

'I hope there'll be milk at Cheviot Cottage.' Tilly sipped and pulled a face. 'Ugh, I've quite lost the taste for tea. Let's go back to the boat; it leaves at noon and we mustn't get left behind. And the smells are making me sick.'

Tilly found the place overwhelming; she had quickly lost her appetite for shopping and meandering around the town. She wished she could shake off her lethargy, but all she wanted to do these days was curl up and sleep. She knew she was being irritable with Sophie but couldn't help it; she envied her cousin's ease of making new friends and her boundless energy. This baby inside had turned her into such a moaner – she didn't recognise herself – but there was nothing she could do to control her emotions.

'You must buy something for James as a souvenir,' Sophie urged. 'What would he like? I thought I'd get Tam some Turkish Delight; he and Boz both have a sweet tooth.'

Tilly was at a loss. 'I've no idea.' The thought made her tearful. 'I'm married to him and I don't even know if he likes Turkish Delight.'

'It doesn't matter,' Sophie said quickly, 'you can buy something for the house.' At once she began bartering with a cheerful young boy for a couple of cushion covers for Tilly. He persuaded them both to buy striped shawls and souvenir spoons too. Sophie bought two boxes of Turkish Delight and then hurried her cousin back to the ship where they were met by an indignant Muriel.

'I thought you'd been abducted! You should never have gone wandering off on your own. You need eyes in the back of your head the further east you go.'

'Difficult when you're wearing a *topee*,' Sophie quipped.

'And look at poor Tilly, quite done in,' Muriel accused. 'You should take better care of your cousin. All you think about, young lady, is yourself.'

'I'm fine,' Tilly said, 'just glad to be back on board.'

Both friends were cheered by letters from their men. James's was short and businesslike, detailing how he would meet her at Calcutta, but if he was delayed she and Mrs Percy-Barratt must book into the Victoria Hotel and wait for him.

'I've just sent a ten-page letter,' Tilly cried, 'and get one page back that looks like it's written on lavatory paper. He's not the least bit romantic. Look at Tam's long letter; it's not fair!'

Sophie found a quiet corner on deck to read hers; six sides of thin paper headed: *Forest Office, Lahore*. It appeared that Tam was mainly based in the countryside at a place called Changa Manga and hadn't seen much of Lahore yet. The letter brimmed full of enthusiasm for his work and his plans for the plantations; a canal that could be diverted to irrigate the nurseries, a wagonway that should be extended and his keenness to experiment with different species.

'Yesterday I shot a blackbuck at dawn. I organised some beaters among the labourers and we flushed it out. Got him with one clean shot in the shoulder at eighty yards. I've had the skin salted and sent over to the Remounts – they're the lads who supply horses to the army – they have a tailor who can make it into a rug for your dainty feet! My sweet one, I can't wait to kiss those feet and all the rest of you.'

Sophie blushed with pleasure and pressed the pages to her lips. 'Me too,' she murmured.

'I've had a bout of fever – nothing to worry yourself about – all us new boys down here have had a dose. It was very hot still when we came out and the "moskies" got busy on me. Just don't

want you turning round and sailing straight home when you catch sight of me at Bombay – I'm a bit of a skeleton compared to when you last saw me. But then maybe I won't recognise you either with your bobbed hair and we'll walk straight past each other! I just want the day to hurry up and come, then we can start our new life together. I'm going up to Lahore in a couple of days to see about renting married quarters in one of the cantonments. I board at the Cecil Hotel when in town – it's run by a kindly old soul called Miss Jones – I know you'll like her and she introduced me to a Christian Science couple, the Floyds.

'Hugh Floyd works for the Revenue in the Punjab government and Deidre Floyd is a mainstay of the C.S. Society in Lahore and they often hold the Sunday reading at their bungalow. She has a friend on your boat, a colonel's wife, Fluffy Hogg. Have you come across her?'

'Fluffy?' Sophie laughed out loud. What an unlikely name for such a formidable woman, she thought. She wouldn't be frightened of her again.

'I've so much to tell you,' Tam's letter continued, '*it feels like I've been here for years already. I prefer it here in the jungle working all hours and learning Urdu. When I go to town and see all the couples dining and dancing and having the time of their lives, I miss you all the more and the hole in my heart grows bigger. Hurry the day I can hold you in my arms again.*

'Yours aye, Tam.'

'I can see from your face,' Tilly said disconsolately when Sophie returned, 'that your letter told you more than train times and how to get through customs.'

'It told me what Mrs Hogg's nickname is.' Sophie grinned. 'Have a guess.'

'Brunhilda?'

'No.'

'Prudence?'

'Not even close.'

'Charity. Oh, I give up.'

'Fluffy!' Sophie cried.

'You're making that up.'

'No I'm not – I have it on the best authority in the Punjab. She must be a Florence or some such but her friends call her Fluffy; isn't that priceless?'

'Yes,' Tilly agreed and then for the first time in weeks she felt a strange sensation bubbling up inside. It came out as a snort and then she was consumed with laughter.

'Tilly's got the giggles at last,' Sophie spluttered as she fell on the bunk beside her and caught the infectious laugh. For several minutes they rolled around in helpless mirth until Muriel came in and threatened to call the ship's doctor if they didn't pull themselves together.

***

The S.S. *City of Baroda* sailed down the Suez Canal and into the Red Sea. The temperature rose suddenly, the crew changed into white 'togs' and the passengers dug out light clothing; white flannels for the men and summer dresses for the women. As they steamed south the heat became oppressive and people preferred to laze and look at the stars rather than to dance. Encouraged by Tam's talk of learning Urdu, Sophie took up Mrs Hogg's offer of teaching her a few phrases while sitting on the port side of the deck out of the direct sun.

'Sets a good example,' said Mrs Hogg, 'if you can talk to your servants in their own tongue – why should they always have to be speaking English? Besides,' she said with a twinkle in the eye, 'it'll mean you'll have some idea of what they're saying about *you*.' She had a dry sense of humour under the *burra memsahib* persona and Sophie grew to like her.

Tilly waved away any suggestion of joining in 'Fluffy's phrase-a-day' as she called it. 'I think James's servants speak Bengali or something else, so what's the point? And I've hardly got the energy to read, let alone take in a language.' Her tetchiness had returned with the heat.

Aden floated by in the twilight as the ship pushed out into open sea, but there was little relief below deck.

Tilly found it impossible to sleep. The fug of the cabin and Muriel's nightly snoring were driving her to despair.

'We'll sleep on deck,' Sophie whispered and, grabbing bedding, bullied her friend upstairs.

Others had had the same idea and the crew had rigged up a sail to divide the deck into two areas; one for women and one for men. They lay in their underclothes, side by side, gazing up at a bright moon. Tilly felt a sudden relief in the mild sea air and reached for Sophie's hand.

'Sophie?'

'Umm.'

'I'm sorry for being such a dragon. I don't know what's come over me.'

Sophie squeezed her hand. 'Pregnancy's come over you.'

'But I shouldn't take it out on you; the nicer you've been to me, the more bad-tempered I've become. I'm horrible pregnant.'

Sophie sat up and rummaged under the blanket. 'Here, this'll sweeten your mood.' She opened a box and tore off a piece of sugary sweetmeat.

'That's Tam's Turkish Delight,' Tilly protested. 'I can't eat your present.'

'There's another box.' Sophie popped a square into Tilly's mouth and took another. It was nutty and delicious. For several minutes they chewed in silence.

'The stars are different from home,' Tilly mused. 'That must be the Southern Cross.'

'Isn't it romantic?' Sophie sighed. 'I wish Tam were here to see it.'

'You'll be with him in a week's time,' Tilly said, 'then you'll never need to be parted again.'

Sophie's insides clenched. 'I've never been so excited or so frightened.'

Tilly snorted. 'You never get frightened about anything. I'm the one who's a bag of nerves. Ever since I knew I was expecting, I keep having these panics and wonder what on earth I've done. Not about the baby really – just about me and James. I bet you don't have doubts it might not work out with Tam and you'll be stuck there for ever?'

'No,' Sophie replied. 'Nothing about getting married to Tam worries me. But I do get nervous at the thought of India; my feelings about the place are so mixed up. I just hope that going back might get rid of the sadness about my parents – lay the ghosts of my childhood.'

'Strange you should say that,' Tilly murmured. 'Rafi Khan said as much.'

'Did he?' Sophie felt a jolt at hearing his name unexpectedly.

'Yes, he seemed to sense your longing. "Laying ghosts to rest" was the phrase he used.'

Sophie felt a slow thud in her chest and then whispered, 'He's right. I suppose, deep down, I'd like to know everything that happened to them.'

Tilly frowned. 'But you know what happened; they both caught enteric fever. You were lucky to survive it too; that's what James said.'

'I know,' Sophie puzzled, 'but I don't remember being ill. I remember my father having fever and keeping to his room – and shouting – I remember him shouting a lot. But not mother or me. My last memory of mother is of her playing hide-and-seek with me. You don't do that if you've got fever, do you?'

'It can happen in a few short hours,' Tilly said. 'That's what is so scary about these diseases.'

'I suppose so,' Sophie struggled with her memory. 'But where was Ayah? I don't remember her comforting me when they died or coming to see me off.'

'Maybe she'd been sent to work for someone else?' Tilly guessed.

Sophie shook her head, baffled. 'There was something going on that night. There was a lot of shouting and the grown-ups seemed worried – wouldn't let me go beyond the veranda steps. I remember lots of noise and fireworks beyond the compound.'

'Yes, I remember you telling me about the drumming when we were young,' Tilly said. 'You thought they were drumming for your birthday, didn't you?'

Sophie nodded. 'Obviously that was nonsense – there must have been something going on in the village. My last memory of Ayah Mimi is her running away down the path with our new kitten. Isn't that a strange thing? Why was she doing that? Or maybe I just remember it wrongly.'

'I don't think it helps to dwell on all that – you'll never know for sure – but it might help if you came to Assam for a visit,' Tilly suggested, 'go and visit your parents' graves.'

'I'm not even sure where they're buried,' Sophie said sadly. 'We were living away from the Oxford gardens when they died. I imagine they were buried somewhere in the hills. Auntie Amy never talked about such things – she didn't want me upset – but perhaps she never knew.'

'James might know,' Tilly said. 'I can ask him if you like.'

Sophie leaned over and kissed her hot cheek. 'Thank you, I'd be really grateful.'

They ate more Turkish Delight and talked about the future.

'Who would have thought we'd both end up going to India?' Tilly mused.

'Or both marrying planters,' Sophie said. 'You always did copy everything I did.'

'Not this time,' Tilly protested. 'I was first to be a planter's bride and book my passage to India.'

'I know.' Sophie chuckled in the dark. 'I was only teasing. And you're definitely going to be a mother long before me. I have no desire for all that yet – I find babies frightening.'

'Frightening?' Tilly asked in surprise. 'You mean giving birth?'

'Not just that,' Sophie said, trying to voice what it was exactly that filled her with fear. 'It's being in charge of something so small and not being able to keep it safe.'

'Oh,' Tilly said, covering her stomach in alarm. In the past week she had felt definite kicks from the baby and was beginning to think of it as real.

'Sorry,' Sophie said quickly, 'that was a stupid thing to say. You and James will be wonderful parents and I bet you go on to have hordes of robust little Robsons. I'm just not ready for a family. Here, let's have one more sweet in honour of baby Robson.'

Half the box was gone before they stopped chatting.

Tilly slept soundly for the first time in two weeks, until the deck scrubbers appeared in the dawn light to hose down the boards, and the cousins crept back to their bunks.

***

The following days were hot and calm; the sea a dazzling peacock blue.

'Looks like a roller has been over it.' Sophie was amazed. 'I've never seen it so flat.'

'Just wish it wasn't so sticky.' Tilly sighed, fanning herself in the shade.

The ship was hailed by two dhows that had been becalmed and the captain stopped to allow the seafarers to come aboard for fresh water and supplies. Sophie watched in fascination as the men paddled across in slim canoes, keeping their balance on the frail craft.

'I don't see why we should be delayed because of some Arab fishermen,' Muriel Percy-Barratt complained loudly. 'It's their own fault for sailing out so far in those primitive boats.'

'It's the code of the sea,' Wesley said brusquely, 'and our captain is duty bound to help them – just as they would help us if we needed rescuing.'

The final few days on board were fractious. People were growing tired of being confined and their thoughts were turning, in anticipation, to arrival. Complaints were made about the carousing of young men in the early mornings on the lower deck, while the young blamed the older men for drinking the most. The ship's captain responded by forbidding any more late night entertainment. Then a cyclonic gale blew up that sent waves crashing over the bows and any would-be revellers retired green-gilled to their cabins. Sophie was one of the few passengers to brave the storm, revelling in the spray that soaked her hair and face.

Weaving her way down towards the stern, she came across Clarrie and Mrs Hogg sitting with a tiny old woman in a sari. Sophie stopped in her tracks at the unexpected sight. She had glimpsed the Indian woman before but noticed how she kept to herself. Up close, Sophie could see that her skin was wrinkled and yellow like parchment, her thin hands like the claws of a bird.

'This is Mrs Besant,' Mrs Hogg introduced her. 'Sophie Logan is a promising student of Urdu. She's on her way to marry a forester called Telfer in the Punjab.'

The old woman greeted her in the Eastern manner with a bow and palms pressed together. She spoke in an upper-class accent. 'Pleased to meet you, Miss Logan. I hope you enjoy India for the short time the Britishers have left in the country.'

'Now, Annie,' Mrs Hogg chided, 'don't tease the girl.'

'Just a statement of fact, Fluffy, my dear.'

It suddenly struck Sophie who this was; the infamous Annie Besant who had spearheaded the Indian independence campaign before the war, advocating the end of British rule. She had read that Mrs Besant had escaped prison only by leaving swiftly for America. Now here she was returning, an unwelcome revolutionary, though to Sophie she looked as harmless as the tiny wren.

'Mrs Besant' – Sophie returned the gesture – 'my aunt knew you in her suffrage days – Amy Anderson from Edinburgh – she talked about sharing the same platform with you once, though you probably don't remember.'

'Of course I do,' the elderly woman said with sudden interest. 'A talented artist as well as a brave campaigner. I remember meeting her when she came out for her sister's wedding. How is your aunt?'

'She died a few months ago,' Sophie answered, her eyes stinging.

'I'm sorry to hear that,' Mrs Besant said, with a brief touch on her hand. 'So you are making a new life in India?'

Sophie nodded.

'All I ask is that you come with an open mind and do what you can for the country,' she advised. 'Too many Britishers come with the sole intention of seeing how much they can get out of India for themselves.'

'Sophie is not the least bit like that,' Clarrie defended. 'And she is no stranger to the country; she grew up in Assam before her parents died. She already has a feel for the place, just like us three.'

Sophie gave Clarrie a grateful smile. It surprised her that three such different women should be friends.

'And perhaps Miss Logan will choose to stay in India no matter who governs in the future,' said Mrs Hogg.

'That almost sounds like sedition, Fluffy.' Mrs Besant smiled. 'Colonel Hogg thinks the Empire will go on for another century, doesn't he?'

'Wishful thinking, Annie. He has no more desire than you do to retire to the south of England and grow roses. That's why we're making our home in Dalhousie hill station.'

'Dalhousie? That amounts to the same thing,' Annie said dryly.

'Dalhousie's more like Scotland from what I've heard,' Clarrie joined in.

'Well, at least I'll feel at home then,' Sophie said, making the other women laugh.

'My dear,' said Mrs Besant, 'I hope you will experience the real India and not hide away in the hills with the government *wallahs*.'

'I want to experience it all,' Sophie was enthusiastic.

'And what are the skills you bring?' she persisted.

Sophie thought for a moment. 'I'm not a great cook but I can dance quite well.' From the frown on Mrs Besant's face, she could see she wasn't impressed. Sophie racked her brains. 'My aunt taught me to use a hammer and chisel, though I don't have her artistic flair.'

'Sophie rides a motorcycle,' Clarrie came to her rescue, 'and she can fix almost anything mechanical, according to her cousin Tilly.'

The older women looked impressed.

'A motorcycle? Well, I never,' Mrs Hogg gasped.

'Sadly I had to leave The Memsahib behind,' Sophie said.

'You called your motor machine The Memsahib?' Mrs Besant raised her eyebrows. 'Why was that?'

'Because she's temperamental and noisy and likes to think she's the boss.'

There was a surprised silence, then Mrs Besant broke into a girlish giggle.

'I like you, Miss Logan.' She laughed. 'I hope India does too.'

***

The day before the steamer put in to Bombay, Sophie watched a school of porpoises diving through the waves in the dusk and sat up all night under a huge yellow moon, unable to sleep. Tam would already have set off on the thirty-six-hour train journey from Lahore to meet her. In a matter of hours, they would be together again. Her stomach did double somersaults.

Tilly found her perched on the hatchway gazing out at the stunning moon as it set into the sea like an imposter of the sun.

'It's four thirty in the morning, Sophie.' Tilly yawned. 'Are you not going to get any sleep?'

'I can't,' said Sophie, 'I'm too excited. Which frock should I wear? The red flowery one that Tam hasn't seen or the blue that he likes me in? And what about my hair? I wish I'd booked a perm on board. What if he hates it short? Do I look too much like a schoolboy?'

Tilly looked at her beautiful friend, her face aglow in the early light, and laughed. 'Not at all like a boy. It shows off your face even more – makes your eyes look huge.'

'Like a broon coo?' Sophie joked.

'Yes, like a cow's,' Tilly teased.

'That's better than a schoolboy anyway.'

Tilly flung an affectionate arm about her shoulders. 'Oh, Sophie, I can't believe this time tomorrow we'll be saying goodbye.'

Sophie hugged her back. 'Try to give old Percy-Battleaxe the slip and come ashore for a few hours – we could all go for lunch and you can chaperone me while we go and pick the wedding ring.'

'Better not,' said Tilly. 'Knowing me, I'd probably get lost and miss the sailing.'

'I wouldn't mind if you did' – Sophie grinned – 'then you'd have to come to Lahore and be my maid of honour.'

The previous storms had delayed the voyage and it was evening before they steamed into Bombay. Passengers gathered at the railings to see the Eastern city in the twilight. Sophie's stomach knotted in excitement as the wide sweep of the bay with its string of imposing buildings and dockside cranes glowed orange in the dying sun. Colonel Hogg pointed out the half-built Gate of India, a massive biscuit-coloured stone gateway that looked more like a fortress.

'That's in honour of King George,' he said. 'Building got delayed 'cause of the war. Maybe next time we sail, it might be from there.'

Darkness fell in minutes and the lights of the city showed up as a glow, but they lay anchored off shore for another night. Sophie was in a frenzy of impatience by the time the ship came alongside Ballard Pier at eight the following morning; she had said countless 'cheerios' several times over as people searched for their baggage and prepared to disembark.

'I can't see Tam.' She peered over the railings at the crowds swarming on the quayside.

'I'm not surprised.' Tilly gazed in awe. 'I've never seen such a busy place.'

A mass of porters, bullocks, carts, traders and officials jostled with those trying to get permission to board to greet their loved ones. They pushed against an endless line of stevedores carrying luggage from the baggage rooms.

'Tam said I should wait on the boat but maybe I should go ashore?' Sophie was suddenly unsure.

Half an hour later, with no sign of Tam, Tilly fetched Clarrie.

'Wesley will go with you and see your baggage through customs,' Clarrie reassured. 'You mustn't worry.'

Wesley picked up Sophie's small suitcase and arranged for porters to carry her large trunk. 'He's probably stuck in the shipping office trying to raise an on-board pass.'

Sophie hugged Tilly and Clarrie one more time. There was no more talk of Tilly sneaking off with her; she was much too daunted by the chaos in the port. But Adela threw herself at Sophie's legs.

''Ophie lift me! I come too.'

Sophie grabbed the girl, kissed her dark curls and swiftly handed her to Clarrie. 'I'll come and visit you soon, I promise.'

Adela began to howl and fling herself about when she realised Sophie and her father were leaving the boat without her.

'Daddy's coming back,' Clarrie tried to soothe her. The girl's wailing pursued them all the way down the gangway and into the cacophony of the harbour.

Sophie caught sight of a tall, familiar figure pushing his way through the crowd of porters, beggars and uniformed officials.

'Boz?' she cried. 'What are you doing here?'

'Sophie! They wouldna' let me through,' he panted, his face puce under his khaki hat.

Sophie introduced him to Wesley. 'It's lovely to see you, Boz, but who are you meeting?'

'You, lassie.' He took off his *topee* and pulled at a large hot ear in agitation.

'Where's Tam?'

'I'm sorry, Sophie, he couldna' come. He sent me in his place.'

Chapter 15

Sophie stood in stunned incomprehension. Perspiration prickled her brow and the hot oily smell of people and street food filled her nostrils and made her feel faint.

'What's happened to Tam?' Sophie panicked. 'Has there been an accident?'

'No, lassie, nothing like that,' Boz said quickly.

'He's ill, isn't he? He's got malaria again.'

Boz shook his head. 'He's had a couple of bouts of fever, right enough; but that's no' the reason. There's nothing to worry about – just a wee misunderstanding.'

'What misunderstanding?'

'Martins, our boss, wouldna give him permission.'

Disappointment punched Sophie in the stomach. 'How could you get time off and Tam couldn't? I don't understand.'

Wesley intervened. 'Let's get you into somewhere cooler and quieter, then your friend can explain.'

In the less noisy surroundings of the shipping waiting room, Wesley guided Sophie into a chair and ordered up tea while Boz delivered his awkward message.

'Tam got on the wrang side o' Martins last month by travelling up tae Pindi for a couple o' days fishing—'

'Fishing?' Sophie puzzled. 'In Pindi? Isn't that miles from Lahore?'

'Aye, but McGinty and Scott are working up there in the pine forests – Tam fancied a jaunt but he didna' get his leave put in writing,' Boz explained. 'Tam says Martins gave him permission to gang but then Bracknall got tae hear about it and wee Martins denied he ever sanctioned it.'

'Who's Bracknall?'

'He's the chief of the whole forestry department in the Punjab – a big gun – mixes with the top nobs in the Indian civil service. Came back from touring the province and started throwing his weight about, showing us new recruits who's boss.'

'But Tam hadn't done anything wrong,' Sophie was indignant.

'No, but you have to dae everything by the book here; that's the biggest rule there is.'

Wesley grunted. 'That's true, and it's why I would never have made a good civil servant. Foolish rules are there to be broken.'

'That's Tam's philosophy too,' Boz said ruefully, 'but Bracknall's a stickler for the rule book. Told Tam it would gang on his record as "extraordinary leave" – so every boss in the future will know he went absent without leave – and to rub salt in the wound he didna' get paid for his five days away.'

'Not a good start,' Wesley murmured.

'Tam was fuming,' Boz admitted. 'Then Martins telt him that it would look bad if he took any more time off to fetch you frae Bombay, seeings as Tam'll be takkin' a week's leave when you get wed.'

'But that's not fair!' Sophie protested. 'It was this Martins's fault that Tam got into trouble in the first place.'

'It's not fair,' Wesley said, 'but William here is not to blame. He's been very kind coming down to meet you, Sophie, and giving up some of his own precious leave.'

'I dinna' mind,' Boz said with a bashful smile.

At once, Sophie was contrite. 'I'm sorry, Boz, I do appreciate it. I was just so looking forward to seeing Tam.'

'Aye,' Boz said, 'he's that disappointed too; he's been like a caged tiger. Tam does no take kindly to orders he does nae agree wi'. But he's always been like that. He canna wait tae see you, lassie.'

Sophie was mollified by Boz's words; it was not Tam's fault that he had a feeble manager who wouldn't stand up for him.

'The last thing I want is to get Tam into more trouble for coming to meet me.' Sophie sighed. 'But right now I could stick pins into this wretched Martins – and that bully Bracknall.'

'That's the spirit,' encouraged Wesley, pushing a cup of hot sweet tea into her hand. 'You can stock up on pins before the train journey.'

Boz grinned. 'Tam calls Martins the wee Martini – says he needs mixing with a large gin to stiffen his backbone.'

Sophie smiled at them both. 'Thank you for cheering me up.'

Soon afterwards, Wesley handed over care of Sophie's luggage to Boz and she took her farewell of Clarrie's handsome husband, promising to visit them at Belgooree whenever she should travel to Assam to see Tilly.

'The Khasi hills are very beautiful,' Wesley said, 'with great riding. Bring Tam; the fishing is excellent. It's how I met Clarrie.' He flashed a wicked smile. 'But that's a long story.'

It took hours to get Sophie's baggage through customs and then to secure a berth in a coupé on the long haul mail train up north to Lahore. Boz seemed to spend hours haggling over the weight of her trunk, the insistence that she travelled first class and the endless paperwork of chits and passes.

The booking finally accomplished, Boz took her to the newly opened Grand Hotel, with its domed tower like a lighthouse, and treated her to a meal of lamb cutlets, greens and potatoes, washed down with pale ale. They bumped into Ella Holland with her stocky, balding husband and discovered they were travelling on the same train as far as Amritsar. Sophie was cheered by the news.

'So when is your wedding day?' Samuel Holland asked Boz.

'Oh, no, he's not my fiancé,' Sophie said hastily. 'Tam couldn't come.' She saw the look of surprise – or was it disapproval? – pass between the Hollands and felt a wave of embarrassment. It hadn't occurred to her that dining with Boz unchaperoned might be seen as bad behaviour. Ella had enjoyed having fun on the boat with the young unattached men, but now with her husband she seemed shy, less assured.

'He's ill,' Boz lied to dispel the awkwardness, 'so sent me instead. I'm tae be Tam's best man and I must deliver Miss Logan safely to her eager bridegroom or my life will no' be worth living.'

'Oh dear, I do hope he'll be fully recovered for the wedding,' Ella said with a pitying look.

Sophie wished she hadn't told Ella quite as much about her hopes and dreams about a future with Tam, or how thrilled she was that Tam had promised to meet her in Bombay, take her to the famous Hanging Gardens and buy her a wedding ring.

Sophie and Ella arranged to meet up on the train later.

Outside again in the glaring sunshine, Sophie watched the S.S. *City of Baroda* steam back into open waters and wondered if Tilly was among those standing at the rail waving to the crowds on the quayside. She felt a stab of loneliness at the thought of her oldest friend sailing away to a different life and envied her the companionship of the kind Robsons.

'I've a couple o' things to buy from the Army and Navy Stores before the train leaves,' Boz broke into her reverie. 'Do you want tae come or would you rather sit in the lassies' waiting room at the station?'

'I'll come with you,' Sophie said, smothering the thought that she should have been with Tam taking a taxi out to Malabar Hill to watch the sunset over the Arabian Sea. There would be other sunsets, she told herself firmly.

They took a cycle-rickshaw through the wide palm-lined streets of the Fort area towards Colaba, past elaborate colonial buildings gleaming in the sun and on into the seething town. Sophie was mesmerised by the sights and sounds: large black motor cars tooting to get past bullocks pulling carts laden with dusty sacks, the cries of street vendors sitting behind multi-coloured piles of spices and vegetables, women on the steps of a temple with mounds of vivid yellow marigolds, the jangle of bells as cyclists dodged wandering cows.

Sophie gasped as a bright green parrot swooped right in front of them and landed in a tree behind a high wall. Through its iron gates, Sophie glimpsed a cool courtyard with a water tank before they swerved on down the street. She wanted to stop and clamber down and explore behind the high wall where the parrot lived. It made her feel like a child again. A holy man with matted hair, dressed in a tattered orange cloth and clutching a metal teapot, stepped through the traffic unharmed like a prophet parting the waves. Three women in colourful saris – blue, saffron and pink – followed in bare feet. A slim ankle, the dark skin, the ring glinting in the young woman's nose. Sophie's heart missed a beat.

'You all right, lassie?' Boz asked in concern.

‘That woman . . .?’ Sophie realised she was clutching his arm. ‘Sorry.’ She let go at once.

‘Don’t be.’ He smiled.

‘She reminded me of my Ayah, that’s all. Silly, ’cause if she’s still alive, Ayah Mimi will probably be grey and toothless by now.’

‘If this is too much for you,’ Boz said, ‘we can go to the station.’

‘No, I’m enjoying it,’ Sophie insisted. ‘And I want to buy some more medicines to go in my first aid box. Mama always used to stock up whenever she went to town.’ She caught her breath. ‘I don’t know how I remember that.’

‘Must ha’ been a big event tae gang tae the toon,’ Boz said. ‘Shillong was it? Or Calcutta?’

‘Shillong I think – it always seemed to be raining and we would have tea in a grand room with a bear’s head on one wall and a tiger’s on the other.’

‘Scary for a wee lassie, eh?’

‘No, I used to talk to them.’ Sophie saw his amused expression. ‘I didn’t have many friends.’ She laughed.

‘I find that hard to believe.’

‘William Boswell, stop flirting with me’ – she tapped his hand, unnerved by his tender look – ‘or I’ll have to tell my fiancé.’

‘Sophie.’ Boz looked suddenly serious. ‘How much has Tam told you about himself?’

‘Lots,’ she said. ‘I’ve met his family and I know all about his life in Edinburgh and his letters tell me everything about the new job.’

‘Has he spoken about France – about the war?’

‘No, not much,’ Sophie admitted. ‘I don’t think he likes to think about all that – none of you do, surely?’

Boz didn’t answer.

‘I did once try to ask him about the scar on his head – how he got it – but he wouldn’t say.’

The look on Boz’s face made her uneasy.

‘How did he get it?’

‘I shouldna’ have said anything. It’s up to Tam tae tell you.’

‘Now you’re making me worried,’ Sophie said. ‘What should I know? Please tell me.’

Boz looked hot and uncomfortable. ‘Our Division were clearing enemy trenches – the Germans were on the run. Tam got bored wi’ too little for us mortar boys tae do, so he gets us a lift on an infantry lorry – takes us up the line. It’s all chaos but we end up in this bombed oot village – trying to help this family o’ Frenchies hiding out in a cellar. God knaws what they’d been surviving on. Well, turns out not all the Boche boys had gone sae quickly – set off a couple o’ shells as they retreated. Tam got hit by a piece of shrapnel – burned a hole in his helmet.’

‘Oh, dear Lord!’ Sophie gasped.

‘The worst of it was,’ Boz said in a tense voice, ‘they were bloody gas shells. I pulled Tam oot as fast as I could, but we both ended up in hospital wi’ sickness and that. Tam didn’t gang back to the Front again – he spent the last three months of the war in hospital then, convalescing.’

‘And you?’ Sophie whispered, appalled.

‘I recovered sooner – didn’t have his head injuries – so I was back with the artillery when the armistice came.’

In the bright teeming town, Sophie could hardly imagine the horror they had experienced. She slipped her gloved hand in Boz’s sweaty palm.

‘How terrible. I’m so sorry.’ She searched his face. ‘Why are you telling me this now?’

Boz hesitated, then said, ‘Tam is my greatest pal – he saved my life early in the war and I saved his near the end. We’ll do anything for each other. But he’s no’ the same since the gas attack. He gets headaches awfu’ bad and sometimes he can lose his temper over nothing. His judgement isn’t always the best. When he was in France on the last—’

‘Thank you for telling me,’ Sophie interrupted. ‘But I don’t need to hear any more tales. It changes nothing. I know the war is bound to have affected him in some way – I’ve worked with the Red Cross and seen how the men’s minds were scarred as well as their bodies. It just makes me love him all the more and want to take care of him. You can't make me change my mind about Tam, however hard you try.'

Boz gave her a sad look. 'I wasnae trying tae do that, lassie.' He pulled his hand away. 'Tam Telfer is a lucky, lucky man. And you, Miss Logan, will be good for him.'

After that, they talked no more about Tam and there was a reserve between them that hadn't been there before. Sophie was thankful when they climbed aboard the clanking, dusty train that evening and she fell exhausted into the sanctuary of the women-only carriage. Peering out of the window at the lively orange sellers trying to catch final trade as the train shunted forward, she saw families setting up stoves on the open platform for their evening meal. She caught a whiff of acrid smoke mingling with the buttery aroma of spicy cooking, and a jolt of familiarity rushed through her. It was a smell she had all but forgotten and yet it immediately brought back the India of her childhood. Sophie breathed in deeply. Her eyes flooded with tears. She sat down trembling.

'Don't worry, dear,' said a plump woman who had introduced herself as Mrs Porter, 'we'll soon be out of this smelly place. Best shut the window, Betty.'

The woman's young daughter sprang up to do so.

'No, please leave it,' Sophie said, her voice wavering. 'I like the smell. It reminds me I'm home.'

Chapter 16

Sophie was on a sun-bleached veranda overgrown with flowering creepers. Her mother was there too, in a red dress, bending down, in a waft of perfume, to kiss her.

Don't go, Mama!

We won't be long, darling.

Her father, in evening dress and smoking a pipe, laughed and pushed her back into the dark house.

Back into bed, you little scamp!

Don't leave me, Papa.

But her parents vanished and she was left in the pitch-black interior, muffled in blankets that smelled of camphor. She couldn't breathe . . .

'Wake up, Miss Logan!' A hand shook her shoulder. 'You're safe with us. Just a bad dream. Best not to make such a noise.'

Sophie came awake with a start. Her carriage companion, Mrs Porter, was peering at her through horn-rimmed spectacles. It took her a moment to realise where she was; on the top bunk of a swaying train heading for Lahore.

'Sorry,' she gasped.

Seven-year-old Betty Porter was perched on the end of her bed. 'Were you dreaming of bandits with scimitars coming to chop your head off?'

'Betty, be quiet,' her mother chided.

'You were screaming,' Betty said. 'Did they throw you down a well or tie you up and set fire to your house?'

'Betty!'

'Well, that's what they do to *memsahibs*; Johnny Tinker says so.'

'Johnny Tinker tells fibs.'

'No he doesn't, Mother. His father is a policeman so he knows everything that's going on.' She turned back to Sophie. 'Johnny says that bandits are very clever at dressing up like ordinary people so you can't really trust any of the natives. Even that man in the uniform who came in with the hot water – he could be a bandit ready to slit your throat—'

‘Stop it now,’ Mrs Porter ordered. ‘Of course he isn’t a bandit. Now come down at once and leave Miss Logan alone. I’m sorry,’ she said to Sophie, ‘my daughter has too much imagination. I don’t know where she gets such thoughts.’

‘Don’t worry, she isn’t bothering me.’ Sophie sat up, relieved to be awake. She eyed Betty. ‘And bandits don’t frighten me either – I can spot the real ones straight away.’

‘How?’ Betty asked, her face expectant.

‘Because my family used to be bandits too.’

The girl gasped. ‘Really?’

‘Yes, they were Scottish Reivers and used to raid across the border into England and steal cattle and burn down houses.’

Betty’s eyes widened. ‘And cut the throats of the little children?’

‘Only if they were annoying and wouldn’t let them get out of bed and have breakfast.’ She made a lunge at the girl.

Betty squealed and scrambled off the bunk. From the safety of the opposite seat she stared at Sophie. ‘Tell me a story about your bandit family.’

‘Betty!’ her mother said in exasperation.

‘Tell me a story about your bandit family, *please*,’ said Betty.

***

The journey passed more quickly than Sophie could have hoped, thanks to the lurid chatter of Betty Porter with her blonde pigtails who demanded stories all day long. Sophie was glad that she had absorbed so many of the family tales from Auntie Amy, and what she couldn’t remember, she made up. Mrs Porter was content to sit and crochet.

‘It’s wonderful having a new supply of wool; I’ve stocked up with half a suitcase. Isn’t the lilac pretty?’

‘Isn’t it too hot for woollens?’ Sophie asked, aware of how sweaty she felt in her limp cotton dress in the stuffy carriage.

‘Not on winter evenings. And if you go to Dalhousie or Murree in the cold season, you jolly well need your woollies.’

When the child had an afternoon nap, Sophie was content just to gaze out of the window and watch the plains of India hurry by; green fields of winter wheat being irrigated by teams of oxen pulling water from wells; villages of beige thatched huts and mud temples, labourers (men and women) carrying baskets of mud from the riverbanks to make bricks. People walked in the sun under umbrellas and skinny tan dogs rushed up to the moving train and barked.

As dusk came, Sophie observed the changes: cows being driven home by small boys with switches, women filling jars of water for the evening wash, men under feathery trees smoking hookahs. She went to the restaurant car for refreshment and met up with Boz and the Hollands for an evening meal. Boz kept them amused with comments about his fellow passengers in second class; mostly soldiers and Indian clerks.

'The Tommies spend their time trying tae fleece the natives at cards and end up having to beg them for cigarettes. And the jokes – too blue to repeat in front o' the lassies – but we've had a few sing-songs.'

'Well, at least you can join in those, having been a soldier.' Sophie grinned.

Boz rolled his eyes. 'Aye, I just hope we all get some sleep the night.'

Having slept deeply on the first night on the train, Sophie found sleep eluded her on the second. She peered out of the latticed shutter at a land bathed in moonlight, ghostly trees dotted among the rolling white hills, and thought how much closer she was getting to Tam with each clanking mile.

Morning came and a breakfast of tea and toast that Sophie could barely swallow.

'You were grinding your teeth in the night,' Betty complained. 'I thought a wild animal had got into the carriage.'

Sophie made a growling noise and lunged for the girl, squeezing her tight around the waist. Betty screamed and giggled.

Having waved the Hollands away at Amritsar, promising to keep in touch, she was too excited to sit; Lahore was the next stop.

'You must call on us, dear,' Mrs Porter said, as they got ready to disembark. 'With Mr Porter being in the Agricultural Department we sometimes have to move around the Punjab, but as long as we're in the Lahore cantonment you're most welcome to visit.' She handed Sophie an address card. 'I can't wait to get home and have a hot bath – wash all this dust off.'

'Thank you.' Sophie was grateful for new friends. 'And you must come to us once we have a house. Tam's trying to rent a bungalow in Davis Road but I imagine we'll be travelling a bit too with his job being in forestry.'

'Will you be going into the jungly mountains where tigers and leopards eat people?' Betty asked.

'Betty.' Her mother sighed.

'Very likely,' Sophie said. 'I'll try to bring you back a tiger cub so you can train up your own man-eater.'

Betty laughed and clapped her hands. 'Oh, yes please!'

The train began to slow and passed out of the glare into the vaulted, smoke-filled station. Boz appeared with a young porter to help the women with their luggage. Jumping down from the train, Sophie scanned the crowded platform for any sign of Tam.

'Daddy!' Betty squealed and flung herself at a ruddy-faced man with a large ginger moustache. He picked her up and gave her a kiss.

'My, you've grown a head taller!'

Sophie turned to Boz. 'Where's Tam? I can't see him.'

'Over there,' Boz said, pointing at a man in khaki shorts and shirt pushing his way towards them.

For a moment Sophie thought Boz must be mistaken. The man was gaunt-faced and sallow, his hair sparse and his clothes hanging loose. He had lost so much weight. Then Tam caught sight of her and his face lit up in his familiar grin. He strode towards her.

'Who is this film star? I was expecting Miss Logan.' He held out his arms.

'Tam!' Sophie hid her shock and fell into his hug. 'I've missed you so much.'

'I hope Mr Boswell has looked after you properly?'

'Of course he has.'

'It was maddening not to be able to fetch you myself.'

'Well, I'm here now.'

'And looking more bonny than ever.' With a quick kiss on her cheek, he let her go and shook Boz's hand. 'Thank you. I owe you a *chota peg* or two.'

'Or three or four.' Boz chuckled. 'But it was nae bother.'

Sophie introduced Tam to the Porters, and as soon as he heard they were heading for the cantonment, Tam immediately took command and organised luggage on to a bullock cart and people into *tongas*; the Porters in front and the others following. As they trotted briskly in their two-wheeled carriage up the wide Mall in the winter sun, Sophie gazed in awe at the imposing buildings. At a junction they passed in front of a huge building of dazzling white pillars.

'This area's called Charing Cross – that's the Shahdin building – excellent restaurant run by a Mr Lorang and a couple of dance halls every bit as good as Edinburgh's.'

'Hope you haven't been doing too much dancing without me.' Sophie nudged him.

'There are twice as many men at any dance, so my chances have been limited.' Tam winked. 'You'll be in huge demand.'

'Well, you'll have to get your name down on my dance card quickly then, won't you?' Sophie teased back.

'Ah, there's the cathedral where we're getting married.' Tam pointed out a large redbrick church set back from the road. 'Four days to go, Miss Logan. Hope you're not having second thoughts.'

Sophie slipped her hand into his. 'I can't wait.'

'Padre Rennie of the Fusiliers has agreed to take the ceremony.' Tam squeezed her hand. 'And the Bracknalls have kindly offered to host the wedding tea party in their garden.'

Sophie was surprised. 'Bracknall who wouldn't let you come to meet me?'

Tam frowned, his thin face scored with lines in the sunlight.

'That was the wee Martini's decision, not Bracknall's. Besides, Bracknall is the chief of our division so it's a great honour that he's throwing us a party. Isn't that right, Boz?'

'Aye.' Boz grunted. He had hardly spoken since they'd left the train. Sophie glanced at him but he just smiled and looked away.

'They've also insisted on you staying under their roof until we're married,' Tam said.

Sophie was dismayed. 'But I thought you said I'd be staying at the same hotel as you and Boz.'

'Edith Bracknall said that was out of the question.' Tam shrugged. 'They take chaperoning very seriously out here, and she thinks it's very hard on you coming out on your own without family. You'll be much better looked after at the Bs than among us crowd of bachelors.'

Shortly afterwards, they dropped off Boz at the Cecil Hotel where he and Tam were boarding, and then turned south into the civil cantonment; a grid of wide, straight streets and orderly lines of bungalows set in pretty gardens.

'The army cantonment is further out,' Tam explained. 'Once you're settled in, we can send out some visiting cards, get you introduced to a few folk. Though by the sounds of it, you've been making plenty of friends on the way. It doesn't surprise me.' He smiled. 'You're the sort of lassie I can take anywhere and you'll find something to talk about. The Bracknalls will love you. And December is a good time to be in Lahore – so many important people come to town for Christmas Week and there's lots of socialising – that's what the Bracknalls say.'

They pulled up outside a large bungalow in Mayo Gardens with a huge sweep of veranda around three sides and tidy lawns under feathery trees bordered by regimented beds of pansies and chrysanthemums.

Edith Bracknall, a small, attractive woman about twenty years senior to Sophie, appeared on the veranda and beckoned to them.

'Do come in, so lovely to meet you, you're every bit as pretty as Tam said. Has the journey been awful? You must be longing to get out of your travelling clothes. I've had the servants boil up hot water – and the iron's been heated up too if you want to press your clothes – people new to India don't realise how much cotton crumples, I always wear crêpe de chine on trains. Tam, you sit and have an iced drink while I show Miss Logan to her room.' She waved an instruction to her bearer.

Sophie could hardly get a word in edgeways as she followed her hostess through a cluttered central sitting room, high white walls covered in dark hangings and landscapes of English countryside in heavy gilt frames.

'Mr B and I have our rooms to the right,' Edith continued. 'You're in the guest room on the left. It's our son Henry's room but he's at school in Cheltenham. Been there three years now so I'm used to him being away. That's a photograph of him in his cricket whites. Handsome boy, isn't he?'

Sophie nodded. He had the same heart-shaped face and dark hair as his mother.

'It wouldn't be fair to keep him in India,' Edith said, 'not with him being an only child. He needs boys around him of his own age – friends for life – that's what my husband says about boarding school.'

Sophie saw the fleeting sadness in the woman's face and then the bright smile returned. 'Your bathroom is through that door – not what you're used to at home no doubt – no flush lavatory I'm afraid, just the thunderbox, as we call it. The sweeper will empty it when you're out. And it's a tin bath but there's endless hot water.'

'It's fine, I'm used to—'

'Ah, that sounds like your baggage arriving. I'll have it brought straight in – you'll want to unpack and rest up – I'll chase Tam away. He can come back for supper of course – such a fine young man – you've chosen very well. Mr B thinks Tam has a good career ahead of himself – as long as he doesn't rock the boat and try to teach his superiors to suck eggs as it were. Best way to get on in India is to listen to the wise words and example of the men who have been running the country for years. But Tam is a sensible chap and knows what's expected.

And with you at his side he'll thrive, I'm sure. You play tennis and ride, I hear?'

'Tennis yes—'

'Splendid, we'll fix up a game of doubles at the Gym this week.'

'Gym?'

'Gymkhana Club of course,' Edith said. 'Mr B is proposing Tam for membership but we can sign you in for tennis as our guests in the meantime. It's the best club in Lahore by far. Army top brass like to use it too.'

Edith bustled out, ordering her house servants to fetch and carry. Sophie hardly had time to say goodbye to Tam before he was being dispatched from the house.

'I'll come back after I've done the office *dak*,' he promised.

Sophie retreated to her room, head pounding, and lay down on the narrow bed marooned in the centre of the bedroom under mosquito nets and promptly fell asleep.

***

She heard Bracknall before she set eyes on him; shouting orders at his servants in a cut-glass accent. Emerging washed and changed into her new red dress, Sophie was plied with a large whisky and soda by Tam's boss, who swept her with an appreciative look.

'Delighted to meet you, Miss Logan.' He was as tall as Boz with an athletic build, thick hair going grey at the temples and pale blue eyes.

'It's so kind of you to have me to stay.' Sophie smiled nervously.

That evening over dinner, Tam was keen to talk to his superior about the shortage of labour in clearing land for planting down in Changa Manga.

'It's tough work,' said Tam, 'and we're really stretched. Do you think we could borrow some labourers from the Farms Department? I've just met Percy Porter today and he seems like a decent man who might help us.'

'Don't want to be beholden to the Agrics, Telfer,' Bracknall was dismissive. 'You'll have to go and talk to the chap at the Criminal Tribes Bureau. See if he can rustle up some crim families as cheaply as possible.'

'But the crims are unreliable in my opinion. I caught one smoking in Compt 21 – the whole place could have gone up in flames.'

'If it happens again, flog 'em.'

'What are crims?' Sophie asked.

'Certain tribes are designated as criminal,' Tam explained, 'because they have criminal tendencies. They're restricted in where they can go or the work they can do—'

'Telfer, I really don't think this is a suitable topic of conversation for the ladies,' Bracknall cut him off. Tam's pale face flushed; Sophie could tell he was holding on to his temper. Her dislike of Tam's boss increased.

'Sound like Border Reivers,' she joked, trying to come to Tam's defence. 'My family are descended—'

'Tomorrow, Tam,' Edith cut in, 'I'm going to take your sweet fiancée shopping in the bazaar so she can choose some furniture for your married quarters. Harnam Das in Anarkali is much cheaper than Mohammed Hayal in the Mall, and it's better to rent your household goods rather than buy at this stage in your career – you can be sent off at a moment's notice and there's enough packing up to do without having to worry about what to do with the furniture. Wouldn't you agree, Henry?'

'You're always right on the domestic front, my dear.' Sophie was unnerved by the way he kept staring at her when others were talking to him.

'You can treat yourself to one or two items, of course,' Edith continued. 'The Elgin Mills have beautiful blue durries and they're practical as floor rugs – you can have them washed and they roll up easily and don't weigh too much – perfect for trekking.'

'I thought I would take Sophie over to view the bungalow in Davis Road tomorrow,' Tam said.

'Of course you must,' Edith agreed, 'but you'll be busy during the day and we girls can get to know each other. I find Bijja Mals is best for crockery – as long as you are prepared to barter. Or we can go to Ram Chand's—'

'I'd rather you didn't,' her husband interrupted.

'Oh? Why is that, Henry dearest?'

'There's a rumour he's been involved with troublemakers.'

'Oh my! What sort of troublemakers?'

'The kind of blackguards who stirred up native troops in the war, trying to get them to revolt.'

'Do you mean Ghadaris?' Tam asked.

Bracknall shot him a look. 'What do you know about them?'

'Nothing really. It's just something we boys discussed on the boat coming out – the 'free Hindustan' movement – there was a debate at uni' before we left. Rafi knew a bit about it.'

'Rafi Khan?' Bracknall frowned.

'Yes. His family are here in Lahore – one of his brothers is a bit of a hothead by all accounts – but Rafi's been out of the country for so long he doesn't really know what he's been up to.'

'Well, Khan had better take care,' Bracknall warned. 'Anyone found being involved with the Ghadar Party or any other such treasonable outfit will be executed as quickly as those war traitors were.'

Sophie could see by Tam's look that he was as taken aback as she was by the harsh warning. She'd never heard of the Ghadar Party.

'Sophie,' Edith said quickly, 'we'll retire to the veranda while the men have a port and cigar, shall we? And I'll tell you some more about the shops in town.'

Sophie threw a look of longing at Tam; he gave a tiny shrug. She knew he didn't like either port or cigars. He sat there looking ill and perspiring under the electric light. Her worry for him mounted; she hoped his overbearing boss wouldn't keep needling him. The sooner they got into their own home and they could shut the door on the world outside, the better.

Chapter 17

Too tired to sleep, Sophie sat up and wrote a letter to Tilly.

'. . . I know Mrs Bracknall means well but I don't know if I can get through three more days of incessant chatter and advice. I think I might be driven to running out of the house stark naked and screaming like a banshee if Mrs B carries on with her outpourings. She probably wouldn't even notice, or, if she did, she would run after me with a blanket from the Elgin Mills and tell me to wrap it round me in case I caught "winter sniffles".

'Do I sound very mean and ungrateful? She's really quite sweet (in the way that we used to be sweet but irritating at ten years old) and I like her better than the Big B. He's a cold fish and full of his own importance. Every time Tam suggests some forestry improvement or new idea, B slaps him down like he's dealing with an over-eager puppy. My heart bleeds for my beloved man and I can see the frustration all over his face. But he's going to have to learn to be patient or end up on a collision course with his boss. Tam's not been well since he got here – keeps catching bouts of fever, Boz says – and to be honest I didn't recognise him at the station, it was quite a shock.

'Tilly, you must write to me as soon as you get to Assam and tell me all about it. By then we will both be planters' wives! I hope you and the baby-to-be are doing well. I know you are as eager to get started on married life as I am. In four days' time, I'll be Mrs Telfer of the Trees. I'm so excited at the thought of seeing your brother Johnny again too and thrilled that he has agreed to give me away in marriage. He's due in Lahore the day before the wedding, Tam says. He and Helena will be staying at the Sunnyview Hotel – and yes, I will write immediately (or maybe after a day or two!) to let you know what my impressions are of your new sister-in-law. We are to travel back with them after the wedding for a few days of honeymoon at Flashman's Hotel in Rawalpindi. If the weather allows, we might get up to the Khyber Pass, which would be a thrill, but just to be alone together at last will be all the honeymoon I want.'

Sophie finished off the letter and propped it against a noisy clock on the bedside table, ready to send.

The next day went swiftly, Sophie relishing her trip to the lively shops around the Mall, entering into the bartering and coming away with a set of dinner plates in green and blue glaze, table mats, a brass ashtray and a solid storage chest called a *yak dan.*

'For all your best dresses,' Edith Bracknall advised, 'so that the white ants don't make a feast of your glad rags.'

She arranged to have the purchases sent on ahead while she took Sophie for tea and sandwiches at Nedous Hotel.

'Nedous is nicer in the spring,' she said. 'They have military bands playing in the garden. Not that we really get spring in Lahore – it just goes from warm to wretchedly hot to unbearably hot and wet. But then you must know about the climate, having lived here as a child?'

'I was in Assam,' Sophie replied, 'so we never got the extreme heat, but I do remember the rains and how the ground disappeared under a blanket of steam when the monsoon finally came and the tea bushes seemed to sprout higher in front of your very eyes.'

'I go to Simla as soon as it starts to get unpleasant here,' Edith said. 'After tiffin we'll go to the Arts and Crafts Depot – you might find some cheap rugs for your floors – and there's always something quaint you can pick up for next to nothing – a papier mâché cigarette box or a mirror. It's good to patronise the Punjabi craftsmen so they can make an honest living, don't you think?'

That afternoon, Sophie saw tantalising glimpses of the old part of the city – tall buildings with ornate balconies and stucco arches peeping over trees and the dome of a large mosque glinting in the mellow sunshine – but Edith Bracknall was astonished she should want to go there.

'It's smelly and dirty like all native towns and the children pester you for money if you so much as glance in their direction. The bazaars around the Mall are as far as you want to go – the shopkeepers know that you don't want to be pestered so they keep the beggars at bay. But if you want to do some sightseeing I can certainly arrange that. You must see Kim's gun and the armoury – if you like that sort of thing – and of course there are the Shalimar Gardens – though they're not at their best at this time of year.'

'Can we call in at the forest office on the way home?' Sophie asked. 'I'd like to see where Tam works.'

'We don't want to disturb the men at their work, dear. I'll take you over to Davis Road later and send a chit to Tam to meet us there. I'd like to take a look at your new home too – make sure the agent isn't taking advantage of Tam's inexperience in such things. And while we're there we can drop off some of your calling cards to let people know you've arrived.'

'I don't have any printed yet,' Sophie said.

'Oh, I'm sure Tam will have sorted that out. I'll tell him to bring some along. And you really should be wearing your *topee* – that straw hat is very stylish, I'm sure, but it won't protect your head from the heat. All the new arrivals make the mistake of thinking they won't get heatstroke in the winter. We don't want you fainting on your wedding day, my girl.'

By the time they got to the bungalow in Davis Road, the sun was already dipping. Tam was waiting impatiently with the agent who introduced himself as Jit Singh. Tam seemed distracted and kept taking off his hat to mop his brow. His shirt was dripping and stained dark with sweat.

'I thought you were never coming,' he muttered.

'So did I.' Sophie gave a rueful smile.

'Oh dear,' Edith Bracknall said, leading the way inside, 'it's really just half a bungalow. I can see that over the wall is already occupied.'

'Yes, madam,' said Mr Singh, 'but it is very spacious for one couple.'

'It's very stuffy, Tam,' she said, walking around and sniffing the air. 'Are there no electric fans?'

'These bungalows are very light and airy with the aid of a *punkah*.' Mr Singh pointed at the large cloth fan that hung like a huge sail from the ceiling. Sophie was immediately reminded of the rhythmic creaking of the *punkah* being pulled by an old man in her childhood home. What was his name? Sunil Ram; that was it. Though she had always called him the Sunny Man.

'You must insist on at least two electric fans being installed, Tam,' said Edith. 'One in the sitting room and one in your bedroom as a minimum.' She turned to Jit Singh. 'And you will have the whole place spruced up with phenyl and whitewash – they can't move in here when it's in such a filthy state.'

'Madam, it has been whitewashed—'

'You've got two days left in which to get it sorted, Mr Singh.' Then she berated Tam. 'Really, you shouldn't have left all this to the last minute.'

Tam's jaw clenched. 'It's not ideal,' he admitted, 'but I've been down at Changa Manga for weeks.'

Edith Bracknall was hurrying outside again and peering across at the separate servants' quarters. 'I presume the compound will accommodate at least a cook, a bearer and a sweeper. You can share our *mali* to begin with; the garden isn't big and you'll be spending much of your time down in Changa Manga.'

She caught sight of a man through the fence walking up the pathway to the other half of the bungalow. He was smartly dressed in a suit and carrying an umbrella over his arm; he waved. Tam and Sophie raised a hand in greeting.

'Who is he?' Edith demanded.

'Dr Pir,' said Jit Singh. 'He's the principal of the Islamic College.'

'They can't have a coloured man here,' she protested. 'They're practically sharing the same house.'

The agent looked embarrassed. 'Dr Pir is a very respectable gentleman.'

'That's not the point,' she snapped, 'he's not a suitable neighbour for the Telfers. He'll have to go.'

'He's signed a lease, madam. I'm sorry, but it is all legal and above board.'

Sophie thought Bracknall's wife was going to explode; she was puce in the face.

‘I’m sure it will be fine,’ Sophie intervened. ‘And it’s too late to change things now. We just want a home to move into by Thursday, don’t we, Tam?’

‘Yes,’ Tam said, his look uncomfortable. ‘And I’ve heard Pir is a sound man. The old *munshi* who is teaching us Urdu at Changa Manga speaks highly of him.’

It suddenly struck Sophie that Tam had known all along whom their neighbour was going to be. With a smile of encouragement, she moved closer and slipped her hand into his. It was clammy.

Edith Bracknall spluttered something about the younger generation and led the way back to the waiting *tonga*.

Tam turned to the flustered agent. ‘I’ll have the furniture delivered tomorrow. The paintwork seems fine to me and electric fans can be installed later. I just want to be able to carry my bride in here on Thursday and have somewhere to put her.’

‘Yes, sahib.’ Jit Singh’s round face broke into a grin of relief. ‘All will be arranged.’

‘Thank you, Mr Singh,’ Sophie said, her cheeks pink at Tam’s allusion to their wedding night.

That night, the Bracknalls threw a dinner party at the gym club for the young couple and invited some of their friends from the Indian civil service. It was a palatial but forbidding building with large rooms for dining and dancing, reading and smoking. Tam looked handsome in formal evening dress and appeared to have shaken off his earlier liverish feeling.

‘We’re going to meet some of the lads at Stiffles later,’ he murmured to her. ‘They have a good dance floor and I can’t wait to get my arms around you, lassie.’

‘How are we going to shake off Mrs B as our chaperone?’ Sophie smirked.

‘Leave that to me.’

After dinner, Tam announced that he was taking Sophie to meet his Christian Science friends in Golf Road for tea and a reading. He wanted to introduce her before the wedding. He would deliver her back before midnight.

Sophie was spluttering with laughter as they escaped down the steps of the club and flagged down a cycle-rickshaw.

'Tea and C.S.! What if some of them decide to go dancing too?'

Tam snorted with laughter. 'Well, it won't be to Stiffles. They allow Indians in there.'

The nightclub was lively and the marble floor crowded with dancers in a dazzling array of shimmering evening dresses.

Boz and Rafi were sharing a table with two Scots nurses from the Medical College; both men stood to greet her. Sophie was light-headed from wine at dinner and the excitement of having escaped the Bracknalls.

'I can't tell you how good it is to see you both.' She grinned, ignoring their proffered hands and kissing them lightly on the cheek.

Tam waved away their offers to buy drinks and took Sophie straight on to the dance floor, pulling her into his arms. They spun around, oblivious to the elbows of other dancers, heady with their daring escape.

'When we're married,' Tam declared, 'we will come dancing every night – Faletti's or Stiffles – and we'll dine at Lorang's and throw dinner parties in our tiny bungalow.'

'And a junior forester's pay will stretch to all that, will it?' Sophie teased.

'Topped up by a bit of army pay I'm due,' Tam replied. 'I'm attached as a reservist to the battery at Dalhousie in the hills, so not only do I get a bit of extra money, but you can escape the hot season down here when I do my annual training.'

'You've got it all worked out,' Sophie said, impressed.

'Oh yes,' Tam was serious, 'I've planned our whole future. And tomorrow I'm going to buy you that wedding ring we should have got in Bombay. Rafi knows a good jeweller in the old quarter; he's offered to take us.'

'That's exciting. I wanted to have a look around the old city today, but Mrs B was horrified at the idea.'

'I have to go out to oversee some thinning work at Tera tomorrow morning – it's just a few miles east of here – but I'll polish off the office work in the early afternoon, then we'll be free for a late lunch and buying the ring. Sound fine?'

‘Sounds grand,’ Sophie said, kissing him quickly on the lips.

Tam tired quickly. When someone bumped into him, he winced and limped back to the table. Sophie tried to look at his leg, but he brushed her off and told her not to fuss, his good humour evaporating. Shortly afterwards, they said their goodnights, arranging to meet Rafi at the Cecil Hotel the following afternoon, and Tam dropped her back at Mayo Gardens. The Bracknalls were still up, sipping whiskies and soda by an open fire, but Sophie feigned sleepiness and went straight to her room. She lay in bed listening to the murmur of their voices and wondered if she and Tam would be as content in each other’s company in twenty years’ time?

***

‘Tam’s no well; he’s laid up in bed at the Cecil with tummy trouble.’

Boz was waiting on the veranda when Sophie and Edith Bracknall returned from delivering cards of introduction to the British fraternity around the cantonment. Her hostess had drawn up a list of suitable people from Sir Edward and Lady Maclagan at Government House down to the Secretary of the annual Horse Show.

‘Oh, dear me,’ said Edith, ‘poor boy. He really has had rotten luck since coming out to India, hasn’t he? The climate doesn’t seem to suit him at all.’

‘I must go and see him,’ Sophie said at once.

‘I don’t think that would help in the least bit,’ Edith contradicted. ‘You can hardly go and see him in bed – not before you are husband and wife.’

‘But he’s ill and I want to see him.’

Boz said, ‘Tam says you’re no to worry – he just canna’ go far from the thunderbox just now.’

Edith sniffed. ‘Perhaps the dinner was a bit rich at the club last night. I’ll send you back with some liver salts, Mr Boswell. Tam must rest up or else he won’t be fit for his wedding day.’

'But we were to buy the ring this afternoon,' Sophie said, her concern mixed with disappointment.

'Tam's asked me to take you instead,' said Boz. 'He'll settle with the jeweller as soon as he's on his feet.'

'Well,' Edith sucked in her breath, 'it's really not convenient for me to come with you this afternoon – I want to talk over the menu for the wedding tea with my cook – there's so much to arrange.'

'That's fine,' Sophie said quickly, 'Boz and Rafi will look after me; Mr Bracknall can vouch for them both.'

Edith looked undecided. Boz put on a grave face. 'I'll tak' personal responsibility for Miss Logan. Time is pressing and it would be an awfu' shame if Tam had no ring to put on her finger the day after tomorrow.'

'Very well,' she gave in, 'but have her back before dark.'

As soon as they reached the Cecil to rendezvous with Rafi, Sophie insisted on going up to see Tam. She found him grey-faced and listless, lying under blankets with the blinds drawn.

'You shouldn't have come.' He sighed. 'I hate you to see me like this.'

'Have you been seen by a doctor?' she asked, putting a hand to his forehead. It felt hot and waxy.

'I don't need a doctor,' he said in irritation. 'It's just a stomach upset.'

'It might be more than that. Do you have a headache too?'

He pushed her hand away. 'I've been neglecting my Science – my body's out of sorts, that's all. I just need a bit of positive thought and prayer.'

'It's not a sign of weakness to take medicine as well,' Sophie said in exasperation.

'It's a sign of my feeble faith,' Tam muttered.

Sophie ran a finger down his cheek, amazed at his stubbornness. 'If prayer doesn't get you up on your feet by tomorrow, I'm sending in the doctor. Agreed?'

He gave a weak grunt. 'Agreed, Nurse Logan.' She leaned over and kissed his hot forehead. As she retreated to the door, he called out in a croaky voice, 'Sorry, lassie; I promise I'll make it up to you.'

'Just get better, that's all I want.' She blew him a kiss and left.

***

Rafi helped Sophie into a *tonga* and instructed the driver in his own language. Boz climbed in the other side and Sophie sat between the two young foresters, her eyes wide with curiosity as they left the wide streets of British Lahore and ventured into the old city. As the streets narrowed around them, the buildings grew taller, their style Moorish but embellished with cupolas and elaborate ironwork. The afternoon light glowed on houses of lemon yellow and salmon pink, their white shuttered windows and doors still shut against the heat. Open stalls were selling garish arrays of sweetmeats, while bubbling vats of fat sizzled with spicy-smelling dumplings.

She plied Rafi with questions: how old were the houses? What was the local speciality? Where did his family live? Could she see inside the mosque? He laughed and said he didn't know the answers to most of her questions.

'I know more about the history of Edinburgh than Lahore,' he admitted with a rueful smile.

'You must at least know where your family live,' Sophie challenged.

'Yes,' Rafi said, 'I haven't forgotten that.' But he didn't elaborate. Leaning forward, he said something to the driver, and a few moments later they had stopped outside a large emporium. 'Here we are at Bhagat's.'

'It doesn't look like a jeweller's,' Sophie said, gazing at the array of china and linen, water pipes and inlaid tables crammed in the entrance way.

'Bhagat sells everything,' Rafi assured, 'but he has an eye for precious stones and his metalworkers are the best in the Punjab.'

Sophie fingered the modest engagement ring that Tam had given her – a single small diamond.

'Well, we don't need anything grand,' she said. 'Just a simple band will do.'

Rafi introduced them to Mr Bhagat, a tall, pale-skinned man with sparse grey hair who welcomed them and took them to a comfortable sitting room where tea was served in delicate green-tinted glasses. Trays of rings were laid out in front of Sophie and she tried them on for size while the men chatted in English about the forthcoming polo matches now that Hodgson's Horse were to be posted to Lahore. To Sophie's surprise, the jeweller asked Rafi if he still played.

'Not since I left the army,' said Rafi.

'But your father still keeps a fine stable?'

'I'm sure he does.' Rafi pulled out his cigarette case and offered it around. 'But there's little call for a thoroughbred down in Changa Manga. Boz and I ride around on bicycles most of the time.'

'Aye, or a lame grey mare.' Boz laughed. 'If we can beg one from the lads at the Remount.'

'Is that the horse depot where Tam plays tennis?' Sophie asked.

'Yes, if you can call a couple of old soldiers, a handful of old nags and a lame dog a Remount,' Rafi said through a gauze of smoke.

'Good.' Sophie smiled. 'I want to learn to ride properly.'

'A lassie who can handle herself on an old motorcycle,' said Boz, 'will have no problem with the Remount horses, eh, Rafi?'

'None at all.' Rafi smiled.

Sophie chose a thin band of rose gold and Tam's friends bought her an opal necklace as their wedding present to her.

'It's beautiful.' Sophie was touched by the men's insistence on buying it. 'But shouldn't you be buying something for Tam instead?'

'The black opal suits you to perfection, Miss Logan,' Mr Bhagat approved.

'And Tam can admire it on you,' said Rafi.

Sophie blushed with pleasure. 'Thank you.'

When they emerged from the shop it was late afternoon and the street was in shadow.

'Anyone else hungry?' asked Boz.

'The smells from these stalls are making me ravenous,' Sophie said. 'Let's buy some and take a picnic to the Shalimar Gardens – I haven't done any sightseeing yet.'

The men agreed and Rafi guided them to a stall where a toothless old man greeted him warmly and filled a dish with piping hot nuggets of vegetable pakora and meat-filled samosas. From another stall they bought almond biscuits, some lurid orange halva and a canister of tea.

In the Shalimar Gardens, next to a rectangular pond shimmering in golden afternoon light, Sophie pulled her mother's thin cashmere shawl from her handbag and laid it out for them to sit on.

'No dribbling hot fat on my only heirloom,' she warned.

The men took off their *topees* and the three of them tucked into the food with relish. Sophie noticed people looking askance at their picnic as they passed.

'They're worried you're going native.' Rafi grunted, wiping his mouth on the back of his hand and licking his fingers. His brown skin was almost glowing in the retreating sun. Sophie had an urge to lean forward and dab the oil from his chin – a chin that was already shadowed with the day's stubble. He caught her look. How had she not noticed that his eyes were not brown but a startling tawny green? Never before had she seen eyes quite like them, framed in dark lashes under thick black eyebrows. She felt a strange sensation in the pit of her stomach.

He gave a puzzled look. 'I didn't mean that you *are* going native. It was a joke.'

'Yes, of course,' Sophie struggled to speak over the quickening pulse in her throat, looking away swiftly.

Boz gave a belch of satisfaction. 'Sorry, Sophie.' He produced cigarettes. As the men smoked, she heard herself chattering inanely about her day's shopping with Edith Bracknall, trying to avoid staring at Rafi.

'Do you think we've time for a quick *chota peg* on the way home,' Boz suggested, 'before Mrs B sends out a search party for you?'

'I know just the place,' Rafi announced, extinguishing his cigarette butt between finger and thumb, and getting to his feet.

Sophie half hoped he would give her a helping hand, but it was Boz who helped her up. By *tonga*, Rafi took them back to the edge of the old city and led them through a wrought-iron gate, through a tiny courtyard and into a tall house. As he led them up three flights of stairs – ancient, creaking, uneven stairs of dark wood with mysterious doors set into the panelling – Sophie's apprehension grew. She threw a look at Boz but he shrugged and grinned, enjoying the surprise.

They emerged on to a roof terrace and Sophie caught her breath at the view. Across the rooftops stood the huge red stone mosque she had only glimpsed in the distance, glowing like fire in the setting sun. It seemed so close in the clear air that she felt she could reach out and touch one of the towering minarets.

'The Badshahi Masjid,' Rafi said, with a proud sweep of his hand. 'Built by Emperor Aurangzeb in the seventeenth century.'

'It's magnificent,' she gasped, 'isn't it, Boz?'

'Aye,' he agreed, 'it's nearly as bonny as St Giles in Edinburgh.'

Rafi laughed and told them to sit.

'So this is your family home?' Sophie asked.

'No,' Rafi said, 'I rent the top floor from a friend – didn't want to go back to the strictures of living under my parents' rule – I've been independent for too long.'

'Isn't that very un-Indian?'

He gave her a sharp look, then the usual relaxed smile returned. 'Very.'

They settled on to old cane chairs with faded cushions while he disappeared behind a curtain. Moments later he was back with three chipped cups and a bottle of whisky.

Boz whistled. 'Glen Livet? Ya beauty! Where did you get this?'

'From bonny Scotland, my dear Boswell.' Rafi grinned. 'Been keeping it for a special occasion.'

He poured out three drams, handed them round and proposed a toast. 'Let's drink to our poor friend Telfer on his sickbed and to his forthcoming marriage to the beautiful and adventurous Miss Logan.'

'To Tam and Sophie!' Boz said and knocked back his drink.

'Thank you,' Sophie said, flushing at the compliment, and raised her glass to them. 'And thank you for this,' she murmured, watching a huge pale moon steal into the deepening sky as the sun blazed orange. 'I'll never forget it.'

They fell silent while they sipped their drinks that tasted of Scotland and thought their own thoughts. Sophie was acutely aware of Rafi next to her – within a hand's reach – and it made her skin tingle. She shouldn't be thinking such thoughts (it was the sunset and whisky surely?) but she didn't want the moment to end.

Then the call to prayer came clear through the dusk, the air chilled and Rafi led them back downstairs. Fifteen minutes later – but a world away – Sophie was being deposited back on a leafy cantonment drive and chivvied by Edith Bracknall to hurry up and dress for dinner. 'Roast beef and ginger sponge pudding,' she announced. 'Mr B's favourite and I knew you'd be hungry having missed afternoon tea.'

Chapter 18

Sophie stood shivering in her flimsy silk wedding dress (paid for by the kind Watsons) at the cathedral door under an umbrella produced by Johnny Watson. It had been pouring all morning and her long white veil that trailed along the ground was soaked and speckled with mud splashes.

'They'll be here any minute,' Johnny encouraged. 'I saw Tam at tiffin; he was in good spirits.'

She was thankful that Tilly's level-headed, cheerful older brother was there to steady her nerves. Tears were prickling behind her eyelids at this latest setback; the late arrival of the groom and his best man, Boz. There weren't many guests in the church: a handful of foresters including Rafi (she didn't want to think about Rafi) with Scott and McGinty who had travelled down from Rawalpindi, Tam's immediate boss Martins (a small, fussy man with protruding teeth), the Bracknalls with some of their friends from the gym club whom Tam had played at tennis, and his Christian Science friends, the Floyds. On the bride's side there was only Johnny's buxom, horsey wife Helena and the Porters, whom Sophie had invited two days ago. She knew they were all watching the clock and wondering at the delay.

Her worry had been about Tam's health; not that he wouldn't turn up. What if he'd got cold feet and jilted her at the altar? She was thousands of miles from home – except that she no longer had a home – a half bungalow in Davis Road was her only shelter in the world now, and only if Tam turned up and married her today. She fiddled with her precious elephant-heads bracelet for luck.

A *tonga* stopped in the road and two men in morning coats clambered out and ran up the path.

'Tam!' Sophie almost wept with relief.

'Sorry, lassie,' he wheezed, shaking rain from his collar, 'the bloody car didn't turn up. Boz's fault. See you inside.'

Boz gave an apologetic look and followed his friend into the dark interior. Johnny took her arm and tucked it firmly into his.

'Come on, Sophie' – he smiled – 'let's show them how brave and bonny a Scottish bride can be.'

Her eyes blurred with tears at his kind words and she clung on to him gratefully as they marched down the long aisle to the small group of well-wishers clustered at the front, her mind filling with regret that neither her parents nor beloved Auntie Amy and Cousin Tilly were there to see the day.

They sang 'All People that on Earth do Dwell' and Padre Rennie said some appropriate words that Sophie hardly registered. When it came to making their vows, she could not control her shaking limbs – from both cold and nervousness – and her teeth chattered as she spoke her lines. But when Tam slipped the ring on to her finger and gave her a wide loving smile, her heart leapt and a flush of warmth flooded through her. They were going to be all right.

Tam was struck by her beauty; the huge solemn brown eyes fixed on him and fleshy pink lips trembling in emotion, the simple lacy headband holding in place her bobbed blonde hair, the swell of her young woman's body under the thin layers of soft silk. All the frustrations and doubts of the past months dissolved as he drank in her loveliness. Many times, in dark moments of the night, he had questioned the path his life was taking: India, forestry and marriage to an Edinburgh girl he barely knew. It hadn't been the original plan. But Nancy's refusal to marry him had put paid to that dream and he must put it behind him once and for all.

It was the bouts of illness that had left him fatigued and depressed, and made him doubt why he was there. Yet illness was an illusion; a state of imbalance that could just as easily be corrected by thinking himself well again. He just needed to be stronger. When he took Sophie's long slender fingers in his hands and twisted on the wedding ring, he felt a surge of relief. She would give him the strength to tackle the demons that plagued his health; together with her, he would be twice as powerful.

***

‘I’ve known Cousin Sophie since she was a small girl coming to stay at our house in Newcastle,’ Johnny told the assembled guests, crammed into the Bracknalls’ parlour out of the cold December rain. ‘A bouncing ball of energy who never stopped talking or running about or asking nosey questions. I have a memory of Sophie sliding down the bannisters with her fair pigtails flying and not understanding why she got a smack from our old nanny for doing so. “Little girls don’t slide,” scolded Nanny. “But I’m an explorer,” wailed Sophie, “and this is the only way down the mountain!”’

Sophie covered her face in embarrassment as people around her laughed. She saw young Betty Porter clapping her hands in glee.

‘The house was always brighter and livelier for having our Scottish cousin to stay – even when I grew older and she and Tilly would pester me and my good friend Will Stock, she was always fun to have around.’

Johnny turned to look at Sophie. ‘I know it’s hard for my cousin not to have her beloved Auntie Amy here to see her married. Auntie Amy was a strong and remarkable lady who took it upon herself to bring Sophie up in Edinburgh after she was tragically orphaned. It’s in large part thanks to her that Sophie has grown from that brave wee girl into the beautiful and warm-hearted woman you see before you today, and I know Auntie Amy would have been so proud. Helena and I are the only ones of our family who are able to be here, but we represent them all when we wish Sophie and Tam the happiest of marriages together.’

Sophie’s eyes flooded with tears at Johnny’s tender words. He raised his glass and proposed a toast to the bride and groom.

‘To the bride and groom!’ the guests echoed, to the chinking of glass and china.

After that, the noise level rose as people’s glasses of champagne were refilled. Johnny, as her only male relative, had insisted on helping pay for the wedding tea party, but Sophie was astonished at the lavishness of the spread and the amount of champagne. She mingled among the guests. Helena came bounding to her side, large-limbed in a lilac suit and a matching hat perched on wavy brown hair.

'Don't know about you, but Johnny's words had me nearly in tears. I'm so happy to be a part of his family – you all sound so delightful – can't wait for us to go on leave and visit his mother and sisters in England.'

Sophie smiled. 'They all live in Scotland now. And they're longing to meet you too.'

'It's a shame Tilly couldn't have come on her way to Assam,' Helena said. 'I'm so looking forward to meeting her. I think she's Johnny's favourite. It's wonderful you've all ended up in old India.'

They chatted for a while about Helena's army upbringing and her passion for horses; she offered to take Sophie out riding while on honeymoon in Rawalpindi. 'Not that you'll want to spend much time with us old marrieds,' Helena said with a nudge.

Sophie tried to catch Tam's eye; she was keen now for the party to end and for them to be alone at last. But Tam and his forester friends were gathered in a corner drinking large whiskies and guffawing like schoolboys around Bracknall who was holding court. Only Rafi stood aloof watching them and sipping at his drink. It had annoyed Sophie how Edith Bracknall had deliberately snubbed Rafi, ignoring his attempts to introduce himself and turning to speak to Jimmy Scott instead.

Sophie was grateful for the generous way the Bracknalls had taken her into their home these past few days, but she was determined they would have as little to do with them socially as possible. Bracknall was Tam's boss and deserved respect, but that didn't mean they had to be at the Bracknalls' beck and call, or put up with Mrs B's petty snobbery.

Finally, Boz extracted Tam from the group. 'Come on, Telfer, there's a taxi and a wife waiting.'

There was much handshaking and kissing of cheeks; Johnny arranged that they would meet at the Sunnyview Hotel in the morning for the journey north together. The rain had stopped and a watery sun was trying to break through the evening clouds.

Sophie sat close to Tam on the worn green leather seats of the open car, which were still damp despite the driver's attempts to wipe them dry. They waved goodbye and a few minutes later they were rounding the corner into Davis Road.

Tam's servants – Hafiz the bearer, Sunbar the cook and a couple of others that Sophie had not met – stood waiting to greet them with smiles and garlands of marigolds.

'Welcome, Telfer Sahib, Telfer Memsahib,' they nodded and hung the garlands around their employers' necks.

'Thank you.' Sophie smiled in delight, nodding in return.

There was a fire crackling merrily in the grate of the high-ceilinged parlour and another in their bedroom. Tam left Sophie to change out of her wedding dress.

'I'll use my dressing room,' he said, straining to loosen the studs of his collar. He looked suddenly exhausted.

Sophie hung up her dress on the back of the door where she could see it and remember the day, and pulled on slacks and a woollen jumper, still chilled from the rain. She noticed with a lurch that one of the servants had laid out their nightclothes on the paisley-pattern quilt in readiness for bed. Returning to the parlour, she asked Hafiz to make a pot of tea and sank into a chintz-covered armchair. She could feel the springs beneath the upholstery, but was too tired to find it uncomfortable.

Tea appeared, but Tam did not. Sophie wished they had a gramophone so that she could have put on soothing music. She was aware of watchful eyes. Two cups of tea later, Sophie got up. Hafiz appeared from nowhere.

'Do – do you think you could see if Mr Telfer needs a hand?' she asked, feeling foolish. Tam was unused to drinking whisky and Bracknall had been pouring it down him all afternoon.

Hafiz returned. 'Sahib is sleeping.' His look was both amused and apologetic.

She followed him back to Tam's dressing room, a small box room perhaps meant for a child, with its own separate bathroom. There lay her husband of a few hours, curled up on a rush mat, morning coat and trousers discarded but shirt still on, snoring lightly. He looked peaceful and boyish and she wondered how he could sleep so easily on a hard floor and scratchy matting.

'Shall I put Sahib to bed?' Hafiz asked.

Sophie hesitated. With a snort of amusement and frustration, she shook her head.

'Don't wake him; just cover him with some warm blankets.' She was tempted to ask the bearer not to mention any of this but knew there was little point. Before sunrise, it would be the talk of the compounds all around that Tam Telfer had spent his wedding night on the floor of his dressing room while his eager bride spent the night alone and virginal in the chilly marriage bed.

Chapter 19

It took a gruelling day of driving on the Grand Trunk Road, with three punctures and frequent stops for Tam to squat behind trees, to reach the northern Punjabi town.

At their picnic lunch spot, Tam vomited up his egg sandwiches and by the time they reached Rawalpindi, his fever was raging again.

'You're burning up,' Sophie said in alarm.

'You can't stay at a hotel in your condition,' Helena was firm, 'you must come to us in the lines.'

'It's just the change in altitude,' Tam said in irritation.

'It's nothing to do with altitude,' Johnny was short. 'You're a sick man. I'm going to run some blood tests, and give you something for the pain and squitters and bring down your temperature.'

They drove straight to the cantonment, Tam fretting about the cost of the Flashman Hotel that was now going to waste.

'I'll send round a chit explaining,' Helena promised.

After that, Tam made no protest and was happy to crawl under the sheets of a hastily made-up bed in the Watsons' spare room, even submitting to the 'filthy medicines' that Johnny insisted he take. A fire was lit but he threw off the covers, drenched in sweat. Sophie sat by his side, wiping his face and neck with a damp cloth, anxious and tearful.

'Oh, lassie,' he croaked, 'I'm so sorry. What a terrible start to our married life.'

'Hush, Tam,' she whispered, 'we've got all our lives ahead together.'

Finally he fell into a fitful sleep and Helena coaxed her out of the room.

'Come and have a nightcap – let the medicine take its course.'

'He sees taking it as a failure.' Sophie sighed, accepting the whisky and soda Johnny offered.

'I hope you don't,' her cousin said sharply.

'I understand why he thinks that way,' Sophie defended, 'given his strong belief in Christian Science.'

'He has a temperature of a hundred and five, dysentery and possible malaria or worse. He's a fool not to have gone to a doctor earlier.'

Sophie swallowed down tears. 'I wanted him to see a doctor two days ago but he seemed to recover.'

'Fever is like that, flaring up if it's not treated.'

'It's not your fault,' Helena said at once. 'Johnny, don't be so hard on the poor girl.'

'Sorry, I didn't mean to be.' He went to her and pulled her into a hug. 'We'll make him better again so stop worrying and drink your dram.'

That night, Tam tossed and sweated in their shared bed, babbling incoherently and crying out. At one point he sat up rigid, staring straight ahead in terror at some unseen horror. Sophie tried to calm him but he struck out at her as if she would do him harm, catching a blow on her temple. After that she got up and wrapped herself in a blanket, sitting by the window until the dawn light seeped under the curtains, Tam's ragged breathing mingling with the sounds of early birds and the creak of water from the outside well as the servants stirred.

Sophie dressed then went out on to the veranda in the freezing air to watch the sun strike the distant snow-capped mountains and was filled with a sudden calm. She had a vague memory of someone – her father? – pointing out the Himalayan peaks to her as a child, though where that was she could not say. It had been her hope that she and Tam would visit Murree in the foothills to see where her own parents had honeymooned but she knew that would not happen now. All she wanted was for Tam to shake off the fever that bedevilled him and to regain his former strength. From first meeting him at the forestry camp in the Scottish Borders, she had been struck by his energy and zest for life; this man wracked by illness and lethargy was a stranger to her. Boz's words about Tam's war injuries came back to trouble her. *He's not the same man since the gas attack . . .*

She pushed them from her mind. Tam was going to get better and she would stick by him no matter what happened; that's what they had promised to do for each other at their wedding.

Concerned by Tam's blood results, Johnny called in the civil surgeon, McManners, to diagnose his fever. He had been on a massive dose of quinine for several days but the fever had not broken. Tam suffered blinding headaches and his limbs felt as if they were being crushed in a vice. At night his temperature soared and he could keep down no food.

At times he did not seem to recognise Sophie and called her Nanny, crying out for her. Only when she lay down beside him and held his head on her breast, stroking away the horrors that plagued his fevered brain, did he become calm.

To her distress, Sophie overheard Johnny and McManners having a tense consultation on the veranda.

'I think it's dengue fever,' said the civil surgeon. 'No amount of quinine will cure him of that.'

'My God, poor Telfer,' Johnny gasped. 'What should we do?'

'By rights the poor devil shouldn't be alive – not judging by his blood tests – but he's got a will of steel. All we can do is keep him comfortable and try to bring his temperature down. The rest is up to God – and that brave girl he's just married – she might be the only one he'll respond to.'

'Oh, dear Sophie,' Johnny sighed, 'she'll not give up on him without a fight.'

After that, Sophie refused to leave Tam's side, terrified that he might slip away at any moment. She sat up through the long nights, bathing his aching limbs, alternately wrapping him in blankets then cooling him down, as he complained of being either too cold or too hot. She sang to him and told him stories like a child, the sound of her voice appearing to soothe him. She helped change him, staring at his vulnerable naked body, wondering if their marriage would ever be consummated, and then chided herself for such selfish thoughts.

Early one morning, she was startled out of a dose by a rattling sound.

'Tam?' she gasped, at once noticing the change in his breathing. She had heard frightening tales of 'the death rattle'. She seized his hand; it was cooling. '*Tam!*'

He winced in pain.

She relaxed her grip. 'Speak to me, Tam!'

'Can – can – I,' he panted, 'have a wee sip of water, lassie?'

'Of course,' she answered, her heart leaping to hear him speak. Quickly she fetched a glass of cooled boiled water from the washstand and helped him drink, supporting his heavy head with the back of her hand.

He sank back from the effort. 'Thank you.'

Sophie put down the glass and sat on the side of the bed, holding his hand. Could this be the fever breaking at last?

He tried to focus on her with glassy eyes. 'Where am I?'

'Johnny and Helena's house.'

'Who?'

'My cousin, Dr Johnny Watson. He gave me away at our wedding, remember? We're at their home in Pindi.'

'Pindi?' Tam frowned. 'Why . . .?'

'We're on our . . . No never mind, we're just visiting.' Sophie smiled.

'I feel as weak as a lamb,' Tam whispered. 'How long have I been like this?'

'Five days.'

Tam's eyes seemed to clear. 'Pindi. Is it our honeymoon?'

Sophie nodded.

'God, what a useless husband I am.' He turned his head away so that she would not see the tears that welled in his eyes.

Sophie leaned over and kissed his forehead. 'No you're not. You've been fighting for your life like a tiger these past few days.'

'Have you been with me the whole time?' he croaked.

She nodded, her throat tightening. How scared she had been at nearly losing him!

'Now' – Sophie smiled through her tears – 'can you manage something to eat? A little soup? You haven't had anything for days.'

He nodded. 'Soup would be nice.'

She stood up and hurried to the door, keen to give the good news to her cousin that Tam was no longer delirious.

'Sophie,' he rasped. She turned to see his haggard face breaking into a smile of relief. 'Thank you, lassie.'

***

It was several more days before Tam was fit enough to get out of bed and walk further than the veranda. He sat in a wicker chair in the chilly air wrapped in blankets and gazing at the far mountains while Helena and Sophie fussed around him, making him eat soft foods and drink plenty of hot sugary tea. Word was sent back to Lahore and he was given an extra week's paid leave while he recovered.

Once his strength began to return, Tam became restless and itched to get back to work. Scott and McGinty came to visit him from their plantation in the hills and fuelled his desire to be busy with forestry. They talked about the new nurseries of Scots pines that they had planted up after the rains and Sophie remembered that it was Tam's reckless visit to them in camp that had got him into trouble with his superiors before she arrived.

When the Watsons laid on a trip out to the ancient ruins at Taxila, Tam took his first faltering steps on the crisp frozen ground and declared he was fit to return to Lahore.

'Give yourself a chance, man,' Johnny advised. 'You've been at death's door and need to build yourself back up.'

'You're all making too much fuss,' he complained, 'I was never that bad, and the best way to rejuvenate is to get back to work and get on with married life.' He threw Sophie a wicked look.

She blushed in the cold. Kind as the Watsons were, she too was impatient for them to be properly husband and wife in their own home.

So they began to make preparations to return to Lahore and two days later, Johnny discovered that a staff car was going south and could give them a lift.

Sophie bade an emotional farewell to Cousin Johnny and Helena, of whom she had quickly become fond, inviting them to visit whenever they had leave.

'I can't begin to repay you for your help and kindness to me and Tam,' she said.

'Not at all, little cuz,' Johnny said, swinging her round in a hug as he used to when she was a girl. 'It was one-tenth medicine and nine-tenths your love and devotion saw that stubborn husband of yours through the worst.' To Tam he said, 'I urge you to keep taking the medicine until your stomach is completely settled but I don't suppose you will.'

Tam grinned and shook his hand warmly. 'Thank you, Johnny, you're a grand man and a good doctor, but all I want now is the attentions of Nurse Telfer.'

***

They entered Lahore as the sun was setting and Hafiz was waiting to greet them on the steps of the Davis Street bungalow, the air cool but milder than in Rawalpindi. They ate a light supper of kedgeree, sitting on the veranda looking across at the twinkling lights of the walled city. The smell of wood smoke wafted from the open fire in the compound where Sunbar's wife was cooking chapattis for their evening meal. Sophie already felt at home in this tranquil part of the vibrant ancient city.

A feeling of nervousness and anticipation hung in the air as the world darkened beyond the candlelit table. Tam eyed her in silence, then sent the servants home, telling them to clear up in the morning.

'Shall we turn in?' he asked, but was already on his feet holding out his hand to her. Sophie took it, trying not to shake with sudden nerves.

A lamp was lit in the bedroom and a china pig of hot water had been placed between the linen sheets to take off the chill. Tam looked about to retire to his dressing room.

'Don't leave me,' Sophie said, 'you can undress in here.' Whatever happened, she was not going to let him fall asleep away from her bed tonight.

Tam gave an awkward smile then began methodically removing his clothes, placing them neatly on the back of a cane chair. He stood in his drawers looking skinny and hunched, watching as Sophie removed her dress and stockings and dropped them hurriedly in a pile on the floor. She half hoped he would come across the room and help her, but he seemed as suddenly bashful as she was. Surely she wasn't the first woman he had lain with? She imagined that all men his age were experienced lovers, but perhaps not. Unsure if she was doing what he wanted, she unzipped her corset, shedding the last of her clothing, and slipped between the sheets without pulling on her winter nightgown.

Tam went over to the dresser to extinguish the paraffin lamp.

'Won't you leave it on for a bit?' Sophie asked.

'Prefer the dark,' he murmured.

The hot mantle glowed for a few moments and then went out. She watched his shadowy figure move across the room, a muted light falling in between the slats of the wooden blinds. He pulled back the covers and immediately positioned himself above her, straddling her with his legs, running his hands over her body and fumbling between her thighs.

'Tam,' she said in alarm, 'kiss me first.'

He stopped. 'We haven't done this yet, have we?' She heard the uncertainty in his voice.

'No, not yet.'

'God knows I've dreamt of it.'

She reached up and felt his face with her hands, pulling his down gently to kiss his lips, ignoring the sourness of his breath that was a remnant of his illness.

Tentative at first, he soon opened his mouth and began to kiss her with enthusiasm. She was reminded of the heady kisses they had shared on the Meadows, returning from dances at the Palais. Sophie closed her eyes and began to relax, shivering with pleasure as he stroked her breasts and ran his fingers down her stomach.

'I've waited so long for this, my darling,' he whispered.

Sophie was pleased at the unexpected endearment and the longing in his voice.

'Me too,' she murmured, running her hands over his body; he was just sinew and bone.

Without warning, he arched over her and thrust his way inside. She gasped at the pain that shot between her legs and cried out. But Tam continued, perhaps mistaking her cry for pleasure. Moments later, he pulled away and rolled off her. Sophie lay stunned and throbbing in red-hot agony. Tam's panting subsided. Of all the sensations she had expected to feel, the shock and creeping numbness that were spreading through her were not it.

Tam climbed out of bed and pulled on his new silk pyjamas that Hafiz had laid out for him earlier.

'Better put on your nightie, lassie,' he instructed, 'in case the servants see you in the morning.'

Sophie lay immobile, heart hammering. He got back into bed, leaned over and pinched her cheek. 'Goodnight, Mrs Telfer.'

Turning his back, he chucked his pillows on the floor and settled down, resting his head straight on the mattress. In minutes he was asleep.

Later, Sophie got up and put on her nightdress, buttoning it up to her throat. With shaking legs she went to the bathroom and sat on the thunderbox; it stung her to urinate. Back in the bedroom she raised the blind and peered out; there was still a glow in the sky from the walled city. She forced her mind not to wander to dangerous thoughts of whether Rafi sat on his rooftop smoking in the dark or with whom he might be. She could smell scented tobacco; the *chowkidar* must be smoking a pipe on the veranda.

She felt overwhelmingly alone. If only Tilly was there to talk to; she would assure her that what had just happened in the marriage bed was normal. *It gets better with practice*, she could hear her friend giggle.

Sophie chided herself for her ridiculously romantic notions of what sex would be like. She had Tam as her companion and husband; that's all that mattered. Their lovemaking would become more enjoyable as they learned about each other's bodies and Tam recovered fully from his illness. He was still too weak and lacking in energy to pleasure her first.

She dropped back the blind and returned to bed, settling in beside Tam, reminding herself that he was still the same man who had won her heart with his broad smiles and charm on a Scottish hillside.

Chapter 20

Tilly was in shock at India. Calcutta had assaulted her senses like a cyclone; the noise, the flood of people, cattle and traffic, the smells of stagnant water and open sewers, the opulence of colonial buildings next to people sleeping on canvas beds in the street. The stench of the streets made her pregnancy sickness worse.

'Where do these people live?' she asked in bewilderment.

'Just where you see them,' said Clarrie, clutching a wide-eyed Adela on her lap as they rode in a *tonga* to their hotel.

Tilly gaped at limbless beggars who looked no older than twelve, and lean mustard-coloured dogs running between bicycles with their tongues lolling. She had seen poverty and stray dogs in Newcastle – she'd helped out at a mission in the West End one summer with her brother Johnny and his friend Will – but never such precarious living on this scale.

But once within the walls of the hotel garden, there was birdsong and the clink of china cups on saucers, murmured conversation and polite servants padding silently on bare feet. Tilly felt guilty relief at such an oasis and refused the Robsons' offer to take her shopping or to see the sights.

'And Clarrie told me you were such a city girl,' Wesley teased as he swung Adela on to his shoulders. 'Last chance to see a proper shop.'

'Thanks but I'm too tired.' Tilly waved them away and retreated to the garden with the first volume of *The Forsyte Saga* from the hotel library.

She didn't need shops, she just wanted to get up country and join James. Now she knew how frustrating it had been for Sophie not having Tam there to meet her from the boat; there had been a telegram from James asking Wesley to accompany Tilly upriver to a steamer port in Assam. *Unavoidably delayed please bring Tilly to Guwahati regards James.*

Wesley had business to attend to in Calcutta so Tilly had worked her way through the whole of *The Forsyte Saga* and taught Clarrie to play *mah-jong* by the time they made their onward journey. The Robsons were kind and good company – Adela was an enchanting chatterbox – but Tilly itched to be reunited with James and prepare for their first Christmas together. The only good thing about the delay was that Muriel Percy-Barratt had arranged to go on ahead.

'P.B. wants me back at once,' Muriel announced to the whole dining room. 'I've been away for so long, you see. And as the Robsons have been chosen to deliver you to James, I don't see the point in hanging around Calcutta, do you?'

Tilly had agreed quickly, which seemed to annoy Muriel all the more.

'I think I was supposed to beg her to stay with me,' Tilly said later to Clarrie.

'Don't worry about her' – Clarrie laughed – 'she didn't want the expense of a week's hotel bills so you were doing her a favour. Our Muriel hates spending money – unless it's someone else's.'

Tilly was surprised at Clarrie's view. 'She was generous to me and Sophie on the voyage out – gave us spending money in Port Said too.'

Clarrie gave her a dry smile. 'Surely you know?'

'Know what?'

'That your husband paid Muriel to chaperone you on the boat.'

'How do you know that?'

'Wesley told me. James wanted him to be in charge once you got to India, just in case something like this happened.'

'So James knew that something might crop up?'

Clarrie's look slid away. 'Perhaps.'

'Clarrie, is there something you're not telling me? James isn't in any sort of danger, is he?'

'No,' she answered firmly, 'so you're not to worry. It's probably just tea garden politics.'

Muriel departed and Clarrie would say no more. Tilly had to curb her impatience.

When they finally pulled out of the crowded station on a train bound for Goalundo, Tilly sank back, heart palpitating.

Clarrie asked in concern, 'Are you unwell? Is it the baby?'

Tilly shook her head. 'Everything is fine, thanks. The baby's kicking like a mule.'

'Good.' Clarrie smiled and squeezed her arm. 'Isn't it exciting to be on our way? I've missed Belgooree so much.'

'Do you think of it as home now rather than England?' Tilly asked.

Clarrie looked thoughtful. 'I love going back to Newcastle and seeing my dear sister Olive and her family, but Belgooree is where I grew up. It broke my heart when we had to leave and the place was put up for sale. Now it's a dream come true that we have it back again and can restore the tea garden to its former glory. I always have a feeling of coming home whenever I get on the train and see the plains give way to the mountains.' She kissed the top of Adela's head as the child distracted her by pointing out of the window in excitement.

'But most of all,' Clarrie continued, 'home is where Wesley and Adela are. Thankfully they both seem to thrive on life in the Khasi hills.'

'We thrive on being with you, Clarissa.' Wesley smiled.

Tilly caught the look of love that passed between husband and wife that she had witnessed so often on the voyage out. She felt a surge of expectation. She had spent her life being looked after by others and told what to do; now she had the chance to forge a new identity that wasn't dependent on being the Watsons' daughter or Johnny's youngest sister. Nobody in Assam would know her as Silly Tilly. She was a married woman – the wife of an important tea planter – and was soon to be responsible for a son or daughter of her own. The idea was daunting yet thrilling.

Tilly gave a sudden snort of laughter.

'Are you laughing at my soft-hearted husband?' Clarrie asked with a wry look.

'No, I've just worked out what it is I want.' She gave another loud laugh.

'What's that?'

'I want to be like you, Clarrie.' She grinned. 'Just like you.'

***

The next day, they transferred from the train on to an old paddle steamer that took them up the Brahmaputra River. Tilly was in awe of her new surroundings; the vastness of the river that was more like a sea and the jungle-covered hills that began to loom around them.

Jackman, the stocky bearded captain of the boat, and his eager son, Sam, pointed out crocodiles dozing on the sandbanks.

'They look primeval.' Tilly shuddered as one flicked its tail and slid into the water.

'They're no bother at this time of the year.' The youth grinned. 'They've eaten their fill and will be half asleep for the winter months. So if you fall in it's unlikely they'll eat you.'

Tilly gave him a playful push. 'I'm going to have nightmares about that now, thank you very much.'

She liked his open face and dancing brown eyes. A small monkey clung to his shoulder and kept up an incessant chatter.

'This is Nelson,' Sam introduced his pet. 'He can tell when we're getting near to the next landing post.'

'How do you know that?' Tilly snorted.

'Because he'll jump off my shoulder and run to the capstan to help untie the rope.'

Tilly was amazed when, two hours later, the monkey did just that. There was a burst of activity as cargo was offloaded, passengers disembarked and new ones came aboard. She sat under an awning at the stern, watching drowsily, and was asleep before they set off again.

Clarrie shook her awake in time for a starlit dinner on the cramped deck. A night breeze was stirring and Tilly pulled on her tweed coat for the first time since Calcutta. Afterwards Clarrie took Adela to their cabin while Wesley stayed above to share a cheroot with Captain Jackman. Sitting in the dark tucked behind a hatchway, Tilly became aware of their conversation.

'. . . scores of them still there, poor blighters,' said Jackman, 'living under scraps of sacking. Like something Biblical.'

'I thought the trouble had died down?' Wesley said.

'Stalemate,' the captain grunted. 'Coolies have no money to pay their way home and they're too scared to leave the camp in case they're rounded up and sent back to the estates. Local people are feeding them, but they're running out of patience too.'

'The government will have to do something for these people,' Wesley was indignant.

'They don't want to get involved,' said Jackman, 'in case it spreads like wildfire and they have an even bigger exodus on their hands. Sets a precedent, you see, if they help this lot.'

'It should never have come to this.' Wesley flicked his cheroot into the water. 'It's only a handful of planters who were dead against a small pay rise but it gave Gandhi and his followers the excuse to come stirring up the workers. I tried to get the Association to see sense, but my stubborn cousin wasn't having any of it; he blocked my proposal.'

Tilly froze. Wesley must mean James. She held her breath, hoping the men wouldn't realise she was still behind them eavesdropping.

'We're making bigger profits now,' Wesley continued, 'and we're prepared to raise wages at Belgooree, but I don't want to rock the boat with the other planters. If it was up to my wife' – he grunted – 'she'd have them paid the same as labourers in the city, but we all know that the tea estates could never afford that.'

As they moved off, Tilly heard Jackman say something about cholera.

'. . . won't be stopping there . . .'

'Don't tell the women, Captain . . .'

'*Koi hai!* Sam, I'll take over . . .'

Their voices drifted away. Tilly hunched down, cradling her unborn baby. *Cholera*? A swift killer that had vanished from Britain but haunted the memories of the elderly. It terrified her that such dangers could be lurking close by; threatening her child before it even took its first breath.

She must have fallen asleep in her chair, for the next thing Tilly knew she was being woken by the excited screeching of Sam's monkey. It was still night but the sky was lit by a lurid smoky glow. Tilly took a moment to work out what it was. She got to her feet and went to peer over the railings. The far bank of the river seemed to be covered in small fires like a rash. There was a buzz of noise. As they steamed past, the swell of voices became more urgent and the monkey Nelson's reply grew shriller.

'What's going on?' she asked Sam.

He stared out with troubled eyes that mirrored the flames. 'It's the camps.'

'What camps?'

'The runaway coolies.'

'Why are they running away?'

'They want to go home but the tea planters don't want them to.'

Tilly peered hard. As they chugged by, she could make out scores of figures massed on the riverbank and crowding on to the jetty. Some were wading out into the water, holding up bundles. Sudden realisation came like a blow to her stomach; the bundles were mewling babies.

'Oh heavens! They want us to take their children,' Tilly gasped. 'How can they be that desperate?'

'We're not stopping,' Sam said. 'There's cholera.'

Nelson leapt from his shoulder and ran along the railings in agitation, gnashing his teeth. Tilly could hardly bear to look but neither could she move or turn away. The desperation of the half-naked figures, shouting out in supplication as they sailed past, appalled her. Yet a small part of her gave thanks that she wasn't one of them.

'What will happen to them?' Tilly whispered.

'I don't know, but we can't do anything,' Sam said. 'If we let one on, the rest would follow and capsize the boat. Nelson doesn't understand that.'

They stood as the boat steered on and the fires and shouting receded into the pitch-black night. Nelson gave up his frantic dance and hopped back on Sam's shoulder with a final shriek of protest.

Tilly stood clutching the rail feeling nauseated; never would she forget the wailing of the parents offering up their infants to be saved. She was glad of the dark so that the youth could not see the tears streaming down her cheeks. Whether she cried for the half-starved people on the smoky *ghat* or in relief that the danger to her unborn baby had passed, she could not tell.

Chapter 21

The next afternoon, they steamed into Guwahati. The sun shone down on a festive crowd gathered on the *ghat.* A band was playing a military air, *The British Grenadiers*, which Tilly remembered her father singing. People were garlanded in vivid flowers of red and orange and skinny boys were cheering and waving.

'Is it some special festival?' Tilly asked, trying to spot James among the throng.

Adela craned forward in her father's arms and giggled with delight. 'Drums!'

'A very special festival,' said Wesley, 'isn't it, Clarrie?'

'Yes.' Clarrie grinned.

'Tell me,' Tilly said, 'so I can seem knowledgeable to James.'

'They're waiting for a VIP.'

'On our boat?' Tilly was incredulous.

Clarrie slipped her arm through Tilly's. 'This fuss is for you.'

Tilly gawped at them. 'Me? Don't be silly!'

Clarrie laughed. 'It's true.'

Wesley chuckled. 'It's a good old-fashioned tea garden welcome for the new Robson Memsahib. You're the star of the show.'

Tilly's hands flew to her face. 'How embarrassing! I'm no good at being the centre of things.'

'You don't have to do anything,' Clarrie assured her, 'just walk off the boat and go to James. Look, there he is.'

Tilly stared at where Clarrie pointed. A burly figure in a white suit and a large *topee* obscuring half his face was standing, hands on hips, waiting. The familiar bullish stance and jutting dimpled chin made her insides flutter with nerves.

'Go on,' Clarrie encouraged, 'give him a wave.'

Tilly raised her hand in a tentative gesture. James caught sight of her, took off his hat and threw it in the air like an excitable boy. He caught it, and gestured eagerly for her to come ashore.

'I'm coming!' Tilly waved back with greater confidence and hurried to the gangway. 'Thank you, Captain Jackman – and

Sam – for looking after us so well.' She shook their hands and Nelson the monkey stuck out his paw. 'And thank you too.' She laughed as the animal tried to grab her hat. Nelson screeched in reply as Sam swung him out of reach.

Tilly hurried down the gangplank, flustered but excited by the rousing greeting on the quayside. James strode forward and shouted over the din of the band; a motley crew of veteran soldiers and youths in hand-me-down military jackets.

'Welcome, wife!' he cried, clamping his hands on her shoulders and giving her a chaste kiss on the forehead. 'Good journey? Come and meet the household.'

He whisked her in front of a line of smiling and bowing servants, who showered her with garlands of flowers and presented her with baskets of fruit. Their names went straight out of her head as she smiled and nodded and thanked them back, quite overwhelmed by their enthusiasm to greet her.

When Wesley and Clarrie had disembarked, James ushered them all into a restaurant garden for refreshments. Tilly was aware of the tension between the men. As tea and pastries were served, Adela went chasing off after James's dog, Rowan.

Clarrie said pointedly, 'There were some sorry sights downriver. Those camps are a disgrace.'

James flushed. 'I quite agree, but it's the left wing agitators who keep them there in squalor to suit their purposes – give us a bad name.'

'You can't believe that,' Clarrie was scathing.

Wesley gave her a warning look. 'Now is not the time, Clarissa. James is our host.'

'And very grateful we are for these fine refreshments,' she said, 'but we all live so far apart, there is no knowing when we will have a chance to talk of these things again.' She turned to James and held his look. 'It's time that all us planters put our hands in our pockets and paid for the relief of these camps – pay for them to journey on – before the death toll gets any worse. Captain Jackman says that cholera is rife.'

James looked furious, barely hanging on to his temper. 'And no doubt you and that busybody Jackman have the answer to our constant need for labour on the estates, as well as the deep pockets to pay for it?'

'Yes,' Clarrie replied. 'The days of importing indentured labour are over – should have been long ago – and we should be nurturing the people we have here already. Give the workers decent housing and health, a patch of land to grow extra food and some schooling for their children, then they'll want to stay and bring up their families here – the next generation of tea pickers.'

'Sounds reasonable to me,' Tilly chipped in. 'There's such distress in those terrible camps—'

'You don't know what you're talking about, girl,' James snapped, 'you haven't been here five minutes. And you, Clarrie, sound like you've spent too long swallowing the sob stories of the Bolshie press in England. I wish you were half as enthusiastic standing up for the British interest in India – it's what gives us our living.'

'Indian tea is what gives us a living,' Clarrie replied.

'Spoken like a—' James bit back his retort.

'What?' Clarrie said, dark eyes blazing. 'A native?'

'Your word, not mine.'

'That's enough,' Wesley said. 'We'll not stay to be insulted. We've done as you've asked and brought Tilly safely here. Come on, Clarissa, we're leaving.'

He strode off to fetch Adela, who wailed at being parted from the patient hound whose tail she kept grabbing. 'Doggy, mine!'

Clarrie threw Tilly a look of regret. 'I'm sorry. Take care of yourself.'

Tilly wanted to rush over and hug her – thank her for all she'd done for her – but she was shocked by the sudden argument and cowed by James's dismissive remark to her. She didn't want to provoke him further, for all their sakes. She stood feeling wretched as her friends gathered their daughter, said stiff goodbyes and left.

After they had gone, James calmed down. 'My dear, I'm sorry, I shouldn't have been short with you. It's that woman; she knows just how to irritate. My idiot cousin is completely under her spell and can't see sense when it comes to the tea trade anymore. He used to be such an astute man of business but she's made him so emotional about everything – and emotion clouds reason – there's no room for it in commerce. Our first duty is towards our shareholders and keeping the company solvent.'

'And the tea workers?' Tilly dared to ask. 'Don't you have a duty to care for them also?'

He gave her a sharp look but answered without anger. 'Yes, of course. But if the company doesn't prosper then the coolies are out of work. So what good does that do them?'

Tilly was happy to let the matter drop. She was feeling uncomfortable on her feet and longed to sit down, so was thankful when James ushered her into an open car and they set off along a dirt track road, Rowan hanging over the back seat and licking her face. The servants had set off ahead with her luggage – two trunks of clothes, one of linen and two heavy with books, stamp albums and framed family photographs – in a series of carts.

'Road's new – so is the car,' James was keen to show off. 'Cuts down the journey to the Oxford Estates by a day. When I first came out to Assam, we had to go further by riverboat to Tezpur or ride horseback. Devil of a journey. Once got stalked by a tiger.'

'Really?' Tilly gasped, gazing around fearfully.

'Don't worry; this car will go faster than a tiger – at least on the straight stretches.' Then he barked with laughter. 'Tilly, your face! I'm joking. There are no tigers on the open road – they prefer to keep to the jungle. Now wild elephants are another matter. Can get very aggressive – tip us off the road and squash us like flies.'

'James, stop it!'

He roared with laughter again and squeezed her knee. Rowan yapped in excitement and tried to scramble forward.

'Down boy!' James ordered. 'He usually sits where you are but he'll have to get used to the new pecking order.'

After three hours of bumping along on the uneven road, Tilly felt carsick. She had long grown tired of looking out over lush vegetation the colour of pea soup, the road often running high above the surrounding flat land on steep embankments. Dust blew up constantly from the unmetalled track, making her eyes gritty and her throat sore. They stopped at a *dak* bungalow – in the middle of nowhere, it seemed to Tilly – where James's bearer, Aslam, had tiffin waiting for them; a cold flask of lemonade, hard-boiled eggs, cheese puffs and small dry cakes.

Tilly hoped her husband might suggest that they stop at the government bungalow for the night, but he was eager to be off and they left some of the servants to tidy up while they re-fuelled and pressed on, taking Aslam with them. The bearer sat in the back with the excitable dog, trying to avoid being licked and sat on. Twenty minutes later Tilly was shouting for James to stop; she just made it to the side of the road before she vomited back her lunch.

'Poor girl,' James said, patting her back and handing over a large handkerchief. 'That's it; get it all up.'

After that, she dozed and jerked awake and dozed again until the sun began to weaken, and the trees grew more regimented on the undulating landscape. Tilly sat up.

'Are those tea bushes?'

'Yes,' James said. 'Have you never seen any before?'

'No, never.'

James smiled. 'I take it all for granted now. But I remember seeing the gardens for the first time. Grand sight, isn't it?'

Tilly thought the endless rows of fat green bushes rather monotonous – give her a golden and russet deciduous wood in autumn any day – but she feigned enthusiasm. At least it meant they must be nearing their destination.

Yet it was another hour before they passed the gates proclaiming they were now entering The Oxford Company Estates. They trundled up a long drive and Tilly cried out with relief at the sight of a neat bungalow and a series of long sheds all fringed with cheery flower beds.

'How pretty!'

'Yes, I suppose it is,' James said in bemusement, as if it had never before occurred to him.

He swung the car around the side and hooted as they passed the bungalow. A balding Indian with wire spectacles came to the door and saluted. Rowan barked and leapt out, rushing up to the man and licking him in greeting. To Tilly's surprise, James waved and kept on driving.

'Why aren't we stopping?'

'Not home yet, dear girl. That's the office. Anant Ram is my chief *mohurer* – excellent bookkeeper.'

Tilly sank back in dismay. She couldn't bear another minute in the bone-shaking car. A few minutes later, Rowan reappeared running alongside and James slowed to let the dog jump into the back seat next to the long-suffering Aslam. Another thirty minutes of grinding uphill was made tolerable by the cooling breeze and the sinking of the sun into a spectacular sunset over the receding valley.

Distracted by its splendour, Tilly was taken by surprise at their abrupt arrival at a large two-storey thatched house perched on a slope and hidden in shadow like a bird of prey looming out of the dark trees.

'Here we are, Mrs Robson' – James beamed – 'your new home, Cheviot View.'

He helped her from the car, her legs so shaky she would have collapsed without his strong hold. They were greeted by a cheerful cook and James's *khitmutgar*, which Tilly gathered was equivalent to a head valet. Aslam rushed ahead, thankful to be out of the car too, and set about giving orders.

They had prepared a large meal but Tilly could not face it. She ached all over. Her stomach was empty but she felt nauseous, while her head pounded and her eyes streamed from the dust.

'Do you think I could just have a lime juice and lie down?'

James looked crestfallen, but Aslam immediately gave out orders to prepare a tray of juice and biscuits for the *memsahib* to have in bed.

Tilly followed James numbly through the gloomy house, which was dimly lit by occasional paraffin lamps, upstairs to the marital bedroom. Left to undress, she was too nervous of what might be lurking in the dark of the far bathroom – she had heard tales of scorpions under sponges – and was thankful to find in the bedside cupboard a chamber pot in which she quickly relieved herself. She would be so much braver in the morning, once she had slept off the terrible car ride.

Shortly afterwards, James found her already asleep, the refreshment tray untouched. Her auburn hair was still half pinned and stuck in messy tendrils to her plump cheeks. He thought her quite beautiful and marvelled again at how he had inadvertently managed to gain her as his wife. He remained sitting close by, gazing at the young woman in his bed.

Already it seemed astonishing that he had lived so long on his own. He was excited at the thought of waking up next to her, of feeling her heat like a warming pan, of repeating the intimacies of those wonderful two days of honeymoon. But perhaps, now that she carried his child, making love to her might be dangerous? Who could he possibly ask about such things?

He would do nothing to bring harm to either Tilly or their child. James was suddenly overcome at the thought of being a father. He cleared his throat; it wouldn't do to get emotional.

'Time for a nightcap,' he said to his sleeping wife. 'Just the one.'

James retreated to the sitting room and its aromatic fire and poured himself a large celebratory whisky. Three drinks later, he was sound asleep and snoring in the large wing-backed chair.

Chapter 22

Tilly awoke to the sound of James whistling *The British Grenadiers*. For a moment she had no idea where she was, then remembered the endless journey and the badly lit house; her new home, Cheviot View. She ached all over and did not have the strength to get out of bed.

'James, are you there?' she croaked.

The whistling continued in the adjoining room; snatches of military marches and music hall ballads.

'James!' she called out louder.

The singing stopped. 'James!' came a shrill echo, and then the whistling began again.

What was he playing at? Tilly struggled out of bed and stood on wobbly legs. Noiselessly, a young woman she hadn't seen before appeared with a tray of tea, set it down on a rickety table, nodded and hurried out. Tilly pulled on her dressing-gown, which had been unpacked and hung on the bedpost while she slept, and went to peer beyond the door. The bedroom opened on to a small dressing room full of men's clothing, which in turn led into a sparsely furnished sitting room. As Tilly ventured into the far room she was startled by a sudden flapping of wings as a small brown bird shrieking 'James!'flew at her.

Tilly screamed and fell backwards. Aslam found her gasping for breath cowering in a faded chintz chair, trying to ward off the garrulous bird. James's bearer coaxed it on to his turban then swiftly grabbed it and popped it squawking back into its cage by the window, where it watched Tilly from a yellow-ringed beady eye.

'Bad boy!' the bird mimicked the scolding servant.

'I'm sorry,' Aslam explained. 'Sahib lets Sinbad out in the morning when he is shaving and having *chota hazri*. He forgets to put him back. He will not harm you, Memsahib.'

'Where is James?' Tilly asked, feeling faint.

'Sahib is down at the tea gardens. He says you must rest.'

'When will he be back?'

Aslam gave a shake of the head. 'Usually he is gone all day.'

Tilly refused his offer of food and retreated back to bed. James, when he returned in the late afternoon, thought her encounter with his pet bird highly amusing.

'I won Sinbad at the races in Tezpur. He's a mynah bird – one of the starling family – and they're better mimics than parrots.'

That evening they ate in a musty dining room downstairs, the shadows hardly pierced by the candlelight. Outside, the garden was full of screeching and barking from unknown creatures. Tilly's nervousness increased when James placed a pistol on the end of the table, saying mysteriously, 'Just in case.'

Halfway through the soup course, there was a scuttling inside the room.

'There's something there in the dark,' Tilly cried in alarm.

James sprang from his seat, lunged for the pistol and fired into the shadows. Tilly screamed at the deafening crack. James seized a guttering candle and held it high.

'Got him!'

'What is it?' Tilly gasped, ears ringing.

'Rat. Quite a big chap.'

Aslam appeared at once and summoned a kitchen boy to remove it. The boy swung it up by its tail and grinned, obviously impressed. It was the size of a weasel. Tilly thought she would be sick. She pushed away her food – it tasted strangely of kerosene anyway – and excused herself. Lying, curled up in bed with the paraffin lamp turned up high filling the room with bright yellow light, she felt this was the only place of safety.

For several days she hardly stirred, seized by lethargy and an irrational fear that if she ventured beyond the bedroom into the unknown, her unborn baby might be harmed. The slim young woman who came with trays of food, and took away her clothes for washing, turned out to be Aslam's wife, Meera.

'She'll be the *ayah* once the baby's born,' James told her. 'She's a timid soul, but doesn't keep strict *purdah*, so I thought she was ideal for helping you.'

Tilly felt she was being watched the whole time and didn't see that she needed a servant. But she didn't have the energy to argue. She slept for long hours or sat at the rough wooden table looking through her stamp albums without the inclination to add to them. Occasionally she heard someone arrive below and the noise of activity as they were given refreshments and waited for her to appear. Later, after they'd gone, Aslam would send in Meera with a calling card on a tray from the wife of a neighbouring planter or office manager.

After a week, and ashamed at her own timidity, she made the effort to dress in outdoor clothes and leave the upper floor for a proper look around, but was horrified at the state of the house. Most of the downstairs was given over to storerooms that James called godowns, full of darkness and strange smells and windows with bars. Looking up she could see that even some of the upstairs windows were boarded over with cardboard instead of being fixed. It was a bachelor's lair of mismatched furniture, chairs that had lost their springs and hunting trophies. At the bottom of the stairs, she had to force herself to pass a roaring tiger's head without screaming. She had imagined that James, like her father, would have a study full of books that she could work her way through, but all she could find was a battered copy of *Sport in British Burma* by Captain Pollok.

She sat on the veranda staring out at an overgrown garden and a dizzying landscape of endless trees and bushes, ringed in the distance by mountain peaks. Like fortress walls, Tilly shuddered. She had the strangest sensation of being hemmed in and yet cast adrift in a sea of green. She tried not to imagine the ferocious beasts that lurked in the undergrowth, but every rustle of grass and frantic bird call was ominous. Tilly fled back to the bedroom to re-read her Walter Scott novels.

James grew baffled. 'You can't put yourself into *purdah*, old girl.' And then concerned. 'Are you unwell? Is it the baby? Shall I call for the garden doctor?'

Tilly grew tearful but could not explain her anxieties. She didn't want a doctor; she wanted her mother and fussing sisters, grey streets, libraries, tea shops and the din of a northern city; hooters, trams and the cries of newspaper sellers. She wanted Sophie's teasing and a dose of her cousin's bravery. Whatever had made her think she could live in such an alien place, so far from her family in this green prison? She wasn't going to last a month. She had even lost the taste for tea; she was a failure as a tea planter's wife.

James sent for Muriel Percy-Barratt.

'A case of newly-wed jitters,' Muriel announced, arriving the next day and bursting into Tilly's bedroom. 'We've all been through it. But there's no point moping up here; leads to melancholia. Seen it happen before; women letting themselves go and not caring about their appearance. Before you know what's what, they're wasting away and heading for the cemetery. Well, I can tell you now, my girl, you are not going to do that to dear James. You're going to pull yourself together and come and have tea at my house; meet some of the other wives. I've sent round a rallying call. I'll give you half an hour to get ready.'

A reluctant Tilly, with Meera's help, had a hasty wash and put on a clean dress. She climbed into the Percy-Barratts' horse-drawn carriage and Muriel gave the command to go. It took nearly an hour to ride across to their nearest neighbour but Tilly found the trip in the mild air lifted her spirits and did not make her as queasy as James's car had done. She only half listened to the older woman's stream of advice on diet in pregnancy, club nights and Christmas activities, but it reminded her of Mona's bossy affection and the loneliness inside eased a fraction.

The Percy-Barratts lived in a beautifully kept bungalow with a neatly thatched roof overhanging a deep veranda, amid manicured lawns with a view down to a pond where a stork stood motionless as a statue. Taking tea, sitting in comfortably upholstered cane chairs, they were soon joined by two other women; plump Jean Bradley, wife of a deputy manager at one of the Oxford gardens, and a younger Ros Mitchell, whose husband worked for an agency called Strachan's.

'Strachan's manage all sorts of businesses in Assam,' Muriel explained, 'tea, coal, shipping.'

'My husband Duncan is overseeing a steamship company at the moment,' Ros managed to interject, 'learning the ropes.'

'The Mitchells moved up from Shillong earlier this year, didn't you, dear?' Muriel continued. 'Though the main office is in Calcutta.'

'Actually the main office is in Newcastle,' Ros corrected.

'Newcastle in England?' Tilly seized on the name.

Ros nodded. 'Not that I've ever been there.'

'Oh.' Tilly sank back in disappointment. 'That's my home.'

'Duncan has, though. He's from the Borders. A little fishing place, St Abbs; you've probably never heard of it.'

'Oh yes! We used to go there on holidays. My brother Johnny loved swimming off the harbour wall even when the rain poured.'

They chatted on, Tilly suddenly garrulous after two weeks of virtual silence, reminiscing about the past. Ros, who had grown up in Calcutta and Shillong, had visited Scotland on leave with her husband. Pulling out a silver cigarette case, Ros offered it around. 'Do you mind if I smoke?'

'I'd rather you didn't, dear,' Muriel said with a disapproving look. 'It looks most unladylike.'

Ros hesitated then put them away. Muriel ordered more tea and reasserted her authority over the conversation, turning it to plans for the Christmas festivities. Polo games, horse racing, a children's party and the fancy dress ball at the club would be the highlights in a week of celebration.

'James is one of our best polo players,' Muriel said.

'Is he?' Tilly said in surprise.

'Captain three years running, didn't you know?'

'No, I—'

'Oh yes, and he always stays over here during Race Week so he doesn't have to go back up to Cheviot View after a hard day's drinking. You know what planters are like once they get together.'

Tilly nodded, though she had no idea.

'In fact, I insist that you both come and stay for Christmas,' Muriel enthused. 'We'll have such fun and it'll be nice to have a young face around now that the children are all away.'

For a moment, Tilly thought she heard a wobble in Muriel's voice. Was it possible that this *burra memsahib* with all her self-confidence and experience of India might still have a vulnerable spot; her children? She swallowed down the tears that welled at the thought of her family gathering in Dunbar for Christmas without her.

'Thank you,' Tilly said, 'I'll see what James says.'

'Oh, he'll want to come here; no doubt about that.'

As the sun dipped and the women made to leave, James arrived to collect her in the car. His anxious expression cleared at the sight of Tilly laughing with Duncan Mitchell's fair-haired wife. The young women arranged to meet for a game of mah-jong at the club on Saturday. Tilly was cheered to hear there was a lending library there too.

'And I've got *dak* for you.' James held up a bundle of letters. 'Looks like Christmas post.'

Tilly tore open a letter from Sophie as soon as they drove off but found her queasiness returning as she tried to read in the car. Over supper in the upstairs sitting room, she read out extracts to James, giggling at her friend's descriptions of her new surroundings, while omitting the references to the marriage bed. She drew guilty comfort that Sophie was not finding it all easy going either.

'Oh, lucky Sophie, seeing a lot of my brother, but what a worry having Tam so ill.' Tilly sighed. 'Do you think he'll be all right?'

'Fever's an occupational hazard in India,' James said, 'but he's a young man and should shake it off. I had malaria every rainy season for the first three years.'

'Did you?' Tilly gasped in concern.

'Been fit as an ox since,' he reassured.

'I couldn't bear it if you got seriously ill,' Tilly blurted out.

James smiled. 'You mustn't worry.'

Tilly folded the letter. 'I'm glad Helena is nice; she looked a bit formidable in her wedding photograph. I was frightened she'd be one of those fierce army wives like you thought she was.'

'I hardly met her.' James covered her hand. 'You worry too much about things and let that imagination of yours run away with you. You need more fresh air and less reading of gothic novels.'

'Stop sounding like my mother.' Tilly laughed and read out a letter from home. Her mother sounded happily settled with Mona, and Jacobina would be joining them for New Year. The thought made her tearful again, so she hurried on to the third letter.

'It's from Clarrie Robson,' she said in surprise, reading the short note. 'Oh, James! She's inviting us up to Belgooree for Christmas. Isn't that kind?'

James's face clouded. 'That's just mischief making.'

'Why do you say that?'

When her husband wouldn't answer, Tilly said, 'I think it would be grand to spend the holiday with the Robsons. They're your only family. I'd jump at the chance if it were my relations.'

'The Belhaven woman is no relation of mine,' James snapped.

'Why are you so unkind about Clarrie?' Tilly asked. 'Is it because she's Anglo-Indian?'

'Race has nothing to do with it; it's about business. Belhavens have always thought they know best – they've never tried to cooperate with the rest of us – old man Jock Belhaven was just as stubborn.'

'We wouldn't have to talk business,' Tilly said. 'I'd love to see Adela again. And Belgooree sounds a lovely place from what Clarrie and Wesley say—'

'It isn't.'

'So you've been there?'

James avoided her look. 'I just think you'd find it too remote – too jungly.'

'It can't be more so than out here – and anyway I'd have Clarrie for company.'

'I don't want you going to Belgooree,' James snapped, 'and that's that. We'll be spending Christmas with the Percy-Barratts like I always do. So you will write to her and say no.'

Tilly watched her husband in dismay as he poured himself a large whisky, his expression as severe and uncompromising as his words. Without another word, he took his drink on to the veranda and left her alone. The disquiet she had felt on hearing Wesley and Captain Jackman talk about James as ruthless and hard-hearted in business returned. She hoped there wasn't a side to her new husband that she would come to fear.

Chapter 23

April 1923

Tilly's baby came swiftly and without much warning just as the first pickings were being plucked from the tea bushes.

'Our very own first flush!' James cried with delight at the sight of Tilly sat up in bed with their pink, crinkled son swaddled and lying in a crib alongside. He was to be called James after his father, but known as Jamie.

Tilly felt tired and sore, yet triumphant at her achievement; she had managed without the interference of the garden doctor. Dr Thomas, a wiry Welshman with a nose like a strawberry from too much whisky and exposure to harsh sun, had, at James's insistence, examined her a month before the birth. Her husband had worried at her sleeplessness and fretting, as her womb grew large and heavy, and she once more became a recluse at the house, too nervy to join her friend Ros at the club.

'It's an hour's drive away,' Tilly had made excuses, 'and I can't even sit with you.'

She hated the way the women were segregated from the men's clubhouse in a dismal tin-roofed building that the planters jovially called the 'hen-house'. With the advent of hot weather it was becoming uncomfortable to sit inside and the so-called library consisted of a few antiquated books on household management and a stack of dated magazines and newspapers.

Tilly had been content to stay at Cheviot View 'preparing her nest', as Muriel put it. Once the festivities of Christmas were over, she had arranged repairs to windows, put up new curtains, had the downstairs dining room whitewashed and ordered a comfortable new sofa from Calcutta, which arrived strapped to a bullock cart, along with a cot for the baby. Ros had taken her on a rare trip to the bazaar in Tezpur to buy crockery that wasn't chipped, cushion covers and floor rugs to brighten up the dowdy bungalow, and from a passing pedlar Tilly bought brass ornaments and a gaudy musical box that played a snatch of *Swan Lake*.

'It'll lull the baby to sleep,' she had told James.

From home, she got Mona to send out baby clothes and she handed a long list of medical supplies to Dr Thomas.

'You won't need half of these,' he had scoffed, more interested in helping himself to James's whisky. When he had failed to provide what she asked for, Tilly had gone to Ros for help, who made a special trip to Shillong to kit out a full medicine cupboard for her anxious friend.

'I don't think you're silly for worrying; not at all,' Ros had said and left Tilly wondering if the childless Ros had experienced some personal loss. Nothing was ever said and Tilly felt she couldn't ask; her new friend was a more private person than the extrovert Sophie.

When Dr Thomas came to visit the newborn baby, Tilly asked him about feeding and bathing the infant, but he seemed quite taken aback by her questions.

'Just do what comes naturally to women,' he had blustered and left quickly to celebrate on the veranda with James.

After the first euphoria of the birth, Tilly panicked that she wasn't feeding Jamie enough. The baby cried a lot and was constantly at Tilly's breast but his sucking was weak.

'I think he's losing weight,' she fretted to her husband. 'Does he look thinner to you?'

James, who was bleary from lack of sleep at the unaccustomed noise and irritated by his wife's insistence that the baby should sleep in their room, grunted. 'Maybe we should hire a wet nurse if you're not up to it. Isn't that what some women do?'

Tilly had no clue and was wretched at the idea but she was growing exhausted too. James began sleeping in his dressing room and was gone long hours. She knew it was now the busiest time at the tea gardens but she couldn't help feeling he was staying away longer than was needed. She cried for her mother who would know just what to do, yet felt she did not know any of the planters' wives well enough to ask for help. Muriel, the one she knew best, would expect her to cope without fuss; it was what *memsahibs* did. She was reticent to ask Ros for help in case such baby talk was painful. She was utterly alone in her plight.

One night, James sent word that he was staying down at the office bungalow; there were problems in the lines. Tilly knew the lines were the rows of houses for the labourers and their families, though she had never seen them; only once had she been to the gardens where James had shown her proudly round well-built sheds full of machinery and she had taken tea with his head clerk, Anant Ram.

The baby had been querulous all day and Tilly was light-headed with lack of sleep and worry. She carried him from room to room, bouncing him in her weary arms, her breasts too sore at the thought of feeding him again.

'Oh do be quiet,' she shushed him as she gazed out, hot and listless, over the miles of darkening tea bushes. The usual rustlings and cries from the surrounding trees mingled with the baby's whimpering and set her teeth on edge.

She was filled with a sudden anger and resentment. She hated this creature that wouldn't shut up; she hated James and India and wished she had never left England. She hated herself for being weak and pathetic and useless at everything.

'Just shut up!' she screamed at the swaddled infant and rushed to the balcony. She held him over the side. '*Shut up* or I'll throw you over, do you hear me? I'll dash you to the ground, you little beast, I will!'

The baby wailed at her raised voice and the sudden violent movement; his eyes opening wide. At the same moment, Aslam appeared below, his face turned up in horror and alarm.

'No, Robson-Mem, do not drop him, I am begging you!'

Tilly stood shaking with rage; it would be so easy just to let go and then the noise would stop and she could sleep forever. She felt her grip loosening . . .

Suddenly she was aware of a presence beside her, a musky scent and murmured words. Small, cool fingers touched her like a breeze. Tilly glanced round in confusion. Meera was there, brown eyes watchful. The next moment the slim young woman was taking the baby from her arms and stepping back, rocking him and soothing with gentle words. Tilly stood shaking and gasping for breath, unable to move.

Meera disappeared and the wailing subsided. All at once, Tilly felt her legs go. She sank to her knees. A huge sob rose up inside and she burst into uncontrollable weeping that she did not know how to stop. She might have stayed like that for ever, but Aslam and Meera returned, helped her up and coaxed her into the sitting room. On the new sofa they made her drink a spicy tea she had never before tasted and eat hot morsels of sugary dough.

Afterwards, Meera put her to bed like a child, tucking her in and leaving the paraffin lamp turned down low. Tilly was vaguely aware that there was no noise from the baby but was too tired to question what had become of him. She fell into blissful, dreamless sleep.

***

Tilly awoke to bright daylight. Emerging from her grogginess, she caught sight of Meera sitting in the corner humming and cradling something under her sari.

'What are you doing?' Tilly asked.

Meera stopped singing and looked up. Gently and swiftly, she extracted a baby from under the folds, popping a round breast back in her chemise. In astonishment, Tilly watched as the servant crossed the room and held out the bundle. It was Jamie. She had never seen him look so contented, his eyes closed, cheeks flushed and small mouth wet with milk.

'How . . .? I-I don't understand,' Tilly floundered.

Meera smiled and gestured for her to take the baby. Tilly froze. The memory of her outburst the night before was suddenly vivid. Shame at the overpowering desire to harm Jamie flooded over her. Aslam would have to tell James and then she would never be trusted with their baby again.

'Please, Robson-Mem,' Meera said, offering up the bundle. He looked so comfortable in her assured hold.

Tilly shook her head. Meera tightened the cotton sheet around him, laid him in the cot, pulled the end of her sari over her head and padded to the door.

'Meera,' Tilly called out. The servant stopped but kept her head bowed. 'Please' – Tilly gulped – 'will you show me how to – you know – feed the baby?'

She wasn't sure how much English Meera knew – they had hardly spoken to each other in all these months – but the woman understood her desperation.

It didn't take her long to show Tilly the best way to nurse Jamie; it was a simple adjustment in the way she held him that made it easy for his small mouth to latch on to her nipple. With gestures and Meera's rudimentary English taught to her by Aslam, Tilly discovered that her servant had a two-year-old boy called Manzur whom she still suckled.

Tilly was ashamed that she did not know this; that the Ahmads lived in a compound beyond the garden in quarters she had never thought to visit, out of sight and out of mind. It had never occurred to her that Meera might be a mother or live a life separate from the household. Why was it, Tilly wondered, that she had busied herself in Newcastle with good works and visited some of the poorest housing in the city, yet had never set foot in an Indian home; a home for which she and James were responsible?

Tearful with gratitude, Tilly thanked Meera and tried to give her the shiny brass bowl she had bought from the itinerant hillsman. With a shy smile, Meera refused. Later, the servant brought up a meal of hard-boiled eggs and tomatoes chopped into flavoured yellow rice, a bowl of stewed fruit and more spicy tea.

'Good for milk.' Meera grinned.

Tilly discovered she was ravenously hungry and ate the lot. She realised how much her appetite had dwindled as her worry over Jamie had grown.

When James returned sweaty and tired at sundown, he was astonished to find Tilly up and dressed, waiting for him on the veranda with a *chota peg* of whisky and soda.

'It sounds strangely quiet,' he said with a curious glance.

'Jamie is sleeping.' She smiled.

Over the next few days and weeks, James could hardly believe the difference in the domestic scene, returning each evening to an increasingly energised Tilly and a son who was fattening out into a contented, if still, in his opinion, rather ugly baby. He had no idea what had brought about the improvement in his wife's mood and put it down to her settling into the job of motherhood. What he did notice was the bond growing between Tilly and Aslam's shy wife – they seemed always to be together – but then he had chosen Meera as Jamie's *ayah*, so that was hardly a surprise the girl should be so ever present.

Chapter 24

Tilly had never experienced heat like it. It muffled everything like a hot wet blanket, slowing down movement and making it hard to catch the breath. Rugs were rolled up and windows encased in fragrant grass screens, plunging the house into a gloomy half-light. Jamie's cradle was stood in bowls of water to stop insects climbing its legs and teams of *punkah wallahs* took it in turns to pull the ropes of the massive cloth fans that stirred the soup-like air and kept the insects at bay.

Tilly suffered from prickly heat that felt like being stabbed with pins in the arms and chest, while at night, the noise of frogs and insects kept her awake. James often returned from riding round the tea gardens with leeches hanging off his legs and drawing blood, but seemed impervious to the discomforts. The tea gardens were busy with the lucrative second pickings and the factories were running at full tilt to process the leaves for packing and shipping before the monsoon.

'Once the rains come,' James told her distractedly, 'the Brahmaputra turns into a sea and half the place gets flooded – then it's a devil of a job to get anything downriver.'

It was such talk of being further marooned by the threat of the approaching wet season that spurred on Tilly to accept Ros's invitation to visit Shillong.

'She says we can stay with her father,' she told James. 'Do you think I should go? It would be cooler for Jamie – he's suffering terrible nappy rash.'

Talk of nappies made James hastily agree. He was proud of his son but found babies boring and didn't know why Tilly didn't hand over more of the tedious work to the *ayah*.

'You'll take Meera, of course,' James agreed.

'But that would mean separating her from little Manzur,' Tilly worried.

'Good God, woman; she's paid to look after you and the baby. Aslam will keep an eye on his son and others in the compound will see to his needs.'

Just before Tilly left, a letter came from Sophie. It was full of relish for her new surroundings – Tam was posted to a rural plantation to the south of Lahore on the edge of thick jungle – and she was enjoying the freedom from the strictures of cantonment life.

'We've given up the tenancy on our half bungalow in Lahore but I love it here. At Changa Manga we go hunting at dawn – Tam hires labourers to flush out blackbuck, but most of the time it's partridge and duck that he bags. He's bought me a rifle and has been teaching me to shoot, but none of the wildlife is in any danger from me! If Tam misses he blames it on inferior ammunition; if I miss it's because I'm a bad shot! But I don't care; it's the riding through the forest that I love and watching the dawn come up and the light filter through the sal and acacia trees. This is the most beautiful country, don't you agree?

'Tam has created a mud tennis court – well, really just a practice wall against the godown – but we go over to the Remount several times a week where they have a proper court, and play tennis against the men. My game has never been so good.

'Sometimes I go with Tam on his trips around the other plantations and we camp or stay in other forest bungalows (I don't bother going to Lahore as the city is getting far too hot now and I prefer to stay here). I know this place is a long way from Assam but it makes me think more and more of my childhood – I have vague memories of my father going hunting and my mother playing tennis. Have you asked James yet about what he remembers of my parents? I'm longing to meet wee Jamie. Perhaps we can manage some leave at the end of the year and come and visit? Some day, I want to see the Oxford Estates and where I grew up. Does Dunsapie Cottage still stand?'

Tilly could feel Sophie's yearning in the letter for any nuggets of information about her past. Sitting on the veranda that evening she read the letter out to James.

'I didn't know the Logans very well,' he blustered, 'I was just a young man making my way at the Oxford. Bill Logan was a senior manager – an experienced hand.'

'And Sophie's mother? What was she like?'

James answered with a shrug.

'Was she anything like Auntie Amy?' Tilly pressed.

'Prettier than Amy Anderson.' James admitted.

'So more like Sophie then?'

'I suppose so.' James shifted in discomfort. 'Sophie has a look of her mother.'

'She looks beautiful in her wedding photograph,' Tilly mused. 'I bet she caused a stir among the planters when Bill Logan brought her to the Oxford.'

'He was very possessive.' James grunted. 'If another man so much as looked at her—'

Tilly glanced at him in surprise. 'James, you're blushing. I hope you didn't give Bill Logan cause to be jealous?'

She had meant it as a joke but James snapped, 'Of course not. He was a queer fish that's all; wouldn't allow anyone else to dance with Jessie at the race meetings, that sort of thing.'

'Poor woman. How boring life must have been for her.' She watched him take a slug of whisky. 'Where is Dunsapie Cottage? I haven't heard anyone mention the Logans' place.'

'Anant Ram lives there now. It's down on the estate.'

'Where we went for tea?' Tilly exclaimed.

James nodded.

'But I thought it was called The Lodge?'

'The name was changed after the Logans died. No one wanted it, so we let Anant rent it.'

'Why did no one want to live there? It's not as if the Logans died in that house.'

'How do you know that?' James asked sharply.

'Sophie told me it was somewhere in the hills.'

'You know what people are like,' James said hurriedly, 'they think bad luck can be caught like a disease. Once it got around that the Logans had died of fever, the house was doomed. Besides, Bill Logan's health had been deteriorating for a while. Anant had the bungalow exorcised by a local shaman or some such nonsense.'

'Poor little Sophie; she must have been so bewildered by it all. To lose her parents and her home.' Tilly sighed. 'What happened to her *ayah*?'

James eyed her. 'Why do you ask that?'

'Sophie has a memory of being deserted by her nurse – just at the time she needed her most.'

James took a sip of his drink. 'We wondered the same thing when we found her.'

'What do you mean, found her?' Tilly questioned. 'Were you up in the hills too? Did you discover the Logans . . .?'

'It was a passing official – or maybe one of the servants – I can't remember,' James was evasive. 'I was summoned from the tea garden.'

'My Lord! How long was Sophie left alone with her parents dead and the wretched *ayah* gone?'

'Not long.'

'How do you know that?'

'Tilly!' James protested. 'Enough questions. I knew it would do no good raking up the past; you're just getting upset. That's why Sophie should stop trying to remember. She should put it behind her and get on with life.'

'She is getting on with life.'

'Good. Then don't encourage her to dwell on her parents' tragedy.' He stood up. 'Come on; let's get to bed.' He held out his hand. 'If you're going to run off and leave me for the next month, I want to make the most of our last night together.'

Tilly laughed and let the matter drop. She sensed that James was deliberately keeping something from her, but now was not the time to press him further. If there were things he did not want her to know, it would only be to protect Sophie from the painful truth. Perhaps her cousin had been left to fend for herself for longer than James would admit? How terrible for the small girl to be hiding out in some remote bungalow, prey to wild beasts and with no one to feed her. Tilly checked on Jamie to assure herself that her precious baby was safely asleep.

‘I’m going to miss you, my girl,’ James murmured in the dark, as he took her in his arms under the bed sheet and made vigorous love.

***

‘And you must go and take tea at the Pinewood Hotel,’ said Major Rankin, Ros’s genial widowed father, ‘after you’ve done the sights, of course. Lot of the old houses wiped out in the earthquake of ’97 – such a pity – but Shillong’s still a pretty place to live. Now, Rosalind, you won’t forget to take Tilly around the lake and point out the bird life?’

‘No, Dad, I won’t. Are you sure you won’t join us?’

‘No, no, I’d only hold you up with my wooden legs. Quite happy just sitting here with the binoculars. Off you go and enjoy yourselves. I’ll keep an eye on baby and *ayah*.’

The friends set off down the steep path from the Rankins’ wooden house, the view of Shillong opening up below them.

‘And don’t forget to show Tilly the museum,’ Major Rankin called after them.

Ros waved back. ‘Course not.’

‘Has your father really got wooden legs?’ Tilly asked as they climbed into the waiting rickshaw.

Ros snorted with amusement. ‘No, it’s his joke; he’s just very arthritic.’

Tilly looked back at the old house with its intricately carved doors and balconies, seasoned almost black with time and weather.

‘He’ll be all right,’ Ros reassured. ‘Jamie, I mean.’

Tilly was glad her friend understood. ‘It’s the first time I’ve left him since he was born. I feel very strange; like something’s missing.’

‘Dad’ll make a fuss of him,’ said Ros, ‘and your *ayah* seems very competent.’

‘She is,’ Tilly admitted. ‘But it doesn’t stop me worrying.’ She told Ros about Sophie’s *ayah* deserting her and fleeing from the dead Logans.

‘That’s shameful,’ Ros agreed, ‘but Meera isn’t like that. I can’t imagine her being so callous, can you?’

‘No,’ Tilly felt bad for having doubts, ‘she loves Jamie like her own son. She even suckled him for a couple of weeks – but don’t tell anyone – James doesn’t know.’

After a week in Shillong, Tilly felt more at home than she had done in the long six months since arriving in India. After two weeks, she daydreamed about moving there and persuading James to grow tea in the nearby hills instead of the hot and humid valleys of Assam.

She loved the bustle of the town; it was lively without being overwhelming and it had a library and quaint shops and a cinema. The wooded hills of pines and the picturesque lake reminded her of Scotland; the sounds of wood pigeons were familiar and a breeze blew through the Rankins’ elevated, creaking house that brought the scent of roses and made her determined to plant some in her own garden when the holiday was over.

Tilly missed James but she was in no hurry to return to the isolation of Cheviot View. She wrote to him daily and received the occasional hasty note in return, telling her how busy he was and glad she was enjoying herself.

It was on a hot, airless day in late June, when the young women were walking in the lakeside park with Meera pushing Jamie behind in his pram, that Tilly was startled by a shout.

‘Tilly! Tilly!’

A small girl with dark pigtails came bowling towards her, arms outstretched and sun bonnet flying off her head.

‘Adela?’ Tilly cried in astonishment, scooping up the child as she flung herself at Tilly’s legs. Adela giggled and planted a sloppy kiss on Tilly’s cheek and then wriggled to be out of her hold.

Clarrie and Wesley caught up with their daughter. Tilly and Clarrie hugged in delight. Tilly introduced Ros and explained their visit.

Clarrie went straight to the pram and peered in. 'And is this Master Jamie? What a little poppet.' In an instant she had the baby out and was rocking him in her arms.

'Wouldn't it be lovely to have a little brother for Adela?' Clarrie winked at Wesley.

'Put it back!' Adela ordered, jumping in front of her mother and trying to grab the baby. Swiftly, Wesley lifted her out of the way and swung her up on his shoulders.

'This little madam is enough for me,' he replied, as Adela instantly forgot her jealousy and began to drum her hands on her father's *topee*.

'Where's 'Ophie?' she demanded, eyeing Ros with suspicion.

'She's living in the jungle,' Tilly told the girl, 'with her husband Tam.'

'Can I see?'

'It's not our jungle,' Wesley said, 'it's far away.'

'I want to see 'Ophie.'

'Not today,' her father replied.

'Yes, Daddy, today.' She banged a hand on his hat.

'Today is your birthday,' he said. 'Don't you want to see the jugglers and the acrobats?'

Adela squealed and kicked her legs with excitement.

'Happy birthday!' Tilly exclaimed, tickling the girl's sturdy calf.

'Tell Tilly how old you are today.'

'Five.'

Clarrie laughed. 'No you're not; you're three.'

'Three and five,' Adela giggled. 'Tilly come too.'

'There's a travelling show of gypsies on the *maidan*,' Wesley said. 'You're very welcome to join us.'

Tilly looked at Ros and her friend nodded. 'I've some errands I want to run. Why don't I meet you later?'

'Yes,' Tilly enthused, 'we could all go to the Pinewood.'

Ros hesitated; she exchanged an embarrassed look with Clarrie. 'Why don't you come back to my father's house for refreshment then Adela can play in the garden?'

There was an awkward pause. Tilly noticed Wesley's look of annoyance and wondered what it meant. Was it possible Clarrie and Adela might be refused entry to the hotel for being Anglo-Indian or was Ros being over-sensitive?

'That would be lovely,' Clarrie said quickly, 'thank you.'

With a wistful look, she put Jamie back in his pram and they walked on together.

'I'm sorry I haven't written much,' Tilly said, still feeling guilty that they had snubbed the Robsons' Christmas invitation.

'Don't be,' Clarrie said, 'I know how busy it is with a new baby. I'm just sorry I haven't been to visit, but I didn't want to make things awkward for you with your husband.'

'It wouldn't be awkward.' Tilly flushed.

Clarrie gave her a look of disbelief. 'Well, we hardly ever get out of Belgooree, let alone across to the Oxford. So it's a real treat to find you here.' She linked arms with Tilly. 'Tell me how you're finding life in Assam. Are you settling in as well as Sophie in the Punjab?'

'To be honest, if it wasn't for this trip with Ros I think I'd have gone mad stuck out at Cheviot View. Does Sophie write to you a lot too?' Tilly asked.

'Yes. I don't know how she finds the time, she sounds so busy.'

***

That afternoon, Tilly and Clarrie spent a happy time catching up and talking about their children. Adela was entranced by the tightrope walkers and jugglers but buried her head in her father's chest and screamed at the sight of the fire-eater swallowing flames.

They arranged to meet Ros at the entrance to the British cemetery; it was a short cut up the hill to the Rankins' house. A hot wind was beginning to blow dust from the baked pathways and clouds were amassing above the far mountain range. They found her arranging a posy of flowers in a vase in front of a grave near the gateway.

'My mother's,' she explained, her eyes tear-filled.

Adela slipped her father's hand, rushed over to a flowering creeper and plucked a large white bloom. She ran back and squashed it in the vase beside Ros's neat bunch of flowers.

'For your mummy.'

Ros looked at Clarrie. 'How does she understand?'

Clarrie smiled. 'She does the same on my parents' graves – they're buried at Belgooree.'

Ros knelt down and pulled Adela into a quick, self-conscious hug. 'Thank you, sweet girl.'

Tilly glanced away, her eyes filling up. She stared hard at the grave stones opposite, trying not to cry. She was still so weepy since having Jamie.

The name made her start: Logan. Tilly wiped her eyes and peered closer. It was just a simple stone, half hidden. She pushed aside a clump of long grass. Her heart lurched. *William Logan – departed this life May 1907*. Underneath it read: *Jessie Anderson, wife of William*, with the same date of death. *May they rest in peace*.

'Oh my Lord!'

'What's the matter?' Clarrie asked, going to her side.

'Sophie's parents,' Tilly gasped.

The others gathered to look.

'What are they doing here in Shillong? It's nearly two days from the Oxford.'

It was Wesley who stated the obvious. 'They must have died near here.'

Chapter 25

The talk each day was of when the rains would come. Tilly was warned that the area around Shillong was one of the wettest in the whole of the Indian sub-continent. She longed for it to come; to remember what rain felt like, to bring freshness back to the air and earth – and to maroon her for longer in the hills away from the sticky heat of the tea gardens.

She dwelled daily on the mystery of the Logans' final months somewhere nearby and their swift death. With Ros's help she tidied up the grave, and took a photograph with her friend's Box Brownie to send to Sophie.

Why had James never mentioned that the Logans were buried here? Especially as he knew she was going to be visiting, and had been full of questions about them, asking for any details he could give her. Did he not know that that was where their bodies had been taken? But he had been involved in rescuing Sophie; he must have known that they lay in the British cemetery in Shillong. It was puzzling why everyone was so reticent about the Logan family. Perhaps they had not been much liked?

Merry on sherry at Christmas, Muriel had let slip that Sophie's mother was too flirtatious for her own good.

'Old Logan hated her talking to any of the men. Even when she was having a difficult birth with Sophie – wouldn't let the doctor in – chased him down the steps. Mind you, he was Indian, so I have some sympathy.'

One day, when visiting the library, Tilly got chatting to one of the librarians.

'I'm trying to find out more about my friend's parents who died here in 1907. Do you keep newspapers from that far back? I was wondering if there might be a death notice or something. A double death like that might have been newsworthy, don't you think?'

The librarian, a retired policeman with a passion for Arthur Conan Doyle mysteries, was intrigued. He disappeared for ten minutes and came back with a heavy bound tome of editions of the *Shillong Gazette* from May 1907. Plonking it on a stand, he heaved it open.

'What was the date of death, did you say?'

'The gravestone just says May.'

'Well, better start at the beginning then.'

He hovered over Tilly while she scanned the first newspaper for notifications of death.

'Course it was a tense time around then,' he said, pulling the ends of his handlebar moustache in thought.

'Why was that?'

'Fiftieth anniversary of the Mutiny, May 1907. Jittery time for us British.'

Tilly looked up in surprise. 'But that was old history, surely? You weren't in any danger of an army uprising.'

'Not from the army – but plenty of agitators wanting to stir up trouble – using the anniversary as a spark to set off unrest and turn Indians against their masters. Busy time for us police – following up rumours of plots.'

Tilly thought it all sounded far-fetched. 'Plots?' she queried in amusement.

'No laughing matter,' said the librarian. 'The planters in particular were worried about an uprising among the coolies. There'd been signs, you know.' He tapped his nose conspiratorially.

'What signs?'

'Strange patterns left on trees – round pats of dung and hair – that people thought was code for an uprising just like the passing round of chapattis had been a sign for the Mutiny. A lot of the planters got windy at that – sent their wives and families away home to Britain for safekeeping. Those that couldn't battened down the hatches. On the night of May the tenth – the date the Mutiny had started – a lot of the British gathered their families in the clubs and the men took it in turns to guard them.'

'How long did that go on for?' Tilly asked, astonished that there should have been such panic. She would have been scared half to death.

'Just a night or two. When the planters saw that nothing was going to happen, they soon went back to their homes and got on with their business. Mind you, us police were rushing about all over the place, making sure everyone was safe. I spent most of the month up at Tezpur.'

'By everyone you mean the ex-pats?' Tilly said dryly.

'Of course.' He sucked at his moustache. 'That might explain why your friend's parents were hiding out in the hills.'

'They weren't hiding out,' Tilly insisted, 'they were there for their health. And besides, the Logans weren't set upon by rampaging coolies. They died of enteric fever.'

'Still,' he said, his eyes lighting at the thought of mystery, 'you can't dismiss a link between their deaths and the fiftieth anniversary, in my opinion.'

Tilly thought that she could. She found his lurid speculation distasteful. All she wanted to find out was where Sophie's parents had been living and died, so that her cousin could come and see for herself and lay their ghosts to rest. Tilly went back to scouring the newspapers.

'Take a look at the eleventh or twelfth,' he persisted.

Tilly stifled a sigh and turned to those editions. If there was no mention of the Logans then he might go and leave her in peace.

Triumphantly, she pointed out that there was no such entry for either date.

'Try the thirteenth.'

Tilly turned to the next edition. Before she got to the death notices, the old policeman jabbed a finger at a heading near the bottom of the page.

"Tragic deaths of planter and wife."

Tilly's insides curdled. The librarian pulled out a magnifying glass, edged her out of the way and began to read out. '*The bodies of William and Jessie Logan were discovered on Sunday the Eleventh of May at White Blossom Cottage by planter James Robson and Superintendent Burke.* Ah, Burke, I remember him, good man, hard as nails.'

Tilly's heart beat faster at the mention of James but she was not going to fuel this man's curiosity by admitting that James was her husband.

'*It's believed*,' he continued, '*that the couple died of enteric fever and passed away on the night of May the Tenth*.' He banged the newspaper with his magnifying glass. 'See, what did I tell you? Anniversary of the Mutiny! There's something fishy going on here.'

'I don't see how,' Tilly said in annoyance. 'It's pure coincidence. Is that all it says?'

He returned to the paper. '*They leave behind a six-year-old daughter, Sophie, who is being cared for by the management of the Oxford Tea Estates, where the deceased Mr Logan was a manager*.'

'Poor Sophie,' Tilly said, feeling a fresh wave of pity for her cousin's brutal loss.

'*The bungalow at Belgooree, which was being rented by the Logans, has been fumigated and boarded up*.'

'What did you say?' Tilly asked in shock.

'Fumigated and—'

'No, the bit about the bungalow. Did you say Belgooree?'

'Yes, that's right. It's about an hour away in the Khasi hills.'

Tilly felt suddenly very hot and faint. 'Yes, I know that.'

Chapter 26

Changa Manga, Punjab

Day after day, the sun shone with a brassy burnished glare; the fields were hard and parched, the grass burnt brown. The windows and doors of the forest bungalow shrank in the heat and dust blew in to cover everything; it lay in cupboards, made the food gritty and got up sleeves, under collars, and into ears, eyes and shoes. Useless to wash, when the dust permeated the basin, soap, towels – even turned the water black. Sophie did not remember such dust or heat from her childhood.

'Ink's dried up in the bloody pen again!' Tam came in from the hut that passed for a forest office. 'How am I supposed to do all that *dak*? And that useless *punkah wallah* is either asleep or pulling so hard that my papers blow all over the room.'

'Try paperweights,' Sophie suggested.

'And the bloody *punkah* squeaks every time he pulls it; I've got a splitting headache.'

'I'll get Hafiz to oil the rings. Come and sit in the shade and have a pomegranate juice.'

'I need a portable typewriter,' Tam grumbled. He drained off the glass that Sophie poured him without sitting down. 'I've too much to do before the timber auction. I want to ride out to the depot. I don't trust them to sell the right stacks of logs and last time they gave it to the merchants before they'd paid up.'

'I'll come with you.'

'You'll fry.'

'Then we'll fry together.'

Before he could argue further, Sophie went and changed out of her frock – it crackled with electricity as she pulled it off – and put on her jodhpurs, a baggy white shirt and wide-brimmed *topee.*

They rode out along the canal, Tam on his grey mare and Sophie on a black pony she had borrowed from the Remount. She wore gloves to stop her hands being scorched by the bridle; sweat glued her clothes to her body. But she would rather be out riding through the jungle with Tam than stuck at the bungalow with her husband in a foul mood.

She worried and watched for a return of the fever that had plagued him six months ago. He drove himself relentlessly with work; up before dawn to check on the plantations, returning after several hours for a late breakfast and then out again before the heat got unbearable. In the afternoons he would wrestle with reports and figures in the office and then ride over to the resin factory, the depot or the irrigation works to check on progress before the sun set.

Gone were the days at the tail end of the cold season when they had hunted buck in the dawn or dusk, gone camping upriver and swum in cool water, played tennis at the Remount and socialised with the horse-handlers.

She saw Tam grow increasingly exhausted and short-tempered. He tried to alter his diet, spurning tea and toast at breakfast for grapenuts and buttermilk for energy, but it led to vomiting and diarrhoea. They cut out meat that turned putrid too easily; Hafiz ordered up vegetable curries and chutneys to lift his master's jaded palate until Tam complained they were giving him nightmares. He would wake screaming out in terror shortly after falling asleep. When Sophie suggested they sleep outside, Tam said it wouldn't be seemly to behave like the servants.

'I need to get better at Science,' he had berated himself. 'It's my own weakness that makes me so tired.'

'It's the heat,' Sophie had said. 'It's no good fighting the Indian climate. Take more rests and drink plenty of juice.'

'I wish there were some fellow Christian Scientists here like in Lahore, then I could draw strength from their example.'

So Sophie tried to follow the exercises for Tam's sake. He seemed happiest when they sat on the veranda at night reading a lesson from Mary Baker Eddy's *Science and Health*. It made him relax. Afterwards they would go to bed and lie under the mosquito nets while Tam made love quickly, mechanically, and Sophie tried not to mind the discomfort. He would sigh with relief and be instantly asleep while she would lie awake for hours listening to the bark of jackals and incessant croaking of bullfrogs, until the squeaking of the well announced the start of a new day.

She had thought she would have been better at sex and wondered if she was a disappointment to Tam. Sometimes she caught him eyeing her with a strange look – was it pity or regret? – then he'd brush her forehead with a chaste kiss and hurry off.

Arriving at the timber depot, the yard was deserted. Tam dismounted quickly and started shouting for the manager. Sophie took the horses under the shade of a mulberry tree to a muddy pool of water diverted from the canal.

'You should be patrolling the stacks!' She heard Tam bawling inside the shed. He emerged with a bleary-eyed manager trying to placate him.

'Do I have to do everything myself? Where are the guards?' Tam stalked off towards the piles of freshly cut logs and firewood. 'What's that burning smell?'

Moments later, noise erupted from behind the stacks. Tam reappeared, dragging a skinny labourer in ragged *dhoti* and turban.

'Smoking! Bloody smoking! You could have the whole place on fire, you useless crim!'

Tam threw him to the ground, his face sweating and contorted with rage. Striding over to his horse, he seized his riding whip and rushed back. The man threw up his arms and cried out in fear. Tam raised the whip and brought it down on the man's arms.

'No, Tam!' Sophie screamed. She was frozen in horror. Tam lashed out again, the whip catching the man on his shoulders and back.

The manager stood back, his face impassive. Sophie could see he was not going to intervene. She ran forward and grabbed Tam's left arm.

'Stop it, please stop!'

He threw her off.

'Get away, woman!'

Sophie stumbled, lost her balance and fell backwards with a thud on the hard ground. She lay winded in the dust. The manager hurried over and peered down.

'Are you all right, Telfer Memsahib?'

Abruptly the whipping stopped and Tam was at her side, pushing the manager away. 'Don't touch her.' He reached down and pulled her into a sitting position. 'Come on, lassie, deep breath. Up you come.'

He was still breathing hard from his frenzied state, but she saw the contrition in his face as he helped her to her feet and into a chair on the depot veranda. The whipped man ran off. Sophie burst into tears. The manager brought hot sweet tea.

Tam spoke to his manager. 'My wife doesn't understand how things are here – the severity of that man's crime – perhaps you would like to explain to her?'

'Very bad man,' the manager nodded. 'Criminal tribes man. All are not to be trusted. Telfer Sahib is a good man to give them jobs but they still do bad things – it is in their nature. He smoke when told not to – very bad crime – he could burn down whole depot then all hell break loose and we have big forest fire on our hands.'

'Exactly,' Tam said. 'By rights I should have ordered him to be flogged – a far worse fate for him than a couple of flicks from my whip. But it's better to deliver swift justice so that his fellow crims will think twice about lighting up their filthy cigarettes when on duty.'

Sophie looked at them both with incredulity, appalled at their callous words. Tam might have regretted rough handling her, but felt nothing for the man he had just horse-whipped – and neither did the manager. To them the unfortunate tribesman was contemptible and belonging to a class so far beneath them he was almost sub-human.

She closed her eyes, trying not to wonder how often such incidents took place. She prayed it was a one-off. They left her sipping tea while they went to inspect the log stacks for the auction. When they finally left, Sophie was stiff and sore, trying not to wince at the pain when sitting back in the saddle. Back at the forest bungalow, she asked a surprised Hafiz to arrange for a tin bath of hot water in the bedroom.

'I know it sounds mad in this heat,' she grimaced, 'but I'm stiff from all the riding.'

Tam disappeared across the garden to the office to finish the day's *dak*. She lay back in the tub and let the warmth suffuse her body till the water went tepid. She emerged pink and glowing, dressed in a pair of Tam's baggy silk pyjamas. Indians had the right idea about loose clothing in the heat. The sky was a blaze of orange, shadows creeping across the garden.

'We have visitors, Telfer-Mem,' Hafiz announced. They could hear horses' hooves approaching slowly through the trees.

'Oh dear,' Sophie laughed, 'they've caught me in pyjamas. Better go and tell Telfer Sahib we have guests. Maybe the canal bungalow is full and they need a room for the night.'

A rider appeared, followed by a pack pony being led by his servant. As she peered from the veranda, she gasped in astonishment. The broad-shouldered man was bare-headed, the last of the fierce sun lighting up his stubbled chin and glinting off his smoked glasses.

'Rafi?' she called out.

He raised a hand in greeting, his handsome face breaking into a broad smile. Sophie's insides flipped over. He dismounted and handed the reins to the Telfers' *syce*, giving his horse a quick and grateful pat.

'Are you having a pyjama party?' he teased, walking up the veranda steps.

'Not unless you've brought music,' Sophie answered, her heart racing.

'I have, as a matter of fact. I'm travelling with my gramophone.'

'Wonderful!'

They shook hands self-consciously. Sophie hoped he didn't feel her shaking. She couldn't read his expression under the dark glasses.

'What brings you here? Lahore too unbearably hot?'

'Bracknall is doing a tour before heading for the hills. He wanted a fluent Urdu and Punjabi speaker with him. I have my uses even to the exalted B.'

'Has Lahore been boring then?'

'It's a city and I'm a forester. I'm enjoying being in the jungle at last and having the excuse to ride every day.'

'So where is the mighty Bracknall and the rest of the entourage?'

'He's taken over the canal bungalow and sent me down here.'

'Sounds typical.' Sophie rolled her eyes. 'Trust him to choose the house with electric fans and an ice-box to keep his whisky sodas chilled.'

'All I ask is a corner of the garden to pitch camp.' Rafi grunted.

'You're welcome to the spare room,' Sophie answered, 'but you might be more comfortable outside.'

Rafi pushed his dark glasses on to his head. 'It's good to see you.' He smiled.

She swallowed. 'You too.'

A shout came from behind. 'Rafi Khan, you old devil! Come to learn a bit of forestry at last?'

Tam took the steps in two swift leaps and clapped his friend on the back; they shook hands vigorously and laughed.

'Rafi's brought his gramophone; isn't that great?'

'As long as we don't have to listen to all his awful Persian love songs that sound like cats being strangled.'

'You're a philistine, Telfer.' Rafi grinned.

'Go and make yourself decent,' Tam told Sophie, 'while the Khan and I have a stiff *chota peg*. It's been a devil of a day.'

It was unusual for Tam to want a drink; perhaps his violent outburst had troubled him too? Sophie wondered.

By the time the sun had set, Rafi's servant had pitched tents, the men had knocked back two large gins and lime and Hafiz was serving up a supper of spiced duck with orange followed by ginger pudding. A huge moon swung above the trees and flooded the veranda with light that made the kerosene lamp redundant. Rafi gave them news of Boz who had been sent off to Quetta.

'You know that Bracknall can't stand your guts when you get sent off to wild Pathan country,' said Tam.

'Poor Boz,' Sophie said, 'what did he do to deserve that?'

Rafi eyed her across the table, then shrugged. 'Too Scots and lower middle class for Bracknall. He has his pet favourites. But don't worry, he speaks highly of your husband. Likes Tam's idea of expanding resin production.'

'Does he?' Tam looked pleased.

Tam and Rafi speculated about what plans Bracknall might have for them.

'Rumour in Lahore is that Bracknall wants to push Martins off to the forest college in Dehra Dun. So there could soon be a promotion to assistant conservator for an ambitious man,' Rafi joked.

'Well, I'd do a better job than old Martini. He's the laziest man in the Indian civil service.'

'Aren't you ambitious, Rafi?' Sophie asked.

Rafi shook his head. 'Not for myself but for India. I want to see our forests well managed – for the people who live in them as much as for those who need the timber.'

'But,' Tam interrupted, 'it's all about planting up trees that will grow quickly and give us a good return for the investment. We aren't going to be here for ever.'

'Some of us hope to be.' Rafi smiled. 'We need to build up our stocks with the next generation in mind, not just ours.'

'Build up stocks, yes,' Tam said, 'but there are huge untapped forests in the Himalayan foothills that are ripe for felling now. And there's a market for the wood in India without having to ship it abroad – pit props and tea chests in Assam – railway sleepers and such like.'

'I would give anything to travel those forests,' Rafi mused, 'get up above the snowline.'

'Let's do it,' Tam declared. 'We're due some leave once the monsoon comes. I've been trying to get Sophie to go up to Dalhousie but she refuses to leave me alone down here in case I go mad in the heat.'

'In case I go mad,' Sophie snorted, 'with all the endless tea and cards with the wives.'

'We'll organise a camping trip,' Tam said. 'You and me, Khan. Go exploring the mountains and survey the forests for Bracknall.'

'Well, I'm coming too,' said Sophie.

'It'll be too risky for a lassie,' Tam was dismissive.

'Nonsense,' Sophie replied. 'I've camped in the Cairngorms with Auntie Amy. I can cope with a few foothills.'

'You see what I have to put up with?' Tam laughed. 'Don't marry a Scotswoman, Khan, they are far too stubborn. A good, biddable Mohammedan wife is what you want.'

Sophie dared to ask, 'Have your parents chosen a wife for you, Rafi?'

'I hope they've given up trying.' Rafi laughed. 'No self-respecting Lahori girl wants to be dragged off to the jungle to live with a forester. I'm a hopeless case in their eyes.'

'Oh, dear, poor you.' Sophie hoped she didn't show the ridiculous relief she felt at his answer. Then she was ashamed of such a thought; she was a married woman and, besides, she didn't want Rafi to be unhappy.

'Enjoy your freedom while you can,' Tam said, then added quickly, 'Of course I'm very happily married now.'

Rafi broke the awkward silence by going to fetch his gramophone. He put on a ragtime record but Tam said it was far too hot for dancing, so they worked through his five other records: Scottish songs, Mozart, Schubert, Roses of Picardy and a Sufi singer.

Sophie thought she had never heard anything more haunting than the yearning, soaring Persian song filling the air over the moonlit jungle garden. Even the birds seemed to hold their breath. When it had finished, no one moved.

'That was beautiful,' Sophie murmured, 'thank you.'

'I prefer a Scots song any day.' Tam grunted and got up. 'It's late; we should let you get to your bed, Khan.'

Rafi stood up too. 'Thanks for a very pleasant dinner.'

'You'll join us for *chota hazri*?' Sophie invited him to breakfast.

'Not sure there'll be time for that,' Tam intervened. 'If Bracknall wants to see round the plantations, we'll need to get a very early start. I've got the timber auction too. I'll get Hafiz to send us off with something.'

Rafi said his goodnights and disappeared to his tent. Sophie could not bear the thought of another restless night in the stifling bedroom. Tam always refused to leave any doors open in case animals wandered in, and tonight she could not get the image of Tam's violent attack on the unfortunate labourer out of her head. It sickened her. She had witnessed a flash of his temper when he'd punched Jimmy Scott at the Palais but nothing like his fury at the timber yard. Was that what Boz had tried to warn her about when, in Bombay, he'd told her of Tam's wartime injuries?

When her husband had fallen asleep, she took a bedroll and sheet from the chest and climbed up to the flat roof. A few months ago there had still been brightly coloured Indian corn drying there, but now it was empty.

Sophie lay gazing at the night sky – it pulsated with stars – and felt a little relief in the wisp of night breeze. Why had they not been doing this all month? She sighed. If Tam had been on his own she knew he would have been sleeping outside; it irked her that things had to be different for the women.

Dreamily, she fingered the black opal, given by Rafi and Boz, which she always wore under her shift. Rolling on to her front, Sophie peered below. The moon had moved round but still shone a bright beam on the compound. The servants lay out on wooden *charpoys*, dogs snuffled; a night guard called out in the distance patrolling a plantation. On the other side of the garden, a body was stretched out on a mat beside Rafi's tent, smoking. He was naked save for a pair of drawers. It must be his servant. Then the man sat up and Sophie gasped as she realised the bulky shoulders and hairy arms were Rafi's.

He looked up at the house, his handsome face bathed in moonlight, while he finished his cigarette. She could not tell if he saw her staring down over the edge of the roof and did not want to move and draw his attention, but her heart began to pound so hard she thought he would hear it. He frowned, deep in thought.

After a long moment, he extinguished the cigarette between finger and thumb and lay back down, resting his head on cupped hands. Sophie stayed watching for a long time; hot with guilt that she found the sight of him so arousing. She had to fight off the desire to hurry down from the roof and stretch out beside him on the burnt grass and put her hands on his broad, naked chest. It left her almost sick with wanting. Tam had never made her feel quite like that.

Sophie rolled away and buried her face in her hands. She was contemptible. She tried to remember what it had felt like to be head over heels in love with Tam in Edinburgh. It was less than a year ago but it felt like the feelings of someone else; some restless girl who had been longing for romance and adventure and was envious that her timid favourite cousin had been the one to suddenly get engaged and plan a future in a faraway land. Tam had caught her attention – he was handsome and a great dancer – and when he disappeared to France he became all the more alluring for being out of reach.

How shallow she was! Sophie mocked herself. She had made a play for Tam partly because she thought she was in love with him, but partly because he was her means of getting back to India. Now she realised how strong her yearning had been to come back; if she felt at home anywhere it was here. These past months had not been easy – the worry over Tam's illness, his swings in mood, the primitive bungalow and learning to be a wife – but she relished the freedom of their jungle life, the surroundings, the people.

She blushed with shame to think that there was one person in particular who made her feel so alive; he was lying feet away in the garden below. She had to admit that was one of the reasons why she had avoided trips to Lahore, in case she bumped into Rafi. Did he have feelings for her too? Sophie knew that when they had first met, Rafi had disapproved of her, had thought her typical *memsahib* material. But now there was a certain look in his mesmerising eyes; she wondered if it was mutual attraction.

Sophie wiped her sweating face on the sheet. She couldn't allow anything to happen. She had made promises to Tam for life; she must make the most of her marriage to him. Somehow, she would rekindle their romance – she sensed he had regrets too – and they would have a baby. She would bury her anxiety about being responsible for a child – it was nonsensical to be so averse to motherhood – and then they would be happy.

Sophie knew she would not be able to sleep lying within sight of Rafi's prone figure. She got up, gathered her bedding and climbed down from the roof. Crawling under the netting of the marital bed, she lay stewing next to Tam until the dawn.

Chapter 27

Three days later the monsoon came. The newspapers had tracked its path north from Ceylon and then from Bombay; Hafiz had accurately predicted its arrival to within half a day. The hot wind strengthened, the clouds rolled in and Sophie heard the hissing of the first fat raindrops as they hit the hot earth.

She dashed outside and threw out her arms, shrieking a welcome. Steam rose around her. Then the sky flashed with light and thunder claps filled the air like gunfire. Hard rain came suddenly in bucketfuls.

'Come inside, lassie,' Tam shouted from the veranda, 'before you're struck by lightning!'

'I don't care' – Sophie laughed, turning her face upwards – 'it's wonderful!'

She ran around the garden, jumping in puddles and cartwheeling across the parched lawn. The earth drank and gurgled like a thirsty creature. The servants watched from under umbrellas, grinning and making comments about the mad memsahib. Rafi's tent billowed and flapped.

Sophie turned to see the men staring at her; Tam, Rafi and Bracknall. Tam looked annoyed, Rafi amused and their boss had a strange, severe look that made her suddenly acutely self-conscious. She was soaked to the skin, hair stuck to her face and clothes drenched. Her dash into the rain seemed childish now, but a few minutes ago she had been seized with a heady madness. She could not have sat still a minute longer listening to Bracknall pontificate about being invited to stay at the Viceregal Lodge in Simla in return for allowing the Viceroy to hunt across Forest Service land in the Punjab jungle.

Tam had been eagerly trying to expound his ideas on irrigation.

'Trenching should follow the contours of the slopes, not be in straight lines along the cliff edge; that's what's led to flooding and erosion in the past. In Germany they—'

'Good God, Telfer,' Bracknall had silenced him, 'we're certainly not going to take advice from the Boche. And as for your plans for felling and grass cutting – they'll have to wait –

need to have them costed up first. The Forest Service doesn't have a blank chequebook, you know.'

They all knew, but didn't say, that the chief conservator's reluctance was more to do with leaving the jungle untamed for the viceregal hunt than the cost.

As Sophie's giddiness subsided, the temperature dropped. She stood clutching her arms and shivering.

'Go and get changed,' Tam said, his look tense.

He had been in a foul mood with her for the past two days, since the timber merchants had boycotted his auction. Tam blamed Sophie for causing a scene at the depot and making him look a fool, but she refused to feel bad for trying to stop him beating the guard. The memory of it sickened her. Rafi had not improved Tam's temper by pointing out that the boycott was in protest at Tam doing a deal with one particular merchant.

As Sophie pulled off her waterlogged shoes, she quipped, 'Well, at least I've saved the sweeper having to lug in bath water tonight.'

As she went, she overheard Tam muttering excuses about it being her first monsoon and the men laughing. Yet it wasn't her first. A memory returned of peering through railings and watching children splashing in a huge pond while the rain pelted down, and wishing she could join in.

Sophie took her time, stripping off wet clothes and rubbing herself down. She lay on the bed wrapped in a towel enjoying the sudden coolness. Let them talk about work while she had a five minute catnap. The drumming of the rain and the rattling of the shutters made it feel snug indoors for the first time in weeks; the sound soporific.

***

When Sophie awoke, the rain was still hammering on the roof but the bedroom was in darkness. She sat up, feeling light-headed. She had not slept so deeply in ages. The damp towel felt clammy on her cool skin; she shivered as she discarded it and pulled on a dry blouse and skirt. The shoes she had worn running around in the mud stood in a puddle by the door, ruined.

As she padded through the sitting room, the house appeared deserted. The veranda was in darkness. Tam had planned to take their guests to view the nursery of shisham and mulberries in the far plantation, but surely they wouldn't have gone out in such weather? Peering over the veranda, Sophie gasped at the sight of their waterlogged garden. The house was almost marooned. How had so much water fallen in such a short time?

'They've gone over to Chickawatin,' a voice startled her. A man rose from a chair in the shadows; Bracknall. 'Sorry if I gave you a fright, dear girl.'

'Chickawatin?' Sophie puzzled.

'I thought it best that someone kept an eye on the canal and, given your husband's obsession with irrigation, he seemed just the man.'

Sophie didn't like his sneering tone.

'Isn't that the job of the canal people in the Public Works Department?' she questioned.

'The canal yes; but the plantation next to it is ours – or more specifically your husband's. If it floods the seedlings will be ruined.'

Sophie hovered by the steps, feeling uneasy. If anything, the rain was increasing again and the light was nearly gone from a metal-grey sky. Rafi's tent sagged under the weight of water, the grass where he'd slept the past three nights turned into a lake.

As if he guessed her thoughts, Bracknall said, 'I sent Khan with Tam. Thought it would be awkward to have him hanging around here with your husband away. You know how servants talk.'

Sophie's discomfort increased. 'How long have they been gone?'

'You've been asleep over five hours. I doubt they'll make it back tonight. Looks like the road is impassable now anyway.'

Abruptly he clapped his hands and a servant hurried out of the shadows whom Sophie didn't recognise. Tam's boss rattled off orders in Urdu and the man dashed away towards the kitchen hut, splashing through water up to his knees.

'Hafiz can get you a drink,' said Sophie, crossing the veranda and calling out, 'Hafiz!'

'Your bearer has gone with Telfer and Khan.' Bracknall gave a sweep of his hand. 'Come and sit down, Sophie – you don't mind me calling you Sophie? – and have a drink with me. I'd like to discuss your husband's future prospects.'

Sophie felt completely wrong-footed by his proprietorial air; it was her house, not his. But then she realised that probably he had more claim to it than she or Tam; the bungalow belonged to the Punjab Forest Service and Bracknall was its chief.

His servant brought back pink gins and a tray of spicy pakora. Sophie began to relax after a few sips of the bitter cocktail. Bracknall talked easily of life in Lahore, his son at boarding school and his passion for polo and tennis.

'It's good to see you joining in the tennis with Tam – it's invaluable to have a supportive wife.'

'I enjoy playing,' Sophie replied. 'I don't do it to please the Forest Service; neither does Tam.'

'Well, I wouldn't be so sure of that.' Bracknall smiled. 'Tam would do a great deal to get on in the Service. He's keen and ambitious, which I applaud. Joining the Masons was another smart move; you have to impress the right people if you are going to make a career in India.'

'Shouldn't it be Tam's knowledge of forestry and his ideas on innovation that should be judged, not whether he can hit a tennis ball?'

Bracknall leaned towards her in the gloom; it was hard to read his expression but his words held a warning.

'Let me give you some advice. Don't let your husband get too enthusiastic about new-fangled ideas. There's nothing more irritating to us old hands than young pups coming out from England thinking they know all the answers and telling us how to run things.'

Sophie was stung into defending Tam. 'He's from Scotland and he's no young pup! Tam is a veteran of the Flanders War. He was experiencing horrors that no man should have to – while his seniors in India were safely furthering their careers. My husband has many good ideas – he's studied hard and learned from experience – and the Service should be glad of what he has to offer.'

She expected Bracknall to take offence; she flushed at her rudeness but the man was insufferable. He said nothing; pulling out a silver cigarette case and offering it to her. She was about to refuse – Tam would hate her smoking – then took one. It might steady her nerves. Bracknall lit hers and then his own, crossed his legs and sat back, surveying her.

'I like that,' he drawled. 'I like your loyalty very much indeed.'

Sophie blew out smoke and took a swig of her drink. She couldn't work him out. Bracknall's servant refilled their glasses and exchanged rapid words with his master that Sophie couldn't follow. The man lit two lamps; their weak light illuminated the sheet of rain beyond the balcony.

'I'm afraid I will have to beg your hospitality for the night,' said Bracknall. 'My bearer tells me the road back to the canal bungalow is flooded. He's going to make us supper.'

Sophie rose. 'I'll ask my own cook to prepare a meal.'

He reached out and stopped her. His grip on her arm made her wince.

'It's all arranged. Sit down and relax, my dear.'

Three drinks later, Sophie was relieved when they were told dinner was served. She felt queasy and couldn't stop shivering, even though the air was still warm. They ate at a table in the sitting room – the house was too small for a separate dining room – and it seemed uncomfortably intimate with the shutters closed and candles lit. She wondered why she hadn't seen any of her own servants. Surely Tam couldn't have taken them all?

Sophie steered the conversation relentlessly back to Mrs Bracknall and away from the senior forester's prying questions about her.

'Mrs B thrives on life up in the hills,' he said. 'Dalhousie is fine; Mussoorie's full of low rank army and inferior civil servants; Murree is pretty but doesn't have enough social life. That's why she loves Simla best. Costs me a small fortune but she's mixing with the right sort.'

'Tam wants me to go up to Dalhousie,' Sophie admitted.

'But you wanted to stay by his side?'

'Yes, of course.' She was annoyed that he might be mocking her.

'It takes a special sort of girl to stick it out through the hot season down here.' He watched her intently. 'Some would say a reckless one. And having seen you cavorting in the rain today, I think perhaps that's what you are.'

Sophie felt the heat rising up from her chest into her cheeks.

'I don't know what came over me,' she muttered.

He slipped a hand across the table and covered hers. She tried to snatch it back but he held on. He fixed her with his pale blue eyes. 'I like a risk-taker. It was enchanting.' Abruptly he let go her hand. 'I'm sorry if I sounded dismissive about Tam's ideas. You're right; we need enthusiastic young men like him coming up the line. Tell me more about his ambitions. You can be quite candid with me.'

Once again, Sophie felt caught off balance by the man. She was uncomfortable in his presence, yet this was a gift of an opportunity to speak about Tam's hopes and further his cause.

She stood up.

'Let's take tea on the veranda and talk more. Help yourself to whisky if you like.'

Opening the doors and peering into the dark, Sophie prayed that Tam and Rafi would still return. Bracknall followed, carrying a large glassful of Tam's best whisky that hadn't been touched since the New Year. Instead of the tea she'd ordered, his servant produced a water-pipe and placed it between them. Bracknall took a drag on the pipe and passed the nozzle to Sophie. She didn't really want to smoke but it gave her nervous hands something to do. It had an immediate calming effect; there was nothing to be gained by fretting over where Tam was.

Sophie grew quite garrulous about Tam's plans; his hopes of being a head conservator by the age of thirty, of becoming an expert in irrigation and silviculture, of lecture tours and professorships. Bracknall nodded and said little, but she felt his approval. She knew how important it was; Bracknall could either help Tam up the career ladder or block his way. They had already seen how Boz had been sidelined. McGinty too had been kept out of the way in the quasi-autonomous lands near the Khyber Pass. '*Too radical*,' Tam had said. '*It doesn't do to have political views in the Service; Khan should take note*.'

When Sophie had asked what he meant by that, Tam had said, '*Rafi dabbled with socialism at Edinburgh – that might be fine in Scotland, but it's seen as sedition in India. He has a hothead of a brother who is mixed up with the independence for India campaign – he needs to distance himself from all that too*.'

Eventually Sophie ran out of words. They sat in silence listening to the rain while Bracknall drank whisky and Sophie smoked on the water-pipe. The drumming on the roof was soporific; the falling water mesmerising.

'They won't be back tonight,' Bracknall said, 'the road's too dangerous. They'll put up at the *dak* bungalow; you mustn't worry.'

Sophie felt strangely sluggish. 'I'll see that the spare room is . . .' She was too tired to finish the sentence.

'I've sent your servants home.'

Sophie focused on him with difficulty. She felt weird, as if she was weightless. 'Why would you do that?'

'I'm offering you an opportunity,' he drawled, 'a way of advancing Tam's career.'

'I don't understand—'

'It's obvious from what you've told me that you're very keen for Tam to get on in the Forest Service. Isn't that so?'

'Yes . . . course.' Sophie's tongue felt too thick for her mouth.

'Let me come to your bed tonight and I can ensure that Tam is given the assistant conservator's position when Martins is sent up to Dehra Dun.'

Sophie thought she had misheard. 'Sorry, what you say . . .?'

'You won't be the first or the last to use your considerable charms to further your husband's position. What's so very wrong in that? We can give each other mutual enjoyment. I find you very desirable, Sophie.'

Sophie struggled to clear her head. His words were ringing in her ears. Her reply came out slurred and slow.

'Bed with you? Won't betray Tam.'

'Not betrayal; you'd be helping him.'

'No, I refuse.' Sophie shook her head but it just made her feel worse. What had he put in the water-pipe?

'That would be a pity for you. I know a frustrated woman when I see one. Your husband doesn't satisfy you, does he? Too many religious hang-ups to let himself enjoy the physical side of things.'

'Stop it,' she slurred. 'Not true—'

'Of course, if you don't want him to get promoted . . .' He let the words hang in the air like a threat, his look regretful. 'It puts a terrible strain on a wobbly marriage to be banished to the North West Frontier. No one will listen to Tam's schemes in a backwater like that.'

'You couldn't,' Sophie said, struggling to her feet. She swayed off balance. He was quick to catch her.

'Oh but I could.' He smiled. 'I have the ear of the highest in the Service – the governor is a personal friend too. The forests of northern India are my personal fiefdom, if you like.'

Sophie was bewildered. She thought Bracknall had been on Tam's side; now suddenly he was making threats to ruin him – and her. How had she misjudged the situation so badly?

'I won't do it. Sickens me.' She pushed him off and tried to walk past. Her legs seemed incapable of taking her in a straight line. She banged into furniture, trying to escape.

He laughed, taking her by the arm and steering her firmly through the house into her bedroom.

'Leave me,' she said. But she had no strength to resist.

'You'll do yourself harm falling about. Just lie down.'

His laughter rang in her head as she reached the bed and fell on it thankfully. Her head spun. She closed her eyes. He was saying something but the words were jumbled. She passed out.

***

Sophie was woken by a shaft of light piercing the half-closed shutter and stabbing her eyes. She felt dreadful; her head throbbed and her eyes felt gritty. For a moment her mind was a complete blank. She squinted and tried to sit up but the movement made her feel sick. She was naked under the sheet. It puzzled her; Tam didn't like her wearing no bedclothes in case the servants saw her. Sophie lay trying to remember what could have happened the previous night to make her feel so ill.

The monsoon. Tam and Rafi had gone. Bracknall had been there. They'd had dinner together. Her pulse began to race uncomfortably. She'd been smoking a water-pipe and talking too much. But she had no memory of getting to bed. Was Bracknall still in the house?

Sophie turned her head. There was an indentation in the pillow next to hers and the sheets were rumpled where someone had slept. Tam must have returned late at night. But even as she willed it to be true, dread clawed her insides. There was a smell of hair oil on the pillow; Tam never used anything but water on his hair. Her chest went tight with anxiety. It smelled of Bracknall.

Fragments of memory began to return; her slurred conversation, Bracknall's propositioning her; '. . . *offering you an opportunity . . . advancing Tam's career . . . let me come to your bed tonight . . .*'

Sophie put a hand over her mouth to stop the bile rising. What had she done? Had she agreed to Bracknall's demands? Getting to bed and what had happened afterwards was a dark void. She struggled to sit up and get out of bed. Last night's clothes lay discarded on the floor. Head thumping, she pulled on a robe and went to the door. The sweeper was crossing the veranda taking away the contents of the thunderbox. The water levels in the garden beyond had receded leaving emerald green shoots. Inching slowly through the house, she found to her relief that Bracknall and his servant were gone.

Only later, as she waited for Tam to return, did a flash of memory that was more like a dream take her breath away. She could see her prone body on the bed as if she looked down on herself from a great height. A man's white fleshy body was rising and falling on top of her, grunting with pleasure. Bracknall.

Chapter 28

Lahore

'Will you listen to your brother!' Abdul Khan exclaimed, running a hand over his thinning grey hair in agitation.

'Why should I listen to that Raj-lover?' Ghulam said with a contemptuous glance at Rafi. 'Look at him dressed in his khaki shorts like a white *sahib*.'

'Don't be disrespectful,' Abdul snapped, 'he is your elder.'

'It's all right, Father,' Rafi tried to calm him, concerned that the argument had brought his agitated parent out in a sweat under the formal suit.

'It's not all right,' Abdul said. 'Everything is not at all right. Ghulam was nearly arrested two days ago protesting outside the courts. If I hadn't intervened—'

'It was a peaceful demonstration – an act of solidarity with our brothers inside,' Ghulam defended.

'You were causing a breach of the peace.'

'There will be no peace until the British leave our land. They have no right to prosecute our brothers just for calling a *hartal*.'

'*Hartal*!' Abdul cried. 'Why are you mixed up in these Hindu practices? They make trouble for us law-abiding Muslims.'

'It's a very Indian kind of protest, Father,' Rafi intervened. 'A spiritual strike if you like – nothing violent.'

'Strikes!' Abdul waved impatiently. 'They are harming our businesses here in Lahore.'

'Only the Britishers are boycotting the shops that join the *hartal*,' Ghulam pointed out, 'and we will soon be doing without their custom once we boot them out of our country.'

Abdul slammed his fist on the table. 'Do not talk such revolution in my house! We have done very well out of British custom – you would not have had such a good education if we had not grown wealthy on their building contracts, don't forget that.'

'I owe the British nothing,' Ghulam said angrily. 'Can't you see how they hold us Indians back and give us only the crumbs from the table? They use your labourers to build their grand houses and clubs, Father, but they don't let you step over their doorsteps or give you membership.'

'I forbid you to attend your clandestine meetings,' Abdul blustered. 'They are outlawed and your so-called brothers are nothing but criminals. They're not interested in peaceful protest; they blow up cars and snatch people off the streets.'

'That's Raj propaganda, Father; they are freedom fighters! And I'm proud to be one of them.'

'If you get arrested, you will shame me and break your mother's heart. Tell him, Rafi!'

'Little brother,' Rafi appealed to his favourite yet troublesome brother. 'As long as you live here, you must respect Father's wishes. There are other ways of advancing independence for India.'

'Such as?' Ghulam scowled.

'By playing the British at their own game. Use your learning to advance yourself in a career in the law – that way you please your parents and you will be ready to take over the reins of power when the British leave.'

'When will that be?' Ghulam was scathing. 'Fifty years? A hundred? No! They will never give up power willingly – imperialists never do – they just string people along with promises that they will never keep. They have no intention of going.'

'That's not true,' Rafi countered. 'Men like Telfer and Boswell are quite open about their intention to train up Indians to take over the Forest Service. It will happen in our lifetime.'

'You've been living among the Britishers for too long, believing all their lies,' Ghulam sneered. 'You even sound like them. People like you make it easier for them to stay – you take their low rank jobs in the hope that one day you will be promoted to the high ranks of the Indian civil service. But they are just laughing at you behind your back – at the way you dress and ape their manners.'

Rafi was stung by his words; the image of Bracknall's patrician air and patronising slap on the back came back vividly. *'You see to the horses, there's a good chap, Khan.'*

'Don't insult your brother!' Abdul shouted, his patience at an end. 'And don't you defy me. I forbid you to consort with these Ghadaris.'

'You can't stop me.'

Abdul shot out of his chair, sending it toppling backwards. 'If you disobey me, I will throw you out of my house, do you hear?'

Ghulam sprang up too. 'I love you, Father,' he said, his fierce eyes glinting with emotion, 'but the cause we are fighting for is bigger than family loyalty. I can't stop and I won't stop.'

He flung Rafi a final challenging look. Rafi felt torn; his brother was going about things the wrong way and courting great danger, but he couldn't help but admire his passion and commitment. He and his student friends like McGinty had talked for hours about a new world order of brotherhood and liberty; Ghulam was prepared to put his words into action.

Sadly, Rafi shook his head. His younger brother spun on his heels and marched out of the room.

For a long moment there was silence between father and son. Abdul went to the window and peered through the latticework at the courtyard below, watching in disbelief as his rebellious son left through the gates, taking nothing with him and without a backward glance.

Rafi righted the toppled chair and came over, pulling out his cigarettes.

'Smoke, Father?'

Abdul shook his head, his eyes brimming with tears.

'What have we done to deserve such disobedient children? First you run off to the army and stay away for years; Rehman is nothing but a playboy; and now Ghulam is a revolutionary. Only Amir and Noor are married. Why can't you all just settle down in good jobs and marry the people we choose?'

Rafi lit up, nervous at the turn of the conversation.

'I have a good job, Father.'

'A *jungli* job,' Abdul was dismissive. 'You live in one room away from your family or in a tent like a Bedouin.'

'My needs are few.' Rafi smiled.

'Well, your needs will be very much more once you are married. The renovations next door are nearly complete; it will make a fine house for your bride.'

Rafi's heart sank; there had been no mention of a wife since the winter and he had hoped that his parents were resigned to his bachelor life. But his father was regaining his former bullishness, latching on to this new project to smother his hurt over Ghulam's rejection.

'You will go now and speak to your mother – she has a very suitable girl in mind – a good Lahori girl with a father in banking. And while you are there, you will talk some sense into your sister Fatima.'

'Fatima?' Rafi asked in surprise. His demure sister was the model daughter, obedient and studious; she had excelled in her schoolwork at St Mary's College, proving wrong the conservative relations who had tutted at money being wasted on educating a girl.

'She wants to be a woman doctor. Have you ever heard of such madness?'

Rafi whistled and stubbed out his cigarette.

His father wagged a finger. 'Let's hope you have more influence over her than you did over—'

'Ghulam?'

'Don't mention that boy's name again in my hearing,' Abdul said, his voice quavering as he turned away to stare out of the window.

***

Rafi always relaxed when he visited the *zenana*, the women's quarters of his father's tall, rambling house. His mother had kept strict *purdah* all her life but somehow knew everything that was going on in the outside world. She had never been formally educated, yet had striven to have her children well schooled and loved them to recite poetry to her. Outwardly, she deferred to her husband in everything; privately she was the driving force behind the family's fortune.

It was through her acquaintance with Miss Drummond, the principal of St Mary's College – his mother had entertained her at the opening of new classrooms built by Khan's Construction – that Fatima had gained a scholarship at the prestigious girls' school. He wondered if his mother had hoped all along that Fatima might become one of Lahore's first women doctors; someone who could administer to women like her in the cloistered world of the *zenana*?

He found his mother and sisters sitting in the shade of the courtyard, the sounds of a fountain trickling and birds twittering in the mulberry tree mingling with their voices.

He embraced his mother.

'Come and drink sherbet with me,' she said, patting the cushion beside her. 'I can see from your face that Ghulam has not done as you asked. Your father will blame me for indulging him too much as a child – and maybe I did – but he has always been in a hurry to change the world.'

Rafi squatted down.

'Don't sit like a peasant,' his sister Noor scolded, 'you're not in the jungle now.' She was hugely pregnant and perspiring.

He flopped back on the cushions, winked at Fatima and helped himself to a fig from a dish of fruit in front of them. As usual Fatima was sitting upright and composed, letting the older women talk while she observed. Perhaps she was shy having him around, but she was always so self-contained that he never knew what she was thinking. Their mother speculated that Ghulam would be staying with his activist friends.

'See if you can persuade him to stay with you, Rafi,' she worried, 'then at least we will know he is not in a police cell.'

'Don't fuss about Ghulam,' Noor was dismissive. 'He will come running back home when he next needs Father to get him out of a scrape. It is Fatima we should be worrying about. Has father told you?'

'About Dr Fatima Khan?' Rafi teased.

Fatima gave him a flicker of a smile.

'Tch!' Noor gave an impatient huff. 'Don't encourage her. She has had enough schooling. It is not natural for a woman to be a doctor; no man will want to marry her. Isn't that right, Mother?'

'That is probably right,' their mother agreed.

'Perhaps another doctor will?' Rafi suggested.

Noor snapped, 'It is not a joking matter. You must make her see sense. It is causing so many arguments in the family. It reflects badly on us all. They say to Father that he cannot control his own daughter.'

'Who says?' Rafi asked.

'Your brothers and uncles – it is the talk all over Gawalmandi.'

Rafi laughed. 'You are right; every shop I go into they are talking of nothing else.'

'Mother!' Noor cried, her eyes filling with furious tears. 'Tell him not to make a fool of me!'

'Rafi,' his mother chided. She put a hand on her fraught daughter's head. 'Now, now, little nightingale, you will make your baby ill with all your shouting.'

'Sorry,' Rafi was quickly contrite, going over to pat his sister's shoulder. 'But I don't share your fears about Fatima. It is a sign of civilised progress that women are training to be nurses and doctors. We need them in India where most men do not want their wives and daughters examined by male doctors. Think how much better the health of our women will be if those like Fatima can look after them. Look at you,' he challenged, 'she could deliver your baby for you.'

'What is wrong with our midwives?' Noor protested. 'You were happy with them, weren't you, Mother?'

For a long moment their mother said nothing. She fingered the brocade on her sari. When she spoke, her voice was soft and full of regret.

'I lost three babies between Amir and you. Your father would not allow a doctor into the *zenana*. That is all I will say on the matter.'

Her criticism of their father was so unexpected that they just stared at her as she adjusted her sari and took a sip of iced sherbet.

'Now, my son,' she continued, fixing him with a determined look, 'what I really want to talk to you about is Sultana Sarfraz, the banker's daughter. She is very pretty and she is a cousin through your great-uncle Jamal. Show your brother the photograph, Noor.'

Rafi rolled his eyes at Fatima, as the older women fussed over the picture. He looked at the posed studio photo of a solemn, slim-faced woman staring at the camera with large, anxious eyes. She looked very young. His heart sank. He felt nothing for her. How could he, when the only woman he could think about was Sophie Telfer? His every waking moment was filled with thoughts of her; the way she smiled and pushed blonde hair out of her lively brown eyes, her quick walk, her throaty laugh, the way she moved in the saddle when she rode her black pony. He noticed how she always wore the dark opal he and Boz had bought her, and how often her slender fingers would stroke it. Try as he might, he could not rid his mind of the sight of Sophie rising from the roof of the forest bungalow, moonlight shining through her flimsy shift as she descended the steep steps. Had she been sleeping up there or just gone up for a breath of air? Just as well he had not known, or he would not have been able to resist rushing up there to lie beside her . . .

Rafi felt consumed with guilt towards his friend Tam for such thoughts, yet he felt anger too at the cold way Tam increasingly treated Sophie. She had been so happy to see her husband when Tam and he had returned from the flooded plantation at Chickawatin, yet Tam had been cross with her for letting Bracknall leave before he got back, and reduced her to tears. '*Really, Sophie, you should have entertained him for me. He'll think us quite rude.*'

Rafi felt wretched to see Sophie upset, but he was in no position to help her; she was married to another. Even if she had been unmarried, in the strict code of the British in India, which made outcasts of white women who married Indians, she would still be out of his reach.

'Yes she is pretty,' Rafi said, trying to summon up some enthusiasm for Sultana Sarfraz. There was too much wrangling in his family for him to add to their unhappiness. Perhaps marriage would be a good idea after all. It might cure him of tortured thoughts of Sophie and give him an outlet for his passion.

His mother gave a broad smile. 'So you will be happy for us to arrange a meeting with the Sarfraz family?'

Rafi hesitated. He saw Noor's expectant look and Fatima's watchful one. He wondered if Fatima could read his thoughts?

'Yes' – Rafi forced a smile – 'if it makes you happy, Mother.'

Chapter 29

Shillong

The rain fell in sheets beyond Major Rankin's veranda. The sky was as dark as night. From the safety of the sitting-room – doors flung open to catch the wind and the view – Tilly thought the storm magnificent.

'I can't stop thinking about the Logans living up at Belgooree,' Tilly said, raising her voice against the claps of thunder.

'Well, it makes sense,' said Ros. 'Somewhere in the hills that was healthier than at the Oxford Estates.They must have rented it for a while.'

'But James must have known it was Belgooree, yet he kept that from me. Why would he do that? He doesn't want me anywhere near the place.'

'Isn't his reluctance to let you go there more to do with his cousin Wesley? They don't see eye to eye, do they?'

'Well, it just makes me want to visit there more than ever,' Tilly was adamant. 'What do you remember, Major Rankin, about 1907? Was there a big fuss about the fiftieth anniversary?'

'There was a good deal of hot air about it, in my opinion. The Indian army is loyal to the hilt – at least in my old regiment – but there was real concern in government that there would be unrest. The planters felt more vulnerable than most, I suppose.'

'Why?' Tilly asked.

'Living upcountry – remote and isolated – but with large numbers of poor coolies on their doorstep.'

'Would it have been any safer at Belgooree for the Logans than staying at the Oxford, do you think?'

'Possibly,' the major conceded. 'Belgooree is a small estate and the Khasi people are friendly. I remember when it was run by Belhaven – an old army man and a genial fellow before he hit the bottle – they never had labour problems as far as I know.'

'That was my friend Clarrie's father, Jock Belhaven,' Tilly said.

'Ah, his daughter Clarissa.' Major Rankin smiled. 'Striking girl – dark good looks and rode well – mother was half Indian. I'm afraid people gave them the cold shoulder socially, but on leave I used to go up to Belgooree for a spot of fishing.'

'But in 1907,' Tilly steered him back to what preoccupied her, 'what was happening up there?'

'Don't know.' The major shrugged. 'Regiment was posted on the North West Frontier that summer. Ros and her mother were here at Shillong, but Ros was too young to recall those days, I imagine.'

'I do remember children at school frightening each other with stories,' Ros mused, 'that natives were going to sneak in at night and knife all the white children in their beds.'

'Children can be little beasts,' Tilly said. 'But was there any trouble?'

'Not that I remember. We were kept very sheltered from the outside world at the cantonment school.'

'And Clarrie won't be able to tell me anything,' Tilly sighed, 'because she was in England by then, that's why the Logans were able to go there. I wonder what happened to the place after the Logans died and before Wesley and Clarrie got it back?'

'Clarissa Belhaven, eh?' The major chuckled. 'Strong-willed girl – didn't give two hoots about what people thought of her – scandalised the gossip-mongers by taking tea in the Pinewood Hotel with her pretty little sister.'

'But Belgooree?' Tilly prompted. 'Did it stay empty all that time?'

The major frowned as he tried to remember. 'I don't remember hearing that anyone lived up there until the Robsons came back.'

'Belgooree,' Ros mused. 'I do remember something about it.'

'Yes?' Tilly asked.

Ros waved a hand. 'Oh, it was nothing really; just silly childish gossip.'

'Go on, tell me.'

'The children in the cantonment used to say there was an old tea bungalow in the hills that was haunted. Everyone who lived there died – but it was just silly tale-telling.'

'There's always a grain of truth in every tale.' Her father grunted. 'Old Belhaven's wife was killed there by a falling tree in the earthquake and then Belhaven drank himself to death.'

Tilly and Ros exchanged looks.

'And then the Logans died,' said Tilly.

They sat brooding in silence as the rain eased and a warm mist rose up from the lake and hid the hills.

***

Tilly went back to the library to read through the *Shillong Gazettes* of that long ago May. She knew that it must be pure chance that the Logans had died on that ominous anniversary date, but she couldn't get the idea out of her head that there was some link.

The tenth had been Sophie's sixth birthday too. Her cousin had remembered that she'd wanted a party but no one had come, yet they had been letting off fireworks beyond the garden fence and drums had been beating. Small Sophie had equated them with birthday celebrations especially for her; but in adulthood that seemed unlikely. *And the drums had got so loud they made me frightened*, Sophie had recalled.

What if the bangs and drums had been something more sinister? Tilly wondered. Had the Logans really been in danger there?

Mama told me to go and play hide-and-seek, Sophie had said. It was one of her few vivid memories of her mother – maybe her last, she had confided in Tilly.

Lister, the retired policeman, was only too pleased to pull out the old newspapers again.

'Knew there was something in it, didn't I tell you?'

'I don't know that there is,' Tilly cautioned, 'I just want to get a better feel of what was going on at that time.'

'I was talking to old Burke at the club about your interest in the Logans' deaths.'

'Burke?'

'The superintendent at the time. He seemed a bit rattled. Wanted to know why you were poking your nose into other people's tragedy after all this time.'

Tilly blushed.

'Sounded to me,' Lister said, pulling on his moustache, 'like a man with something to hide.'

She asked him to carry the bound volume of newspapers to a table in the main section where people read in silence, knowing that he wouldn't be able to hover and talk. Tilly immersed herself in the newspapers. Most of the articles were deadly dull; reports of cantonment life, a production of *HMS Pinafore*, a parade, prices fetched at a timber auction. The most exciting event appeared to be the spotting of a leopard lying on a tombstone in the cemetery.

What was she looking for? Proof that there was something untoward going on at Belgooree while the Logans were there? But, from Sophie's hazy memory, it sounded as if their final day together was routinely uneventful. A birthday with no party; a game of hide-and-seek. Tilly vowed that she would make a huge fuss of Jamie on every birthday.

A strange feeling settled on her. Jessie Logan, Sophie's beautiful mother marooned at Belgooree with a dying husband, was soon to succumb to fever herself. But a woman who was playing hide-and-seek with her six-year-old didn't sound like someone in the grip of fever. Such doubt had plagued Sophie too.

Who was the doctor who had pronounced them dead? There was no mention of him in the report of their deaths. *It is presumed that they died of enteric fever.* So who presumed? A double death should surely have attracted more attention than it had. Tilly conjured up the distressing image of small Sophie, running off to hide and waiting for her mother to seek her but never coming. And the *ayah* running away with a kitten. She found that almost as odd as Jessie's sudden fatal fever. *Ayahs* were usually devoted to their charges and Sophie remembered hers with an affection bordering on devotion. That was why she felt so betrayed by her *ayah*'s disappearance. Had the woman been terrified of catching the fever too? But why save a kitten and leave Sophie behind? It just didn't make sense.

Tilly sighed. She was not going to find anything in these old newspapers to shed any light after all this time. On the point of closing the folder, she flicked through the edition for the day before the Logans' death.

Tilly let out a gasp at the sight of James's name.

'Planters urged to be cautious: *Mindful of the imminent anniversary of the Indian Mutiny, planters and businessmen are being urged to be vigilant. Touring the tea gardens, assistant manager at the Oxford Estates Mr James Robson warned his fellow tea planters to take extra precautions to keep their wives and families safe.*

'Visiting the Shillong area, Mr Robson said, "The advice is for British in the mofussil *not to stay in isolated bungalows but to band together on the larger estates. Don't put your wives and families at risk."'*

So James had been in the area at the time of the Logans' death, Tilly realised with shock. If he was going around warning the planters, he must surely have visited Belgooree too? But he had told her that he was only there later when summoned by the police.

She went and found Lister the librarian. 'What's the *mofussil*?'

'It's Anglo-Indian for the provinces; anywhere outside the safety of the town.' He gave Tilly a curious look. 'Have you uncovered something interesting?'

Tilly shook her head. She was not going to share her sudden suspicion of her husband's behaviour. But her stomach fluttered with tension. James had been there – or at least near at hand – at the time of the Logans' death. He must have had an inkling that by staying on at Belgooree alone and unguarded, they were in danger. Had he tried to persuade them to leave? If he had found them ill with fever, surely he would have organised their rescue? But he hadn't; and they had died.

Tilly shivered with sudden cold in the dim library. What if something terrible had happened on the anniversary of the Mutiny? What if the Logans had not died of fever but had been attacked and killed? She had a sudden image of a tough young James doing all he could to cover up what had happened at Belgooree. What was it that James knew but was determined to keep from her and Sophie?

Chapter 30

Dalhousie Hill Station

It was a relief to get away from the plains and the claustrophobic forest bungalow. It held no enchantment for Sophie anymore; only ugly memories. White ants ate through their furniture, insects dropped into their food, and the doors and windows swelled and would not close. As the rains turned the jungle to mosquito-ridden swamp and the house to a mildewed mess, Tam had suffered a further bout of debilitating fever.

He screamed in horror about Germans pouring into his trench and laughed hysterically that the trees were talking. Sophie had taken him back to Lahore to be seen by the civil surgeon.

'When you are this susceptible to fever,' he had told Tam, 'only a few months back in Europe can cure you. You need to get it out of your system. Somewhere at high altitude where the air is bracing but dry – the Tyrol perhaps.'

'Damn it,' Tam had fulminated, 'I've hardly been in India a year. I'm not due home leave for a couple of years. It's out of the question.'

'Well, get yourself to the hills here then,' the doctor had ordered.

So Tam had agreed to go with her to Dalhousie. Just before they left, a package had come from Tilly containing a photograph. Sophie had stared in shock at the weathered gravestone bearing the names and dates of her parents; they were buried in Shillong. She was glad to know but it left her more upset than she had imagined. Why Shillong? Tilly said she would try to find out more.

Up in Dalhousie, Sophie delighted in the cool air, misty mountains and the gurgling of fresh running water. They stayed in a cottage on a steep slope above the post office with views of distant snow-capped mountains, where Tam had revived. At moments when she had nursed him, he had been almost tender with her again and she was filled with optimism that they could rekindle their former feelings. But his interest in making love to her had dwindled to nothing since the monsoons had brought on his illness. Each night Sophie lay anxious that they shared no intimacy, yet relieved that he did not touch her. The thought of sex brought back horrible bouts of anxiety over what she might have done with Bracknall.

Outwardly, she and Tam appeared a happy, sociable couple, attending tea dances, picnics and fancy dress parties. Tam bought her a second-hand guitar and encouraged her to play and sing when they had company. It was as if all he wanted from her was a wife to show off and partner him at tennis and dinner dances, while he flirted with the daughters of colonels and flattered their matronly mothers. Sophie knew Tam meant nothing by such flirtation; it was just the way the British behaved on holiday in the hills. And, with painful clarity, she realised that that was all he had really intended with her in Edinburgh; a summer flirtation. It was she who had pushed him into a proposal.

But what did she want from him? Sophie puzzled. She no longer knew. She saw with resignation that he was at his most content escaping both her and hill station society to the army mess of the Ghurkha regiment, posted at the barracks further up the hillside. Tam would go there for mess dinners and return drunk on rum, unaccustomed to drink, weeping like a child and calling her his angel nurse. Once sober, she never pressed him as to what had made him so upset.

When Tam went out alone, Sophie would call on Fluffy Hogg and talk about Mrs Besant and the recent strikes in the Lahore shops. 'No point boycotting them,' Fluffy was fatalistic, 'they'll press ahead with their protests whatever we do.' Sophie enjoyed these conversations as Tam wasn't interested in talking about current affairs.

No sooner was he feeling half restored than Tam was planning a hunting trip to the mountains towards Chamba, bordering Kashmir.

'It'll give me the ideal opportunity to collect data on the deodar plantations and the chir pine forests up near the snow line,' he enthused. 'I can do a spot of game hunting too. There's plenty of company for you here while I'm away.'

'I'm coming with you,' Sophie insisted, yearning for a camping adventure beyond the confines of the hill station. Her greatest pleasure was riding the steep paths on a sturdy Bhutan pony she had hired for their stay; now she would be able to go further and higher.

Two days before they set off, Sophie returned from the bazaar to an unpleasant shock. Bracknall was coming down the steps of their veranda talking to Tam. He smiled and swept her with a predatory look that gave her palpitations.

'I couldn't pass up this opportunity of a trek into the Himalayas – I came as soon as I got Tam's invitation.'

Sophie looked at Tam in horror. How could he have done such a thing? She couldn't possibly go. The thought of the man being anywhere near filled her with disgust.

'M-Mr Bracknall,' Sophie stuttered. 'Tam never said.'

'I told you she'd be overwhelmed at your coming, sir,' Tam said in delight. 'You do us both a great honour.'

Sophie felt nauseated at Tam's ingratiating tone. She wanted to spit at the vile Bracknall. He had drugged her and probably taken his pleasure; in her memory it was like a bad dream but she feared it had taken place. How had she got into such a position? She had never given Bracknall the slightest encouragement. Oh, why had Tam gone off and left her alone with such a man! She felt angry with her husband; the day the monsoon broke he should have woken her before he left and given her the chance to go with him. But Tam's cross words, flung at her after the terrible trip to the depot, still rang in her head.

'That's the last time I take you with me on my rounds. You shouldn't have been there – and you shouldn't have interfered – your actions totally undermined me in the eyes of the depot manager. Word got round to the timber merchants and that's why they ganged up against me.'

Tam had punished her for his humiliation. But he would be horrified if he knew what his boss had done behind his back.

Yet Bracknall still had not confirmed Tam as Martins' successor. Tam had been told unofficially that the job was his; Bracknall had hinted as much at a Masons' dinner that Tam had dragged himself to in Lahore a few weeks previously. Well, if Bracknall thought he could coerce her into going to bed with him again, then he was mistaken. Better that Tam remained in the job he had; she bitterly regretted that his boss had tricked her and taken advantage of her state of intoxication. Shame washed over her anew at just seeing him again.

'It's a great pleasure,' Bracknall replied with a satisfied smile. 'I'm so glad that Mrs Telfer is going to be one of the party.'

It was only as she turned from him to hide the distaste she knew must show on her face that she saw another man standing smoking at a distance, stroking the nose of his horse.

'Rafi?' Sophie cried.

He ground out his cigarette and came forward. 'Hello, Sophie,' he said, his smile tentative. He did not hold out his hand.

She was aware of the awkwardness between the three men. Then it struck her; Rafi had been left outside with the horses like a common *syce* while Bracknall had gone into the house to share a drink with Tam. She felt indignation rise. How could Tam be so discourteous to his friend?

'Will you come inside for a refreshment?' she asked, pointedly.

Before he could answer, Bracknall said offhandedly, 'He hasn't time. There's a lot to arrange before we set off for Chamba. Isn't that right, Khan?'

Rafi touched his *topee* in a mocking salute. 'Yes, sir.'

'So you're coming too?'

He smiled and nodded.

Sophie could not hide her relief. 'That's wonderful! Isn't it, Tam?'

Too late, she realised that both Tam and Bracknall were giving her stony looks at her grin of delight.

***

They argued that night. Tam accused her of being rude to Bracknall.

'You didn't even shake his hand.'

'I was laden down with shopping.'

'One parcel.'

'Oh, Tam, why can't we just go on this trip ourselves? I thought it would be a good chance for us to be alone – enjoy our own company.'

'You seemed more than happy that Khan is coming,' he snapped.

'He's our friend,' Sophie pointed out, 'whereas Bracknall is your boss – you won't relax.' She noticed how Tam never referred to Rafi by his first name anymore, distancing himself.

'This is a working trip – I'm not here to relax. And I want to impress the chief. Promise me you will be civil to him?'

Sophie reluctantly nodded but Tam remained in a bad mood, taking himself off to sleep in his dressing room. She lay sleepless and feeling out of sorts – bilious and head pounding – and wondered if she was succumbing to a fever.

Perhaps it was creeping dread of the forthcoming trip with Bracknall but she felt no better the following day. It was only as she was looking out clothing and toiletries for a servant to pack that it struck home. Her sanitary towels were still washed and unused in a linen bag, untouched since Changa Manga.

Her heart began a slow thud. When had she last used them? Five, six weeks ago? She hadn't had her monthly bleed since coming to Dalhousie. They were always like clockwork even when travelling; she should have had one two weeks ago. How could she not have noticed? Sophie had been too caught up with life in the hill station and worrying about Tam to give her own body a second thought.

Sophie sat down on the bed, weak-kneed. Could she be pregnant? She swallowed down the odd metallic taste in her mouth, noticing the nausea even more. Somehow she just knew it. To her surprise, she felt elated. Tam would be over the moon. This would bring them together. She gave a small gasp of excitement. She had expected to feel frightened but she wasn't at all. She wanted a baby. *A baby*!

Sophie hugged herself. She need not pack the sanitary towels. But if she didn't, the servants would talk. She wanted to keep the discovery to herself until she was certain. Then Tam would be the first to be told; or maybe she would write to Tilly in the meantime and share the news. She had to tell someone! How, at that moment, she longed for her Auntie Amy to be alive to share her good fortune. She would have come out on the boat at once to help her through the pregnancy and stay for the birth.

Tam would insist that she be put under the watchful eye of the civil surgeon or maybe one of the army doctors – Cousin Johnny for instance. They would examine her and keep her and the baby healthy. Could they give a precise date of the birth? she wondered. Sophie was light-headed with sudden plans. The baby would be born at the start of the hot weather in April. Tam would be in his new post in Lahore by then . . .

Sophie clamped a hand to her mouth in sudden fright. She was counting off nine months from mid-July when they had arrived in Dalhousie and her periods had stopped. But she and Tam had not made love since before the rains. The baby could only be . . .

Sophie rushed from the bedroom into the dingy washroom and vomited into the drain. She heaved and heaved, until her stomach was hollow and her throat burning. But she could not empty her head of the spectre of Bracknall's white bulk on top of her as she lay beneath pliant and detached. She must be carrying Bracknall's bastard.

Chapter 31

Rafi did not mind the petty snide remarks from his insufferable boss about the incompetence of Indians or that he was never invited to dine in Bracknall's tent at night as Tam was. He relished living out of doors, riding the steep paths in the heat of day and sleeping like a hillsman wrapped in a black blanket in the chilly nights, falling asleep to the sound of horses munching forage, the shrill cry of a hill deer and the distant grunt of a bear.

He had forgotten what a beautiful country he lived in, and each day brought new delights. The lower hills were covered in feathery mimosa, wild lemon trees, yellow flowered cassia and groves of wild orchids by fast rivers. Steadily they had climbed through dark forests of sal to the higher slopes of ancient oaks, cypress trees growing in isolated sunny spots amid silver firs, and up to the vast stretches of chir pines with their light green tufts of long needles.

'They're like Scotch firs,' Sophie had gasped in awe at the massive trees that miraculously clung on to sheer cliffs, their roots twisting like corkscrews around the rocks.

She had caught his look for a moment, given a wistful smile and then quickly looked away. They had hardly spoken on the trek; she seemed deeply preoccupied. Perhaps Tam had warned her off being too friendly; his old friend was ignoring him too in his efforts to please Bracknall. It saddened him. Yet it was Bracknall's over-familiarity with Sophie that made him angry. Tam did not seem to notice how tense and uncomfortable Sophie became in their boss's presence. He was always trying to touch her and make remarks that carried a double meaning. Rafi had not noticed this before, though he had heard stories about Bracknall being predatory with Anglo-Indian women when his wife went to the hills each summer. If he were Tam he would defend Sophie's honour with his fists and to hell with any promotion. But he wasn't, and he had no claim to protect Tam's beautiful wife.

So Rafi often rode on ahead with the bearers who were tasked with choosing the next night's camping ground or detoured up side ravines to shoot partridge and deer for the evening meal. He made sure the mules and horses were well rested at the end of the day, ignoring Bracknall's command that their tired legs be bound together to stop them wandering off over steep cliffs.

On one cold night, when his boss was drinking at his tent door, Rafi went and loosened the reins of Bracknall's highly strung Arab mare. The beast was quite unsuitable for their tour into the mountains and it had been tied to a high branch so it could not graze the lush vegetation at its hooves. The sweat of the day had cooled the animal's flanks and the horse was shaking with the cold.

'There you are, girl,' Rafi murmured softly in the mare's ear, as he rubbed it down and covered its trembling body with a blanket. The horse whinnied, plunged its nose into a basin of water Rafi had fetched and drank thirstily.

Suddenly Bracknall was weaving himself towards them, stumbling on a guy rope.

'What the bloody hell do you think you're doing, Khan?' he bellowed.

'Ariadne was tied too tightly,' Rafi held his temper. 'I'm giving her a drink and a rub down.'

Bracknall pushed him aside. 'Get your thieving hands off 'er.' He swayed and slurred. 'Trying to take her for y'self, were ya?'

'Of course not, sir.'

'*Syce*!' he called for his groom. 'Ya lazy savage! Get here now.'

Rafi watched in fury as Blacknall took the reins of his horse and yanked the beast round, slapping it hard on the rump and shoving it towards the scurrying *syce*.

'Tie it up again,' the drunken chief forester ordered, then staggered back to his tent.

Rafi helped the anxious Lahori boy calm the over-wrought animal, speaking quietly but firmly in Punjabi. 'This is the way you secure the horse; no tighter. And never let it stand here all night without a cover. The temperature in the mountains can fall below freezing even in the season of monsoon. It's hard for us men from Lahore to imagine a cold night at this time of year, isn't it?'

The young groom nodded and smiled at Rafi's confiding tone.

'The horse won't wander off if it's well fed and watered, my friend, understand?'

***

Sophie found the narrow tracks carved into the mountainside unnerving; bound on one side by dark walls of rock and on the other by dizzying drops to the valley far below. They seemed to have been travelling for days without the view ahead changing; a deep gorge with its raging torrent, side streams and waterfalls that they crossed on swaying rope bridges, and endless dark forest stretching away to snow-clad mountains and distant glaciers. It was gloomy and oppressive; the stamping of their long line of pack animals and the clinking of metal pans magnified by the silence.

Sometimes they would come across Tibetan traders in thick woollen clothes, baskets of goods strapped to their heads and spinning prayer mills. Bracknall would order them out of the way and somehow they would cling to the cliff edges with strong bare feet a few inches from the void and let the camping expedition go by.

With each passing day, Sophie loathed Tam's boss more. Even her husband was beginning to mutter about Bracknall's drinking and his bawdy remarks.

'It's a side he keeps well hidden at work. I suppose it's his way of letting off steam.'

Sophie could not bear to be near the man, yet he sought her out and always rode close by. She had overheard the altercation between Bracknall and Rafi a few nights before, and noticed how the Indian forester grew ever more impatient with his boss's harsh treatment of his skittish horse Ariadne.

They were coming to another dizzying rope bridge now. Sophie watched in alarm as Ariadne stamped at the ground and refused to go forward, unsettling the other horses. Instantly,

Bracknall raised his whip and lashed at the mare; once, twice, three times. It reared up and nearly threw off her rider. Bracknall clung on, the whip slipping from his hand and disappearing over the precipice.

Rafi dismounted and leapt forward. 'Give her to me, sir,' he cried. 'She's terrified.'

Without waiting for permission, Rafi stripped off his shirt, threw it over the horse's eyes and seized the reins. Sophie watched transfixed as the muscled forester risked a kicking from the crazed mare and fought to bring it under control. It dragged him perilously close to the edge; Sophie's heart froze in her chest. The other beasts stamped fretfully, infected by Ariadne's fear.

'Easy, easy,' Rafi cajoled. Within minutes the horse was pacified and he was guiding it gently across the swaying bridge. Bracknall followed, puce with humiliation, his expression thunderous.

'I think Ariadne is short-sighted,' Rafi explained, helping his boss remount. 'She sensed the huge drop but couldn't see to the other side. I'll get the *syce* to make some blinkers, then she won't give you any more problems.'

'Short-sighted?' Bracknall barked. 'I've never heard such nonsense. I'll handle my own horse, Khan.' He leaned down, eyes narrowing, and added under his breath, 'You'll regret making a fool of me, you jumped up *babu*! Your card is marked.'

Sophie saw Rafi recoil as if struck, his green eyes stormy, and wondered what offensive remark Bracknall had made.

They rode on in single file, Rafi going back over the bridge for his own hill pony. Sophie wanted to hang back and talk to him but there was no room to manoeuvre round and she had to keep going.

The heat bounced off the walls of rock around them, sweat running in rivulets under her shirt and jodhpurs. She felt increasingly sick and faint. Rounding a bend, they went from white light into abrupt shade. The temperature plummeted. A waterfall was frozen; shards of ice hung down from the overhanging rock.

All at once, Sophie's pony skidded on icy stones towards the sheer drop. She cried out in horror. The river boiled below her, a lurid grey-green from the melted glacier.

'Help!' she screamed, yanking her pony away from the cliff edge towards the rock face.

Tam was already around the next bend and out of sight. Bracknall leaned round, startled. His horse jumped, spooked by the noise.

'Control it, damn you!' he bawled and kicked Ariadne forward, trying to put distance between their horses.

Sophie fought to bring the pony towards the rockface, but stubbornly it began to back away. All at once, Rafi was behind, shouting.

'Pull her round to face the drop! Let her see the drop!'

'I can't!' Sophie wailed.

'Do it!' Rafi urged.

Seeing how Sophie was paralysed with fear, he pushed forward, his pony scrambling on the edge to keep its feet. He lunged at Sophie's bridle and jerked the wild-eyed pony towards him.

Just before the terrified animal pushed them both off the path, it caught sight of the ravine and stopped in its tracks. The young *syce* from Lahore ran along the path and held its head, talking to it gently as he'd seen Rafi do. In moments, the pony was walking on sedately as if nothing had happened.

Sophie's heart raced as if she had scaled the mountain; she gulped for breath, forcing back tears. Shortly afterwards, the path plateaued and they stopped for tiffin, the cooks frying up fritters and boiling tea.

Sophie could hardly speak, she was still so shaken by how close to death she had come – how close Rafi had too.

Bracknall put on a show of concern, forcing a whisky flask under her nose that made her retch.

'Have a swig – make you feel better. You look grey as putty.'

Tam came over. 'What happened, lassie?'

'Her pony got frisky,' Bracknall said. 'I think Khan fussing made it worse. Nearly took them both over.'

'Rafi?' Tam turned and glared. 'Did you put my wife's life in danger?'

Rafi looked furious, but Sophie could tell he was not going to defend himself.

She pushed Bracknall's flask away and faced Tam. 'That couldn't be further from the truth,' she said hotly. 'Rafi saved my life back there – and risked his own to do it.' She turned to Rafi. 'I can't thank you enough.'

Abruptly, she burst into tears of relief. Tam hesitated, then awkwardly went over to pat her shoulder.

Chapter 32

At the end of a week, they came across two engineers surveying the mountainside for a possible road over the high pass.

'It's Miss Logan, isn't it?' the junior engineer exclaimed as Sophie dismounted.

She recognised the cheerful army captain, Cecil Roberts, from the voyage to India the previous year. They had helped organise the children's deck games together.

'Captain Roberts, fancy meeting you here!' she smiled. 'I'm Mrs Telfer now.'

'Lucky Mr Telfer.' He grinned.

Tam stepped forward and introduced himself and the others. He was immediately interested in their work and what they could tell him about the way ahead.

'Come and take a look at our survey maps,' the older man named Ford offered. 'They show all the peaks and ridges and the best places to cross the river courses.'

'Splendid,' cried Tam. 'We can use them as a basis for our forestry mapping, can't we, sir?' He looked to Bracknall for approval.

His boss had already flopped on to the engineers' most comfortable camp chair. 'Yes, yes,' he answered with a dismissive wave. 'We'll set up camp here. I've had quite enough of being in the saddle. Looks like you sappers have found the best spot, eh?'

While the servants set up camp, collected firewood and water, Tam and Rafi went off to a forest village the engineers had discovered, to help buy milk, flour and a sheep for slaughter.

'Listen, Khan,' Tam said bashfully, 'I'm sorry I snapped at you the other day. I didn't really think you'd put Sophie's life at risk. It's just Bracknall made the accusation and I had to challenge you. I blame myself for not being there to protect her.'

Rafi eyed his friend, wondering if there was more troubling him than the incident on the cliff edge. He looked harrowed and emaciated, yet he still drove himself relentlessly, his enthusiasm for work undimmed.

'No offence taken,' Rafi said, putting a hand on Tam's shoulder. 'But you shouldn't believe everything Bracknall says. It seems to me he is taking an unhealthy interest in Sophie.'

'Why do you say that?' Tam asked sharply.

'Open your eyes, Telfer! He never lets her alone.'

'He just likes female company,' Tam retorted.

'He has a bad reputation.'

'The chief would never do anything dishonourable – it's just your over-active mind, Khan.' Tam gave him a hard look. 'It's high time you got yourself a wife and stopped fussing over mine.'

Rafi reddened. 'Well, you'll be pleased to hear my parents have found me someone suitable' – he gave a wry smile – 'Sultana Sarfraz, a banker's daughter.'

Tam was immediately conciliatory, clapping Rafi on the back. 'Congratulations, Khan! That is good news. It'll help you get on in the Service. The chief likes his men to be married.'

It's the wives Bracknall likes, Rafi thought but didn't say.

By evening the tents and camp beds were erected, cooking fires lit and an evening meal of curried lamb prepared. They sat around a camp fire, Tam poring over maps with the engineers in the light of lamps hung in the trees.

'Have you been on to the glacier?' Tam asked eagerly.

'I have,' said Ford. 'Roberts here is dying to get up there and see his first snow leopard.'

'Could you show us?' Rafi joined in, excited at the thought. It might be his only chance of climbing in the Himalayas. Bracknall would probably banish him to the desert once they returned; the man did nothing to conceal his dislike of him now.

'Be delighted to,' Ford said. 'We're planning to push on up to the glacier in a couple of days. You won't be able to take all this encampment with you – just what you and a porter or two can carry – it's hard going. But it's the best time of year to survey these parts.'

'Worth taking our guns for a spot of game shooting?' Tam asked.

Ford nodded. 'There's musk deer and a particularly aggressive wild goat called *Thar*. But you'll need guns to protect yourselves from bears and leopards.'

'Well, I shan't be joining you.' Bracknall grunted, helping himself to more of Ford's whisky. 'There's plenty of game in these forests to keep me occupied while you scramble around on the ice. And I'll look after Mrs Telfer, of course.'

Rafi saw the alarm on Sophie's face as it drained of colour.

'That's very good of you, sir,' Tam said, though he flashed Rafi a questioning look.

'No,' Sophie said in panic, 'I'm not staying here.' She swallowed and forced a smile. 'I mean I want to climb too. It's such a golden opportunity.'

'It's not suitable for a woman' – Bracknall laughed – 'is it, Ford? The girl would be a liability.'

'Well,' Ford sounded unsure, 'it depends on your experience, Mrs Telfer.'

'I've climbed in the Alps,' Sophie said quickly. 'And I'm quite capable of carrying my own pack. I won't hold you up, I promise.'

'What do you say, Telfer?' Ford asked.

Tam snorted. 'My wife is like a mountain goat. If she wants to come, you'll have the devil of a job stopping her.'

'Then I'd be delighted to have you along, Mrs Telfer.' Ford smiled.

'Thank you.' Sophie grinned. 'Show me the route we'll take.' She joined the men leaning over the table to scrutinise the map.

Only Rafi caught the thunderous look on Bracknall's face, illuminated in the firelight. Sophie would not be forgiven for outwitting him – nor Tam for allowing Sophie to choose the climb instead of staying in camp with him.

***

They took small tents just big enough for camp beds – Rafi loaded their packs on to his sure-footed Tibetan pony – and hammered nails into their shooting boots for grip. Ford hired a *shikari*, a local guide, to take them up to the glacier; Sophie noticed how the local man travelled simply with a blanket, kettle and grass shoes that didn't slip on rock.

They left at dawn as the early gleams of sun over the eastern hilltops were striking the white tents of the main camp and dew-covered spiders' webs were glistening as the mist on the trees dissolved. Sophie was thankful that Bracknall was still snoring in his tent and hadn't bothered to see them off. She tried to hide from Tam how sick she was feeling, forcing down a cup of sweet tea and a piece of dry chapatti to keep the nausea at bay. She didn't want to think about the baby growing inside; it revolted her now to think it could be the hateful Bracknall's. Nobody must ever suspect. She would lie about her due date and refuse to be seen by a doctor.

'Are you sure you're up to this?' Tam asked, giving her an anxious glance. 'You seem a bit out of sorts, lassie.'

'I'm fine.' Sophie smiled, swallowing down the bile in her throat.

The guide moved noiselessly on the steep paths without dislodging stones on to those who followed; Sophie tried to imitate his steady pace. They climbed steeply all morning before stopping for a late breakfast on a narrow terrace. Cecil Roberts got out his binoculars and scanned the slopes below.

'Good Lord! Look at that! A black bear.'

He passed the glasses to Sophie. She gasped in excitement at the ambling creature, moving with surprising speed like a mechanical toy.

'It's about five thousand feet below us,' Ford said. 'You feel like an eagle up here, don't you?'

They pressed on towards the amphitheatre of snowy peaks, sweating under a fierce sun. Sophie found it increasingly difficult to breathe in the rarefied atmosphere.

'The mountain tops look close enough to touch,' she panted, as they stopped mid-afternoon for a meal of cold fowl and vegetable samosas.

‘They’re actually about twelve miles away – all over twenty thousand feet,’ said Ford. ‘But we’re aiming for the glacier at fifteen thousand.’

‘What’s that roaring noise?’ Sophie asked in concern. ‘It’s not a thunderstorm on its way, is it?’

Rafi had a quick exchange with the guide. ‘He says it’s an avalanche echoing across the mountain,’ he said in excitement. ‘Must be getting near the glacier.’

‘You sound like you’re enjoying the thought of danger ahead.’ Sophie snorted.

‘I’m enjoying it all.’ He grinned. ‘And the *shikari* says we must watch out for falls of rock on the way up too.’

That night they camped in the shelter of juniper trees on a grassy slope on the edge of the snowline. Sophie shivered on her narrow canvas bed, unable to get warm.

‘Tam, can I climb in with you?’ she whispered.

‘No room,’ he answered drowsily and was soon asleep.

She lay awake agonising about her situation. The idea of carrying Bracknall’s child made her physically sick. How could she get rid of it? Perhaps if she had a fall on the rock that would do it? She really had no idea. There had been a nurse at the Red Cross depot during the war who had got rid of an unwanted baby before her fiancé returned from the navy. She had gone to see someone. But that was in Edinburgh. Here, Sophie had no one to turn to. She was utterly alone with her problem. Better to throw herself off a high ledge than to go through months of mental torture and a lifetime of being shackled to Bracknall’s baby having to pretend it was Tam’s. She would never be able to love it for she would always remember the hateful night of its conception and the burning shame of what she had done.

The servants put the kettle on with the morning star. Sophie was exhausted from lack of sleep but thankful to see the dawn. Sunlight pushed away the dark thoughts of the night. Warming her hands on a bowl of tea, she took a sip, which made her want to retch. She dashed behind a stunted fir tree and vomited.

Just when she thought she couldn’t feel more wretched, a swift movement caught her eye. She looked up to see a snow fox padding by. It paused briefly to sniff the air and stare at her, tail stiff, ears alert.

'Good morning.' Sophie smiled and pressed her hands together in greeting.

The fox flicked its tail as if in response and then darted away down a rocky ravine.

'Who are you talking to?'

Sophie swung round. A figure stepped out of the shadows, pulling on a cigarette. Rafi. Her heart squeezed. It was almost unbearable to be with him at such close quarters and yet not to be able to touch him and tell him how she felt. Yet the thought of the trip finishing and not being able to see him every day was even worse.

'I was saying hello to a fox.' She smiled.

'Lucky fox,' Rafi murmured, blowing smoke. He walked up to her and bent to pick up the discarded tea bowl. 'Are you okay?'

Sophie grimaced. 'I've felt better. Last night's meal disagreed with me. I'll be fine once we get going again.'

She was unnerved by his scrutinising look. She couldn't bear him to guess her predicament. Grabbing the bowl from him, she muttered about getting ready and hurried away.

That day, they left the belt of juniper and birch where a base camp of tents and Rafi's pony were left with the cook and two other servants to prepare the evening meal. With rifles for a day of hunting, they followed the tracks of the stocky, shaggy black goats, which the locals called *thar*, up the grassy slopes. Soon they were scrambling across slippery rock polished by the elements, with huge precipices dropping away into the void. Ford used two walking sticks made out of bamboo to take the strain and Roberts took off his boots and edged across in stockinged feet. To Sophie's amusement, the local hillsmen hired to carry their packs walked nimbly in bare feet behind the guide who was following the droppings of the elusive *thar*.

'They must be hiding in caves or behind the larger rocks,' Ford panted, as the guide led them on to the glacier. They soon picked up tracks in freshly fallen snow, which disappeared up a chimney-like ravine that seemed to lead straight into a wall of rock.

The guide began to pull himself up from boulder to boulder and beckoned the others to follow. Sophie looked aghast at where they were heading; it didn't seem humanly possible to scale such a vertical face of rock.

'If you want to go back, I'll take you,' Cecil Roberts said. He looked sweaty and anxious.

Heart pumping, she took a deep breath and shook her head. 'I want to go on, thanks.'

With Tam giving her a helping hand, Sophie made it quickly up the narrow gorge. They emerged breathless on to a grassy plateau surrounded by a jagged ridge. A flock of stone-coloured ewes and their kids were grazing peacefully. In a nervous rush, Cecil raised his rifle and fired at a fat young buck. The report rang around like a thunderclap. The *thar* moved as one, fleeing across the plateau and up the crag, defying the law of gravity in their escape.

'Idiot!' Tam barked.

'Sorry.' Cecil flushed.

'At least we know where they've gone.' Sophie gave a reassuring look and pointed upwards. 'There's obviously a cave up there.'

Cecil gave her a grateful glance and pushed his binoculars at Tam. 'She's right. Here, have a look.'

'We can track them later after we've had something to eat,' Ford suggested.

As they ate a picnic of egg sandwiches and boiled up water for tea, Ford plunged a thermometer into the bubbling water.

'Look; water's boiling at 182 degrees instead of the usual 212 degrees; that's thirty degrees difference. If you estimate about five hundred feet to each of those thirty degrees, it means we've reached about fifteen thousand feet in altitude.'

'That's clever,' Sophie said.

'Saves carrying bulky measuring equipment that could cause injury on these crags.' Ford smiled. 'Old surveying trick.'

The sun edged round and their grassy shelf grew hot. Rafi, taking his pack and rifle with him, went off to explore with the guide. The other men were keen to stalk the wild *thar*.

'I'll stay here,' Sophie said, tired now from lack of sleep and the strenuous climb.

'Do you want me to stay behind?' Tam asked. She was grateful that he offered but knew he was desperate to follow the chase.

'I'll be fine with the servants,' she assured.

They scrambled off in the direction of the *thar* caves and were soon out of sight. Sophie was just dozing off when Rafi returned.

'The *shikari* has found the spoor of a snow leopard,' he cried. 'Come and see.'

He grinned like an excitable boy and waved her over. Sophie quickly pulled on her walking boots and got to her feet, her weariness evaporating. She followed Rafi on to the narrow footpath chiselled out of the rock by years of passing *thar,* but ten minutes out on the rockface, she was suddenly overwhelmed by the precipitous view. Fifteen thousand feet up in the sky. The river and its streams looked like shiny threads on a map. Her head began to spin. Her lungs tried to suck in air but she couldn't breathe. It was then that she heard an ominous rumble shake the stillness. Sophie knew now that the sound was that of melting snow on the move. They were halfway across to the next overhang of rock and grassy slope – a few hundred yards – but it might just as well have been a hundred miles as she knew she could not reach it. Neither could she move backwards.

'Where's the guide?' she asked anxiously.

'He's climbed up to tell the others about the leopard.' Rafi cast a glance over his shoulder and stopped short at the sight of her face tight with fear. 'It's not far.'

Sophie felt sweat breaking out on her face; she clawed at the rock and screwed her eyes shut. If she looked at the drop, she knew she would not be able to resist stepping off the ledge. It pulled at her like a magnet.

'I'm stuck,' she gasped. 'I-I can't move.'

Rafi slung his rifle over his shoulder and backtracked till he was beside her. He held out his hand.

'Here, hold on to me.' His broad smile of encouragement made her feel brave. She grabbed at his hand and held on tight.

Together they edged along the cliff face until it broadened out into a deep gulley. They crossed over a stream that bubbled out of the rock. To Sophie's dismay, Rafi pulled his hand away and crouched down to drink.

'It's safe to drink this,' he said, scooping handfuls and slurping it thirstily then splashing it over his face and hair. 'It's the melted ice that you have to avoid – too full of impurities.'

He flicked water playfully at Sophie. She gasped in shock.

'That's freezing!' she squealed. She lunged forward and splashed him back. Rafi laughed and held up his hands in surrender. In those few moments, Sophie lost her fear of the mountain and shuddered to think how close she had come to hurling herself off it.

Rafi led the way under the rocky overhang, past a clump of junipers and dwarf pines springing out of thin soil. The afternoon sun shone in their faces, making them squint and shade their eyes in the glare. Around them the sounds of ice cracking and water trickling filled the silence.

Abruptly, Rafi halted and put a finger to his lips. He pulled Sophie behind a boulder and pointed. At first she could see nothing. Then her eye caught it; the swinging of a tail from a stunted fir tree. The more she stared, the easier it was to make out the feline shape of the leopard clinging on to a branch that overhung a patch of grass where the snow had melted. Under it grazed a stout, black-haired *thar* buck with thick curling horns, oblivious to the danger.

Swiftly and silently, Rafi crouched, slipped the rifle from his shoulder, steadied it on the rock and took aim. For a moment Sophie thought he was going to shoot the leopard, but with a practised steady squeeze on the trigger, the gun went off and the *thar* buckled to its knees. In an instant, the leopard was leaping from its perch and bounding off into a cave.

'He can help himself to the leftovers when I've skinned it and taken what we want,' Rafi said cheerfully, as they hurried over to inspect the dead *thar*.

With horror, Sophie watched as he drew a sharp hunting knife and cut the buck's throat. Ruby red blood spurted out and turned the snow crimson. Methodically, Rafi began to skin the goat. Sophie's throat watered. She turned away and scrambled behind the tree but it was too late to stop her stomach going into spasm. She was violently sick, retching again and again until all she could bring up was thin green bile.

Rafi dropped the knife and rushed over.

'I'm sorry; I didn't realise you were that sensitive to blood.'

'I'm not,' Sophie gasped, mortified that he should witness her being sick. She took the handkerchief he held out, and wiped at her mouth. She felt ghastly; hollowed out and cold but perspiring.

He rubbed her back. 'I don't think you're well. You've been sick nearly every day for the past two weeks.'

She gave him a startled look. 'How do you know?'

'I notice things. I notice everything about you.'

Sophie felt the heat rise into her cheeks. He reached out and pushed a strand of hair from her mouth. She wanted to grab his hand and hold it against her burning face, to press her lips to the large palm. But she mustn't weaken.

She turned from him. 'There's nothing wrong with me. It's just the altitude.'

Abruptly, there was a loud boom from above. Sophie jumped in fright. Her first thought was gunfire. Then the rock beneath her trembled and a noise began to grow as if a train approached. Suddenly Rafi was pushing her under the tree and to the ground, flinging himself on top of her. Sophie screamed and struggled but he held on.

'Stay still!' he ordered.

Seconds later an avalanche of falling rocks and stones came tumbling down, pulverising the spot where they had just stood. The noise was like cannon fire. Then just as quickly as it had started, it was over. Rafi rolled off Sophie.

'Are you okay?' he gasped, coughing in the dust. 'I'm sorry—'

'Don't be,' Sophie said quickly. 'I shouldn't have screamed like a baby.' She looked dazedly at where they had been moments before. It was piled high with loose rocks. 'You saved my life again.'

Rafi gave her a wry smile. 'There's no one I'd rather rescue.'

Sophie laughed off the compliment. He was just being gallant. 'Oh, Rafi, look.' She stared beyond him in sudden alarm. 'The path back is blocked.'

They went to investigate. Rafi began to scramble up the rockfall but it shifted dangerously under his grip. He came back down and looked around, squinting in the direction in which the snow leopard had disappeared.

'There's another way on to the ridge that way.' He pointed upwards. 'We can work our way above the rockfall and come down the far side. That's the way the *shikari* went. We'll just have to leave the *thar* behind.' He gave a regretful glance at the half-skinned animal just beyond the fresh tumble of rocks.

The sun had already left the slope and the temperature was dropping.

'Lead on, Macduff.' Sophie smiled, hiding her nervousness.

Rafi shouldered his pack and led the way. They made quick progress up the crag, following *thar* tracks. But the air was cooling rapidly and the light vanishing. As they drew near the top of the ridge, clouds began to gather on the peaks and the wind picked up. She saw Rafi giving anxious glances at the sky as the bank of cloud built around them.

There was a rushing sound and Sophie watched in confusion as a pillar of leaves and pine needles was sucked up from below and whirled past them.

'What's happening?' she panted, trying to match Rafi's pace.

'A storm's on its way,' he called. 'We need to hurry.'

But the further up they climbed, the worse it got. Soon they were surrounded in white mist. It chilled to the bone. One moment they could see magnificent iced peaks, the next nothing. Rafi seized Sophie's hand.

'We won't make the top before it comes. We'll find shelter till it blows over.'

Sophie tried to smother panic. 'But there isn't anywhere.'

'If we drop down a little – we passed a cave.'

She gripped on to Rafi, as he inched their way down the crag. One wrong step and they would be falling off the mountain to certain death. Sophie stifled a sob. Amid the feeling of utter panic, she had a moment of clarity; she didn't want to die. She wanted to live and love and see the baby inside her born, no matter how abhorrent its conception. It was her baby and that was all that mattered. She clung to Rafi, her lifeline.

Just as the first heavy drops of rain began to hit them, Rafi saw the mouth of a low cave rear out of the mist. He pushed Sophie under the rocky shelter with his pack and rifle.

'Stay here, I'll be back in a minute.'

'No! Don't leave me,' she begged.

But he was gone, swallowed up in the mist again. Sophie didn't want to shuffle in any further in case Rafi should miss the opening. She squatted down and sang 'It's a Long Way to Tipperary' at the top of her voice, to keep up her spirits and to guide Rafi back through the rain.

It seemed an age but was probably minutes before he reappeared out of the swirling cloud. He was soaking but clutching an armful of juniper branches. He fell to his knees laughing and panting.

'I don't know how you find anything to laugh about,' Sophie cried, nearly throwing herself at him in relief.

'You singing that song.' Rafi chuckled. 'Never in my wildest dreams did I think I'd hear that being sung so lustily from a Himalayan cave!'

Sophie sank down beside him and dissolved into laughter too.

They made a nest of juniper branches under the overhang, pressing as far back into the shallow cave as they could, while the storm broke around them. From his pack, Rafi produced toffees.

'Real Scots toffee,' Sophie exclaimed. 'Where did you get this?'

'McGinty's mother sends them to me.' He grinned. 'She knows my sweet tooth.'

They sucked on the sticky sweets and Sophie had a pang of longing for Edinburgh and Auntie Amy. Rafi seemed to understand, for he began reminiscing about his days in Scotland as torrents of rain raged down the mountain slopes; thunder deafened like a hundred ton gun and lightning flared in blinding flashes.

Soon the rain turned to hail – huge balls of ice that bounced on the rock – and then snow. Sophie sat with her shoulder pressed against Rafi's damp one for comfort, watching in awe as the storm raged just feet from their sanctuary, blinding and deafening, as if it would cleave the very mountain in two and hurl them into the chasm.

It went on for hours.

'Tam will be so worried,' Sophie fretted. 'He might think we're dead. No one caught out on the mountain could survive in this.'

'He'll know we'd look for shelter,' Rafi tried to calm her. 'And that I'd take care of you.'

'What if they got caught in this?' Sophie cried.

'They won't have. The *shikari* will have led them to safety long ago. They'll be back at camp. We would have been there too if it hadn't been for that fall of rock.'

Eventually Sophie succumbed to exhaustion. She curled up, wrapped in Rafi's blanket, comforted by the fragrant smell of juniper.

The silence woke her. The storm had passed on. There were distant fitful rumblings as it died away. In alarm, she felt the gap where Rafi had been. She was alone in the darkness.

Chapter 33

'Rafi?' she called out. 'Rafi!'

He answered from beyond the cave. 'Sophie, come and have a look.' She could hear the wonder in his voice.

Keeping the thick wool blanket about her shoulders, she crawled out. Clear cold air hit her face. The sky was crowded with brilliant stars and a crescent moon shone over white summits and fields of snow. Far below was darkness – outlines of forests and crags – and a faint murmur of the distant river in the stillness.

'Have you ever seen anything so magnificent?' Rafi marvelled.

'It's like a fairy-tale land,' Sophie whispered.

They stood spellbound in a glittering silver world, listening to the occasional rumble and crash of glaciers moving. After a while, Rafi collected up some of the juniper branches and lit a fire in the cave mouth. Melting some snow in his camping kettle, he brewed tea and they shared the same wooden cup.

'How were you so prepared?' Sophie asked, amazed.

'Old Lahore Horse, remember?' He grinned. 'Trained to survive anywhere.'

In the frosty night, huddled close to the small fire, they found themselves talking of many things; their differing Indian childhoods, their shared love of the outdoors, of poetry, music and fishing.

'Where,' Rafi asked in amusement, 'did the young Miss Logan learn to fish?'

'Great Uncle Daniel in Perth taught me.' She laughed. 'I'm good with a rod and I don't mind gutting fish either. Not like Tilly who used to pretend she had a headache and run off with a book.'

'Well, when the snow melts and we get out of here,' Rafi said, 'we'll go fishing for mahseer. Boz says we foresters have an open invitation from Wesley Robson to go to the Khasi hills for some sport. Best fishing in the land, according to Robson. You could visit your friend Clarrie and combine it with a trip to see Cousin Tilly.'

She let him daydream and make impossible plans as if both of them were free from all ties and obligations to anyone else. Under the magical stars anything seemed possible. A couple of days ago, Tam had announced that Rafi was betrothed to a Lahori banker's daughter, making a fuss of him in front of the others. Rafi had been embarrassed and Sophie had slipped off so that no one would see how upset she was at the news. But that night, they mentioned neither his forthcoming marriage nor Tam.

Eventually, they lay down to sleep, though Sophie never wanted the night to end.

'You keep the blanket,' Rafi said, burrowing down in the juniper branches.

'We can share it,' Sophie said, glad that the dark hid her blushing. She opened it out and threw an end over him.

She lay with her back to him. He snuggled closer but didn't touch. Her heart banged in her chest. How she wanted him! Sometime later, she asked quietly, 'Rafi, are you awake?'

'Yes.'

Sophie swallowed. 'Will you hold me please?'

There was silence. She cursed herself for embarrassing him. What would he think of her? 'It's just I'm cold.' She tried to make light of it. 'I don't expect anything more – I just want your warmth.'

Then a strong arm came around her waist and Rafi pressed himself up against her back. Sophie held on to his hand.

'Thank you,' she whispered.

She could feel his breath on her hair and the strong, fast beat of his heart. She knew then that if she just said the word, Rafi would make love to her. She could feel the tension in him, the desire in the way he held her, breathed in her scent and sighed her name. Sophie was sick with yearning too. But she had already made a mess of her marriage to Tam – Bracknall had seen to that – and to be unfaithful with Rafi would be the finish of it. Neither would she ruin Rafi's future life with his soon-to-be wife. She suspected his sense of honour to his friend Tam would hold him back anyway. There would never be a future for them together, so giving themselves to each other now would only be destructive.

They fell asleep in each other's arms.

***

Sophie woke to find Rafi gone. She sat up in alarm. The space behind her was cold, the glow of the fire almost out. Outside was daylight; pink light making the snow look like cake icing.

Then she spotted Rafi trudging back up the frosty slope with pine branches and tree roots. His breath billowed in clouds at his exertion. He saw her and gave his broad smile, his green eyes shining. Sophie's heart sang. She would give anything for that to be the face she woke up to every morning. She had a sharp stab of envy for this Sultana Sarfraz chosen to marry him.

'I've been back to the dead carcass,' he panted. 'No sign of the leopard. Do you like kidneys?'

'Normally I love them,' Sophie said. 'But I've gone off meat lately.'

'They will taste delicious cooked over a scented pine fire and eaten in the open, believe me.'

He set about stoking up the fire, balancing the kettle on a couple of stones and roasting the kidneys on a stick. The smell of cooking meat made her feel sick, but Rafi encouraged her to eat and Sophie found herself enjoying the taste after all. They sat cross-legged and drank tea, toasted old chapatti and chewed more toffee.

'I think it'll be safe to go back the way we came,' Rafi said. 'Looks like the fresh fall of snow has created a bridge over the rockfall – frozen it solid. But we'll have to get going before the sun heats up. There'll be a risk of avalanches later.'

'Part of me,' Sophie dared to admit, 'wishes we could stay here for ever.'

Rafi fixed her with his green eyes. 'Those are dangerous thoughts.'

‘I know.’ Sophie held his look. ‘We could hunt and fish and travel the Himalayas on Tibetan ponies.’ She spoke flippantly, though really she meant it.

Suddenly she dreaded going back to her old life; Tam’s moods and fevers, biting her tongue in Bracknall’s presence, a life of social etiquette in Lahore’s clubs and sitting rooms. How could she bear it?

‘You could do all that with Tam,’ Rafi said quietly.

Sophie shook her head. ‘I thought that was the life we would lead when I came out to India – to be trekking and exploring – but that’s not what Tam wants from me.’

‘Which is?’

‘A hostess and tennis partner – someone to help him climb the ladder. His career is his passion – you know what he’s like – he lives and breathes forestry.’ Sophie sighed. ‘I feel disloyal talking about him behind his back but he doesn’t love me. I sometimes feel as if he resents me for agreeing to marry him.’

‘I’m sure Tam loves you,’ Rafi said.

‘I think he tries, but deep down he can’t. Boz tried to warn me – in Bombay – he told me about Tam’s war injuries and how that had changed him. But I wouldn’t listen.’

Rafi snorted. ‘Boz was just trying to put you off because he was in love with you.’

‘No.’ Sophie blushed. ‘He was trying to tell me something. Now I think it was that Tam didn’t really want to marry me but didn’t know how to get out of it.’

Rafi leaned over and took her hand in his. ‘I think you are worrying unnecessarily. Tam is not an easy man to live with but I don’t doubt that he cares for you. He talked about nothing else when we were out here before you came. Tam’s a good man.’

‘Oh, Rafi,’ she whispered, tears prickling the back of her throat. ‘You are such a good friend. Tam hasn’t always treated you well these past months, yet you’ll say nothing against him.’

Rafi withdrew his hand. ‘It’s British society out here that won’t accept our friendship in the way it did in Edinburgh. Tam can’t be blamed for the imperialist mentality that we have to work under. But things are changing.’

‘Not fast enough for me,’ Sophie said. ‘I hate it that you can’t socialise with us – can’t dance or dine in most of the clubs – that Bracknall snubs you at every opportunity.’

‘Bracknall,’ Rafi sneered. ‘I’m happy not to be invited to his tedious dinners.’

‘But he has power over you and your job – has power over all of us,’ she added bitterly.

‘Has Bracknall done something to you?’ Rafi demanded.

Sophie looked away. ‘I just loathe the man.’

Abruptly Rafi stood up and held out his hand. ‘He can’t stop us dancing in the Himalayas. Would you do me the pleasure of this dance, Mrs Telfer?’ He started whistling a waltz.

Sophie got up laughing. ‘Of course I would.’

On the frosty slope in the early sunshine, they shuffled around humming and grinning. Slowly they came to a standstill, their arms still around each other, gazing into the other’s eyes. Sophie leaned up and brushed his lips with a kiss.

‘I’ve wanted to do that for so long.’

His look was suddenly fierce; he dropped his hold and pushed her gently away.

‘I’m sorry’ – she gulped – ‘I thought you felt the same.’

‘My God, woman,’ he exclaimed, ‘you have no idea how much I want you. But up till now, we’ve done nothing to be ashamed of. I can look Telfer in the eye and tell him that nothing improper has happened between us.’

‘It doesn’t feel like that to me,’ Sophie retorted. ‘For me, everything changed last night. Standing under the stars with you—’

‘Don’t say it!’ Rafi cried. ‘Don’t say anything more.’

He turned from her and began kicking out the fire. She watched him in distress as he packed his knapsack and rolled up the blanket they had shared. How could he say that nothing had happened? They might have just managed to keep their desire in check physically, but in her mind she had given herself willingly to Rafi a hundred times.

They did not speak again as they descended, Sophie placing her footsteps in the tracks that Rafi left in the virgin snow. The sound of ice cracking and snow melting made them hurry on past the remains of the dead buck that the leopard had recently dragged under its tree. As Rafi predicted, the snow had compacted into a bridge over the rock-strewn ravine that had been impassable the day before. It was a difficult scramble but they made it across.

At the sheer rock face beyond, Sophie halted in horror.

'Where's the ledge?'

Rafi looked concerned too. 'It's covered in snow. I don't like the look of this.'

Sophie's heart hammered as she tried to keep down her panic. 'What shall we do?'

Rafi scanned the icy slope. 'Watch for *thar* – see which way they cross the crag.'

'I'm scared.'

He threw her a look. 'Still want to roam the Himalayas on a mule?'

'Don't tease me.'

'Come on, we'll see if we can find the track the *shikari* followed across the top.'

They spent the rest of the morning scrambling up the frozen ravine trying to find a route back to the camping ground. The sun was high and they could hear the glacier groaning as it shifted under the strong rays.

Finally they gained the summit, Rafi hauling Sophie up the last muscle-burning climb. She fought for breath, her head pounding and legs buckling. But as she clung to the rock she felt a thrill of victory that they had made it to the top.

The white peaks dazzled and shimmered. Below, the valley had disappeared under clouds. The mountain range stretched away like an archipelago in a sea of mist, leaving them cut off from the rest of the world.

'Over there,' Rafi pointed out. 'A flock of *thar*.'

Squinting, Sophie saw a line of wild goats threading their way between giant boulders down the slope.

'Doesn't look too difficult.' She forced a smile.

‘We’ll eat first,’ Rafi said, hunkering down and pulling the remains of their breakfast out of his pack; cold kidney and stale bread.

One whiff and Sophie was vomiting into the rock. Rafi scooped a handful of snow and held it out to her.

‘Suck this.’

Sophie dipped her face and licked. The snow numbed her mouth and burned its way down her throat. But it stopped the retching. She took some more. Rafi rubbed her back.

Sophie groaned. ‘I’m sorry. It was just the smell.’

He regarded her. ‘It’s not altitude sickness, is it?’

She didn’t answer.

‘You’re expecting, aren’t you?’

Sophie gave him a startled look. ‘How do you know about such things?’

‘My sister Noor was always being sick when her baby was on the way.’

Sophie sighed. ‘Yes I am.’

‘Does Tam know?’

‘Not yet.’

Rafi’s eyes glittered. ‘That will make him happy – and perhaps you too.’

Sophie gave a wistful smile. ‘Yes, perhaps.’

Rafi shoved the unwanted food back in the pack. He appeared to have lost his appetite too.

Just before they set off on the descent, he said, ‘I’m glad now that we did nothing to be ashamed of. Tam will make a good father for your child.’

It wrung Sophie’s heart to hear the finality in his words. He was right; they had come so close to betraying Tam but had resisted. It was the hardest thing now to nod in agreement and let Rafi go without telling him how much she loved him, how much she regretted not making love to him when they had had the chance. He was a better person than her by far, Sophie thought.

She turned from him quickly so that he would not see the tears that welled in her eyes, and led the way down the mountain.

Chapter 34

Rafi looked around in disbelief. The tents were gone, ripped from their moorings with only a few pegs left in the hard ground. Debris of pots, candles and food lay scattered in the melting snow. A group of *thar* ran off, disturbed from picking over the remains.

'What's happened?' Sophie gasped.

'The storm's wrecked everything.' He pulled a hand over his tired eyes as if he could change what was in front of him. He looked around in vain for his pony.

'Oh, dear God!' Sophie wailed.

Rafi gripped her arm. 'This doesn't mean they aren't safe. There are plenty of places to shelter down here among the fir trees.'

'What do we do? Should we start looking for them or go for help? I must know if Tam's all right!'

Rafi saw the look of distress on her face, the huge brown eyes haunted with guilt. He knew now that she must regret the things she had said; their strange night of intimacy among the snow fields and stars seemed quite unreal now.

'We'll find him, I promise. Let's head back to the main camp – if they're not there, we'll get up a search party.'

Rafi kept to himself the niggling question: why was no one out looking for him and Sophie?

Nightfall caught them still halfway back to the main encampment where they had left Bracknall. Rafi made a makeshift shelter under the branches of a chir pine tree, propping up fallen branches and insulating it with feathery needles. They shared an apple and some biscuits salvaged from the storm-blown camp and huddled down together under the blanket for a second night.

They hardly spoke. Sophie was distant with him, preoccupied. He longed to put his arms around her again but she did not ask it. She would never know what a supreme effort it had been for him not to declare his love for her; to admit his need to be near her, hear her laughter and look into her passionate brown eyes. As he lay there sleepless, listening to her even breathing, he ground his teeth in jealousy that she was carrying Tam's child and not his.

'Rafi,' she spoke suddenly. She had not been asleep after all.

'Yes?'

'You asked me if Bracknall had done something to me,' she whispered.

Rafi sat up and peered through the dark. He could not see her expression but her voice wavered. 'Well, he – he did.'

'Tell me,' Rafi said gently.

Sophie could only bear to speak the words because she was cocooned in darkness, and the burden of not telling anyone was too great.

'That night of the monsoon – when you and Tam were away and I was left alone with – that man.' She swallowed. 'He drugged me. I think he had it all planned – sent away my servants and kept his own – said the road to the canal bungalow was flooded so he had to stay the night. I hardly remember what happened,' she said in distress, 'but I know he took advantage – came to my room and forced himself on me—'

A huge sob broke from her. At once, Rafi had his arms around her, pulling her to him and holding her tight.

'My God, Sophie,' he hissed, 'that bastard!'

She shook and wept in his arms. 'How could I have let such a thing happen? I feel so guilty.'

'Don't say that' – Rafi gripped her – 'you're not to blame. It's all Bracknall's doing. He's a loathsome excuse for a man.'

For a while he just held her while she sobbed into his shoulder; the relief she felt at having spoken her horror aloud was like a dam bursting.

Eventually Rafi asked, 'Does Tam know?'

Sophie shook her head. 'You're the only person I've told. And Tam must never know.'

'But, Sophie, something must be done about Bracknall. I want to tear his sneering head off!'

'No!' Sophie pulled away in agitation. 'You mustn't do anything foolish. He would just deny it and take it out on Tam.'

'I'd stand up for you, and Tam would too.'

'I could never tell Tam,' Sophie cried, 'because of the baby. He might suspect . . .'

Rafi felt his heart go leaden. 'Suspect what?'

Sophie hesitated and then forced herself to say, 'I think the baby is Bracknall's.'

Rafi let out an oath. She could tell how shocked he was. He had nothing to say. She should not have told him; it was unfair to have shared her burden when he could do nothing for her.

'I'm sorry, I shouldn't have told you. What must you think of me?'

Quickly he took her head between his hands. 'I think you are the bravest woman I know,' he whispered and kissed her gently on her forehead. 'I'm so sorry.'

She leaned into him and they lay down side by side, holding each other until they both fell asleep.

***

A party of hillsmen led by Cecil found them early the next morning. They were startled from exhausted sleep, not realising that the sun had been up for two hours.

'Thank God!' Cecil cried. 'We've been looking since yesterday. A herdsman said he'd seen a couple on the higher slopes.'

Sophie, dishevelled and stiff with cold, asked anxiously, 'Where's Tam? Is he all right?'

'Twisted his ankle – took a tumble coming down in the rain. But he's all right – apart from fretting about you.'

'I'm fine. Rafi kept me safe.'

Rafi noticed the awkward glances and felt he had to explain. 'We got cut off by a fall of rock – had to take refuge in a cave—'

'You can tell all this to Telfer,' Cecil interrupted, looking embarrassed. 'The main thing is that Mrs Telfer is unharmed.'

Rafi flushed. 'She was never in danger of being harmed.'

Cecil gave him a frosty look. 'She was in great danger from all kinds of things – out in a storm on a mountainside without her husband's protection.'

Rafi was offended. It was quite clear the young engineer saw him as an added danger. He saw the way Cecil had peered at them in suspicion on finding them alone in the shelter. But a pleading look from Sophie made him bite back a retort.

At Cecil's insistence, Sophie was bundled on to a mule and taken ahead with the army engineer, while Rafi followed on behind with the local search party. By the time he reached the camp, the mood was tense. There was no sign of Sophie. The engineers avoided him. Bracknall summoned him into his tent. Rafi could hardly bear to look at his boss; he was so full of disgust at what the man had done to Sophie.

Tam hobbled up from a chair to greet him, his thin face etched with pain. Rafi wondered if he had broken his ankle.

Shaking him by the hand he said, 'Thank you, Khan, for bringing Sophie safely back.'

'Where is she?'

'She's resting; looks terrible. I don't know what she was thinking of going off without the rest of us.'

'My fault, I'm afraid,' Rafi admitted. 'I wanted to show her the leopard.'

'Leopard.' Bracknall snorted. 'An unlikely tale.'

Rafi bristled but bit his tongue.

'Still,' Tam said, looking unsure, 'she should have waited for me and the other chaps.'

Bracknall was quick to criticise. 'I think it's damnable! You go missing for two nights with Mrs Telfer while her husband here is going out of his mind with worry. And Cecil finds you in a cosy little nest in the woods. Explain yourself, Khan!'

Rafi stood, furious. None of this would be happening if he had been white and British. His brother Ghulam was right; their rulers had no intention of handing over power to men like him. Bracknall and his insinuations were odious. He refused to answer.

'You had better start speaking if you want me to prevent a scandal from breaking over us all,' Bracknall snapped, his look malicious. 'It would be very stupid to lose your job over this.'

'My job?' Rafi was incredulous.

'My wife assures me that nothing improper went on,' Tam said, blushing deeply. 'Just want to hear it from you.'

Rafi gaped at him. So Sophie had already been subjected to questioning. It suddenly struck him how Sophie had been right about Bracknall having too much power over them all.

'And you believe your wife, do you?' Bracknall butted in.

'Of course.' Tam looked flustered.

'Well, I'm sorry to say it, Telfer,' Bracknall leered, 'but that minx is not the innocent little Scotch girl you think she is.'

Rafi saw Tam flinch as if struck in the face. Anger churned in his stomach.

'Please don't speak about her like that,' Tam said.

'It's true.'

'What do you mean, sir?' Tam demanded.

'I mean you need to keep your wife under a firm hand. It's embarrassing the way she flirts with other men. Even a middle-aged man like me isn't safe. You must have noticed.'

'No—'

'Don't listen to his lies, Tam,' Rafi snarled, his fists clenching.

'Did she try to seduce you too, eh?' Bracknall needled, his cold eyes lighting with glee. 'I bet she did. The guilt is written all over your brown face.'

In an instant, Rafi was launching himself at his boss, knocking him out of his camp chair. 'How dare you, after what you did!'

He pinned him to the ground. Bracknall stared up at him, eyes wide with shock.

'Get him off me!'

'I despise you!' Rafi raised his fist to strike.

'Khan, don't be a damn fool!' Tam was immediately catching at his arm and attempting to pull him off.

At the commotion, Cecil ran in. He punched Rafi hard in the face; Rafi reeled backwards, releasing his grip. Tam hauled him up while Cecil helped a shaken Bracknall to his feet.

Rafi stood breathing hard, his cheek stinging from Cecil's blow. For a moment, no one spoke. Bracknall brushed at his shirt and smoothed his hair. His look turned from fear to cold fury.

‘Telfer,’ he said, his voice icily calm, ‘you will discipline your wife as you see fit.’ He fixed Rafi with a look of pure loathing. ‘Khan, you’re finished. Now get out of my sight.’

Sick at heart, Rafi stormed from the tent.

Chapter 35

The journey back to Dalhousie was torturous. Sophie saw how much pain Tam was in from his ankle, yet he snapped at her if she fussed. He rode ahead, making no secret of his wish to get back as quickly as possible.

Sophie had heard the row in Bracknall's tent when Rafi had got back with the porters but hadn't been able to make out what they said. In an agony of indecision about whether to intervene, she had decided that anything she said would only make things worse. Now she wished she had. Tam had told her how Rafi had attacked Bracknall like a madman over something he had said about her. Tam would not tell her exactly what that was but his coldness towards her was wounding.

'You shouldn't have gone off with Khan alone,' he had accused. 'The man's going to be sacked because of it – wouldn't be surprised if Bracknall hands him over to the police too.'

It sickened her that Rafi was to take the brunt of Bracknall's vindictiveness, and she was furious at her own powerlessness to prevent it. Her word counted for nothing. She'd longed to speak to him – she'd feared he might have said something impulsive about Bracknall molesting her – but Rafi had been despatched ahead to await his fate in Lahore. Rafi went without a goodbye. The last glimpse she had of him, he was unshaven, hair unkempt and cheek swollen as if he'd been punched. It broke her heart to see the sadness in his handsome face as he mounted his horse. There had been no chance to speak to each other. Impotently, she had watched him go. Sophie felt desolate. Would she ever see him again?

Before they reached Dalhousie, rumours had already preceded them that the trip had nearly ended in disaster. Within a week of being back in the hill station, scandalous speculation was circulating around the hotel tea rooms and clubhouses about Sophie.

Telfer's headstrong young wife – you know the one who preferred to hang around with the men in the plains than join the women in the hills? – well, she went missing on the Chamba route with another forester, don't you know?

A native forester at that!

What was she thinking?

Handsome, of course. Mohammedan.

Turned up safe as houses. Rumour has it, they were hiding in the forest all the time.

Poor Telfer. It'll blight his service record. Well, it puts Bracknall in an impossible position, doesn't it? They say the Scotsman showed promise.

Bit too full of himself, I'd heard.

The Indian will be sacked, of course.

Can't just do that – not these days. Father's a big shot in Lahore. Just have to send him off somewhere remote.

The little madam!

Don't be too harsh. It's not her fault she doesn't understand India – she's barely been out a year. And you know how seductive these chaps can be.

Sophie overheard the gossips; they disgusted her. Rafi's attack on Bracknall was the only part of the awful affair that didn't seem to have leaked out. Perhaps the chief forester thought it would show him up as weak and unmanly if it became known that an Indian subordinate had got the upper hand in a fight? Whatever the reason, she prayed it meant that Rafi was not to be arrested for assault.

Tam spent his time out in the forests riding, filling every hour with work, ignoring the pain in his swollen ankle. Soon he was due to go back to Changa Manga.

'It'll still be unbearably hot down there,' he said, 'but it might be best if you come with me. Social invitations seem to have dried up anyhow – apart from that eccentric friend of yours, Fluffy Hogg.'

'Of course I'll come back with you,' Sophie replied. 'I want to. I can't bear it here. People are saying such awful things about us – about Rafi.'

Tam gave her an unhappy look. 'You promise me there's nothing in the rumours?'

'Tam! How many times do I have to tell you?'

'Cause I couldn't bear the thought of you with any other man.' His tone was hard and unforgiving. 'It would break me.'

Sophie's insides froze. She forced the thought of the hateful Bracknall from her mind. She could never tell her husband the truth of that night; Tam would never be able to bear it. She regretted bitterly that she had told Rafi, for surely that was why he had lost his temper with Bracknall. She should have gone through life nursing the awful secret alone.

'There's just you, Tam.'

'I'm sorry.' He sighed.

They stared at each other, wondering if their fragile marriage could survive the doubts and accusations.

It was time to tell him, Sophie decided. She went and sat next to him on the veranda. The air was full of the scent of rambling roses. She slipped her hand in his.

'Tam, I do have something important to say. Unless you've guessed already?'

'Guessed what?' He looked alarmed.

'It's nothing bad. We're going to have a baby. I'm with child.'

He gaped at her, speechless.

'It's true.' She smiled. 'Are you pleased?'

She saw tears spring into his eyes. He swallowed hard. 'That's wonderful,' he croaked. 'How long have you been—?'

The sudden doubt on his face made Sophie's stomach leaden. He still did not trust himself to believe that nothing had happened with Rafi.

'You should know,' she chided. 'Since Changa Manga.'

'That's grand.' He seized her hands and kissed them, hardly able to speak. She had never seen him so emotional. Tam put a hand to her face. 'I need you, lassie. This proves your love for me, doesn't it?'

Sophie nodded, though she felt empty inside.

Tam gave out a triumphant cry. 'I'm going to be a father! Oh, Mrs Telfer, I'm over the moon about the baby.'

Sophie reached out to him. 'So am I.'

They hugged.

‘This setback won’t last,’ Tam was bullish, ‘it’s just hill station gossip that will die off in the cold season. I’ll still get the promotion. I’m the best man for the job.’

Chapter 36

Shillong

A month into the monsoon season, Tilly received a note at the Rankins' house.

'It's from Burke, the old police officer,' Tilly told Ros. 'He wants to meet me. What should I do?'

She felt a mix of fear and excitement.

'Perhaps he's going to give you some more information,' Ros said. 'Probably all of Shillong know of your interest by now.'

'You think I've become obsessed, don't you?'

Ros gave her a long look. 'I think you're spending too much time at the library letting Lister fill your head full of lurid imaginings. You're here to enjoy yourself with baby Jamie. Don't waste away your time on the dead.'

Tilly felt chastened. 'I'm sorry; I'm being a boring friend. You and your father are being so kind. I'll tell him not to call.'

'Oh, I know that'll half kill you.' Ros snorted with laughter. 'You might as well see him and see what he has to say,' she relented. 'Then you can put it all behind you and get on with our holiday.'

'I will, I promise.' Tilly grinned.

***

Ronald Burke was as wide as he was tall; a bear of a man with wiry grey hair, trim moustache and a glass eye that glared with permanent suspicion. An old Jack Russell followed at his heels, growling and drooling. It snapped at Tilly when she tried to pet it.

'Doesn't like women,' Burke said.

Tilly and the Rankins took tea with him on the veranda. The major chatted amiably about fishing, but Burke showed little interest and had no small talk. Something he had in common with James, Tilly thought.

She watched him demolish a plate of sandwiches, some of which he fed to the bad-tempered dog. Ros caught Tilly's look and rolled her eyes. Tilly wished she hadn't invited the man; she must end the awkward tea party as soon possible.

'So, Mr Burke, you know my husband, James?' she ended the silence.

Through masticating jaws, Burke nodded. 'Sensible man. Last saw him when he was up for a wedding last year. Army doctor.'

'That was my brother Johnny's wedding!' Tilly exclaimed. 'Do you know him too?'

'No. Wasn't there myself. Robson and I had a chinwag at the club. Didn't tell me he was married.'

'We weren't then.' Tilly blushed. 'It all happened very quickly when he was on leave.'

'Does Robson know you're asking questions about the Logans?'

'N-not as such. But he knows I want to find out as much as I can for my cousin Sophie.'

He fixed her with his good eye. 'And what has your husband told you?'

'That you called him to the bungalow – he didn't say it was Belgooree – and that you found the Logans dead of fever and Sophie on her own.'

'And that's all there is to it,' Burke said, slurping off his tea. 'Terribly tragic.'

'But there are too many things that don't add up,' Tilly said. 'It was Sophie's birthday and she remembers playing hide-and-seek with her mother – she doesn't remember her being ill at all.'

'Fever can strike and kill in hours,' he replied. Tilly ignored the stock response.

'But what was the *ayah* doing running away with a kitten and leaving Sophie—'

'Kitten?' Burke frowned. 'She thought it was a kitten?'

'Yes,' Tilly answered, surprised by his reaction. 'Wasn't it?'

'I wouldn't know,' Burke blustered. 'The *ayah* was gone by the time we arrived on the scene.'

'So who got word to you that they were dead?' Ros interjected.

He trained his suspicious eye on Tilly's friend. 'I don't recall.'

'And was there a doctor?' Ros asked.

'Or was there foul play?' Tilly dared to ask.

Abruptly, he stood up, thanked them curtly for tea, shook the major by the hand and made for the door, his dog padding behind. Tilly went after him.

'Mr Burke, it was you who wanted to see me,' she reminded, 'but you're going without telling me anything new.'

A servant held out his *topee* and walking stick at the front door. He took them without acknowledgement, facing Tilly.

'Go back to your husband, Mrs Robson, and stop stirring up the past. You won't find anything and Robson won't thank you for trying.' He leaned closer, his tone threatening. 'You don't know what you're dabbling with. You could be putting James in a dangerous position if you continue to ignore our advice to leave well alone.'

'Danger? How?' Tilly gasped.

He pulled on his hat. 'Go home,' he ordered and barrelled out of the door.

Chapter 37

Punjab

Back at Changa Manga, Sophie's relationship with Tam improved. He fussed over her with a tenderness she had not thought he possessed.

'No tennis for you, lassie,' he ordered, 'and no riding around on horseback. I'm going to cosset you and our child. You can have anything you want. I'll get Hafiz to bake you cake – I know you can't bear the smell of curry just now. Shall I send for Tilly to keep you company? Or Clarrie Robson?'

Sophie laughed, touched by his eagerness and concern. 'No, we can't expect them to drop everything and come halfway across India just because you are keeping me in *purdah* and won't let me do anything.'

'Perhaps we should move to Lahore now?' Tam worried. 'It's too unhealthy here in the jungle. We can go up for a couple of days and look around for a new bungalow – Golf Road or somewhere with a big enough garden for the baby and its friends to play in.'

Sophie cupped his face in her hands. He had aged in the past year but was still wolfishly handsome.

'The baby won't need a garden for ages.' She smiled. Silently she thought it foolish to go renting anywhere until they knew for definite where Tam's next posting would be. But he was touchy about the subject – there was still no confirmation of promotion – and Sophie knew better than to mention it.

'You're right, we mustn't jump the gun.' Tam kissed her forehead.

But all their conversations revolved around the longed-for son or daughter. Sophie wondered what they had talked about before.

'Where do you want the baby to be born?' Tam asked her one evening, stretching out his tired limbs on the veranda, enjoying the cool of evening. His ankle still gave him trouble but he always brushed away Sophie's concern.

'It depends where we are next spring,' she answered with a cautious glance.

'I thought you might like to go back to Scotland for the birth.'

'Scotland?' Sophie was taken aback. 'I'd never thought of that.'

'It's common practice to go home for such things,' Tam said, 'and I like the thought of our child being born on Scottish soil.'

'But I don't have a home there anymore.'

'Yes you do,' Tam insisted. 'You would go to my mother's and my sister can help with your confinement.'

Sophie tried to absorb the idea. 'Would you come too?'

'You know I'm not due leave for another couple of years.'

'Then I don't want to go.'

'That's just being pig-headed,' Tam said in exasperation.

'That's rich coming from you.' Sophie gave a wry laugh.

'I'll just worry about you and the baby if you stay.'

'And I'll worry about you if I go. You need a spell in Europe more than me – remember what the doctor said?'

They came to no conclusion. Sophie knew Tam would not give up on the idea, so instead she suggested, 'Why don't you invite your mother and sister out for a visit? They could come before the end of the cold season and stay for the birth. I know you miss them.'

Tam's face lit up. 'I'd like that very much. But you're the one who would have to entertain them. Would you want them here when the baby's born?'

Sophie nodded. 'Carrying this child just brings home to me how important family are. I want him or her to know their granny and aunt in the same way that I knew my own special Auntie Amy.'

'Thank you.' Tam smiled in gratitude.

'And I want Cousins Johnny and Tilly to come to the christening,' she added, her eyes glittering with emotion.

***

Their spell of contentment was short-lived. Tam's fever returned. He could not crawl from bed, complaining that his limbs and head were being crushed in a vice. His temperature soared and he could keep down no food. He babbled incoherently. In lucid moments he gave Sophie despairing looks, his eyes set in hollows.

'I'm going to die, aren't I?'

Sophie clung to his burning hand. 'I'm not going to let you! You're going to be a good father to our baby.'

A doctor from the Remount rode over daily and administered large doses of quinine. 'Should be in hospital but he's too weak to move.'

'What else can I do?' Sophie agonised.

'Keep him cool and pray hard.'

After five days, the fever broke, leaving Tam weak and depressed. He was a sallow ghost of his former self. Sophie had seen him debilitated before, but not so listless and downhearted.

'Let's go up to Lahore for a few days – see some friends,' Sophie suggested.

But he just gave her a bleak look and shook his head. 'I've too much work to catch up on. They're badgering me from Lahore for reports.'

Day after day he forced himself out of bed early to ride the plantations, overseeing the new growth that had sprung up since the rains. Sophie knew it was pointless to try to hold him back; Tam lived for work. Only the prospect that he should soon be posted to Lahore kept her hopeful. At least there they would be near a good hospital and his job would be more office based.

To pass the time, Sophie took up woodwork and carving again, brushing up the skills that Auntie Amy had taught her. She made a toy box for the baby out of offcuts from the timber yard and then embarked on a tiny stool.

Tam came limping across from the forest office one October afternoon waving a letter. His face was lit with excitement for the first time since his illness.

'It's come – Bracknall's promotion!'

Sophie was out on the veranda carving. Her heart jumped. Bracknall had kept his promise. She could hardly believe it.

'That's wonderful! Let me see.'

Tam thrust it at her, babbling about the things he would do once they were back in Lahore. Sophie read the letter. She looked up in confusion.

'But it doesn't actually say you've got Martins' job.'

'Not in so many words,' Tam blustered. 'But it's calling me to Lahore to be given my next post. What else could it mean? Bracknall will be wanting to do things properly – welcome me as his assistant – not just send a note.'

'Yes, I see.' Sophie tried to hide her disquiet.

'And the date,' Tam continued, 'ties in with our lodge dinner next week. No doubt I'll be made a fuss of on the night.'

'That's good.' She smiled.

'I'll book us into a room at Nedous Hotel,' said Tam. 'Something grander than the old Cecil.'

'Will some of the other foresters be coming to town too?'

'Such as?'

'Well, Boz and McGinty.' She felt herself redden under Tam's sharp look. She dared not ask about Rafi, though not a day went by when she didn't think of him. She assumed that he had been sacked from the Forest Service but Tam had told her nothing. He never spoke of his old friend.

'Yes, I imagine they will. The forest staff are back from the hills and everyone will be wanting to know where they go next.'

'It'll be good to see them,' Sophie said, 'and see a bit of city life again.' With Tam insisting that she mustn't ride, she was finding life dull and restricted.

Tam bent and squeezed her cheek. 'Perhaps I'll take you dancing, Mrs Telfer. Nothing too energetic, just a sedate waltz or two.'

Sophie had a sudden image of waltzing with Rafi in the snow high up the mountain. The memory winded her.

'So better start packing up this house, lassie.' Tam grinned. 'We're on the move.'

***

Tam left to check on the plantations at Chickawatin and beyond. 'Want to leave things in good shape for my successor. I'll be back in a couple of days.'

Sophie was left to organise the packing of their china, glass and pictures into tea chests. Her enthusiasm soon waned. She returned to her carving, which she found absorbing, and thought often of her dear aunt who had taught her to chisel.

The child's stool was finished, now the toy box needed some toys to go in it. What she wanted was a light piece of pine to fashion into a boat. There was nothing suitable in the garden or the forests around. She asked Hafiz if he had anything to hand.

'In the *daftar*,' he suggested, pointing at the forest office across the compound. 'Telfer Sahib keeps bits and pieces in many boxes.'

Sophie had never been into Tam's office; he did not like to be disturbed when working and had made it clear early on that it was his domain. After the terrible confrontation at the timber depot, she had steered clear of Tam's working life. But it would be locked and she didn't have a key.

'Can you let me in?'

Hafiz nodded. 'I will fetch the key.'

'There's no need to tell Telfer Sahib about this,' Sophie said.

Hafiz smiled. 'My lips are sealed, Memsahib.'

The office was dark, the shutters closed and a musty smell greeted her. There were folders and ledger books piled on a large wooden desk. Stacked beside it were small metal trunks, presumably full of *dak* – the endless post and papers that came in daily – which Tam wrestled with and resented for keeping him indoors.

There were boxes of timber samples and offcuts lining the far wall. Sophie rummaged quickly; she didn't want to stay there long. She found a few pieces that would do for a boat and a train with carriages. Wondering if she might try a motorcycle too, she was startled by a cry and the sound of a bell at the door.

The *chaprassy* was standing there with a bundle of post. Sophie hesitated then held out her hands.

'I'll take the *dak*, thank you.' She wondered if Tam usually gave him some refreshment. In her rudimentary Urdu she said, 'Go to the kitchen. Hafiz give you chapatti.'

He saluted and disappeared. Sophie put the bundle of papers on the desk; reports that Tam would be passing on to someone else. It occurred to her that there might be further instructions about the summons to Lahore; maybe even confirmation of the new position. She could not help a nagging anxiety that Bracknall would renege on his promise. He had been frosty towards them at Dalhousie and had swiftly left for Simla. There had been no social invitations to visit Mayo Gardens from Mrs Bracknall.

Sophie went back to the desk and searched through the post. There was nothing official-looking from the Lahore Forest Headquarters. A slim letter slipped out. It was different from the others, sealed in a thin envelope for sending airmail. It must be from the senior Mrs Telfer or Flora. In excitement, Sophie wondered if it would have the reply to their invitation to visit India in the New Year.

In the gloom, Sophie peered closer. It was addressed only to Tam. Usually Flora wrote to them both. And bafflingly it was sent care of the forest office and not to their home address. She walked to the open door to scrutinise it in the light. It was then that she noticed the foreign stamp and postmark: France.

Turning it over, she saw it was from an N. Bannerman. She was curious. Who was this Bannerman writing to Tam? Perhaps someone from the war or his forestry course? But the name wasn't French and Tam had never mentioned a comrade of that name. What did the N stand for? Her heart began to thud. She hated herself for her suspicion but something about the writing looked feminine.

Sophie replaced the letter in the pile and gathered up her bits of wood. She hesitated. Why would this Bannerman write to Tam at the office address? Was it so that Sophie would never know? She put the wood back down. Quickly she began to rummage across the desk and through its drawers for any other sign of previous Bannerman letters. Nothing. Despising her own suspiciousness, she looked in a trunk; it was full of buff folders, all work related. Searching the other trunks and shelves produced nothing. She felt guilty relief.

As she closed the blinds again, she saw a cash box pushed down the back of the desk. Pulling the heavy desk away from the wall she retrieved it and lifted the metal catch.

Her throat went dry. The box was full of letters with the same blue envelopes, same handwriting. Sophie's heart drummed. She knew she had a choice; to close the lid and dismiss the letters as those between old war friends, or to read them and perhaps discover things about Tam she never wanted to know.

She picked one at random from the middle of the pile. The thin page gave off a faint scent of roses.

'*My dearest,*' it began. Sophie scanned down the page, skipping over news of people she'd never heard of. There was mention of a winery and a dinner for clients. Then she caught sight of her own name.

'… *How very terrible for you to have Sophie interfere with your work. It sounds like you handled the situation with your usual firm fairness but you'll have to make it clear to her that it's up to you how you deal with the coolies. Just don't let her go with you to the depot. Anyway, that's just my opinion.*

I have my own cross to bear; Papa is as irascible as ever and shows no sign of failing. I carry on doing my 'good works' as he calls the running of my nursing home and we rub along. He's still talking of selling up the business and moving back to New York, but he won't. He loves France too much, as do I.

I do hope you are keeping healthy and that your young wife is taking good care of you. Sweet of you to say that no one can nurse a man back to life like I can! They were extraordinary times, weren't they?

Love and kind regards,

Your Normandy Rose, Nancy.'

She pulled out another letter – a more recent one – and read about Nancy nursing her father who was ill with pleurisy but wishing she could be experiencing life at Dalhousie instead. She asked him if he was staying healthy by doing his Christian Science exercises just as she was doing them on his behalf. So was it Nancy who had made him a convert to the American-born philosophy? She remembered now how Tam had mentioned that an American friend in France had introduced him to it. A third letter sympathised with the fuss over Sophie and Rafi.

'*. . . just too bad! What was she thinking of going off with that Indian? I think girls her age have come to expect too much freedom since the war and don't understand etiquette. It's a changing world, my dearest.*'

Always, she signed herself off as his Normandy Rose. Sophie clutched her stomach feeling sick. She could not bear to read any more. Judging by the dates on the envelopes, Tam had been keeping up a correspondence with this American woman since he had arrived in India – long before she joined him to get married.

What did Nancy mean to him? She sounded older – almost like a bossy elder sister at times – but also loving. The letters were confiding and tender. Were his letters loving and intimate in return? Or was he just using her as a sounding board for frustrations with his wife and India?

Sophie felt ashamed for having read through letters never meant for her eyes, yet angry that Tam should be writing about her to another woman. He had obviously been critical of her. What else did he say? That he regretted marrying her and that she was a disappointment as a wife?

Sophie shoved the letters back in the box, secured it behind the desk and locked up the office, taking the afternoon's *dak* with her. She left the wood behind; she couldn't settle to carving anything now.

When Tam returned that evening, she handed him the pile of post.

'The *chaprassy* came with your *dak*.'

‘I’ll see to it tomorrow.’ He waved it away, his face scored with exhaustion.

‘There’s one from someone called Bannerman.’ She watched his startled look.

He turned away, making for the door. ‘Ah, is there?’

‘Tam—’

‘I’m going for a wash. Just put it on the table.’

Nothing was said at dinner. The post lay untouched. Sophie went to bed early and listened to him cutting open the letter. She heard him chuckling to himself, a sound she hadn’t heard for an age. Nancy made him laugh. Later she heard him pacing the veranda sighing.

In the morning the letter was gone and Tam was out riding early. She waited for him to say something – anything – to explain away the correspondence, but he said nothing. She agonised over whether to tell him that she knew that Bannerman was a woman. But it would open up such a gulf between them and destroy the recent harmony.

If Tam had any romantic intentions towards this Nancy, surely he would have acted on them long before he met her? She was just a pen friend from his past – someone to whom he could pour out his troubles – things with which he didn’t want to upset his wife.

Tam had chosen her, not the older-sounding Nancy, and they were going to have a child. Everything changed with the baby. She would put up with this illicit correspondence as long as Tam was the devoted father she thought he could be. He had lost his own father when young and she knew how he longed to become one himself.

And Sophie’s guilt over her feelings for Rafi held her back from speaking out too. How could she criticise Tam when she had yearnings for another man? They had heard nothing from Rafi since the camping trip, though there had been scandal in the *Civil and Military Gazette* about a Ghulam Khan getting arrested on suspicion of setting fire to the governor’s car. Sophie knew from her mountain conversation with Rafi about his family that this was Rafi's hotheaded younger brother, but didn't dare raise the subject with Tam. Ghulam Khan was languishing in prison.

Just as she had fought and overcome her strong feelings for Rafi for Tam's sake and the baby's; she believed that Tam would do the same for her.

A few days later they loaded up a bullock cart and rode through the jungle to the canal where they got a ride on a plate-layer's trolley on the newly built tramway. By midday they were at the station and boarding a train north to Lahore.

Chapter 38

To Sophie's delight, Boz and McGinty were in town. They were staying at the Cecil Hotel but bumped into each other at a tea dance in Nedous. Sophie could tell from their shocked expressions how ill they thought Tam looked. Jimmy Scott was with them too, being as bumptious as ever, Sophie thought, but Tam seemed pleased to see them all.

'Mrs Telfer, you look bonny and well.' Boz beamed, his face ruddy with sunburn. 'Tam,' he greeted his old friend, 'you must hae come into money to be staying here.'

'Nothing but the best for my wife.' Tam grinned and held out a bony hand. He dropped his voice. 'We're not broadcasting it yet, but there'll be a Telfer nipper in the spring.'

Boz pumped his hand vigorously, making Tam wince. 'Congratulations.' Then he bent and gave Sophie a kiss on the cheek.

The foresters gathered round the table and began to talk about their jobs, catching up on the past months. Jimmy was full of how well he had done in Rawalpindi. 'Doubled the production in the resin factory,' he boasted. 'Had to sack half the local staff – lazy, thieving lot.'

Boz complained about the heat of Baluchistan. 'Like putting your heid in the oven every day. I'd give ma right arm for a wee bit o' monsoon.'

But it appeared that he liked the people and there was plenty of entertainment in the large army cantonment. 'My polo's improving.'

'That'll impress Bracknall,' Tam said.

'It'll take more than that.' Boz grunted. 'What I need is a bonny wife like yours.'

Sophie blushed, uncomfortable at the mention of their boss.

'Sorry to hear you've been sick again, Telfer. And coming after that scandal on your Chamba trip – very bad luck,' Jimmy said, eyeing her. 'Khan behaving dishonourably.'

Tam reddened.

'Lay off, Jimmy,' Boz warned.

'Must have been awful for you, Mrs Telfer,' he needled. 'Cut off on a mountainside with a wog forester.'

Tam leaned over the table and grabbed his arm. 'Don't you speak to my wife like that. Nothing happened. It's just bloody gossip.'

Jimmy shook him off easily. 'I'm sorry,' he said, though his tone was mocking. 'Still, Bracknall couldn't take any chances; Khan was bringing his department into disrepute. And on top of all that, having a brother for a traitor – that one who got arrested for setting fire to the governor's car.'

'That was nothing to do with Rafi,' Sophie protested. 'He doesn't agree with any of that.'

Tam gave her a strange look. He was breaking out in a sweat.

Jimmy went on. 'So the chief had to get rid of him, didn't he?'

'Get rid?' Sophie echoed. 'He's left the Service, then?'

Jimmy gave a pitying look. 'Sacked weeks ago. Does Tam not keep you informed down in – where have you been? – Changa something?'

Boz cut in. 'Shut up, Scott.' He glanced at his friends awkwardly. 'It's a sad business.'

Sophie felt kicked in the stomach. She could tell from Tam's lack of surprise that he already knew.

'Bracknall couldn't put up with his insubordination,' Jimmy said with glee, 'and the way he tried to kidnap you—'

'Kidnap?' Sophie cried. 'He did no such thing.'

'Well, he'll never get work in the Indian civil service again, that's for sure,' Jimmy said. 'You should be pleased, Telfer, that Bracknall was defending the honour of your wife. Khan won't be able to bother her again.'

Sophie felt her head swim, her heart palpitating. She had ruined Rafi's career. It had been pure chance that they had been stuck on the mountain together, but she had welcomed it. She had never felt so alive and in love as during those magical hours with just her and Rafi talking and laughing under a starlit sky. If only she hadn't confided in him about Bracknall and the baby, perhaps Rafi would have kept his temper and the whole affair might have blown over.

Bracknall was never going to defend his young forester from the firestorm of gossip once Rafi had laid hands on him. Besides, she had seen the raw jealousy in his face whenever Rafi talked to her; now Bracknall had taken his revenge. The only consolation was that Bracknall appeared not to have pressed charges for assault.

'Is he still in Lahore?' Tam asked, as if he read her thoughts.

'God knows,' said Jimmy, 'and who cares?' He slid Sophie a triumphant look.

'It's a waste of a good forester and a good man,' said Boz.

'Well, I wouldn't waste any sympathy over him. His family have potfuls of money. He probably doesn't need to work. That's the trouble with rich Indians; they just play at having a job. They don't have the work ethic of us British.'

Boz snapped. 'Rafi was as hard-working as any of us – loved his job. I for one am sad to see him gang. He'll be much missed in the department. That's what we're here for, isn't it? To work wi' men like Rafi and bring on the native foresters so they can run it for themselves.'

Sophie wanted to hug him for defending his old friend. She waited for Tam to back him up, but he said nothing.

'That'll be a long time coming,' Jimmy was disdainful. 'They'll not be ready for that while we're in the job.'

Sophie was reminded of Rafi's optimism that India would see independence from Britain in his lifetime. She wondered if his sacking had smothered his hopes and dreams.

'Stop fretting over Khan,' Jimmy went on. 'No doubt his rich new father-in-law Sarfraz will give him a comfy job in his bank.'

Sophie's throat dried. 'He's married then?'

Boz nodded. 'It was in the *C and M Gazette* last week. Khan and the banker Sarfraz's daughter.'

'Probably only got a mention' – Jimmy sniffed – 'because of his notorious brother.'

Sophie could bear no more of his poisonous words. She stood up.

'I'm not feeling well,' she told Tam. 'I'll just go and lie down for a bit.'

'Shall I take you, lassie?' Tam asked in concern.

'No, you stay and catch up with your friends.'

She couldn't get away from them fast enough. In the sanctuary of the plush bedroom, Sophie sank on to the bed.

'Oh, Rafi! I'm so sorry.' She gulped and gave way to tears of desolation.

***

The following day, Tam suggested they take a walk in the Shalimar Gardens, but Sophie couldn't bear the thought of going back to the place Rafi had taken her on a picnic. She didn't want to go anywhere near the old city either, though she had no idea if he was still living there.

'Let's take a walk around Golf Road,' she suggested, 'and see what's for rent.'

Tam was pleased with the suggestion. They didn't talk about the unpleasant encounter with Jimmy Scott, and Rafi was never mentioned, though Sophie was sure Tam must have been thinking about him too.

That evening as Tam made ready for the dinner that Bracknall was laying on at the gymkhana club for his department, he said, 'Will you be all right on your own here? I wish I could take you along but wives are not invited.'

'I'll be fine. It's a lovely evening. I might go out for a stroll before dinner – walk up the Mall and see where we were married.'

'You sentimental lassie.' Tam gave a wan smile, adjusting his bow tie in the mirror. His collar was far too loose around his neck now and his dinner suit looked too big. 'Don't go too far. And if it's getting dark, take a *tonga* back.'

He kissed her head and left whistling.

'Good luck,' she called after him.

On her way past the Cecil Hotel, Sophie spotted Boz having a cigarette on the steps.

'Just delaying the moment when I have to gang and lick Bracknall's boots.'

‘That man,’ Sophie said, her teeth clenching. ‘I wish they’d promote him to Delhi and we’d all be rid of him.’

Boz raised his eyebrows. ‘Thought the Bracknalls were like parents to you and Tam?’

Sophie shook her head. ‘I hate him. He’s vindictive and sly – nice to your face but not behind your back. Look at the way he’s treated Rafi. And sending you to Quetta because you’re not posh enough for Lahore. I’m just frightened that—’

‘What?’ Boz ground out his cigarette and steered Sophie on to a bench under an acacia tree. ‘Tell me.’

‘That Tam won’t get the job he wants because of the fuss over me and Rafi,’ Sophie whispered.

‘Bracknall knows Tam’s a good forester. But, to be truthful, I’m shocked to see how his health’s got worse. If he doesn’t get the job it won’t be because of you, Sophie, it’ll be ’cause the chief doesn’t think he’s physically up to it.’

‘Oh Boz, I don’t think Tam could cope with not getting promotion. It would be the last straw.’

Boz touched her hand. ‘Whatever happens, Tam is lucky tae have you by his side, lassie. I’m glad about the bairn. It’s what he’s always wanted for as long as I’ve known him. So things are good for you both, no?’

Sophie didn’t answer. They stood up. ‘Boz,’ Sophie stopped him. ‘What do you mean he’s always wanted a child?’

‘I think it was the war brought it hame to him – the thought that you could be snuffed oot at any minute.’

‘Was there someone special to Tam in France?’

Boz looked uncomfortable. ‘It’s not for me to say.’

‘Someone he wanted to have a child with?’ she pressed.

‘Tam wouldnae want us talking of this.’

‘But that time in Bombay you tried to tell me something about Tam in France, didn’t you?’ When he didn’t deny it, she went on. ‘Please, Boz.’

Boz sighed. ‘There was a lassie he was fond of, aye. Her father was an American wine merchant – gave us lads entertainment when we were on local leave in the war. Then when Tam got injured, she nursed him. But she was older and thought Tam too young for her. Her father was against their getting wed too. But that's all in the past; it's you he's married.'

'But he wanted to marry her?' Sophie swallowed. When Boz didn't deny it, she pressed him. 'When Tam went back to France on your final field trip – after he'd started seeing me – did he go to her? Was that what you were trying to tell me – warn me about before I got married?'

'Oh, lassie, it's not right to talk about it now. You chose Tam, and I could see that nothing would put you off.'

'Knowing about Nancy Bannerman might have.'

He flinched in shock. 'You know her name then?' he said, flustered.

'I came across a boxful of letters. They've been writing to each other since he came out here. They didn't stop after the wedding.'

'Oh, the daft man!'

'So you didn't know?'

'Of course not,' Boz insisted. 'We argued about him seeing her in France. I told him he was being unfair to you.'

Sophie's stomach clenched. 'Why did he see her? Was he still trying to get her to marry him?'

Boz's look was full of pity. 'Aye.'

'But she turned him down?'

Boz nodded. 'As long as her father was alive she wouldn't go against his wishes. Old Bannerman wanted her to marry into money.'

'So I was always his second choice,' Sophie said with a bitter laugh.

'The best choice,' Boz said, seizing her hand. 'Tam knows that now.'

'So why is he still writing to his former sweetheart?' Sophie demanded.

Boz shook his head with incomprehension. 'Maybe he just sees her now as an old friend – a confidante – and means nothing by it.'

'That's what I was hoping.'

'Well then, dinna' let Nancy come between you two. Tell him you know about the letters and you want them to stop.'

'Thank you, Boz.' She squeezed his hand then let go. 'I hope you find someone good enough for you one day.'

For a moment he stood looking down at her with a look of regret in his eyes and Sophie remembered that Tam's tall friend had once been sweet on her. Then they parted.

The call to prayer was sounding out across the rooftops. Sophie's mind was in turmoil. She felt that she was hanging on to her life in India by her fingernails; she and Tam had too many secrets from each other. She wondered suddenly if her own parents had been like this? If she forced herself to remember, the adult world had been one not of kisses and sweet words but of shouting and tears.

Would she and Tam make unhappy parents for their child? Sophie's insides lurched to think how her own parents had died of fever – how her father had often been sick and bad-tempered like Tam. She felt a great weight of foreboding. Backtracking to the hotel, she no longer had any wish to revisit the Anglican cathedral where she had wed Tam with such high hopes for their future together. What fools they had been, she thought savagely. Tam had probably been writing to Nancy on the eve of his wedding – and she had already been falling in love with Rafi.

Sophie ran a bath – such a luxury after months in the jungle – and tried to wash away her unhappy thoughts in the steamy water. Feeling too sick to eat anything, she crawled under the covers and fell asleep.

Chapter 39

Sophie woke with a start. Someone was crashing through the door. It was flung open and Tam lurched in. Electric light flooded the room. Sophie was blinded.

'What time is it?' she asked groggily.

'Didn't get it,' Tam shouted. 'Didn't get the bloody job!'

'Tam?' Sophie sat up; she had been dreaming of eating snow.

Tam limped around the room, ripping off his bow tie. 'Ruddy Jimmy Scott is Bracknall's new assistant.'

'No,' Sophie cried. 'I don't believe it. He promised you.'

'Gentleman's agreement, he said,' Tam spat out the words. 'Shook hands on it at the lodge meeting.'

Sophie forced herself up and out of bed. 'Oh, Tam, I'm so sorry.' She held out her arms.

But he advanced on her, his face livid. She could smell sour liquor on his breath. 'Humiliated me in front of the others – and all because of you.'

'Me?' Dread clawed at her insides. Surely the poisonous Bracknall would not have said anything about that night in Changa Manga? He had too much position to lose.

'You and Khan,' Tam accused. 'Told me that I should keep my head down for a year or two until something else came up. Best thing was to get you in the family way – show you your place – stop you getting so friendly with the natives.'

'That man disgusts me,' Sophie said. 'Rafi was our friend. You've known him for years.'

'I'm not sure I did know him,' Tam cried. 'He was always after you, wasn't he? Always sniffing round like a dog on heat.'

'Stop it, Tam. That's Bracknall talking.'

'What did you do to upset the chief? You should have shown him more respect. That's all I asked of you, woman, to help me get on. Just a bit of loyalty and support.' Spittle landed on her cheek. She wiped it away. Tam caught her hand. 'Do you know what my punishment is? Instead of running things here like I should be, I'm being banished to Peshawar.'

'The North West Frontier?' Sophie gasped in dismay.

'Bandit country,' Tam railed. 'A fine place to bring up my child, eh? My mother and sister won't want to visit us there.'

Sophie tried to calm him. 'We'll make the best of it. We've still got the baby to look forward to, haven't we?'

'And what colour will it be?' Tam said venomously. 'A half-caste?'

'Don't be so vile,' she gasped, trying to pull her hand away.

He held on hard. 'Then look me in the eye and tell me you aren't in love with Rafi Khan?'

Sophie gulped. 'Rafi's married to someone else – and it's you I chose, Tam.'

'That's not an answer!'

Her patience snapped. 'And what about you and Nancy Bannerman? Are you still in love with her?'

He gaped at her.

'You've kept in touch with her right through our marriage, Tam – piles of love letters I found in your office.'

'You've been through my letters?' he hissed. 'You had no right.'

'I'm your wife,' Sophie blazed, 'I have every right. I know you were in love with her – wanted to marry her – but she wouldn't have you. So why are you still writing to her?'

'Because I'm still in love with her!'

Sophie shrank back. 'Then why did you marry me? You shouldn't have led me on to think you loved me.'

'I never told you I loved you. It was you who threw yourself at me! I thought we could make a go of it – wanted to love you – God I've tried hard enough. But you're not Nancy – you'll never be a patch on her.'

He shoved her away from him. Sophie lost her footing, knocked against the sharp corner of a bedside table and fell to the floor.

Tam fled the room, slamming the door. Sophie covered her face with trembling hands. She was too shocked to move; too numb to cry.

She must have lain on the cold floor for twenty minutes before she dragged herself up. Tam had not returned. Filled with impotent rage at her situation, Sophie picked herself up, got dressed and went out into the night.

***

Hailing a *tonga*, Sophie headed for the old city. The streets narrowed and closed in around her, still warm from the heat of the day. Some shops remained open; blanketed figures loomed out of the dark to stare at the passing memsahib. She knew it was reckless to try to find Rafi's old house but she was drawn on by a need deep inside. He had stood up for her when her own husband had not; how she admired him for that! They had not even said goodbye to each other and she wanted to say how sorry she was and ask his forgiveness for her part in his sacking. She wanted to tell him about her terrible argument with Tam – and even if it was the last time she ever set eyes on him, she wanted Rafi to know how deeply she loved him. If they never found anyone else in their lives to love, they at least could be honest with each other and know that they had had a brief moment of pure joy on a Himalayan mountainside.

As she drew near to the street with the jeweller's, Sophie wondered if she would remember the way. Even if he was not there, perhaps someone could tell her what had become of him.

The *tonga* driver, an elderly man, was finding it difficult to control his pony. The animal was skittish in the dark lanes. It suddenly struck Sophie how futile was her search. She would only embarrass Rafi if she did find him. How would he explain the eccentric Scotswoman rushing around after dark trying to find him? He was married now. He would be making a new life away from the Forest Service, cutting off the old world that had rejected him. She had to come to terms with never seeing him again, however devastating that was. She felt overwhelmingly alone.

Sophie told the driver to turn around and take her back to Nedous Hotel. She would have to face Tam; try to salvage something from the destructive night. For the sake of the baby they would have to work out a way of living together.

As the old man manoeuvred the nervous horse, she thought she got a glimpse of the house she had been looking for; a tall building of crumbling stucco and rusting ironwork.

'Wait a minute!' She half rose from the open carriage.

At that moment, a boy dropped a brass tray, which clattered to the ground right beside them. The pony jumped sideways knocking over a stall of hot food. It reared up and bolted, bumping the *tonga* over the scattering pots. Sophie was flung off the seat. She landed on her hip, hitting the hard earth with a jolt. Pain shot through her.

At once people rushed to help her up. Further up the lane the old man was trying to control the pony with whips and curses. A local policeman was soon at the scene and pushing back the crowd that had gathered.

'I will take you to hospital, Memsahib,' he said.

'No, please,' Sophie groaned, 'I'm all right. Just a bit shaken. I'd be very grateful if you could just take me to my hotel.'

He helped her up. 'You should not be out in the bazaar at this time,' he admonished.

'I know. I think we lost our way,' Sophie mumbled.

What an idiot she had been! By the time her rescuer delivered her to the doors of Nedous she was feeling terrible.

'I will ask the hotel to call in a doctor,' he said.

'No, please, I don't want any fuss. You've been very kind. Thank you.'

The *chowkidar* let her in.

She took off her shoes and limped up to her room, every step jarring her right side from the hip to the ankle. Tam was still not back. She was too drained and sore to care where he might have gone. Stripping off in the bathroom, she saw with relief that there was only a slight graze on her hip. But she knew it would bruise.

***

In the early hours, Sophie woke with a searing pain in her abdomen. She doubled up and cried out for Tam. He wasn't there. Fear gripped her. What was happening? She felt waves of nausea rise up, but worse were the red hot needles that stabbed at her side and belly. She lay trying to calm herself, breathing deeply. But the sharp pains spread down between her legs. It grew unbearable. She broke out in a sweat of panic.

Crawling out of bed, she got as far as the bell-ring and rang for help.

The youth who answered turned on the light, took one look at her and dashed off shouting. Sophie looked down and saw with horror that her nightdress was stained with blood. The stench of it filled her nostrils.

Two hotel staff helped her back on to the bed. By the time a doctor arrived, Sophie knew that something terrible was happening to her baby.

'You're miscarrying,' the young Indian doctor told her, 'I'm sorry. I'll give you something to help the pain.'

'No,' Sophie sobbed, 'I can't be! Please don't let me lose my baby.'

An hour later, it was all over. Sophie watched in disbelief as the messy remains of her pregnancy were bundled into a sheet and carried away.

***

Tam returned with the dawn, ashen and hungover. Word of the tragic mishap to Telfer Memsahib in the night reached him before Sophie could tell him herself.

He stood beside her, looking down at her desolate face, her eyes dark-ringed and puffy from weeping.

'Tell me it isn't true,' he croaked.

Sophie closed her eyes so she didn't have to look at his guilt-ridden face.

'Oh, lassie,' he moaned. 'I'm so sorry.'

'It wasn't your fault,' Sophie whispered.

'Yes it was,' Tam said bitterly. He sat down on the bed and began to sob. She did not have the strength to comfort him. All she wanted right then was to go to sleep and never wake up.

***

Word soon spread of the Telfers' tragedy. Mrs Bracknall insisted that Sophie should come to Mayo Gardens to convalesce.

'Not there,' Sophie was adamant. 'I know she means to be kind but I couldn't bear it. Please take me back to Changa Manga.'

Somehow the thought of being back in the jungle, looked after by the kind Hafiz, was all that she could face. Her life with Tam was held in limbo in the days that followed. Neither referred to their terrible row or the loss of their baby or whether they had a future. Her feelings were shredded – her insides felt gouged out that motherhood had been snatched away – yet a small part of her felt guilty relief that Bracknall could no longer exert a mental hold over her. At least she would not have to go through life pretending the baby was Tam's. It was bleak consolation. She wrote to Tilly, a long outpouring of all that had happened. How she longed for the kind comforting presence of her oldest friend.

One night, standing watching fireflies from the veranda, Tam admitted, 'It wasn't the scandal over you and Rafi that lost me the job. Bracknall just threw that in as a cautionary tale.'

Tam turned to her. 'He said I am to take leave – six to eight months – and not to come back until the fever is out of my system. Then I'm to go to Peshawar because the heat will be dry and I'm less likely to have a relapse.' He snorted. 'Of course that was the last thing I wanted to be told. I'd survived the trenches – I wasn't going to have my career ruined by India's climate.'

'Oh, Tam, why didn't you tell me that?'

'I'm sorry, lassie. I had no right to blame you for it. I was just lashing out.'

So she told him about her reckless ride in the *tonga*.

'You're right; I was in love with Rafi. After the argument – hearing how you still loved Nancy – all I wanted was to see him – just set eyes on him. Remind myself that someone did love me, even if we can never be together.' Her feelings felt cauterised. 'So you see, you mustn't blame yourself for the miscarriage. It was a horrible accident.'

Tam shook his head. 'I drove you to it. I will always blame myself.'

A week later, as Tam prepared to go back to Lahore and arrange a passage home, a letter came from Tilly in answer to Sophie's outpourings on her situation. Sophie reached a decision. She steeled herself to say it.

'I'm not coming with you. I think we should separate.'

He looked fearful. 'But we could try again – try for another child.'

'No, Tam,' she said gently. 'We'd be doing that for the wrong reasons. A child needs to know it's born out of love.'

He looked about to argue so she quickly went on. 'This way you are free to go to Nancy if that's what you want. It sounds to me as if that's what *she* wants. And I won't stand in your way. Looking back, I see now that it was me who pushed you into marriage. I thought I was in love – perhaps I was for a bit – but it was India I really wanted.'

Tam's expression softened. 'But what will you do?'

'I can't have our baby anymore,' she said, her voice wavering, 'but I can have India. I feel I belong here still. I'll go and stay with Tilly and decide what to do from there. She's been asking me to go for ages – says she has information about my parents. I've been putting off going – maybe I'm afraid of what she's found out – but nothing can hurt as much as losing our baby. I'm going back to Assam.'

She heard Tam swallow down a sob. He came to her on the cane sofa, sat down and took her hand.

'I know I haven't been an easy man to live with.'

'You've been ill a lot of the time,' Sophie sympathised, 'but it's partly because I don't make you happy either. When I first met you, you were full of fun and enthusiasm for life. If Nancy makes you happy like that then that's what I want you to be.'

'Thank you, lassie.' He gave her a sad smile. 'It's just that Nancy knew me before the gas attack. She knows the old Tam – and that's what I'm trying to hang on to.'

For a long time they sat in silence, listening to the screech of parakeets as the sun dipped behind the trees.

Chapter 40

Assam

After Tilly had returned to Cheviot View at the end of August, she had settled better than before into the life of a tea planter's wife. She had been away two months; Jamie was sitting up, had grown a tuft of dark red hair and two teeth had appeared in his lower gums that gleamed when he grinned and giggled, which was often. James had been overjoyed to have them back.

'I'd almost forgotten what you looked like,' he had teased, hugging his wife and tickling his son under his plump, milky chin, making him squeal.

'We've missed you too.' Tilly had smiled, glad to feel his broad arms around her and to see the delight in his weathered face.

Meera was happy to be with her family again too. Tilly had felt guilt at keeping her from her little boy just so that she could pursue her obsession with Sophie's parents in Shillong. She had decided to put it all behind her. She didn't really want to know what James's involvement had been; it was sixteen years ago and she didn't want to judge his younger self. She knew James did not want to talk about it again, so she would not spoil their happy reunion with fruitless questions. She had never known him more loving or demonstrative – reluctant to leave her bed in the morning and quick to return from the tea gardens at dusk rather than linger with the men – and he was becoming more interested in baby Jamie.

'Come here, you little fat pup,' he would cry as he bounded up the veranda steps, seized his son and swung him into the air.

Jamie's startled face would either crumple into a howl of alarm or light up in a huge gummy grin. His father laughed and kissed him whatever the reaction. Jamie would jam his fingers into James's mouth and giggle while his father made nonsense noises to entertain him.

Tilly felt more settled than she had ever been before, inviting round Ros, Muriel and Jean Bradley for tea, games of cards, lending books and swapping plant cuttings from each other's gardens. In Shillong she had discovered that Ros and her father were keen stamp collectors. Now Tilly and Ros spent happy hours helping each other add to their albums.

Tilly even welcomed the sound of Sinbad singing and shrieking at her when she got up for breakfast. As September gave way to October, the humidity dropped and the days became pleasant. Sometimes James would take them out in his car and they would picnic above the river, watching the local boatmen toing and froing with their passengers and cargo, while elephants wallowed at the edges and cooled themselves with trunkfuls of water.

Then a letter came from Sophie.

James returned to find his wife distraught and red-eyed from crying. She rushed at him, burying her face in his chest. 'It's awful! Poor Sophie. The baby. And Tam!'

James tried to calm her, steering her into the house and sitting her down in a chair.

'Fetch a lime and soda,' he bade an anxious Aslam. 'Now, take a deep breath and tell me: what's happened to Sophie?'

'I thought it strange I hadn't heard from her for weeks' – Tilly sniffed – 'not since she told me she was expecting and Tam was hoping for promotion. She was all excited about going on a trek into the Himalayas. I just thought everything must be fine and she was too busy to write. I kept writing to her from Shillong . . .'

'You're not to blame for her lapse in letter writing.' James grunted. 'But she's written now?'

Tilly straightened out the crumpled letter she had been clutching since opening it two hours ago. She gulped back tears. 'She's miscarried.'

'I'm sorry to hear that,' James said, looking embarrassed. 'But it's not uncommon, is it? Hardly the end of the world. They can try again.'

Tilly winced at his lack of understanding.

'She's planning to leave Tam,' Tilly's voice wavered.

'What! Leave him? Why, in God's name, would she do that?'

She handed the letter over. James looked warily at the screeds of large looping writing.

'I'm not sure I should be prying into your private correspondence.'

'Read it,' Tilly pleaded.

She forced down the cold drink that Aslam brought, her stomach knotting with its fizziness, while James frowned in concentration over the letter. It told everything: the fateful trek; her two nights with Rafi and what she felt for him; the ensuing scandal; Tam's fresh bout of fever; his humiliation at being passed over for promotion; the revelations about American Nancy in France and their secret correspondence; hearing that Rafi was married; and the final devastating loss of her baby.

'. . . I would have put up with almost anything to have given birth to and raised our child – even his love letters to Nancy – but that life has gone now. Tam is being sent back to Europe to recuperate from the fever that so debilitates him out here. I don't intend going with him. I want him to be free from me so he can go to Nancy if that's what will give him peace of mind. We certainly don't make each other happy.

'If you would allow it, I'd like to come and stay with you in Assam for a while. When I thought I was going to be a mother, I was constantly thinking about my own one. Am I like her? What would she think of me and the mistakes I've made in my life? I've yearned for her comforting arms.

'Tilly, you are my nearest and dearest relation on this earth and I can think of no one else I'd rather be with at this time. Please can I come to you and James? I won't outstay my welcome – just long enough to find my feet again. I've been longing to meet my wee cousin Jamie too – and you can tell me what it is about my parents that you have found out. I treasure the photograph you sent of their gravestone in Shillong. I will welcome any scraps of information you can give me.

'Please write back quickly.
Your loving friend
Cousin Sophie.'

James gave Tilly a shattered look. 'What a mess.'

'I want Sophie to come here,' she said. 'Would you agree to that?'

James nodded. 'Of course, she can stay as long as she wants.' He stared down at the letter and then back at Tilly, his face grim. 'What is all this about the Logans? How did you know where they were buried?'

'I came across their grave by accident – Ros's mother is buried nearby. You must have known that was where they were taken, but you never thought to tell me.'

'Why does it matter to you?' James demanded.

'Because it matters to Sophie. She is desperate to know anything about them.'

'She knows all there is to know.'

'That's not true, is it, James? I think you know a lot more but you're keeping it from me.'

His jaw clenched. 'What do you mean by that?'

'I know where the Logans were living when the tragedy happened; White Blossom Cottage.'

'I told you that.'

'You never said it was the bungalow at Belgooree!'

James gaped. 'How did you . . .?'

'I found a report about their deaths in an old copy of *The Shillong Gazette*. I also know that you were in the area at the time – visiting tea planters and trying to get them to leave their isolated homes and go to safety. It was the anniversary of the Mutiny and all the planters were frightened they were going to be attacked – I've read about it and talked to people in Shillong.'

'My God, woman, what have you done?'

Tilly jumped up, her heart drumming as she confronted him. 'No, what have *you* done, James! You didn't just get summoned after their deaths – you were there right beforehand – perhaps you were there on the day they died? Were you?'

She saw from his shocked expression that she was right. He didn't deny it.

'Then why didn't you get them help if they were sick with fever? Or was that just a story put about to cover up what really went on? Mr Logan might have been ill but I don't think Sophie's mother was. She was fit and healthy and playing hide-and-seek with her daughter on her birthday.' Tilly trembled under his furious look but pressed on. 'I think she died a violent death – that villagers came and attacked them in revenge for the Mutiny. Maybe the *ayah* was in on the plot – tipped off the local agitators and ran off leaving Sophie alone.'

'No!' James shouted. 'You don't know what you're saying.'

'I think you came back with Superintendent Burke and found them dead and—'

'Burke?' James said appalled. 'How could you possibly know—?'

'It names him in the newspaper. And he came to the Rankins' house to warn me off – told me you'd be in danger if I tried to find out any more.'

'Burke threatened you?'

'Yes. That's why I let the matter drop and came home.' She steeled herself to accuse him. 'But now you have to tell me the truth. They were attacked by coolies – Sophie heard the drumming and noise of them coming – and you and Burke covered it up to stop a scandal and made up a story about a fever in case there were reprisals. And the poor Logans died a horrible death and no one was brought to justice – not the *ayah* or anyone – so that other planters didn't take the law into their own hands and make things worse. I can see from your face that I'm right.'

James sprang forward and grabbed her arms.

'I'll tell you what happened,' he cried. 'Bill Logan got up from his sick bed, loaded his revolver and shot his wife dead! Then he turned the gun on himself and ended his miserable life. If Sophie hadn't been hiding, he would probably have killed her too.'

Tilly reeled with incomprehension. 'Sophie's father?' she gasped.

'Yes!'

'But why would he do such a terrible thing?'

'Bill Logan was a sick and deluded man – and intensely jealous over Jessie – he thought she had been unfaithful to him.'

Tilly winced at his iron grip. 'And had she?'

'Not that I know of. Don't look at me like that, girl. I meant nothing to Jessie Logan.'

'You had feelings for her?'

James suddenly let go his hold. 'It was a long time ago. Perhaps I did. I know that I wanted her safely away from Belgooree – not just from possible attack from bands of agitators but from Logan. My going there that day – Sophie's birthday – just made things worse. Logan flew into one of his rages and accused me of getting his wife with child. So I left without taking her with me. I went to fetch Burke – thought he could persuade Logan to see sense – but when we came back the following day we found this terrible—'

James broke off, his jaw clamping. Tilly put a hand on his arm and pulled him on to a wicker sofa.

'Oh, James.'

'If only I'd insisted on Jessie leaving the day before. I will never forgive myself for not doing more. Burke was adamant we were not to let the truth get out. Everyone was nervous and rumours were flying. If word had spread that a planter and his wife had been shot, we knew that Indians would be blamed. It would be just as people had predicted. Then there would have been tit for tat and Burke feared real unrest.'

'And little Sophie was hiding all this time?'

James nodded. 'We found the poor lass curled up in a linen chest, shaking and speechless. God knows what she'd seen. But I think Jessie deliberately got her to hide, knowing that her daughter's life was in danger.'

'Was Sophie's father really that unhinged?'

'I think so.'

Tilly sat stunned. 'Why did Mrs Logan stay with him if he was a danger to her and Sophie?'

James gave her a harrowed look. 'She thought being at Belgooree would be good for his health and stop him being so jealous over her – there would be no social life – it was a kind of self-imposed *purdah*.'

'Then why would Logan accuse you of making Sophie's mother with child?' Tilly asked, blushing.

James swallowed hard. She thought he wasn't going to answer. Then he said in a strained voice, 'You see, they'd cut themselves off from us other planters for months and no one knew. I didn't realise until I went to Belgooree on Sophie's birthday.'

'Realise what?'

'Jessie had given birth the week before. When I went the first time there was a newborn baby. By the following day,' he said grimly, 'it had gone.'

Chapter 41

'That's Guwahati,' said the amiable Sam, the steamboat captain's son, pointing at the distant *ghat*. Sophie squinted into the sun. Sam's frantic monkey ran along the deck rail screeching and pointing too.

Sophie felt her insides knot. She was back in Assam.

'I'll fetch your luggage if you like?'

She smiled at the youth. She had enjoyed his company on the slow voyage upriver, impatient to be with Tilly yet filled with a sense of dread that she couldn't explain. Sam's lively chatter and interest in their surroundings had stopped her from brooding. From one of Tilly's early letters, she knew her cousin had travelled up the Bramhaputra on the same boat and with the same engaging Sam with his pet monkey.

Only at night in the cramped cabin was she plagued by doubts. Was she mad to have left Tam? What was the point of staying on in India without a husband or a home? She would be shunned by everyone she knew. Already the Bracknalls had sent a curt note to say she was no longer welcome in Lahore society for abandoning Tam. It would be so much easier just to retreat back to Scotland and start again. She could get her job back with Miss Gorrie and the Scottish Servants' Charity. She would buy another motorbike and take off to Perthshire and go fishing.

Thoughts spun in her head but always came back to Assam and her reason for staying in India; to revisit the place where she had been a child and try to lay to rest the ghosts of her elusive parents. Lying in the dark listening to Sam's monkey running about the deck overhead, Sophie ran her fingers over the smooth dark opal she wore next to her skin, and knew she couldn't leave India without trying to see Rafi one last time too.

Standing at the rail, she caught sight of Tilly and James on the quayside. As the steamboat edged alongside, her friend waved and her plump face broke into a smile. Sophie couldn't get down the gangplank quick enough. They fell into each other's arms and hugged; both bursting into tears. For several minutes Sophie couldn't speak, while Tilly gabbled incoherently about how much she'd missed her and something to do with Cheviot Cottage and babies and a friend called Ros.

James patted his wife and pulled her away. 'Let the girl get her breath, Tilly. You can tell her all your news on the journey to Belgooree.'

'Belgooree?' Sophie asked in surprise. 'How lovely.'

James gave her a self-conscious kiss on the cheek.

'Yes, your cousin is insisting we go there first.'

'It's all been arranged with Clarrie and Wesley.'

'And you are coming too?' Sophie scrutinised James.

He cleared his throat and nodded.

'Clarrie and I are determined that the Robson men are going to bury the hatchet once and for all.'

'This has got nothing to do with Wesley,' James said crossly. 'I'm doing this for you, Tilly – and Sophie.'

'For me?' Sophie was baffled. 'I don't understand.'

'I'll explain all in good time,' Tilly said, slipping her arm through her friend's. Something about Tilly's pitying expression made Sophie's dread return. 'Now let's have some refreshment before we travel on. You must be ravenous. And you're looking too thin and peaky. Clarrie and I are going to spoil you rotten, we've decided.'

'Oh, Tilly, how I've missed you fussing over me.' Sophie gave a tearful smile.

In a restaurant garden, Tilly beckoned to a slim Indian woman who came towards them pushing a pram.

Sophie's stomach went taut as she realised she was staring in at Jamie. Tilly reached in and proudly held him up.

'Say hello to your cousin Sophie,' she crooned at the plump red-headed baby. Jamie gurgled and gave her a drooling smile.

'Would you like to hold him?'

Sophie froze. She couldn't do it. James swiftly intervened and took the boy in his arms. Sophie felt winded. For a moment she imagined it was Tam bouncing their longed-for baby in delight. Tears welled in her eyes and she turned away.

'Sorry.' She gulped.

Tilly steered her back into the restaurant. 'No, it's me who's sorry; so very sorry.'

***

It was nearly sundown by the time they were bumping up the track to Belgooree in a pre-war Wolseley hired in Shillong. Sophie knew that her friends were keeping something from her – something too important to discuss en route – and her stomach felt leaden.

As they pulled up outside a neatly painted bungalow, swamped in a riot of flowering creepers, she had a frisson of déjà vu. Adela came flying down the bleached steps, arms outstretched.

''Ophie!' she squealed.

Sophie swept her up and swung her round, burying her face in the girl's warm neck.

'Hello, my wee angel,' she said, kissing the girl on her flushed cheek. 'I've missed you.'

'I'm here, silly,' Adela laughed and wriggled down again, running round to Tilly for a hug. Tilly made a fuss of her too. James stood watching, looking awkward.

'Who are you?' Adela demanded.

'He's your Cousin James,' Clarrie called out, coming down the steps. 'Say hello to him nicely.'

'Hello,' the girl said, already losing interest and jumping back to Sophie.

Clarrie embraced Sophie warmly and led them all up to the veranda where tea was served. Wesley returned from the tea leaf withering sheds. There was tension in the air and looks were exchanged; Sophie wondered if it was frostiness between the rival men or to do with her. Soon after, they were shown to their rooms to wash and change for dinner.

There was a chill to the night air as they sat around the dining table on the deep-set veranda, night birds restless in the jungle beyond. Sophie could hardly eat a thing, beset by the strange sensation that she had been here before. In such an ethereal place she could believe in reincarnation.

And then realisation began to dawn. She looked around the table at their anxious faces. Her question came out as a whisper.

'Is – is this place White Blossom Cottage?'

Again the looks flew between the others.

Clarrie said gently, 'It is. At least that is what your father renamed it when he brought you and your mother to live here. I don't think he liked the native name Belgooree.'

Sophie's heart drummed. Her thoughts plunged back to that long-ago birthday. She saw her small self in a blue dress, standing at the top of those very steps waiting for her party to begin, the sound of tom-toms beating beyond the compound.

'Tell me what you know,' she rasped. 'Tell me everything.'

***

Minutes later, Sophie lurched down the steps and doubled over, retching into the dark flower bed. Her head reeled with what she had just been told; her father was a murderer and her mother had suffered a terrifying death. Had she pleaded for her life as he swung the revolver at her head? Had she begged him not to harm their daughter?

She gasped for breath as she remembered how she had hidden in the suffocating linen chest. She sobbed and struggled to breathe as she vomited again. Tilly and Clarrie quickly had their arms around her, soothing her and cajoling her back inside.

They lay her down on a lumpy sofa and sat either side, Clarrie stroking her hair away from her face and Tilly making her sip sugary water.

Sophie lay feeling utterly torn apart. James and Wesley stood looking on helplessly.

Clarrie said,'When we first came back to Belgooree there was a local rumour that a planter had died here years back, but I thought it was probably about my father.'

'We knew none of this till Tilly told us in a letter,' Wesley said, flinging an accusing look at James.

'I told you,' said James, 'it was Burke who made the decision to cover up the shootings. Once it was done, we couldn't go back on it.' He threw Sophie a pleading look. 'And I wanted to protect you from the awful truth of what your father did. You were so young and upset as it was.'

Sophie stared at him. 'It was you who found me in the chest, wasn't it? How long had I been there?'

'All night,' James admitted. 'We hoped to God you hadn't climbed out and seen—' He broke off.

'I heard the bangs,' Sophie said, no longer able to keep the memories of that fearful night at bay. 'I thought they were fireworks. And the drums sounded as if they were in the house. I tried to make myself as small as I could. Were there people coming to harm us?'

James shook his head. 'I don't think so. May is a time of weddings – they were probably just celebrating. That's why no one in the compound heard the gunshots – it was too noisy or they had slipped off to the feasting.'

Sophie closed her eyes but she couldn't blank out the image of Ayah Mimi running away. It had still been daylight. If her nurse had suspected trouble, why did she not attempt to take her with her?

'I can't forgive Ayah for leaving me like that,' she said bitterly, 'and saving the wretched kitten.'

Tilly covered Sophie's hand with hers. 'James has something else to tell you that he's never spoken of until he told me two weeks ago. I don't know whether it will make you feel better or worse; but I think you have a right to know.'

James came forward and straddled a chair. 'I don't think your *ayah* was running away with a kitten. I think it was a baby.'

'A baby?' Clarrie said, startled. 'You never said—'

'Let him speak, Clarissa,' Wesley cautioned.

James held Sophie's look. 'Your mother had just given birth shortly before your birthday. When I came to try to persuade them to leave, your father seemed agitated by the newborn – in his fevered state he made accusations that the baby wasn't his. It's crying just enraged him all the more.'

Tilly squeezed Sophie's hand. 'James thinks your mother must have sent Ayah to the village with the baby for protection. She feared her husband was so unstable he might do it harm.'

'A baby?' Sophie whispered in confusion. 'How do I not remember a baby brother or sister?'

'Perhaps your mother called it her little kitten,' Clarrie suggested, 'and you took it literally. You were very young.'

'And she may have been frightened to talk about the baby in your father's hearing,' Tilly added.

Sophie fought back tears. 'I remember calling out to Ayah to wait for me, but she didn't even turn round. And she never came back for me, did she?'

Clarrie said, 'You don't know that. She might have stayed hidden, caring for the little one – finding someone to suckle him or her – and only come back after you'd been rescued.'

'Yes,' Wesley agreed. 'She wouldn't have known where you had gone or how to find you.'

'Don't spend your life being angry with her,' Clarrie said gently.

***

In the middle of the night, unable to sleep for the memories that crowded in and would not give her peace, Sophie went out on the veranda. Wrapping herself in a blanket, she stared out at the outline of huts across the compound where Ayah Mimi must once have lived. Scented wood smoke filled the darkness. Suddenly she was overwhelmed with grief – for her mother, her Ayah, her lost baby, the brother or sister she would never know – and racking sobs seized her.

Meera found her in an exhausted dozing state, huddled on the veranda steps, as the grey light of pre-dawn filtered through the trees. Sophie sat up in alarm at the sight of Tilly's *ayah* cradling Jamie, as the baby sucked lustily on his bottle.

Her heart squeezed with fresh pain. Meera removed the empty bottle, put Jamie against her shoulder and rubbed his back. The infant gazed dreamily at Sophie. New tears leaked down her wan face. Meera offered him to her to hold. Sophie shook her head and tightened the blanket around her shoulders. She didn't know if she could bear to stay under the same roof as Tilly's baby; she hated the envy she felt and the clawing grief that left her hollow.

It had been a mistake to come back to Assam. And now she had to live with this appalling knowledge of what her father had done. Her memory of him as an aloof figure of adoration was for ever spoilt. He had been a jealous, unkind, cowardly husband and a cold-hearted father.

As Meera took the baby away, Clarrie appeared in riding dress.

'Whenever I was sick at heart,' she said softly, 'and overwhelmed with the troubles of living with an ill father, I would go out riding in the early morning on my beloved pony Prince.'

She bent and touched Sophie's head; it felt motherly and comforting.

'Come riding with me now,' Clarrie urged.

Sophie looked up with huge dark-ringed eyes. 'I'd like that,' she answered.

***

They took the track through the tea gardens and wound their way uphill through thick forest, Sophie following Clarrie on a sturdy brown Bhutanese pony that Wesley had bought for Adela. The trees were alive with the call of birds. With every step, the sky lightened and Sophie's grief lessened a fraction.

After twenty minutes they came into a clearing. She gasped at the sudden view of the distant mountains; the dawn light turning the peaks apricot. Clarrie dismounted and led her pony to a gurgling stream that spouted from some fern-covered rocks into a dark pool. The animal dipped its head to drink.

Sophie did likewise, patting the stocky horse and whispering her thanks into its ear. Looking about the grassy enclosure, she saw scattered stones and strangely carved pillars lying prone as if some giant of the hills had trodden on an ancient temple.

Clarrie unpacked a cloth parcel from her saddlebag and laid it on a flat stone close to the freshwater pool.

'Are you putting out food for the gods?' Sophie smiled.

'Just for the *sadhvi* who lives here,' Clarrie said.

'*Sadhvi*? That's a holy woman, isn't it?'

Clarrie nodded. 'The locals think she's a *shaitan* – a bad spirit – and the village children are frightened of her, but I think she's a widow with nowhere else to go.'

Only then did Sophie notice a low, thatched hut almost totally obscured by creepers and overhanging branches. There were traces of an old fire – charred sticks and ash – in front of the closed bamboo door.

'When I was young there was an old holy man lived here,' Clarrie said, pulling out a rose-coloured stone on a chain from under her riding jacket. 'He blessed this stone and gave it to me – I think to bring me luck and keep me safe – and I kept it through all the hard times in England. I always believed that one day it would bring me back to India.' Clarrie smiled, her face radiant in the dawn. 'And here I am back at Belgooree, in the place I love best and with the people I love most.'

Sophie's throat constricted. She stared beyond to the golden light flooding across the far mountains and felt her heart squeeze. It reminded her too vividly of her brief magical time with Rafi. No lucky stone could recapture that happiness for her now. But even as she thought her heart could never be sorer, Sophie felt a strange comfort in being there close to the hermit's hut in its beautiful flower-filled dell with a striking sunrise rippling along the mountain chain.

Yesterday, she knew neither the truth about her parents' death nor that she had once had a sibling. Today her world had altered for ever. But knowing about the baby brother or sister made her feel less alone. Had he or she survived? Were they still in the area being brought up by another family? She would be sixteen by now (somehow Sophie imagined it would be a sister). Did she look like her? Would she recognise her if she passed her in the village, or Shillong or Calcutta? Sophie determined there and then that she would make every attempt to find her lost sibling. The idea burned inside her and gave her courage.

Watching the daylight come, Sophie stood with Clarrie and shared her thoughts.

'We could start by asking in the village,' Clarrie offered.

Sophie felt a wave of gratitude that the older woman did not dismiss the idea as impossible. They sat on a fallen pillar and talked. She pulled out the black opal. 'Like you, I have a special stone,' said Sophie, and found herself unburdening about her love for Rafi and the fateful trek in the mountains.

'I wish I had known Rafi better in Edinburgh,' Sophie said sadly. 'Auntie Amy liked him a lot – he used to go round to visit her – but I was a bit offhand. Maybe even then I was frightened of my attraction to him.'

'Where do you think he is?' Clarrie asked.

Sophie shrugged. 'I wish I knew. I imagine he's in Lahore working for his father or maybe he's gone back in the army. He talked with affection of his days with the Lahore Horse. Or maybe he's just living off his rich new father-in-law like Jimmy Scott said.'

'Of all the foresters, which one would he keep in touch with?'

'Boz or McGinty,' Sophie guessed.

Clarrie squeezed her hand. 'Why don't you write to Boz and ask if he knows? Even if it's true that Rafi is married now, I can see you are not going to have peace of mind until you've heard from him.'

'Why do you say, even if it's true, as if there's some doubt?'

Clarrie said, 'Wesley and I nearly threw away our happiness together because of misunderstandings between us. I thought he had married a rich heiress and he thought I had affections for Tilly's brother Johnny.'

'Really?' Sophie's eyes widened. 'And did you?'

'No.' Clarrie laughed. 'I only ever loved Wesley. The first time we met was in this very clearing – he was out hunting and his friend nearly shot me.'

'Never!'

'Yes. Wesley rescued me but we got off on the wrong foot and argued badly. It took me years to admit how deeply in love I was.'

Sophie's eyes glistened. 'I'm so glad you overcame the misunderstandings. I don't think I've ever seen a couple as loving as you two.'

'Thank you.' Clarrie smiled.

'The trouble is,' Sophie sighed, 'that Jimmy Scott and Boz both saw a notice in the *Civil and Military Gazette* about Rafi's marriage to a banker's daughter – making comment about him being a brother of the notorious Ghulam who'd been arrested for arson.'

'But you didn't see it?'

'No, but Boz wouldn't lie about something like that.'

'It's just strange,' Clarrie puzzled, 'that he didn't invite any of his forester friends to his wedding.'

'I suppose it is,' Sophie said, 'I've never thought of that. But there again, Rafi had been sacked by his boss and cold-shouldered by his colleagues.'

'But not by Boz and McGinty, from what you've told me.'

'No,' Sophie agreed, 'not by them.'

As the sunlight spread across the ruined temple and they remounted their ponies, Sophie determined she would write to Boz for news of Rafi.

Chapter 42

Early each morning, Sophie would ride out to the temple clearing with Clarrie to witness the sunrise. Sometimes Wesley would go with them. The days grew colder and the air stung their cheeks but it was like balm to Sophie's wounded heart. She looked forward to the rides and began to recover her zest for life. Clarrie carried a parcel of rice or flour each time, in case the hermit had returned, but the hut remained empty.

'Perhaps she's on pilgrimage,' Clarrie wondered.

'Or moved on,' said Wesley.

James soon grew impatient with being at Belgooree and, refusing Wesley's offer of a fishing trip, set off back to the Oxford Estates, taking Tilly and the baby with him.

'He doesn't want us to be separated again so soon after my Shillong visit,' Tilly explained to Sophie. 'Are you sure you won't come with us?'

'Clarrie says I can stay,' Sophie replied, 'and I want to try to find out more about my sister or brother.'

'It's not because of Jamie, is it?' Tilly worried. 'I know you find it difficult with a baby around.'

Sophie gave a bleak smile. 'Sorry, I know it's silly and he's such a lovely wee boy—'

Tilly grabbed her hands. 'It's not silly at all. I can't imagine what it's like for you. I just know that you're strong enough to come through this dark time. When you're ready, you will come and stay with us at Cheviot View for as long as you want. There will always be a home for you wherever I live.'

Sophie's eyes stung with tears at the kind words. She pulled her cousin into a hug.

'Oh, Tilly, you are the best of friends!'

A week after the Robsons departed, Sophie noticed a difference as she rode with Clarrie into the jungle clearing. Scented wood smoke filled the air and a small fire crackled and sparked, illuminating the *sadhvi*'s hut. The door was open.

They dismounted and Clarrie went forward with her parcel of food. As she laid it on the flat stone between the hut and the pool, a figure appeared from under the low door, wrapped in a grubby saffron-coloured robe. A tiny woman with claw-like hands, pulling the end of her sari over sparse hair, approached them. In the half-light, Sophie thought she looked like the malevolent spirit that the local children feared, her forehead daubed in white and ochre, her nails like talons.

She put her hands together and bowed in greeting. Clarrie and Sophie responded. The holy woman beckoned them towards her fire. Sophie hesitated but Clarrie said softly, 'She'll want to give us something in return for the food. Best to accept.'

The *sadhvi* moved with a calm gracefulness, pulling out a battered rush mat from her hut for them to sit on and pouring tea from a kettle suspended over the fire into clay cups. From under her veil she gave them quick darting looks, murmuring to herself. The sun rose. The tea was laced with something spicy – perhaps cardamom, Sophie guessed – and filled her with a strange sense of familiarity.

No one spoke as the golden light on the far peaks dazzled their eyes. Sophie took a sip of the aromatic drink. She caught the *sadhvi* staring at her with keen dark eyes that belied her careworn, wrinkled face. Sophie's heart began to thud. The holy woman rose from her squatting position and stepped around the fire, her gaze never faltering. Emotion welled up in Sophie's chest. She saw the mole on the woman's wrinkled chin.

'Ayah Mimi?' she whispered.

The woman stretched out her bony hands and cupped them around Sophie's face.

'Sophie, my little chick,' she croaked in a voice not used to speaking.

'Ayah!'

Tears spilled down Sophie's face as the woman's thin arms went around her and stroked her hair. Ayah began a high-pitched song of joy that rose up to mingle with the twittering of birds in the dense trees.

'Sophie,' Ayah crooned. 'I knew you would come back one day. I just had to be patient.'

Sophie held on to her and wept and wept.

***

Ayah rode back to Belgooree with the British women, perched behind Sophie on the stout pony. Adela was fascinated by the woman with the ochre streaks on her face whom Sophie had conjured out of the forest, and she stared at her from the safety of her mother's skirts. It wasn't long before Ayah Mimi had won Adela's confidence with her singing and easy smiles, and Sophie felt a tender tug to see the small girl sitting cross-legged on the veranda with the old nurse eating rice with her fingers; something she remembered her own parents forbidding her to do.

Over the next couple of days, they pieced together what had happened that fateful night when the Logans had died. After Robson Sahib had tried but failed to get the Logans to leave Belgooree, Bill Logan had gone out to the compound with a gun and told the servants to make themselves scarce. Alarmed, Ayah had been sent by Jessie Logan to the village with the week-old baby – a boy whom the Logans had yet to name – for safekeeping.

'Logan-Mem was frightened for the baby. But also thought Sahib would calm down if the baby was out of the way. He was very jealous of Baby.'

Mimi had been told to stay at the house of Ama, a wise old Khasi woman, whose son was the *mali* at White Blossom Cottage and whom Jessie trusted.

'Ama?' Clarrie had cried. 'She was my old nurse!'

She had found Ama's family in the midst of a wedding party but Ama had taken them in and found a young mother in her tribe to suckle the Logan infant.

Two days later, the celebrations over and worried that no word had come from Jessie, Ayah went back to the tea bungalow with Ama's son, the Belgooree gardener. They found the house boarded up with a Sikh policeman on guard who chased them away. A week later, a police officer from Shillong tracked Ayah down to the village and forced her to hand over the baby.

'He told me that the Logans had died of fever and that their daughter no longer had need of me. I begged him to tell me where they had taken you, Sophie, but he said it was none of my business.'

'Was he called Burke?' Sophie asked.

Ayah nodded. 'He said that he would throw me in prison for stealing a white man's baby if I tried to follow you. He paid off the other servants and told them the same story about fever. I tried to find you. I walked to Shillong and sold my gold earrings and bracelets, then made my way back to Assam. But it took many weeks and I was held up by the rains. By the time I got there, the Logan bungalow had been given to another family and you were gone. The old sweeper thought you had been taken to Calcutta. When I asked about the baby, he said there had never been one; you had left alone.'

Ayah broke down in tears, wailing about her failure to Logan Memsahib to keep her baby safe or to care for her daughter.

'What did you do next?' Sophie asked gently, putting her arm around the distraught woman.

'I went to Shillong and got work at one of the orphanages, sewing and looking after the babies. I hoped I might come across Baby Logan but didn't. When I heard that a family had come back to Belgooree, I left and came back to the hills, hoping it might be you.'

'How disappointed you must have been to find us instead,' Clarrie sympathised.

Ayah shook her head. 'You have been kind to me. Some weeks I would not have eaten if it was not for your gifts. And I never gave up hope. I prayed every day that my little chick would be returned to me or, if that was not to be, that the gods of the mountains would protect you wherever you lived and breathed.'

Sophie and Ayah sat rocking in each other's arms, absorbing the shock of finding one another again. If she could be reunited with her beloved old nurse against all the odds, Sophie thought, then why not with her missing younger brother?

Wesley broke into their reverie. 'So the only person who really knows what happened to Baby Logan is the retired police officer Burke?'

'Yes,' Ayah said, 'but I was too frightened to approach him again.'

'Well, I'm not,' Sophie said. 'If he doesn't tell me what happened to my brother, I'll expose him for covering up murder.'

Clarrie put out a steadying hand. 'Be careful; you would be getting James into trouble too. And it's obvious from what Ayah is saying that he knew nothing about Burke going off with the baby.'

Sophie bit her lip in frustration. The last thing she wanted was to cause problems for Tilly's husband; he had protected her, brought her safely to Edinburgh and helped pay for her education. He might have his differences with his cousin Wesley but he was a good man and Tilly adored him.

'Sophie has a right to know,' Wesley said stoutly, 'and it needn't come to threats. I'd be happy to go with you to see him.'

Sophie smiled at the handsome, craggy-faced tea planter. 'Thank you.'

***

It was another ten days before the trip to Shillong was arranged. Sophie wrote to Tilly asking for Burke's address, giving her the astonishing news about finding Ayah Mimi and the information about a baby brother. While she waited for Tilly's reply, a letter came from France. Sophie took it out into the garden to read. Clarrie found her teary-eyed.

'Tam left the ship at Marseilles,' Sophie said quietly. 'Nancy was there to meet him. They're wintering in the French Alps.'

Clarrie squeezed her shoulder. 'It must be upsetting.'

Sophie shook her head and swallowed. 'I'm happy for him. It's a relief in a way. I'm just sad he wasn't honest with me at the beginning.'

After that, Tam was never mentioned. Sophie focused on looking to the future and finding her brother. Back came an excited reply from Tilly wishing her the best of luck in tackling the hard-bitten police officer.

'His card was a bit vague,' Tilly wrote back, *'it just said Superintendent R Burke, The Lines, Shillong. No doubt he thinks himself so important that everyone should know where he lives.'*

On the eve of her going, a message came that the landowner of the neighbouring principality of Gulgat was on a hunting trip in the Khasi hills. The Rajah of Gulgat was asking permission to use the camping ground at Um Shirpi by the river on the Belgooree estate in a few days' time. Wesley sent back a chit granting permission and asking if he could join the party on his return from town.

'He's an amusing man,' Wesley told Sophie, 'with a huge menagerie of exotic pets including a white tiger. Went to Edinburgh University and studied philosophy. You'll have to meet him.'

The next morning, Sophie and Wesley saddled up ready to leave. Sophie put on her bracelet of elephant heads to bring luck in the search. Ayah Mimi gasped at the sight.

'From Logan Memsahib!'

'Yes,' Sophie answered. 'Do you remember it?'

Her old nurse nodded, her eyes haunted. 'There were two. I had forgotten. The other one—' She put a trembling hand to her mouth.

'Tell me, Ayah Mimi,' Sophie said gently.

'The baby,' she whispered. 'Your mother wrapped the other one in the baby's shawl. I was to sell it if I needed to pay for anything for the boy.'

'Did it stay with the baby?' Sophie asked, her heart jolting.

Ayah nodded. 'I put it with the little one when Burke took him away.' Her eyes lit with hope. 'Perhaps it might help you find the boy?'

Sophie knew the chances of the bracelet having been handed on with her brother were slim; Burke would probably have got rid of anything that might link the boy with the Logans – if he'd found it. But she saw the longing in the old woman's face.

'Thank you' – she smiled in encouragement – 'it might well help us.'

At the moment of departure, Adela burst into tears.

'I want to go too!'

She would not believe her mother's entreaties that her father and adored Sophie would be coming back in a few days. Only Ayah Mimi's enticing the small girl over to the giant babul tree and mimicking the jungle birds distracted the girl long enough for the riders to trot away.

As soon as they got to town – impatient to get the confrontation over – Sophie sent a card of introduction straight round to the lines in the cantonment. She spent a sleepless night in the boarding house and could hardly touch her breakfast the next day.

'We could call on Tilly's friend Major Rankin while we wait for a reply,' Wesley suggested. 'Or we could go to the cemetery to pay your respects . . .?'

Sophie's insides knotted. She didn't feel like making small talk with a stranger, however kind the major was, and she knew that she had to go to her parents' grave – wanted to – and yet dreaded the moment. Her feelings for her father were so confused.

'I'd rather wait for Burke's reply,' she answered.

She spent the morning pacing about the veranda scanning the steep path leading to the boarding house for signs of a *chaprassy* with a chit inviting her to visit Burke's house. By dusk nothing had come. The next day, Wesley insisted on taking her out sightseeing around the lakeside. Sophie tried to enjoy the beauty of the place – Tilly had been right about it being reminiscent of the Scottish Highlands – but she hurried back for news rather than go for tea at the Pinewood Hotel.

'I can't believe he's ignoring my request,' she said in annoyance on finding no note from Burke.

'Perhaps he's away?' Wesley said.

'Tomorrow we'll go to the cantonment and find out for ourselves,' Sophie was insistent. 'I'm not going to be put off another day.'

Wesley gave a snort of amusement. 'It's like listening to a young Clarissa. You Logans aren't related to the Belhavens by any chance?'

It was a drizzly misty morning as they made their way downhill to the cantonment and the uniform lines of British bungalows.

'Rather than tramp around in the rain,' said Wesley, 'why don't we go straight to the club and ask. He's bound to be well known there.'

Sophie stood defiantly in the doorway of the men-only club so she could hear what was said.

'Ronny Burke?' a portly man queried, peering over his newspaper.

Wesley nodded.

'I'm afraid you're too late. Dropped down dead of a heart attack two weeks ago. You'll find him in the cemetery. Are you family?'

Sophie was so full of bitter disappointment that she could not speak. Wesley steered her away from the club into the soft mizzle of rain. She bent her head and walked in silence, not caring where they went. It was only when Wesley stopped abruptly that she realised they were at the gates to the British cemetery.

'I know where they are,' he said quietly. 'We were there when Tilly found the grave.'

Sophie took a deep breath and followed where he pointed.

It was a simple stone with their names and date of death, but more imposing than it had looked in Tilly's snapshot. The only adornment – perhaps arranged by James? – was a Celtic cross engraved into the polished stone. She stooped and ran her finger along her mother's name: Jessie Anderson, wife of William. She thought of the woman she had last seen on the veranda at Belgooree telling her to go and hide; a hand gently pushing her away, a rustle of gauzy clothing, a distracted smile.

Sophie wondered if her mother had really longed to grab her hand and run off down the path after Ayah and the baby. She wished with all her might that her mother had had the courage to do that. But maybe the more courageous act was to let her daughter go and to turn around and try to placate her fevered, irrational husband.

Crouching down, Sophie whispered, 'Auntie Amy brought me up well. She was as loving as any mother could be. But all my growing up I tried to remember what you were like. You were my real Mama and it's you I always wanted.' She swallowed hard. 'I found Ayah Mimi and I longed with all my heart to find my wee brother – so he would know about you – and I would have someone of my own flesh and blood to love. But I don't know how I can do that now. I'm sorry.'

She bent forward and kissed the cold, damp stone with trembling lips. 'Goodbye, Mama.' Tears coursed down her face and dropped from her chin. She stood up.

Wesley put a hand on her shoulder. 'Your father was an ill man. It's not making excuses for what he did, but there must have been a time when he loved you. It's impossible for fathers not to love their daughters.'

Sophie turned and gave him a regretful smile. 'That's because you are a good father. I don't remember my father being like that. Yet I'd like to believe it – so thank you.'

As they left the dank cemetery, a shaft of watery sunlight broke through the blanket of cloud. By the time they had climbed back to the boarding house, the clouds had rolled back and the hills were once more in view.

'*Your parents honeymooned in a hill station called Murree,*' Auntie Amy had once said. '*Your mother always loved the hills.*'

Sophie knew wherever she went next she would always find comfort in mountains. Auntie Amy had loved them, and it gave her solace to think that her mother had too.

Chapter 43

Adela was the first down the steps to greet them on their return to Belgooree.

'Daddy! 'Ophie!'

Clarrie had to grab her hand to stop her running under the horses' hooves. She flung herself into her father's arms and he swung her round.

'How I've missed my little kitten!' He planted a loud kiss on her cheek.

She giggled and wiped it away. Sophie's heart squeezed at their delight in each other and the endearment that echoed her mother's name for her baby brother.

Adela wriggled out of his hold and sprang at Sophie.

'There's a prince in a tent,' she said, wide-eyed in excitement. 'He's got a wolf on a gold chain. 'Ophie come and see.'

Clarrie explained. 'It's the Rajah of Gulgat. He arrived yesterday. We went to watch them set up camp. The wolf is actually a hunting dog.'

'Yes, wolf,' Adela repeated. 'Come on, 'Ophie.'

'Give her time to rest and bathe,' Clarrie said. 'She's had a long ride.' She gave Sophie an expectant look. Sophie shook her head.

'Burke died two weeks ago,' Wesley explained. 'We can talk of it later.'

Adela looked between them in confusion. ''Ophie, why are you sad?'

Sophie bent down. 'I'm sad because I've spent five days away from you. Give me a hug.'

Adela giggled and put her warm arms around Sophie's neck, threading her fingers in her hair. Sophie's silky fair hair fascinated the little girl.

'We can invite the Rajah and his hunting friends to tea tomorrow,' Clarrie said, 'now that you're back. They're just a small group by the looks of it.'

'I'll go down this evening and ask them,' Wesley agreed.

As the shadows were lengthening, refreshed from a hot bath and changed into a clean dress, Sophie accompanied the Robsons down to the river to meet the Rajah. She was surprised by the simplicity of the camp – eight tents the size of those Tam would use for a jungle tour – around an open fire over which two cooks were busy preparing the evening meal.

Four men were splashing about in the river, shouting.

'Ladies,' Wesley said in alarm, 'you must look away – the men have nothing on.'

Laughing at his prudishness, Clarrie and Sophie went behind a large oak tree. Adela thought it was a game and squealed in delight. Wesley went down to greet the men and returned several minutes later to say it was safe to come out.

Camp chairs were hastily found for the women and the Rajah reappeared from his tent in tunic and trousers to shake their hands. He was a slim handsome man of about thirty. Sophie immediately liked his lack of airs and graces.

'Welcome to my palace.' He winked at Adela.

'Where is the wolf?' asked the girl, gazing around.

'Gone off to find Red Riding Hood,' he said, laughing at his own joke.

He ordered up *chota pegs*. As glasses of lemonade or whisky were handed round, the other swimmers appeared out of the gloom.

'My brother Ravi and my good friend Colonel Baxter – and this is my new aide-de-camp, Khan.'

Sophie caught her breath. She stared at the muscled figure with tousled wet hair who had hastily pulled on shirt and trousers. He was bearded but, as he stepped forward in the dying light, she knew it.

'Rafi?' she gasped.

He came forward and took her hand in his. 'Sophie, how are you?' He didn't seem as shocked to see her as she was at his sudden appearance.

Her heart hammered. She could hardly reply. How could he be so casual?

'You know each other?' the Rajah asked with interest.

‘From Edinburgh and the Forest Service,’ Rafi explained. He let go her hand and Sophie sat down quickly on a camp chair before her legs gave way.

She caught Clarrie’s look and knew she understood. Had she known since yesterday that Rafi was here? The Rajah began to reminisce about Edinburgh and question Sophie about her life there, while Clarrie engaged Rafi in conversation about the tea gardens. Sophie had a thousand questions on her lips for Rafi, yet she was thankful when the Robsons took their leave, issued their tea invitation and retrieved Adela from hampering the cooks’ chapatti-making.

As they left, Clarrie said casually to Rafi, ‘If you come riding with us at dawn I can show you the wild walnut trees we talked about.’

Rafi nodded in acceptance.

Later, back at Belgooree, Sophie sat up late with Clarrie, quite unable to sleep.

‘Is it pure coincidence? He didn’t seem in the least surprised. But maybe that’s because he doesn’t feel the way I do. Oh, Clarrie, I don’t know what to think. It’s all hopeless anyway.’

Nothing Clarrie said could calm Sophie’s mental turmoil.

‘Try to sleep.’ She yawned, giving up and going to bed. ‘It’ll be dawn in a few hours.’

***

Riding out in the frosty December morning, Sophie felt relief that the long night was over and she was out doing something active. Her spirits lifted. Whether Rafi appeared or not, she was going to enjoy the sunrise as she did every morning. Clarrie and Wesley went with her. The darkness was filled with the scent of early morning fires from the village, as the ponies picked their way through the tea gardens.

Where the path turned into the forest, Sophie saw the outline of a horse and rider against the charcoal sky. Rafi had come.

‘You go ahead,’ Clarrie told Sophie. ‘We’ll ride behind. The path is too narrow for us all.’

Sophie greeted Rafi and their horses fell into step. Neither said a word, as if each feared what the other might have to say. Twenty minutes later, they arrived at the temple clearing where Clarrie wanted to show Rafi the wild walnut trees. Only then did Sophie realise that the Robsons were no longer behind them.

As they dismounted and waited for the sunrise, Sophie found herself telling Rafi all about finding Ayah Mimi in the hermit's hut, discovering the truth of her parents' death and her fruitless search for her younger brother. It all came spilling out.

'I think that's why I was so afraid of having a baby myself – deep down I remembered my baby brother – or rather I remembered the feeling of losing him. Somehow, in my childish mind, I felt responsible for not keeping him safe.'

Suddenly Sophie was weeping uncontrollably. Rafi, who had hardly spoken a word, put his strong arms around her and pulled her into a comforting hold. They stood like that while dawn light seeped into the enclosure, making the frost on the trees and grass sparkle like jewels.

As the sun grew in strength, melting the thin ice on the pool, Sophie broke away, self-conscious of their intimate hold. It was sweet agony to have found him again but to know they could not be together.

'I'm so sorry for the trouble I caused you, Rafi,' she said. 'Ruining your forestry career.'

'Don't be,' he said. 'I couldn't have worked for Bracknall any longer – knowing what he'd done to you – and I'm happier where I am now with the Rajah. We knew each other briefly in Edinburgh. He offered me the job of his chief assistant when he heard I was back in India. So when Bracknall sacked me, I took up the offer. I'm his chief forester too.' Rafi gave a wry smile.

'I'm glad about that,' Sophie said, feeling an easing of her guilt. But her heart was still heavy. 'I have things to tell you – about Tam – and – the baby . . .'

Rafi said quickly, 'You don't have to explain.'

Sophie looked into his handsome face, her insides leaden. He didn't want to know. He was forging a new life at Gulgat. His tenderness of moments before was mere kindness.

'I see,' she said, stepping back.

'No, you don't.' Rafi caught her hand and held her. 'I mean that I know all about what's happened between you and Tam – your terrible loss – his going on leave. Boz wrote and told me everything.'

'Boz?'

'Yes. As soon as he heard from you and knew you were at Belgooree he tracked me down. He told me you wanted to find me.'

She flushed. 'Well, yes, just to apologise—'

'Sophie,' he said, pulling her back towards him, 'it's not chance that the Rajah's hunting party is in this part of the Khasi hills – I arranged it. I wanted so much to see you again.'

'You did?' She swallowed, her heart racing.

'Of course.' He touched her cheek. It sent shivers through her. 'But I need to know about you and Tam. Is there any chance of a reconciliation between you? If there is, then I will go with a sore heart, and not stand in your way.'

'Tam has gone to be with the woman he has loved all along,' Sophie whispered. 'I ought to feel jealous but I don't. I've only ever really cared for one man; I just didn't realise it in time.' Her eyes stung with tears as she looked into his intense green eyes. 'I love you, Rafi, but I feel guilty at the joy I feel just being here with you. Guilty towards—'

'Stop,' Rafi said forcefully, gripping her hand. 'I have things to tell you too. Boz told me about the wedding announcement in the newspaper with Sultana Sarfraz.'

'Was that not true?' Sophie asked, not daring to hope.

'It's true there was a wedding,' Rafi answered, 'but not to me. It was my brother Rehman who married. I refused – I couldn't go through with it – and he was happy to step into my shoes. The *Gazette* couldn't distinguish between one brother and the other – they were only interested in the connection with Ghulam and his notoriety.'

'So you're not married?' Sophie's heart leapt.

'No,' Rafi said, titling her chin and gazing at her with his passionate eyes. 'I vowed to stay single all my days if I couldn't have the woman I loved. You, Sophie, you're the only one I could be happy with. Your Auntie Amy knew it – it's you who couldn't see how much in love I'd fallen.'

She felt dizzy at his words. 'Oh, Rafi, kiss me.'

He bent and embraced her with firm lips that she had dreamed about kissing for so long. She felt her heart would burst with joy.

When the kissing stopped, Rafi's voice was raw with emotion.

'Come and live with me at Gulgat,' he urged.

'Will the Rajah not be shocked?' She laughed, heady at the idea. 'I'd be bringing further scandal to your door.'

'Not shocked' – Rafi grinned – 'just envious.'

They gazed at each other, unable to believe their luck. A shadow passed over his handsome face. 'You have more to lose. It is you who will be cast out from British society in India for ever if you choose me.'

'I care nothing for that,' Sophie said with spirit. 'And the people I love won't turn their backs on us.'

Rafi's face broke into a tender smile. 'Let our new life start today then, my love.'

Under the dazzling wintry sun, they remounted the grazing ponies and left the jungle clearing, hand clasped in hand, to face the future together.

Some Anglo-Indian Terms

ayah	nanny
babu	clerk (derogatory)
boxwallah	merchant (derogatory)
burra memsahib	senior lady
chaprassy	messenger
charpoy	wooden/hemp bedframe
chota hazri	breakfast
chota peg	drink, sundowner
chowkidar	nightwatchman, guard
daftar	forest office
dak	post, mail
dak bungalow	travellers' rest house
dhoti	loincloth
ghat	quay, wharf
hartal	labour strike, general strike
jungli	of the jungle, wild
khitmutgar	head valet, server at table
koi hai!	Is anyone there?
maidan	open ground, field in a town
mali	gardener
memsahib	madam
mofussil	countryside, provinces
mohurer	head bookkeeper
munshi	language teacher
pukka	first class, proper
punkah	cloth ceiling fan
purdah	seclusion of women
raja	landowner
sadhvi	Hindu holy woman
sahib	sir, master
shikari	hunter, guide
syce	groom (of horses)
tonga	two-wheeled carriage
topee	tropical sunhat
wallah	person, worker
yak dan	storage chest
zenana	women's quarters

GIRL FROM THE TEA GARDEN

An emotional and uplifting novel set in the momentous times of the 1930s and the Second World War: India Tea Series – Book 3

Assam, India, 1933: Bullied at school for being Anglo-Indian, pretty and spirited thirteen-year-old Adela Robson escapes St Ninian's in the boot of a car belonging to handsome young river captain Sam Jackman. Discovering his stowaway, maverick Sam is persuaded by Adela to take her home to her parents' remote tea garden at Belgooree. By the time they arrive, Adela has fallen deeply in love with her rescuer, but the shock of their appearance sends Adela's mother Clarrie into labour and baby Harry is born. Sam disappears from the area having forfeited his steamboat in a game of cards, leaving Adela bereft and longing for adult life to begin so she can fulfil her ambition to be an actress.

Exhausted to be a mother again at forty-seven, Clarrie is insistent that her vivacious daughter must finish her education, so Adela is sent to school in Simla, the prestigious summer capital of the British government in India. For a while Adela is supremely happy, acting at the Gaiety Theatre, coming of age in the glittering society of the Raj in its dying days and taking a job in the forest office. Best of all, she rediscovers Sam working for a mission in the hills, planting apple trees. Determined to see more of him, she volunteers for Dr Fatima Khan's mobile clinic. But in that summer of 1938, she meets spoilt and charming Sanjay Singh, nephew of the Rajah of Gulgat, and a chain of events is set in motion that leads to a devastating loss. Adela is sent to Britain – a country she cannot remember – not knowing if she will ever see Sam again. War is looming and Adela's great courage and endurance will be tested to the limit.

Acknowledgements

I owe a debt of gratitude to my maternal grandparents for keeping diaries and writing interesting letters home to Scotland from India, as well as taking pioneering cine film in the 1920s. This recently rediscovered treasure-trove has inspired much of the background to this novel.

Thanks to my eagle-eyed and perceptive editor, Janey Floyd for her practical help and wise comments over the original manuscript. Thanks also to husband Graeme for keeping body and soul together with great meals and many cups of tea and coffee. And to Amy and Charlie for their constant cheerful encouragement.

About the Author

Janet MacLeod Trotter is the author of numerous bestselling and acclaimed novels, including *The Hungry Hills*, which was nominated for the *Sunday Times* Young Writer of the Year Award, *The Tea Planter's Daughter*, which was nominated for the Romantic Novelists' Association Novel of the Year Award and *In the Far Pashmina Mountains*, which was shortlisted for the RNA Historical Romance of the Year Award. Her novels have been translated into nine different languages. Much informed by her own experiences, MacLeod Trotter was raised in the north-east of England by Scottish parents and travelled in India as a young woman. Fascinated by family links between Scotland and India, she discovered diaries and letters belonging to her grandparents, who married in Lahore and lived and worked in northern India for nearly thirty years, which served as her inspiration for the India Tea Series. Find out more about the author and her novels at www.janetmacleodtrotter.com

Printed in Great Britain
by Amazon

26543341R00212